Pokémon™

ADVENTURES
BLACK & WHITE

VOLUME SIX

Story by
Hidenori Kusaka

Art by
Satoshi Yamamoto

BLACK & WHITE

A STORY ABOUT YOUNG PEOPLE ENTRUSTED WITH POKÉDEXES BY THE WORLD'S LEADING POKÉMON RESEARCHERS. TOGETHER WITH THEIR POKÉMON, THEY TRAVEL, BATTLE, AND EVOLVE!

SOME PLACE IN SOME TIME... A YOUNG TRAINER NAMED BLACK, WHO DREAMS OF WINNING THE POKÉMON LEAGUE, RECEIVES A POKÉDEX FROM PROFESSOR JUNIPER AND SETS OFF ON HIS TRAINING JOURNEY TO COLLECT THE EIGHT GYM BADGES HE NEEDS TO ENTER NEXT YEAR'S POKÉMON LEAGUE. ON THE WAY, BLACK MEETS WHITE, THE OWNER OF A POKÉMON TALENT AGENCY, AND THE TWO TRAVEL TOGETHER. MEANWHILE, AN EVIL ORGANIZATION NAMED TEAM PLASMA IS TELLING PEOPLE TO GIVE UP THEIR POKÉMON AND RETURN THEM TO THE WILD. WHAT IS THEIR ULTERIOR MOTIVE?
AFTER MEETING N, THE KING OF TEAM PLASMA, WHITE DECIDES TO LEARN SOME BATTLE SKILLS. SHE BOARDS THE BATTLE SUBWAY, AND SHE AND BLACK PART WAYS. MEANWHILE, THE UNOVA REGION GYM LEADERS JOIN FORCES WITH BLACK TO PREVENT TEAM PLASMA FROM STEALING THE MYSTERIOUS DARK STONE FROM THE NACRENE MUSEUM... WHAT DO THEY WANT WITH IT, ANYWAY...?

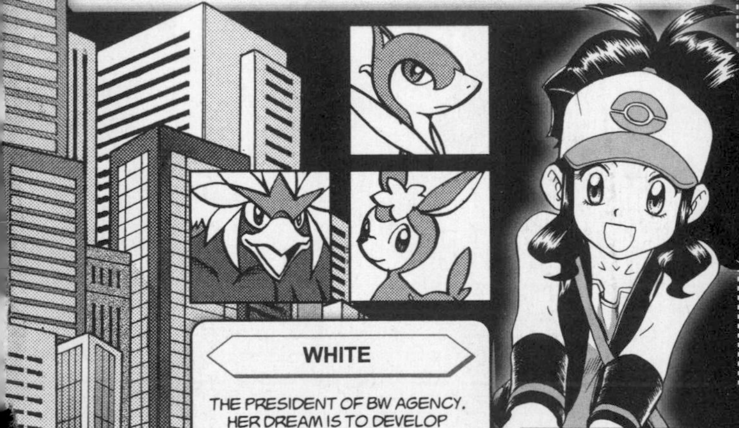

WHITE

THE PRESIDENT OF BW AGENCY. HER DREAM IS TO DEVELOP THE CAREERS OF POKÉMON STARS. SHE TAKES HER WORK VERY SERIOUSLY AND WILL DO WHATEVER IT TAKES TO SUPPORT HER POKÉMON ACTORS.

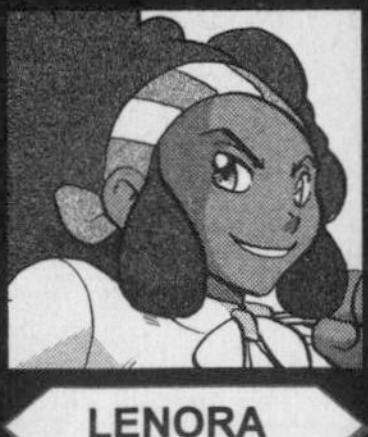

LENORA

THE NACRENE CITY GYM LEADER AND NACRENE MUSEUM DIRECTOR.

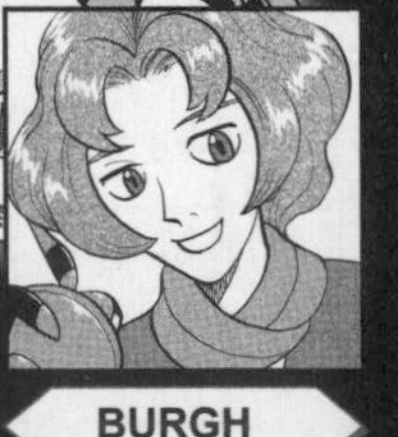

BURGH

AN ARTIST AND CASTELIA CITY'S GYM LEADER.

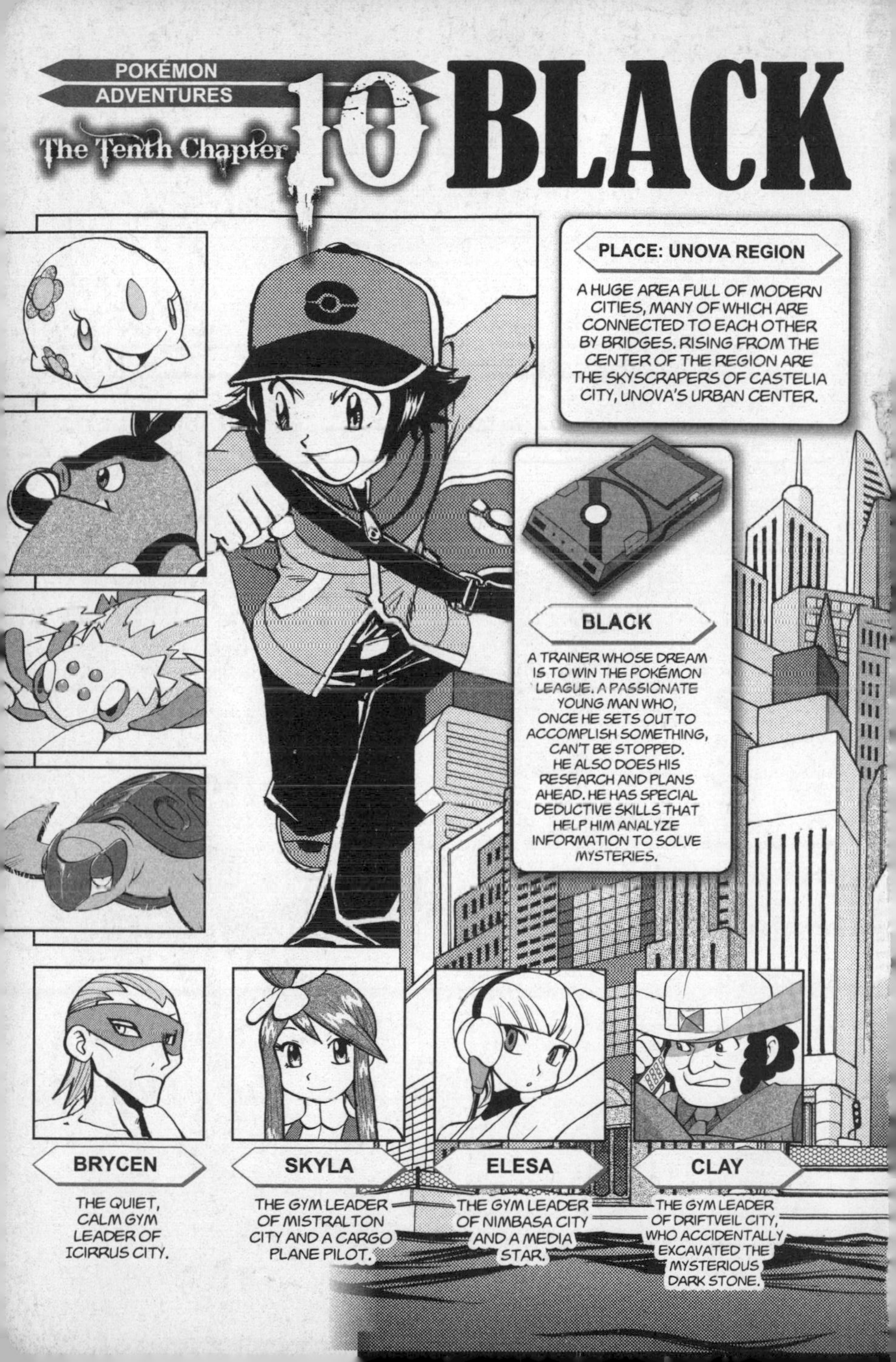
POKÉMON ADVENTURES
The Tenth Chapter 10 BLACK
PLACE: UNOVA REGION
A HUGE AREA FULL OF MODERN CITIES, MANY OF WHICH ARE CONNECTED TO EACH OTHER BY BRIDGES. RISING FROM THE CENTER OF THE REGION ARE THE SKYSCRAPERS OF CASTELIA CITY, UNOVA'S URBAN CENTER.
BLACK
A TRAINER WHOSE DREAM IS TO WIN THE POKÉMON LEAGUE. A PASSIONATE YOUNG MAN WHO, ONCE HE SETS OUT TO ACCOMPLISH SOMETHING, CAN'T BE STOPPED. HE ALSO DOES HIS RESEARCH AND PLANS AHEAD. HE HAS SPECIAL DEDUCTIVE SKILLS THAT HELP HIM ANALYZE INFORMATION TO SOLVE MYSTERIES.
CLAY
THE GYM LEADER OF DRIFTVEIL CITY, WHO ACCIDENTALLY EXCAVATED THE MYSTERIOUS DARK STONE.
ELESA
THE GYM LEADER OF NIMBASA CITY AND A MEDIA STAR.
SKYLA
THE GYM LEADER OF MISTRALTON CITY AND A CARGO PLANE PILOT.
BRYCEN
THE QUIET, CALM GYM LEADER OF ICIRRUS CITY.

POKÉMON™ ADVENTURES BLACK & WHITE

6 VOLUME SIX

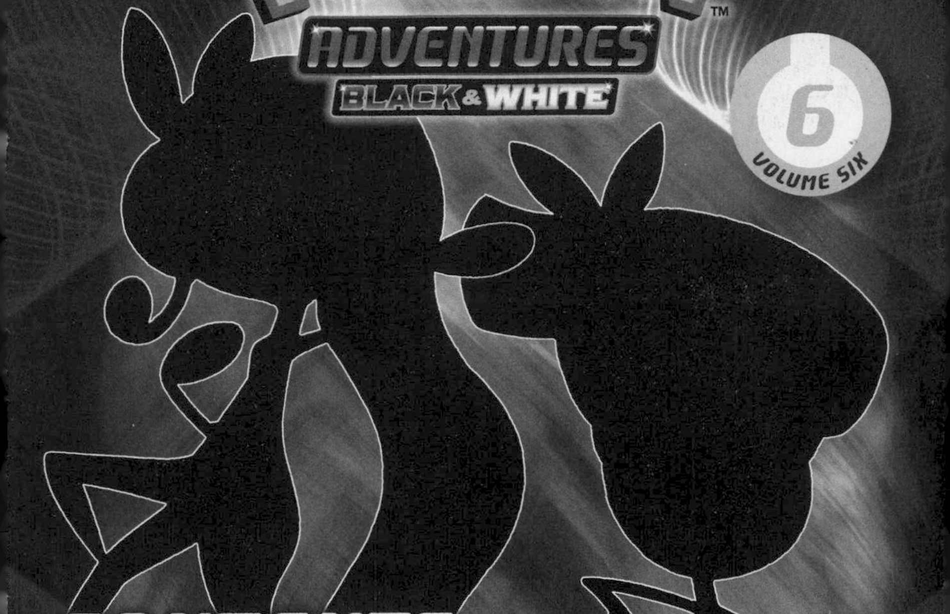

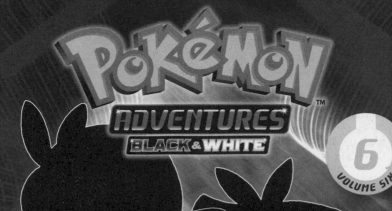

CONTENTS

POKÉMON™
ADVENTURES
BLACK & WHITE

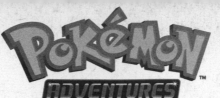

TORNADUS, THUNDURUS, LANDORUS
I

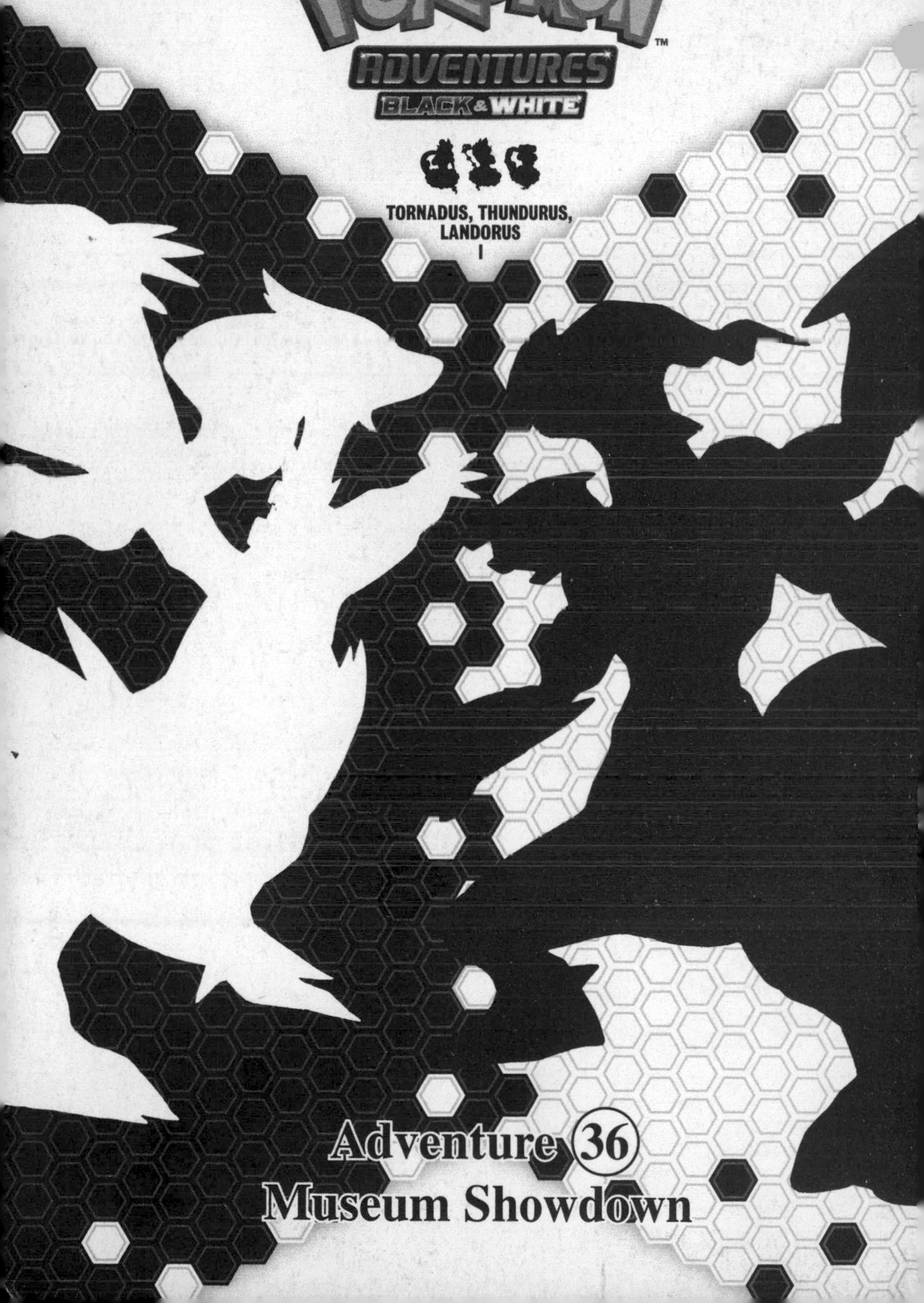

Adventure 36
Museum Showdown

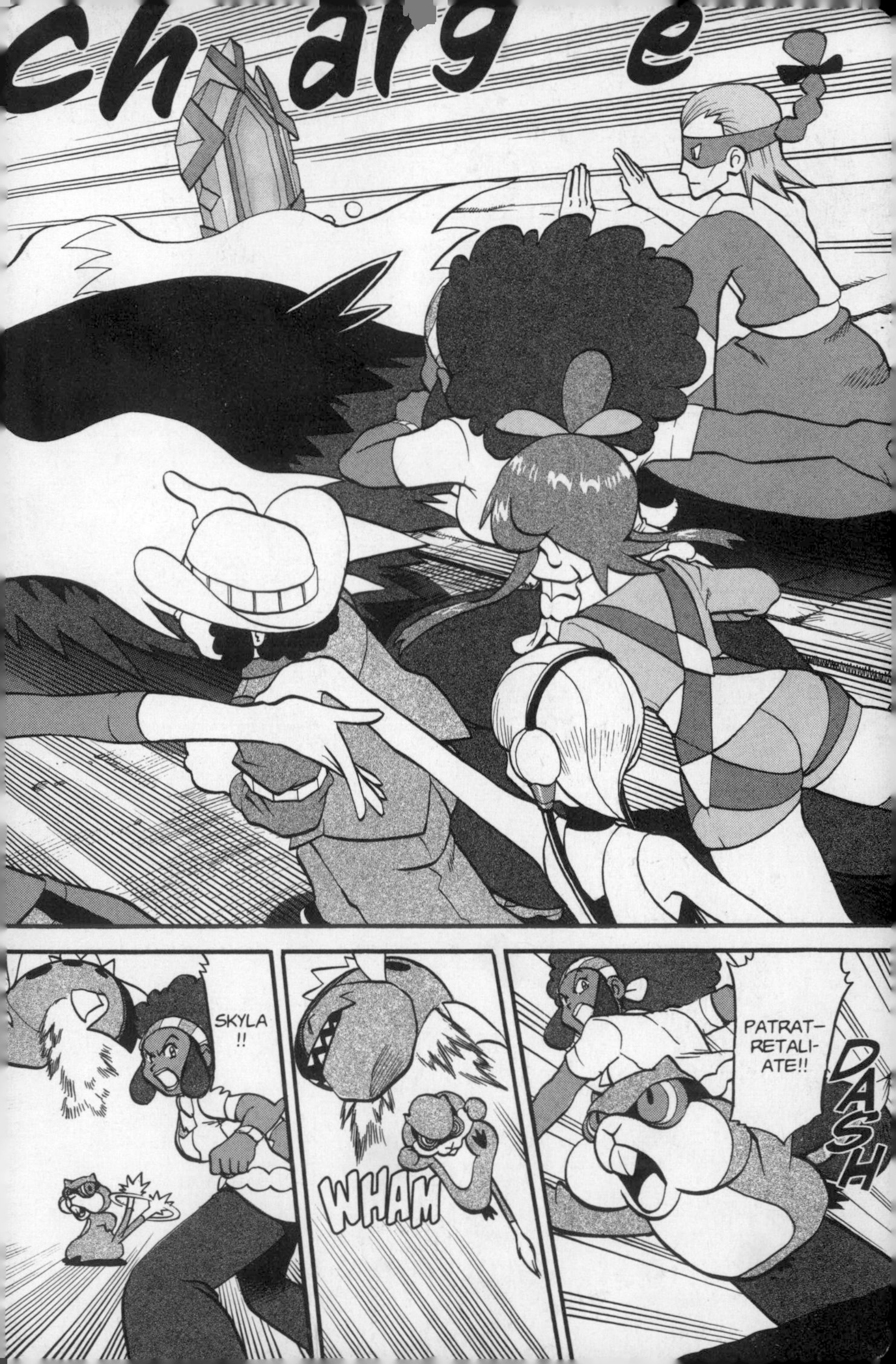
charge
PATRAT-RETALIATE!!
DASH
WHAM
SKYLA!!

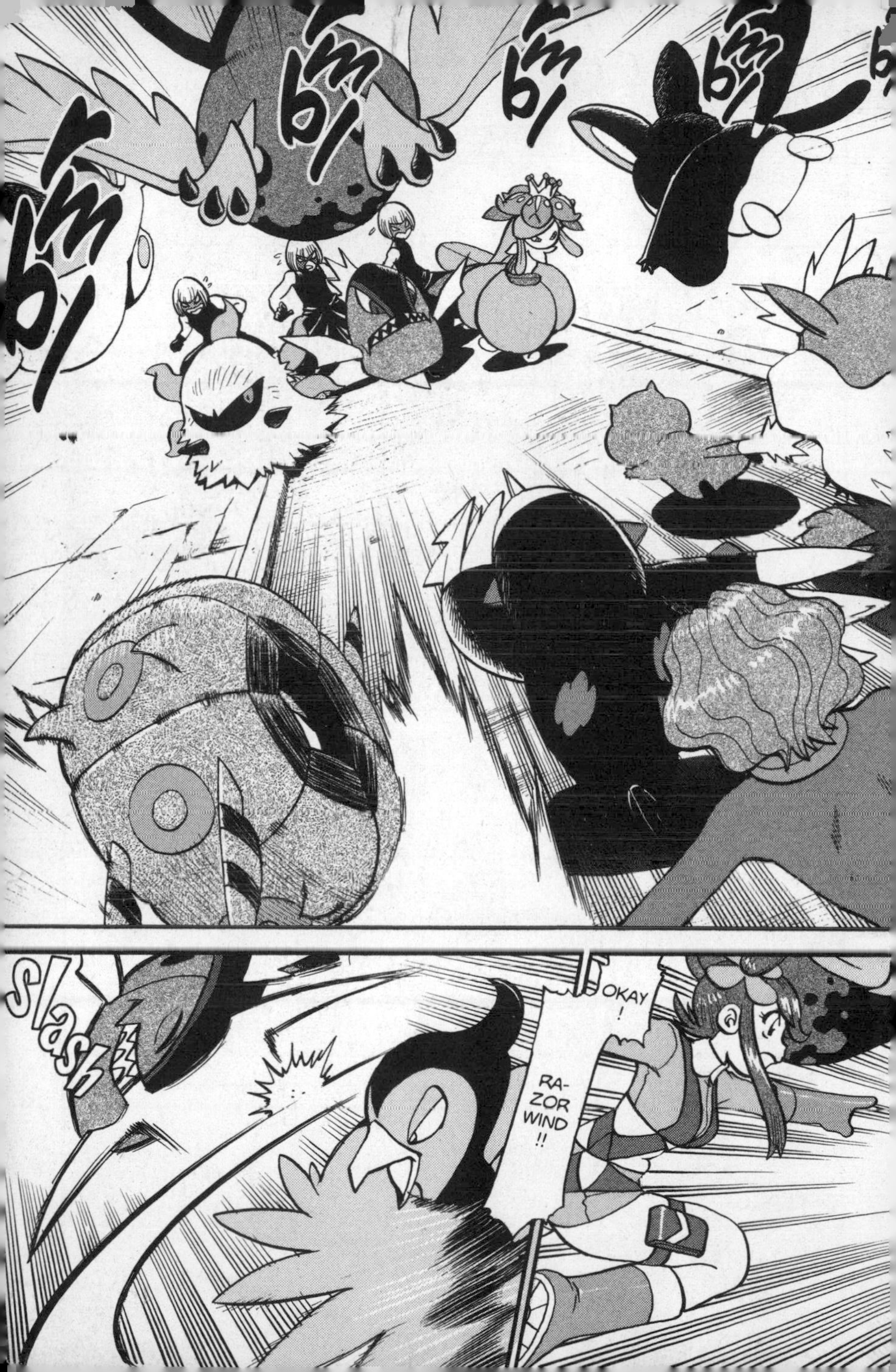
...
OKAY!
RA-
ZOR
WIND
!!
slash

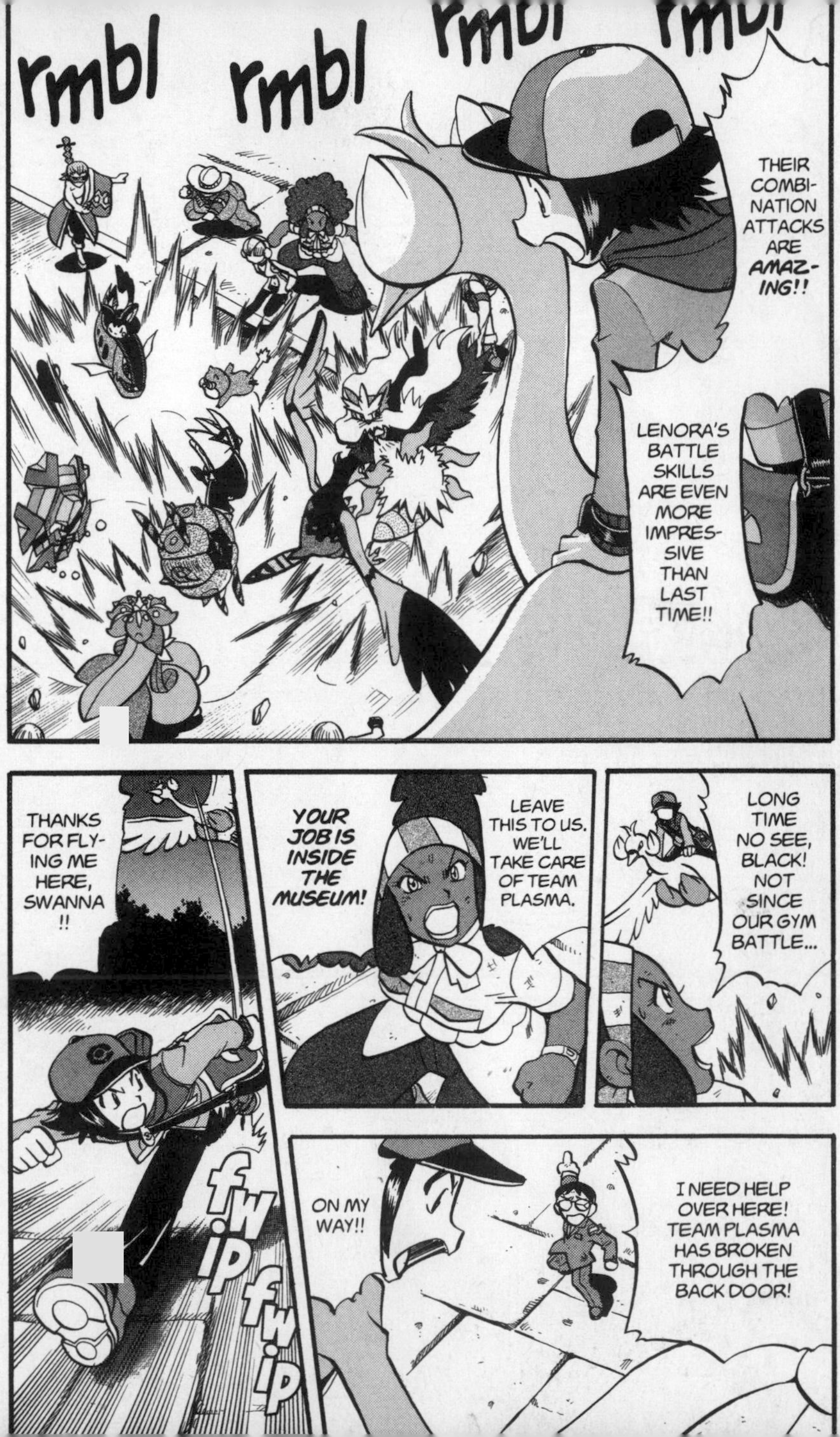
rmbl
rmbl
rmbl
rmbl
THEIR COMBINATION ATTACKS ARE AMAZING!!
LENORA'S BATTLE SKILLS ARE EVEN MORE IMPRESSIVE THAN LAST TIME!!
LONG TIME NO SEE, BLACK! NOT SINCE OUR GYM BATTLE...
LEAVE THIS TO US. WE'LL TAKE CARE OF TEAM PLASMA.
YOUR JOB IS INSIDE THE MUSEUM!
I NEED HELP OVER HERE! TEAM PLASMA HAS BROKEN THROUGH THE BACK DOOR!
ON MY WAY!!
THANKS FOR FLYING ME HERE, SWANNA!!
fwip
fwip

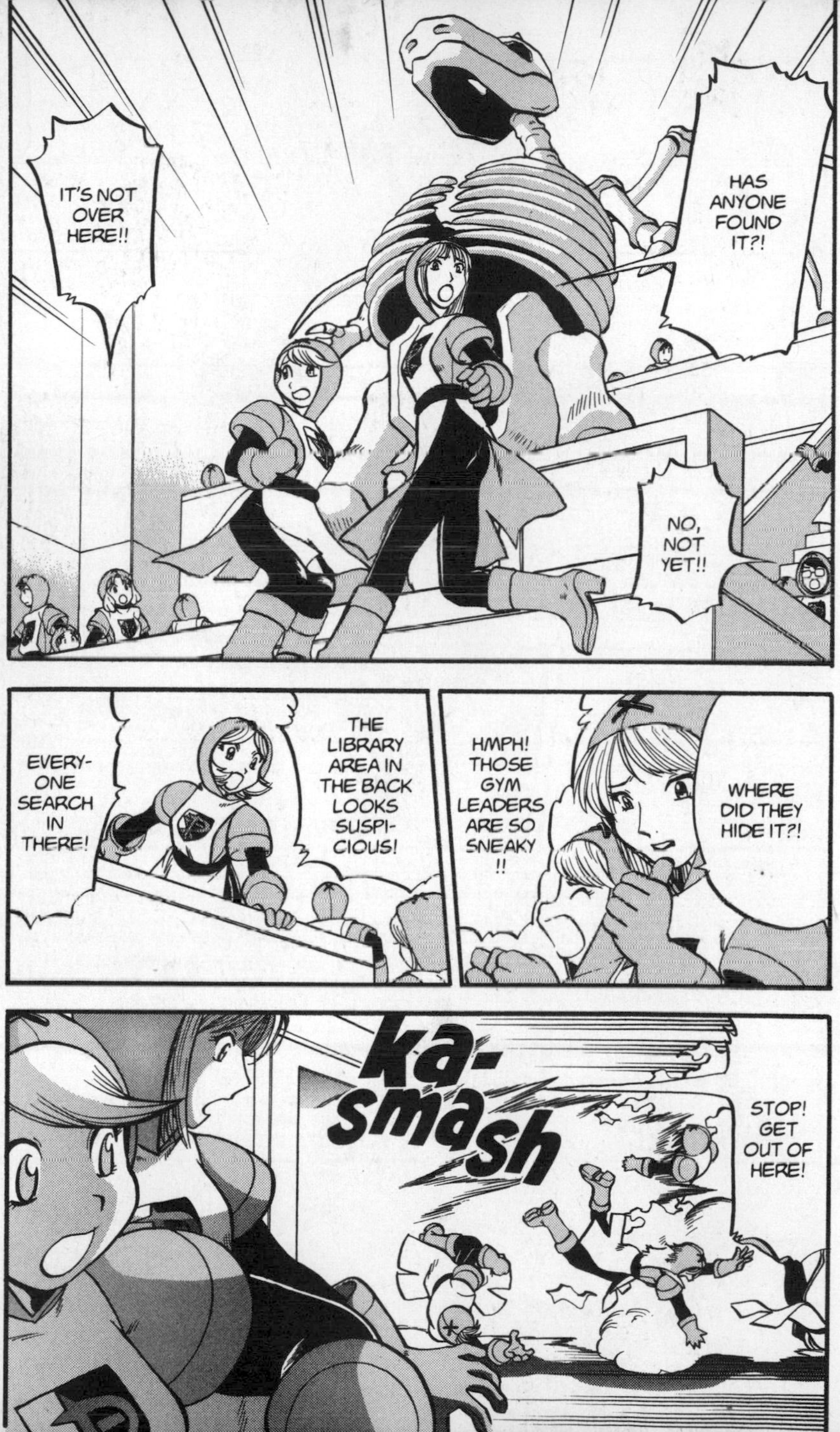
HAS ANYONE FOUND IT?!
IT'S NOT OVER HERE!!
NO, NOT YET!!
WHERE DID THEY HIDE IT?!
HMPH! THOSE GYM LEADERS ARE SO SNEAKY!!
THE LIBRARY AREA IN THE BACK LOOKS SUSPI-CIOUS!
EVERY-ONE SEARCH IN THERE!
STOP! GET OUT OF HERE!
ka-smash

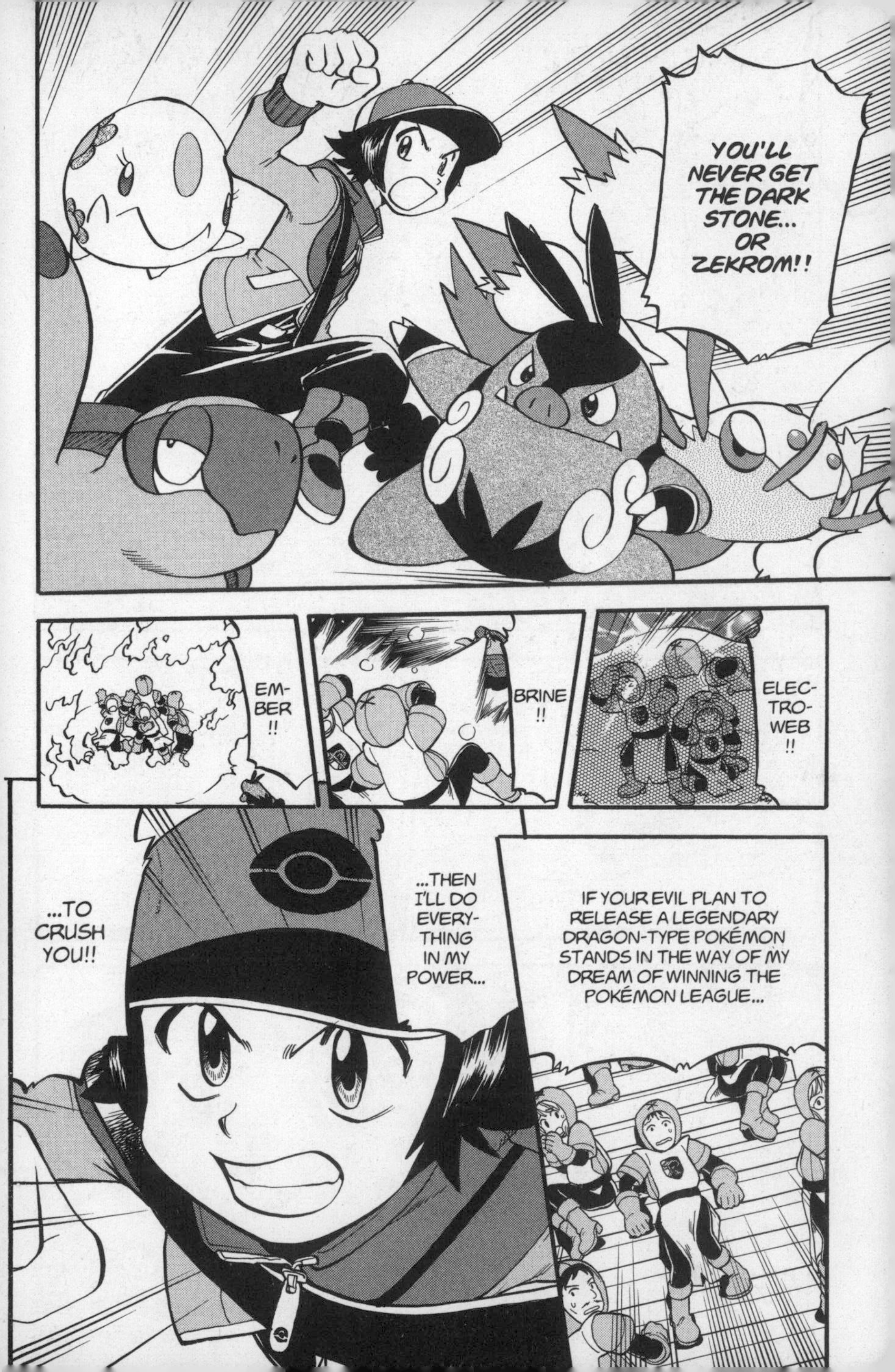
YOU'LL NEVER GET THE DARK STONE... OR ZEKROM!!
ELEC-TRO-WEB!!
BRINE!!
EM-BER!!
IF YOUR EVIL PLAN TO RELEASE A LEGENDARY DRAGON-TYPE POKÉMON STANDS IN THE WAY OF MY DREAM OF WINNING THE POKÉMON LEAGUE...
...THEN I'LL DO EVERY-THING IN MY POWER...
...TO CRUSH YOU!!

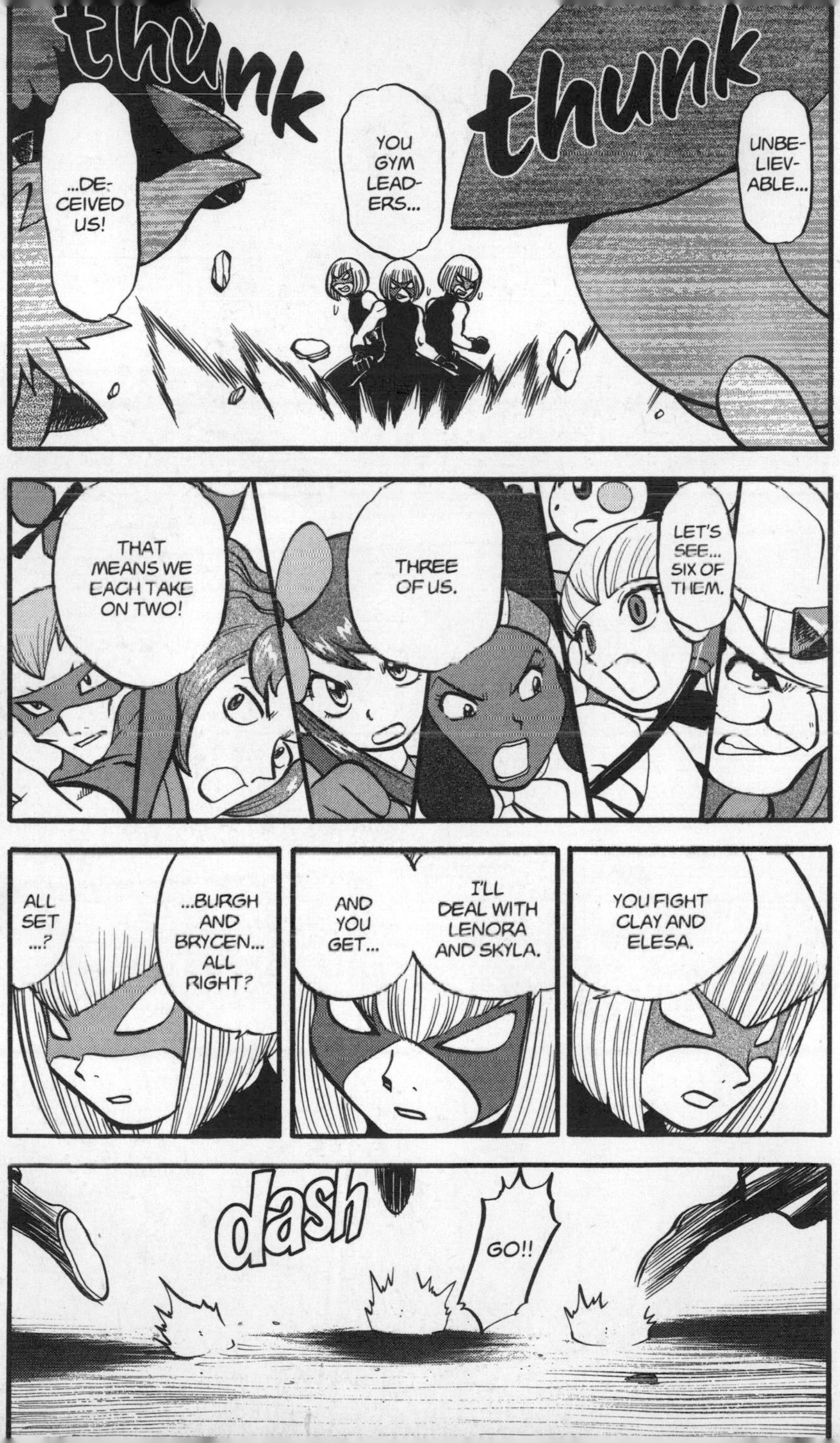
thunk
UNBE-LIEV-ABLE...
YOU GYM LEADERS...
thunk
...DE-CEIVED US!
LET'S SEE... SIX OF THEM.
THREE OF US.
THAT MEANS WE EACH TAKE ON TWO!
YOU FIGHT CLAY AND ELESA.
I'LL DEAL WITH LENORA AND SKYLA.
AND YOU GET...
...BURGH AND BRYCEN... ALL RIGHT?
ALL SET ...?
GO!!
dash

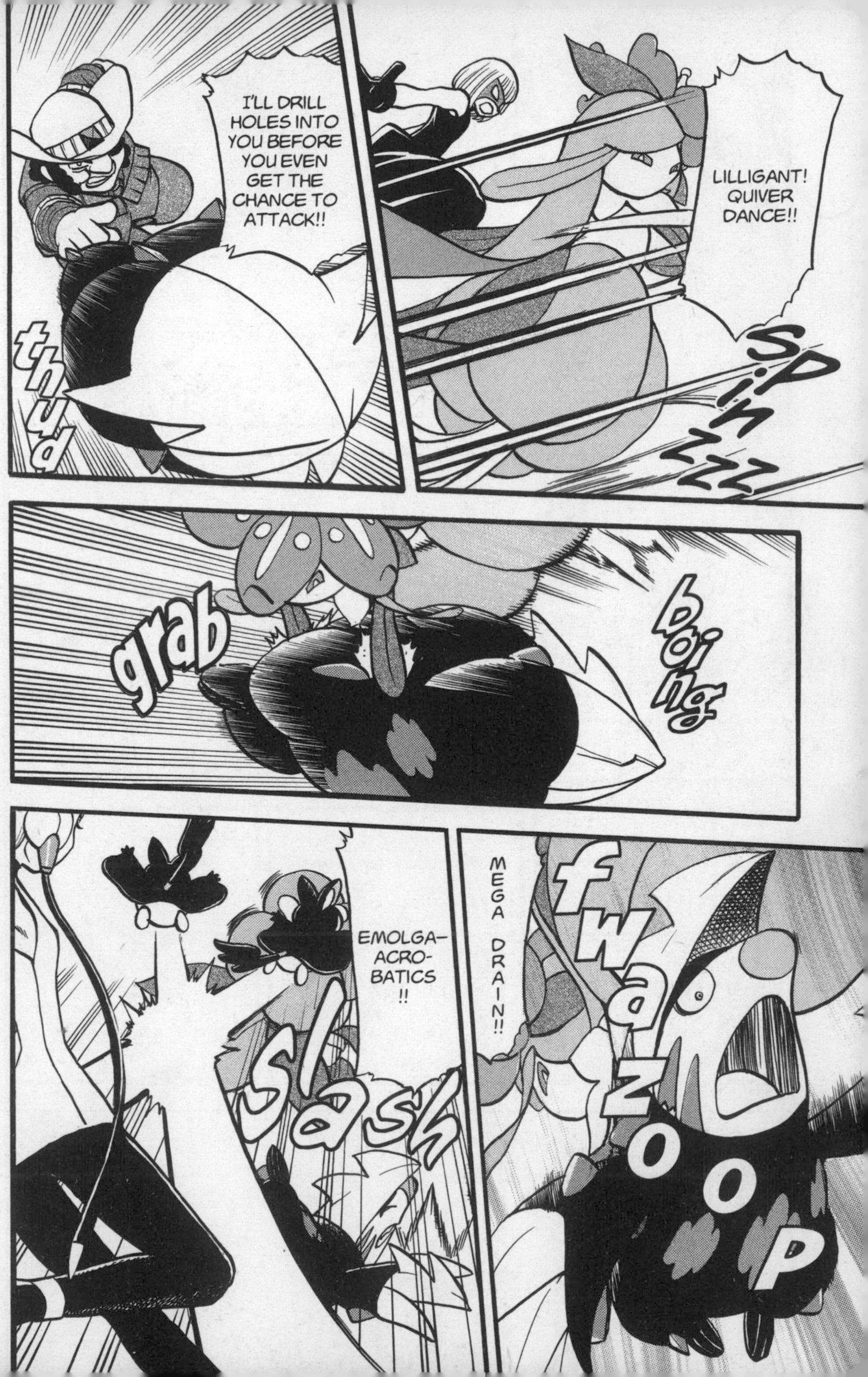
LILLIGANT! QUIVER DANCE!!
SPINZZZ
I'LL DRILL HOLES INTO YOU BEFORE YOU EVEN GET THE CHANCE TO ATTACK!!
thud
boing
grab
MEGA DRAIN!!
fwa
ZOOOP
EMOLGA-ACRO-BATICS !!
slash

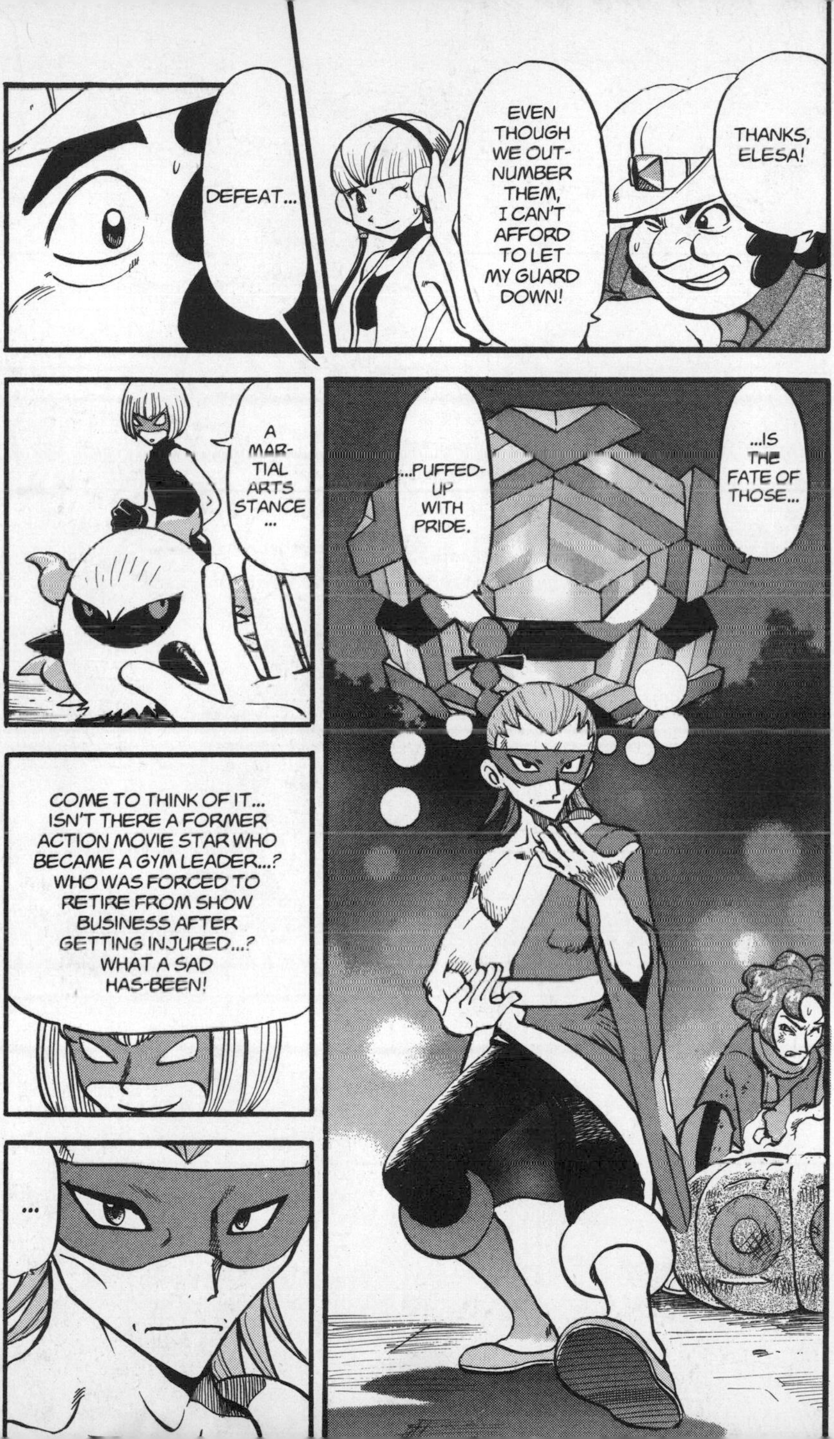
THANKS, ELESA!
EVEN THOUGH WE OUT-NUMBER THEM, I CAN'T AFFORD TO LET MY GUARD DOWN!
DEFEAT...
...IS THE FATE OF THOSE...
...PUFFED-UP WITH PRIDE.
A MAR-TIAL ARTS STANCE...
COME TO THINK OF IT... ISN'T THERE A FORMER ACTION MOVIE STAR WHO BECAME A GYM LEADER...? WHO WAS FORCED TO RETIRE FROM SHOW BUSINESS AFTER GETTING INJURED...? WHAT A SAD HAS-BEEN!
...

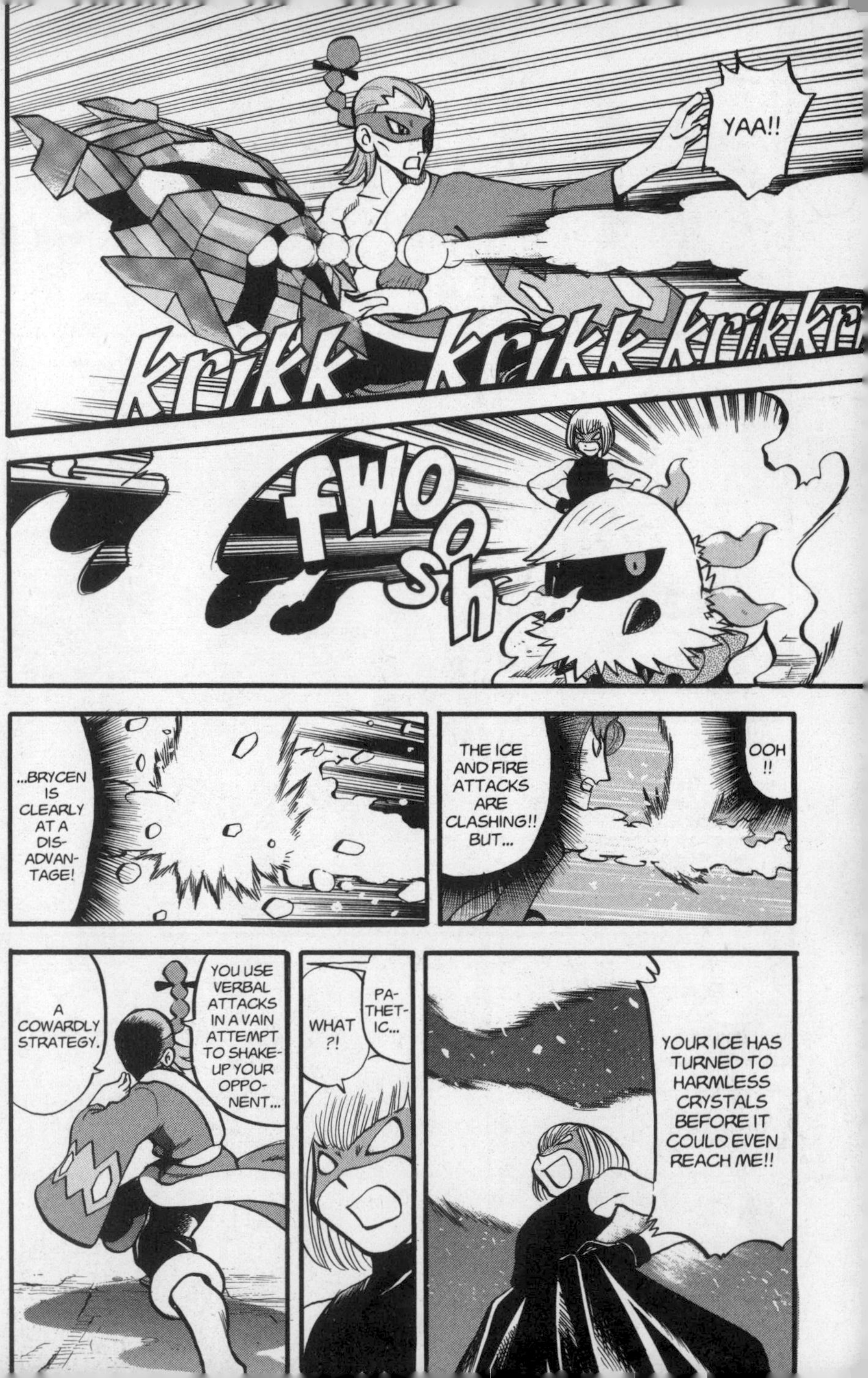
YAA!!
krikk krikk krikkr
fwoosh
OOH!!
THE ICE AND FIRE ATTACKS ARE CLASHING!! BUT...
...BRYCEN IS CLEARLY AT A DIS-ADVAN-TAGE!
YOUR ICE HAS TURNED TO HARMLESS CRYSTALS BEFORE IT COULD EVEN REACH ME!!
PA-THET-IC...
WHAT?!
YOU USE VERBAL ATTACKS IN A VAIN ATTEMPT TO SHAKE-UP YOUR OPPO-NENT...
A COWARDLY STRATEGY.

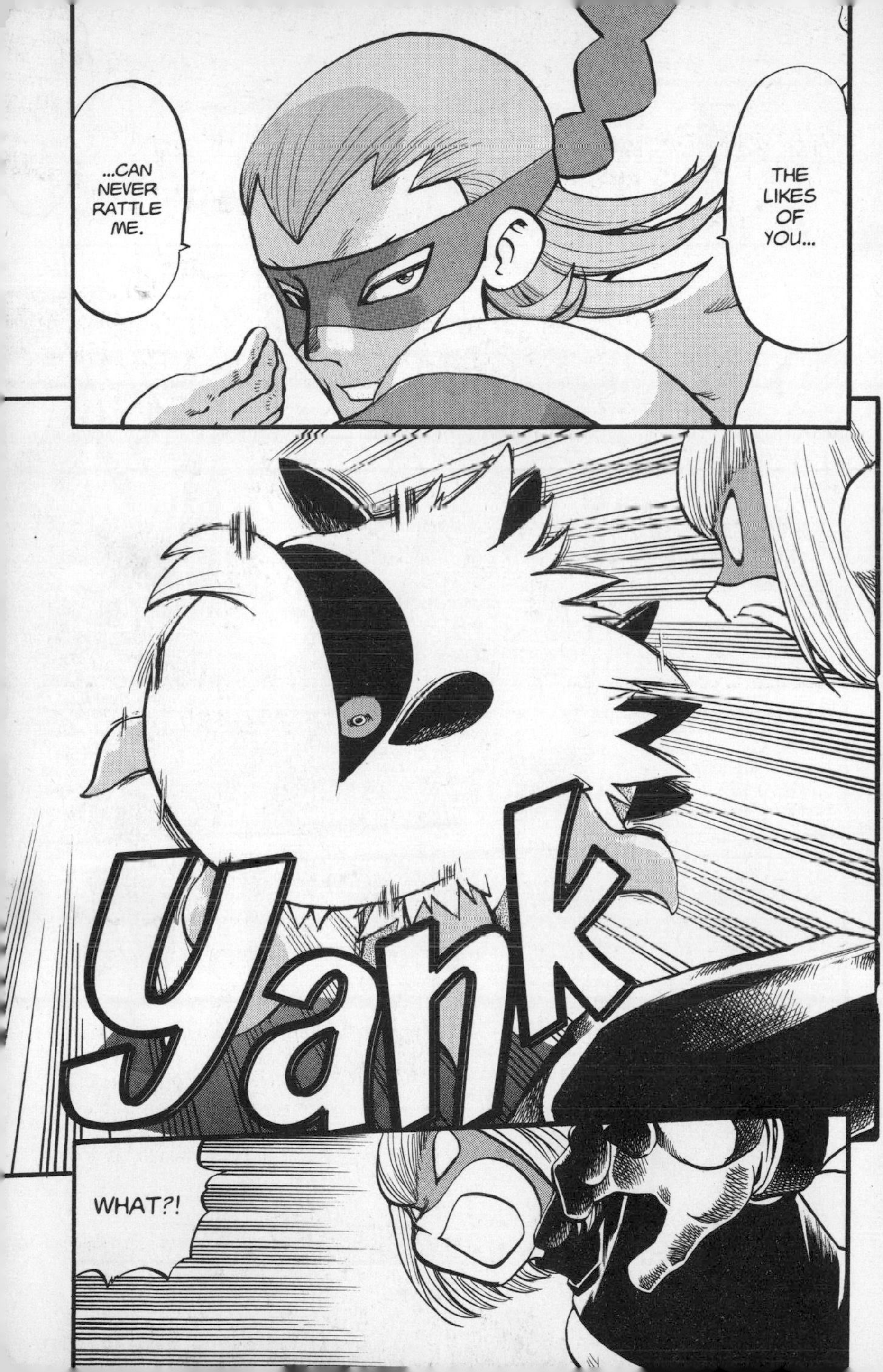
THE LIKES OF YOU...
...CAN NEVER RATTLE ME.
Yank
WHAT?!

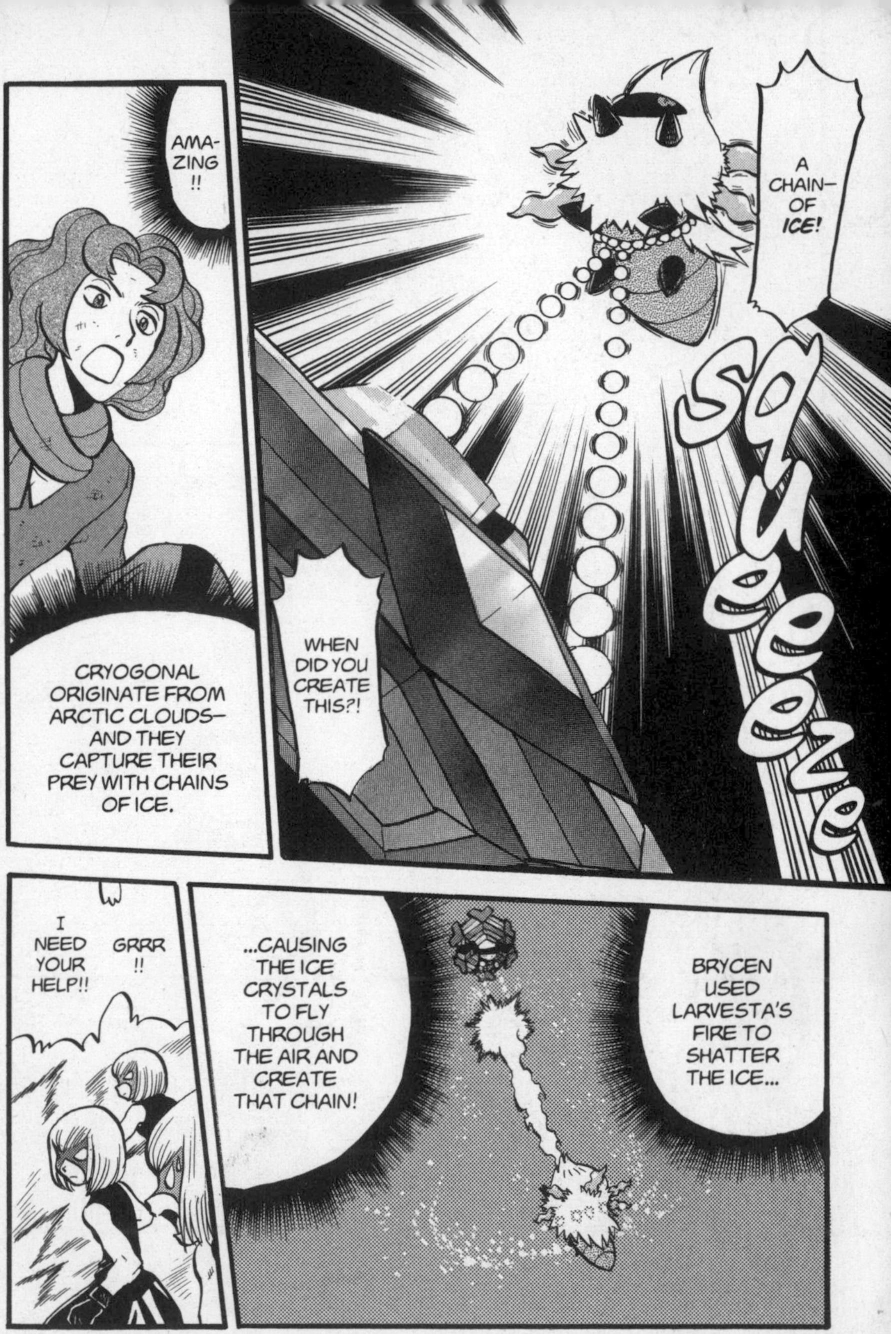
A CHAIN—OF ICE!
SQUEEZE
WHEN DID YOU CREATE THIS?!
AMAZING!!
CRYOGONAL ORIGINATE FROM ARCTIC CLOUDS—AND THEY CAPTURE THEIR PREY WITH CHAINS OF ICE.
BRYCEN USED LARVESTA'S FIRE TO SHATTER THE ICE...
...CAUSING THE ICE CRYSTALS TO FLY THROUGH THE AIR AND CREATE THAT CHAIN!
GRRR!!
I NEED YOUR HELP!!

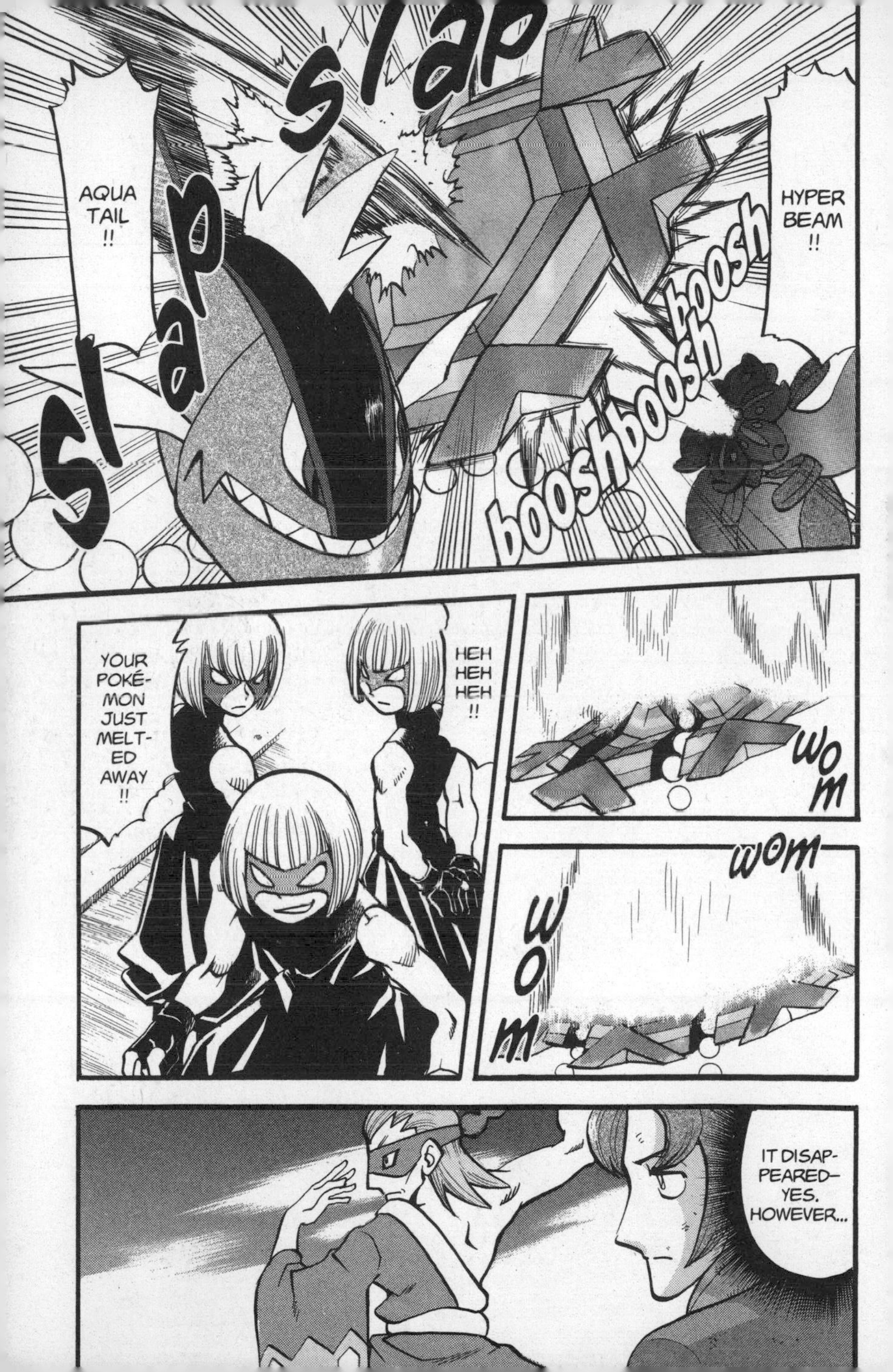
HYPER BEAM !!
booshbooshboosh
slap
slap
AQUA TAIL !!
wom
wom
wom
wom
HEH HEH HEH !!
YOUR POKÉ-MON JUST MELT-ED AWAY !!
IT DISAP-PEARED—YES. HOWEVER...

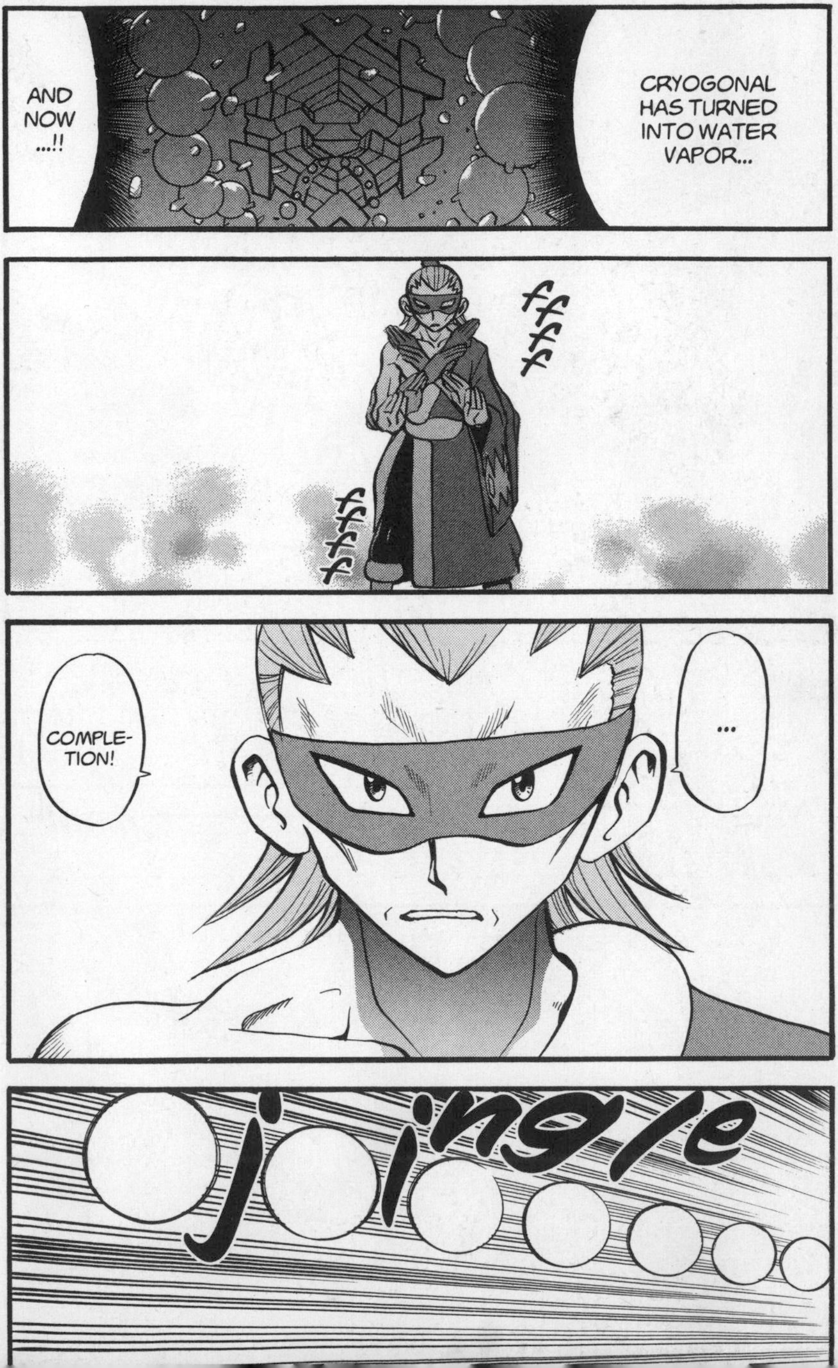
CRYOGONAL HAS TURNED INTO WATER VAPOR...
AND NOW ...!!
ffff
ffff
...
COMPLE-TION!
jingle

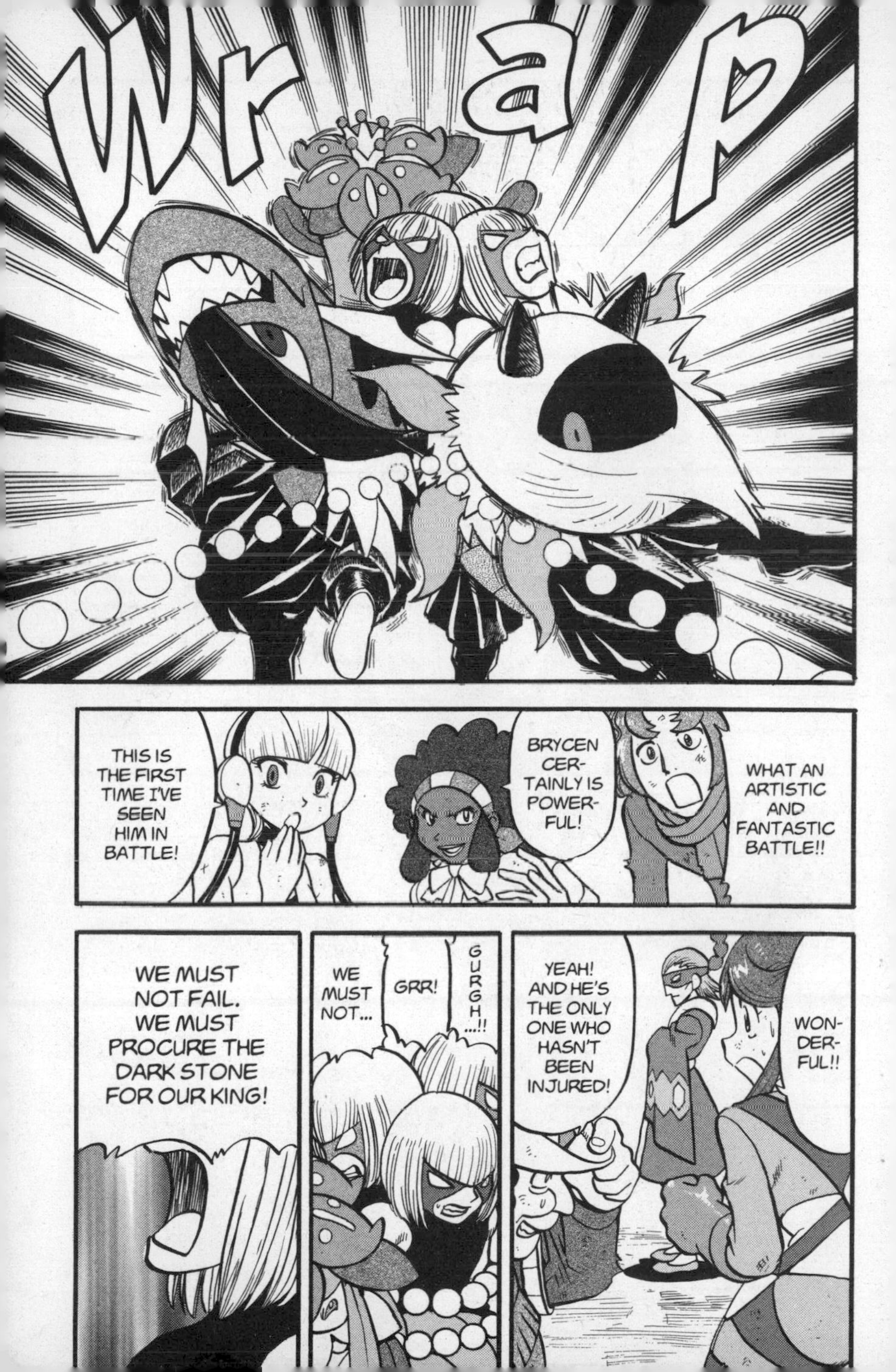
Wrap
WHAT AN ARTISTIC AND FANTASTIC BATTLE!!
BRYCEN CER-TAINLY IS POWER-FUL!
THIS IS THE FIRST TIME I'VE SEEN HIM IN BATTLE!
WON-DER-FUL!!
YEAH! AND HE'S THE ONLY ONE WHO HASN'T BEEN INJURED!
GURGH...!!
GRR!
WE MUST NOT...
WE MUST NOT FAIL. WE MUST PROCURE THE DARK STONE FOR OUR KING!

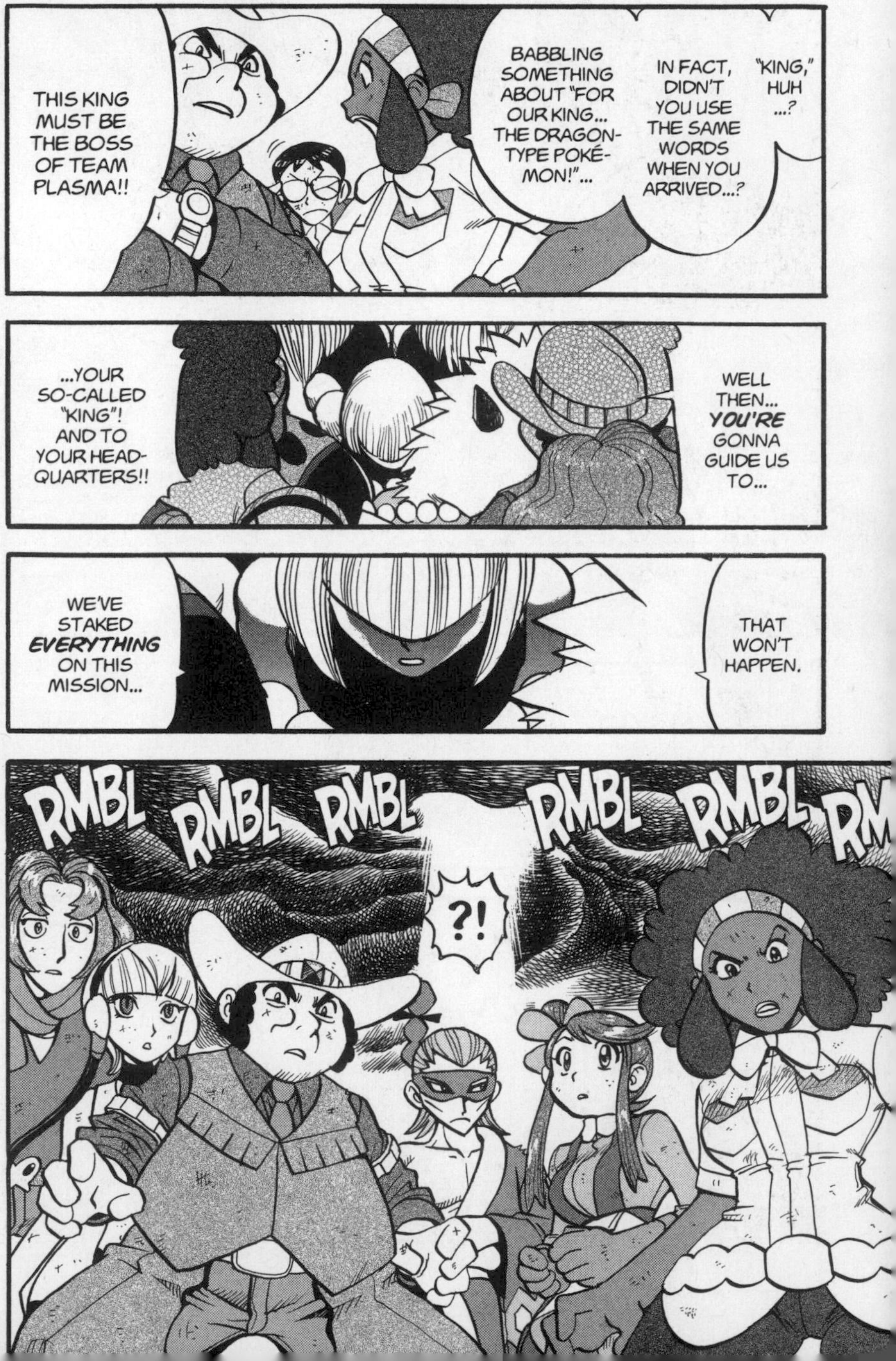
"KING," HUH ...?
IN FACT, DIDN'T YOU USE THE SAME WORDS WHEN YOU ARRIVED...?
BABBLING SOMETHING ABOUT "FOR OUR KING... THE DRAGON-TYPE POKÉ-MON!"...
THIS KING MUST BE THE BOSS OF TEAM PLASMA!!
WELL THEN... *YOU'RE* GONNA GUIDE US TO...
...YOUR SO-CALLED "KING"! AND TO YOUR HEAD-QUARTERS!!
THAT WON'T HAPPEN.
WE'VE STAKED *EVERYTHING* ON THIS MISSION...
RMBL RMBL RMBL RMBL RMBL RM
?!

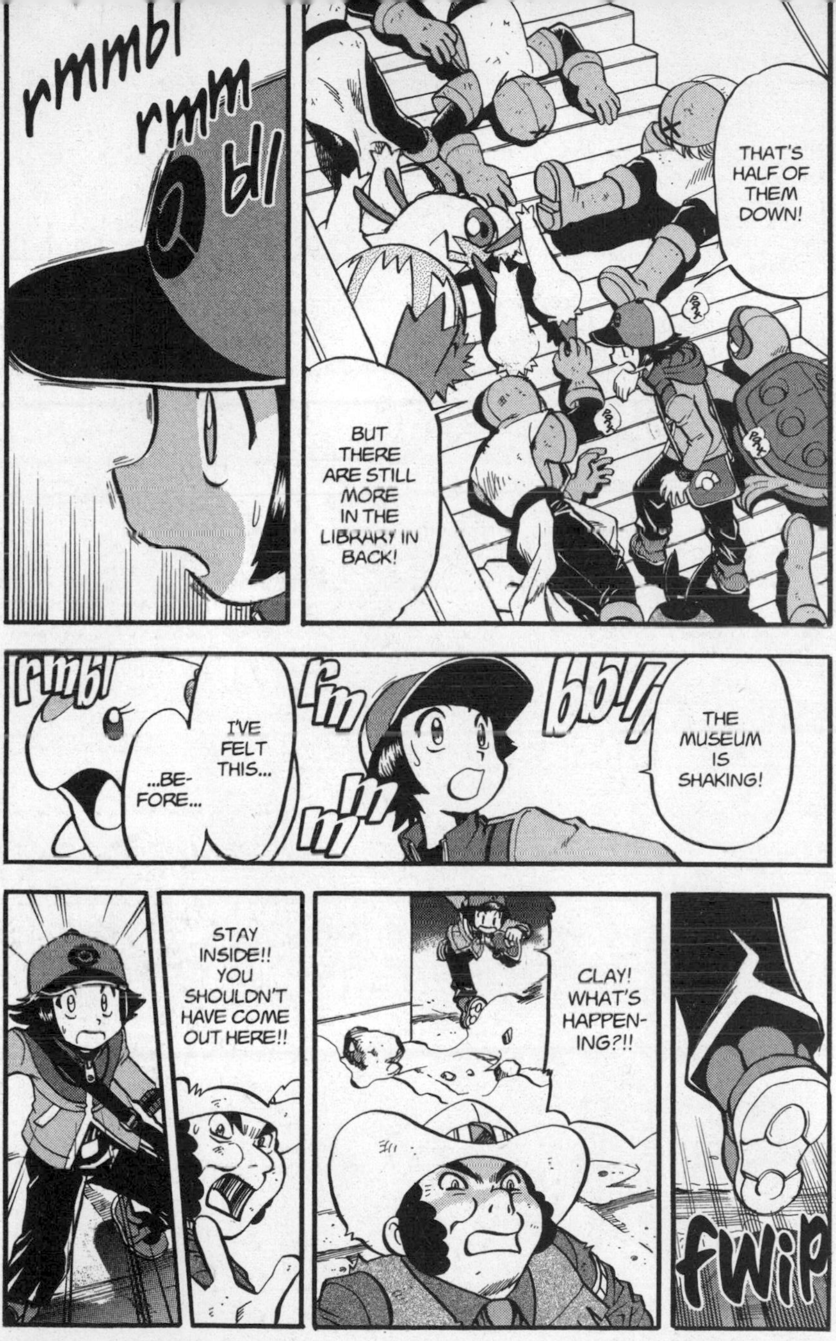
THAT'S HALF OF THEM DOWN!
BUT THERE ARE STILL MORE IN THE LIBRARY IN BACK!
rmmbl rmm bl
bb
THE MUSEUM IS SHAKING!
rm
mm
I'VE FELT THIS...
...BE-FORE...
rmbl
fwip
CLAY! WHAT'S HAPPEN-ING?!!
STAY INSIDE!! YOU SHOULDN'T HAVE COME OUT HERE!!

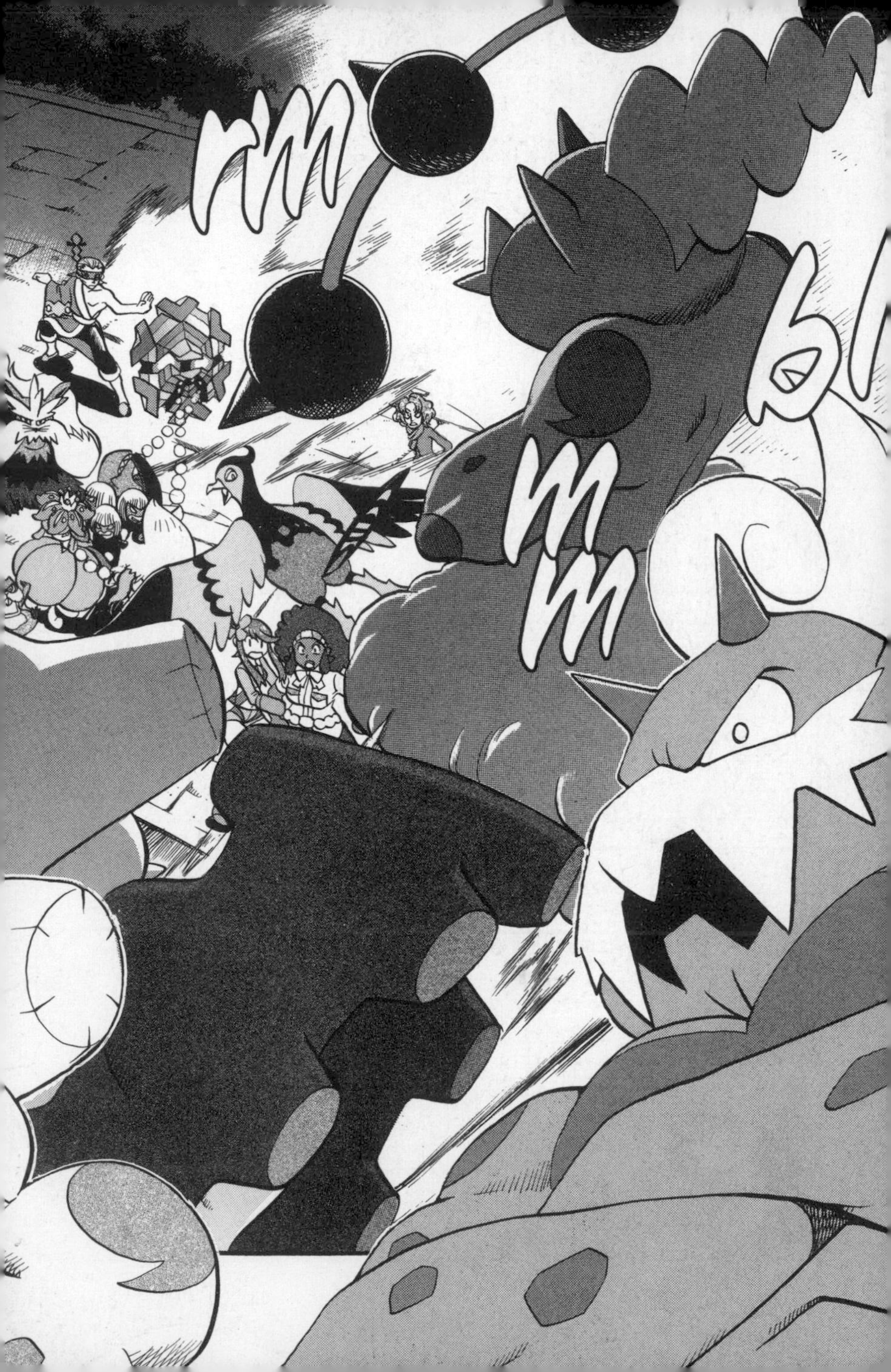
rm
mmm
bl

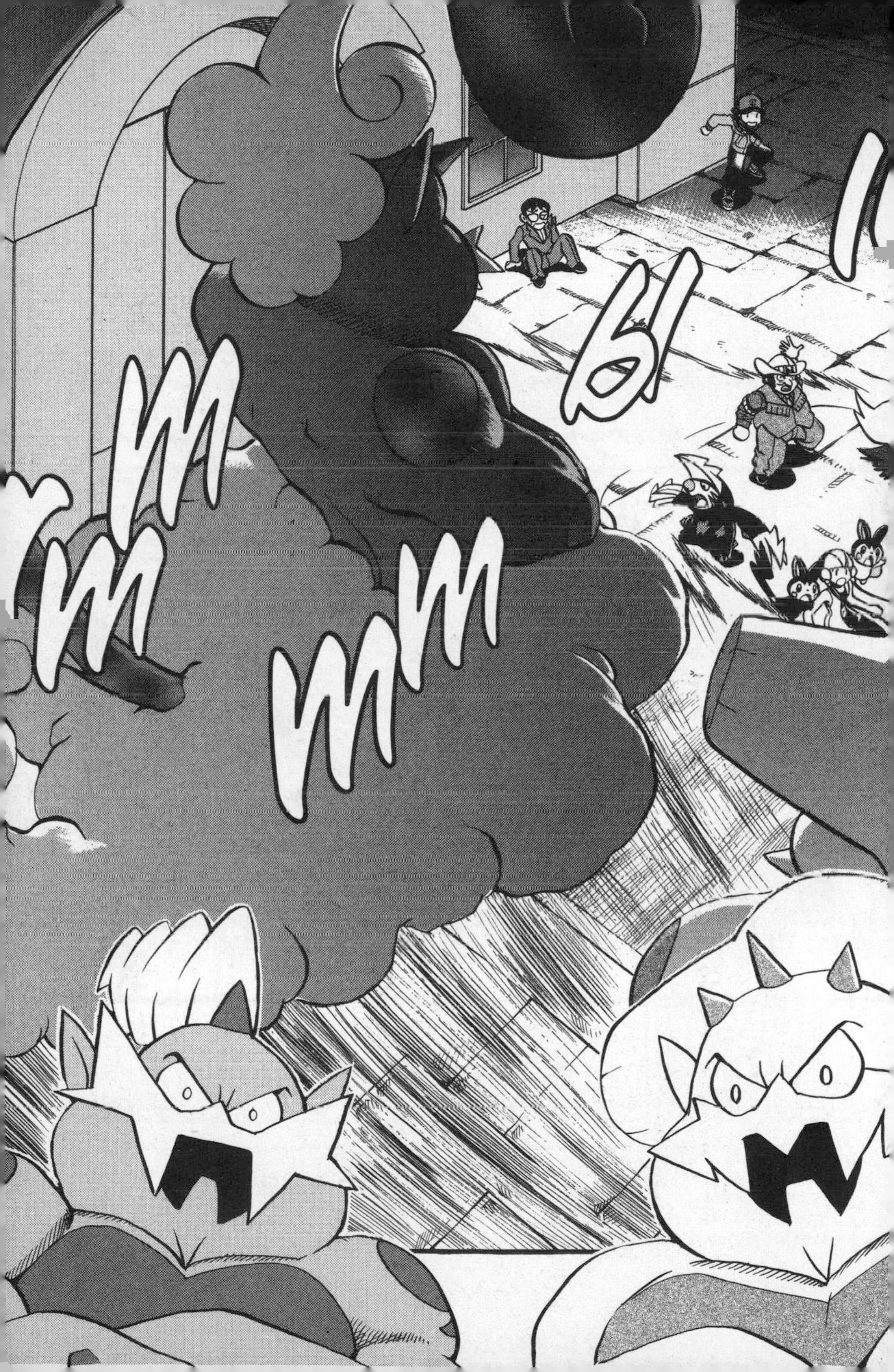

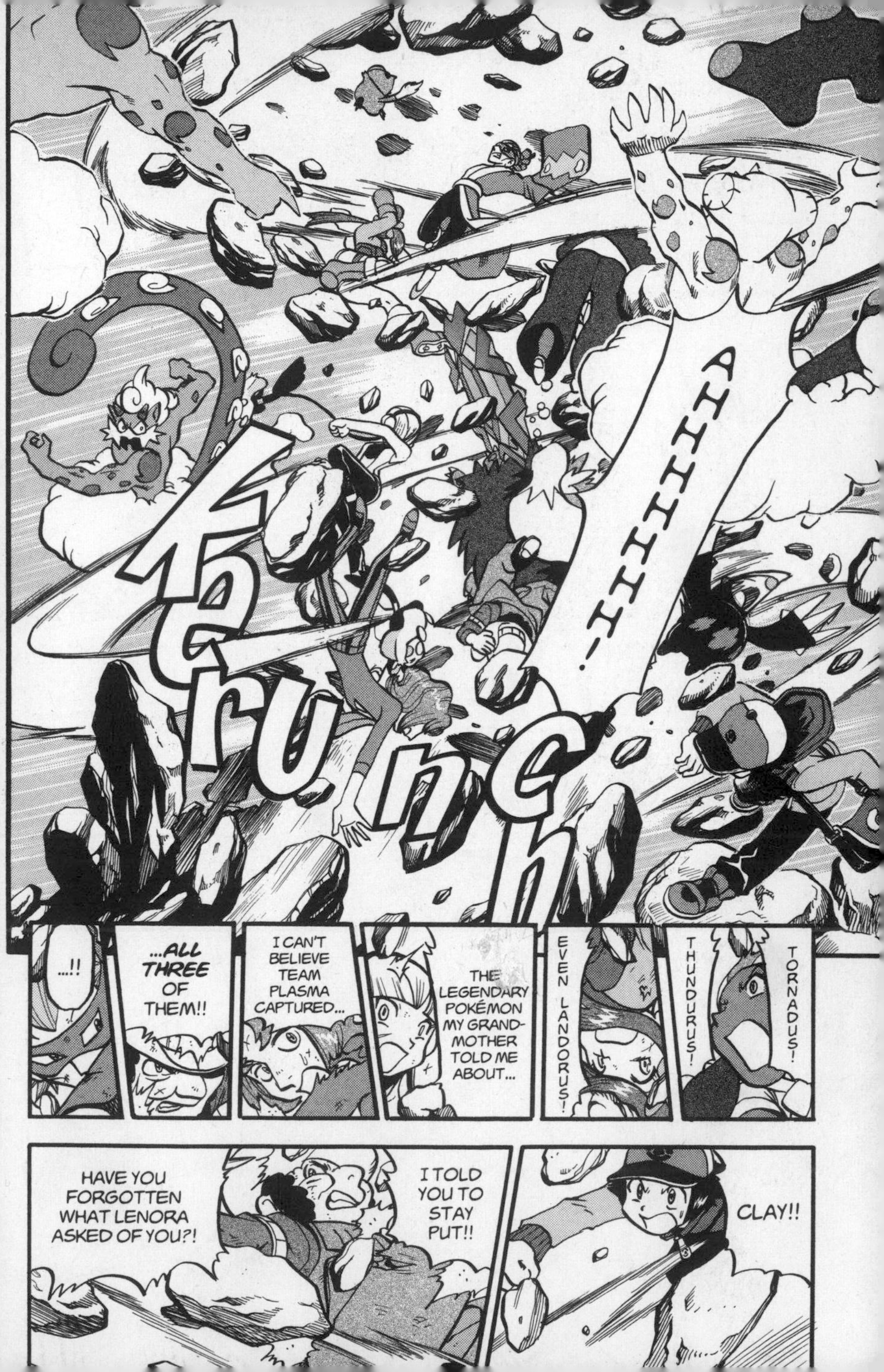
AHHHHHHH!
crunch
TORNADUS!
THUNDURUS!
EVEN LANDORUS!
THE LEGENDARY POKÉMON MY GRAND-MOTHER TOLD ME ABOUT...
I CAN'T BELIEVE TEAM PLASMA CAPTURED...
...ALL THREE OF THEM!!
...!!
CLAY!!
I TOLD YOU TO STAY PUT!!
HAVE YOU FORGOTTEN WHAT LENORA ASKED OF YOU?!

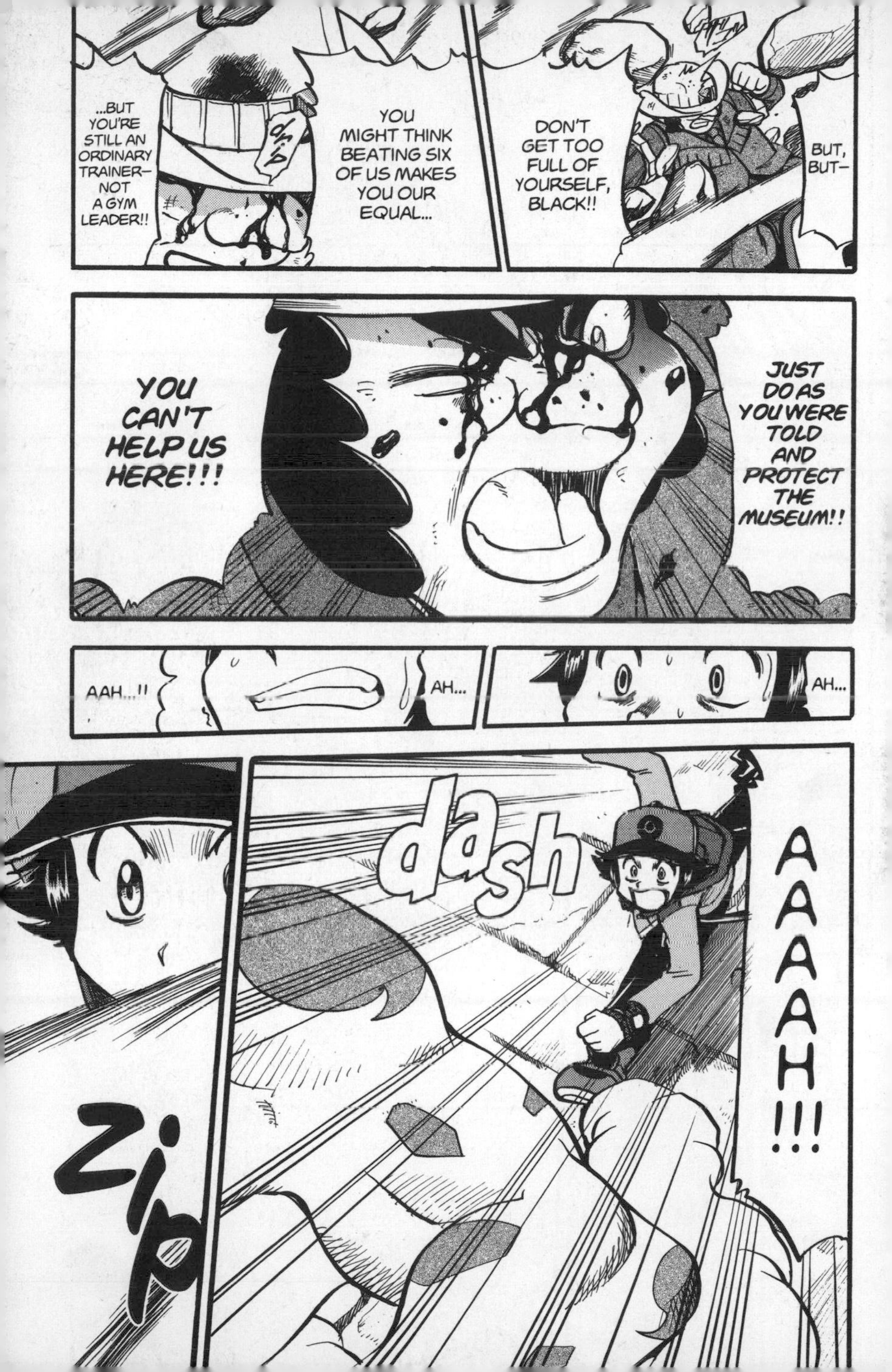
BUT, BUT–
DON'T GET TOO FULL OF YOURSELF, BLACK!!
YOU MIGHT THINK BEATING SIX OF US MAKES YOU OUR EQUAL...
drip
...BUT YOU'RE STILL AN ORDINARY TRAINER— NOT A GYM LEADER!!
JUST DO AS YOU WERE TOLD AND PROTECT THE MUSEUM!!
YOU CAN'T HELP US HERE!!!
AH...
AH...
AAH...!!
AAAAH!!!
dash
zip

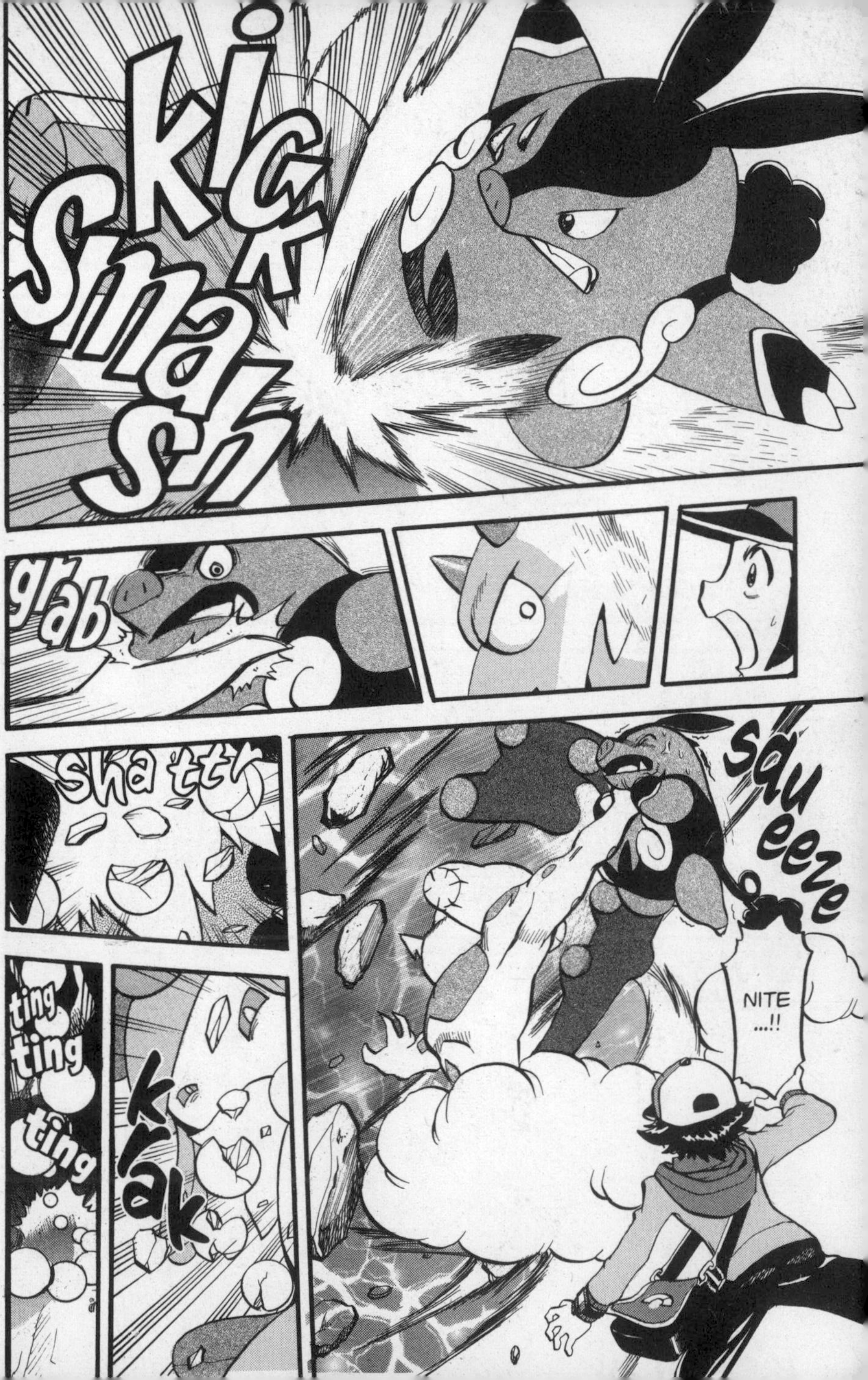
kick
smash
grab
squeeze
NITE ...!!
shattr
krak
ting ting ting

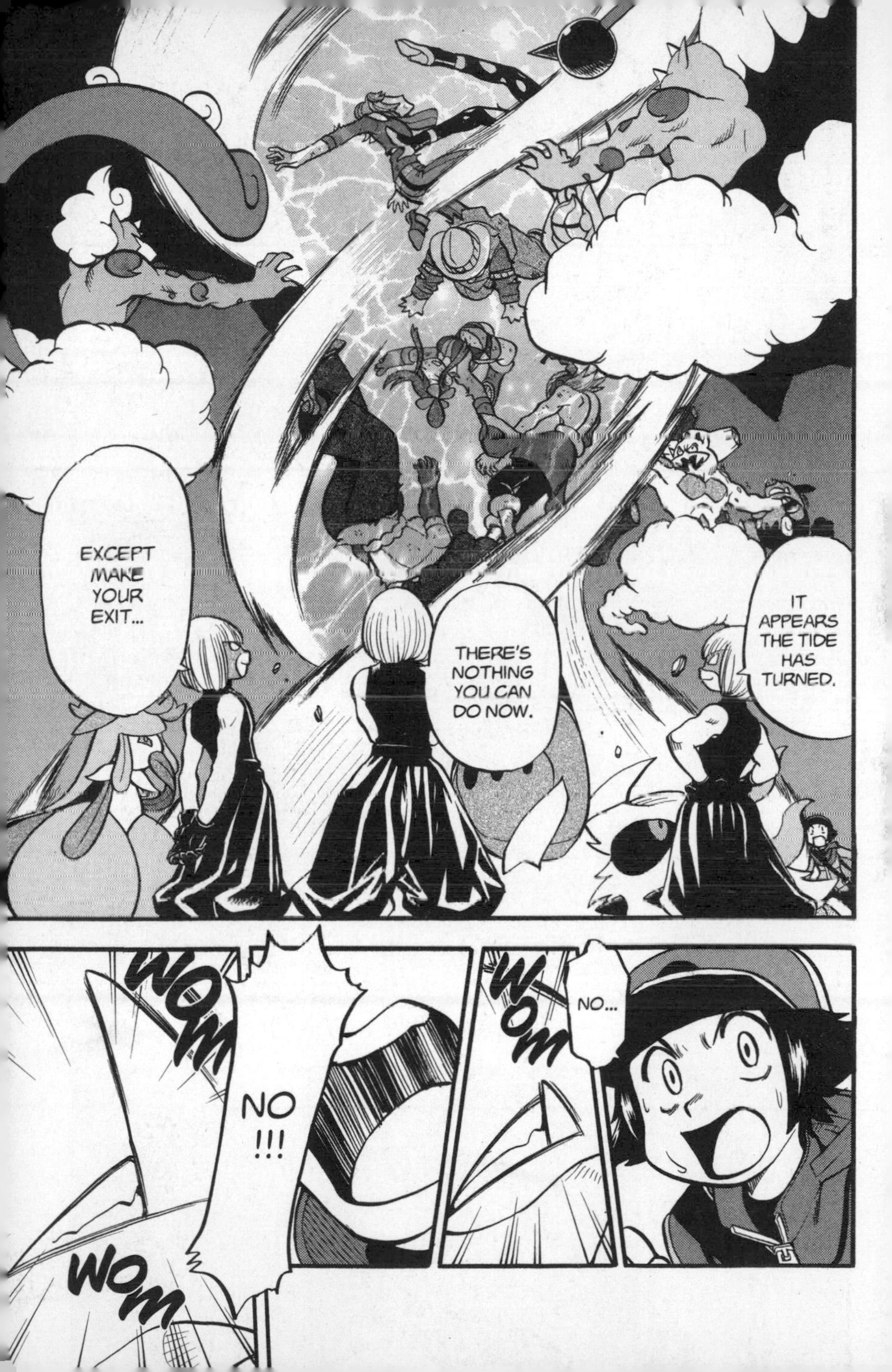
IT APPEARS THE TIDE HAS TURNED.
THERE'S NOTHING YOU CAN DO NOW.
EXCEPT MAKE YOUR EXIT...
NO...
WOM
WOM
NO !!!
WOM

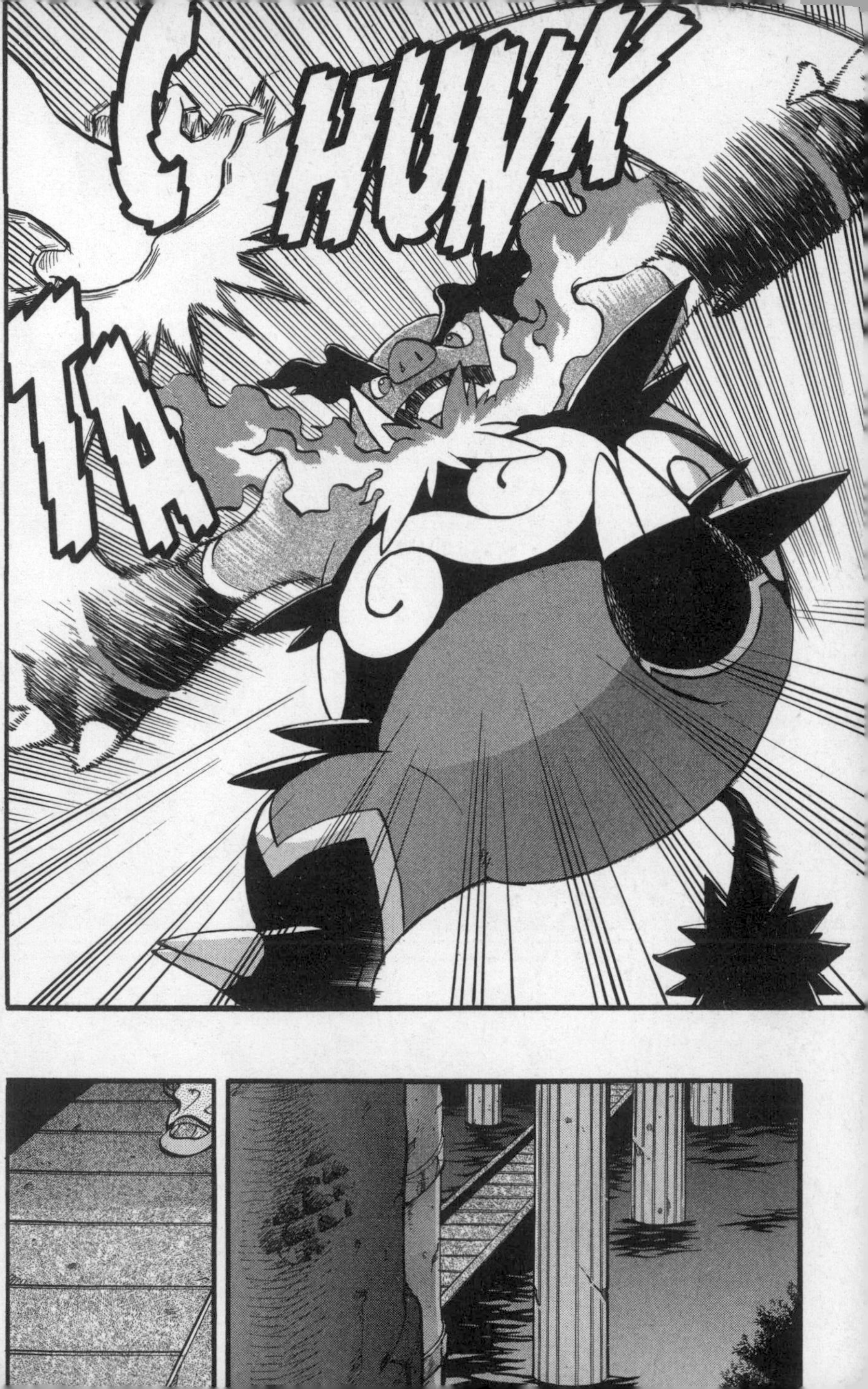
CHUNK
TA

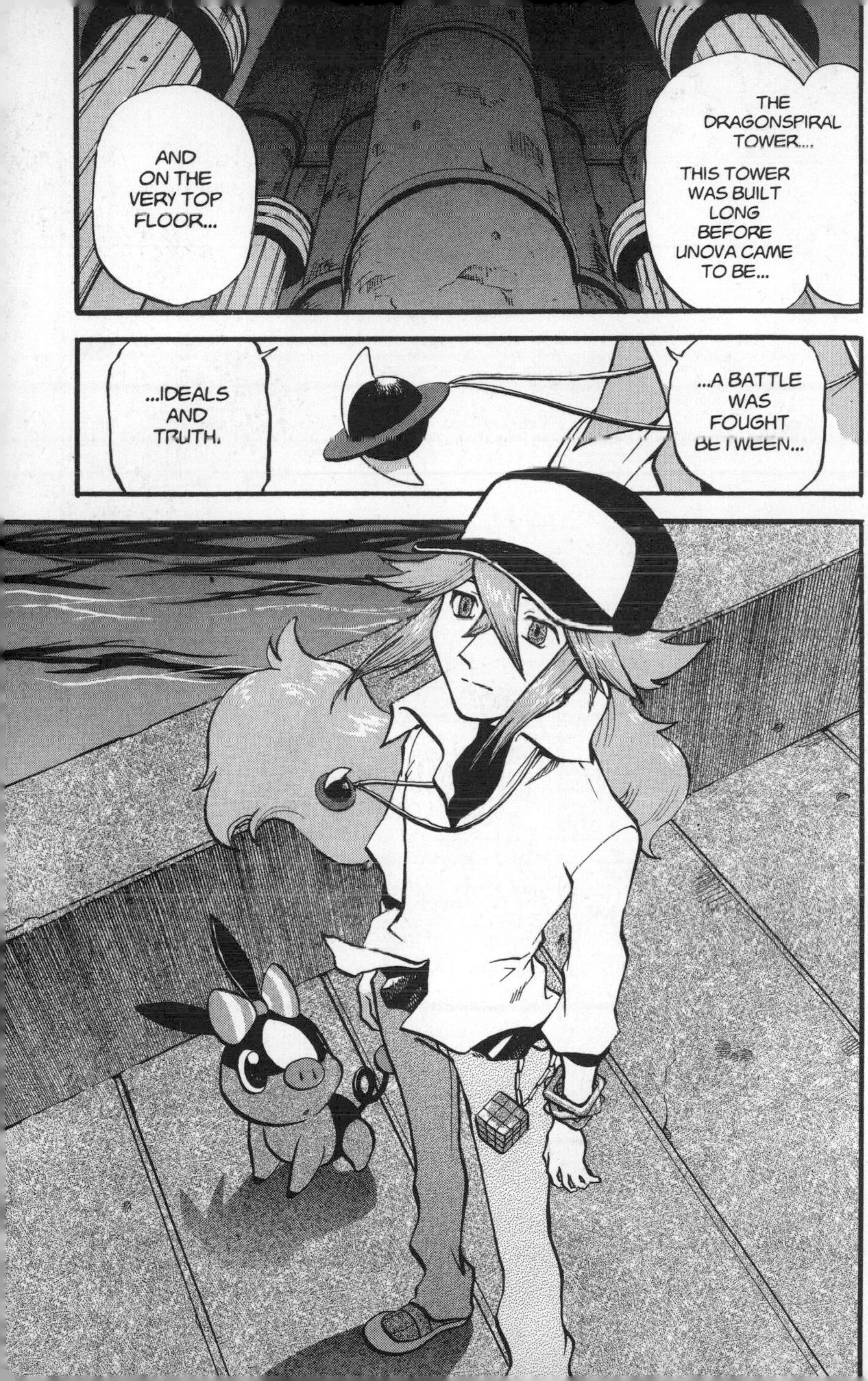
THE DRAGONSPIRAL TOWER....
THIS TOWER WAS BUILT LONG BEFORE UNOVA CAME TO BE...
AND ON THE VERY TOP FLOOR...
...A BATTLE WAS FOUGHT BETWEEN...
...IDEALS AND TRUTH.

ADVENTURE MAP

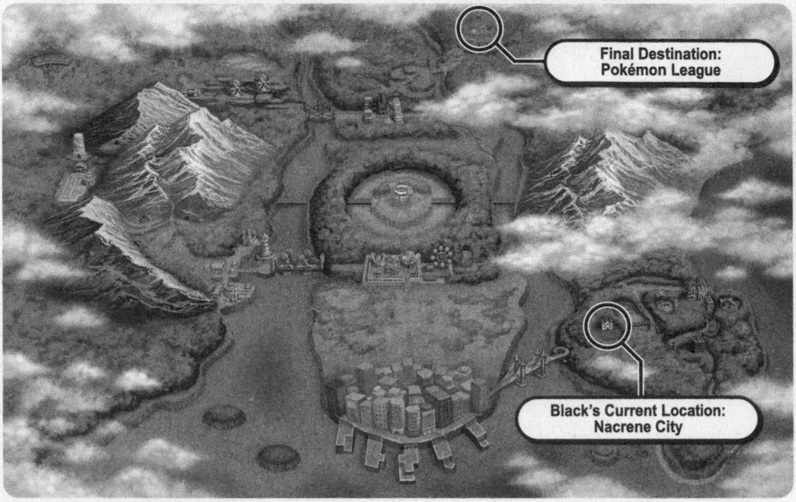
Final Destination:
Pokémon League
Black's Current Location:
Nacrene City

BLACK

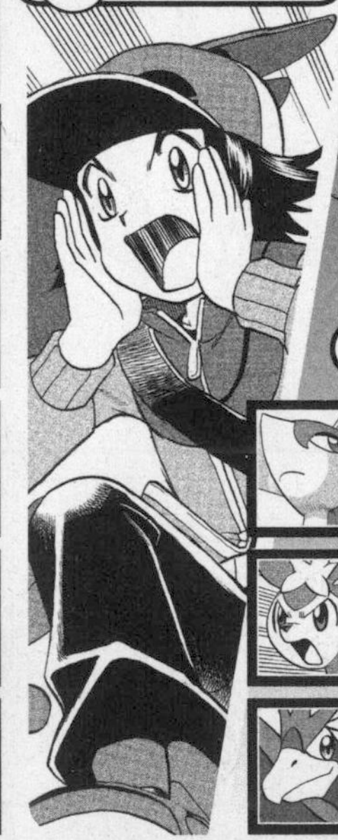

Mega Fire Pig Pokémon	**Nite**
Emboar ♂	Fire / Fighting
Lv.36	Ability: Blaze

Dream Eater Pokémon	**Musha**
Munna ♂	Psychic
Lv.52	Ability: Forewarn

EleSpider Pokémon	**Tula**
Galvantula ♂	Bug / Electric
Lv.53	Ability: Unnerve

Prototurtle Pokémon	**Costa**
Tirtouga ♂	Water / Rock
Lv.34	Ability: Solid Rock

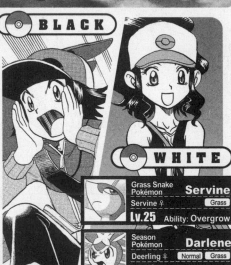

WHITE

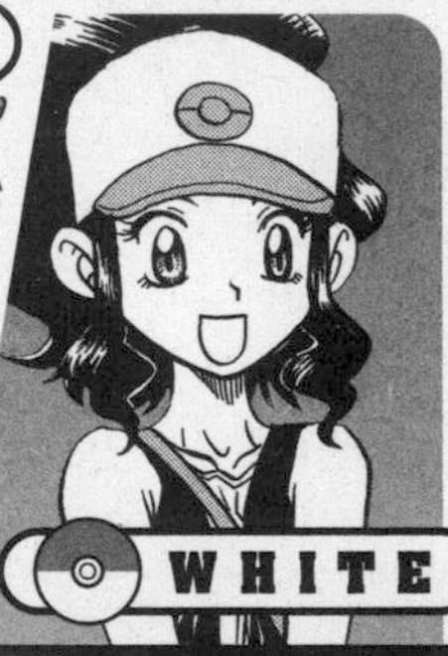

Grass Snake Pokémon	**Servine**
Servine ♀	Grass
Lv.25	Ability: Overgrow

Season Pokémon	**Darlene**
Deerling ♀	Normal / Grass
Lv.23	Ability: Chlorophyll

Valiant Pokémon	**Brav**
Braviary ♂	Normal / Flying
Lv.54	Ability: Sheer Force

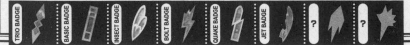

TRIO BADGE · BASIC BADGE · INSECT BADGE · BOLT BADGE · QUAKE BADGE · JET BADGE · ? · ?

POKÉMON ADVENTURES BLACK & WHITE

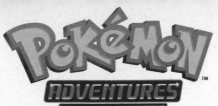

TORNADUS, THUNDURUS, LANDORUS
II

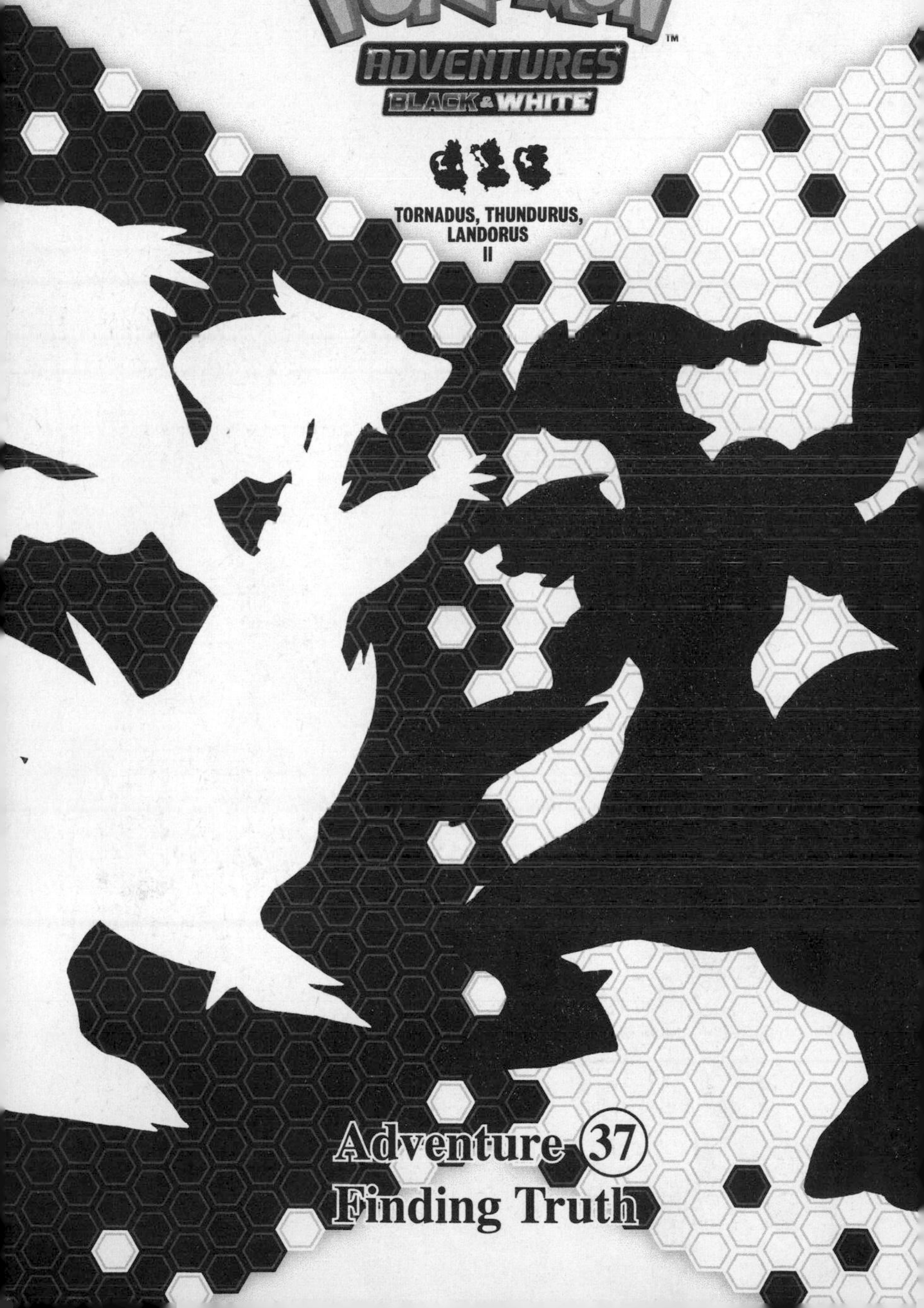

Adventure 37
Finding Truth

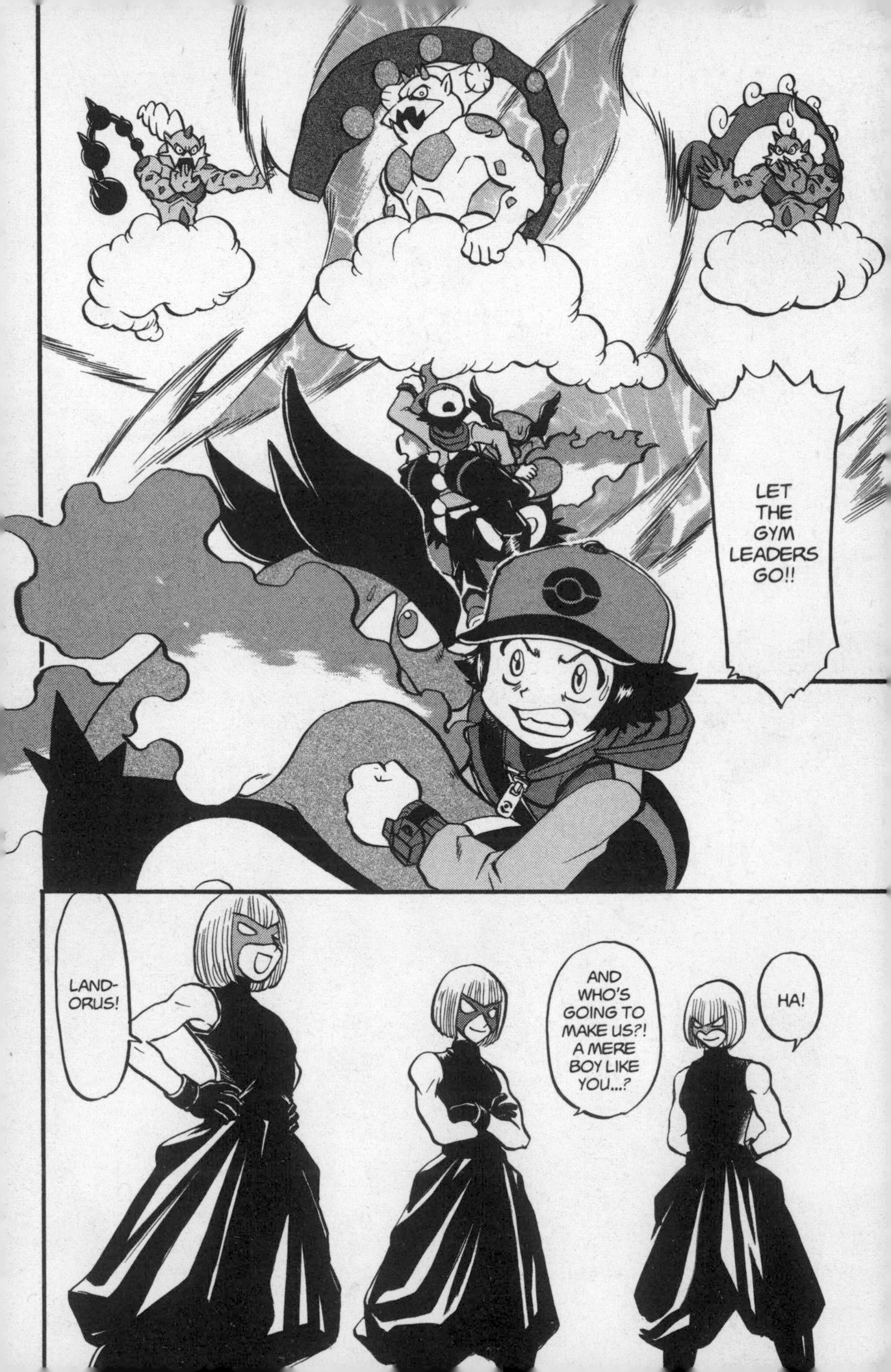

LET THE GYM LEADERS GO!!
HA!
AND WHO'S GOING TO MAKE US?! A MERE BOY LIKE YOU...?
LAND-ORUS!

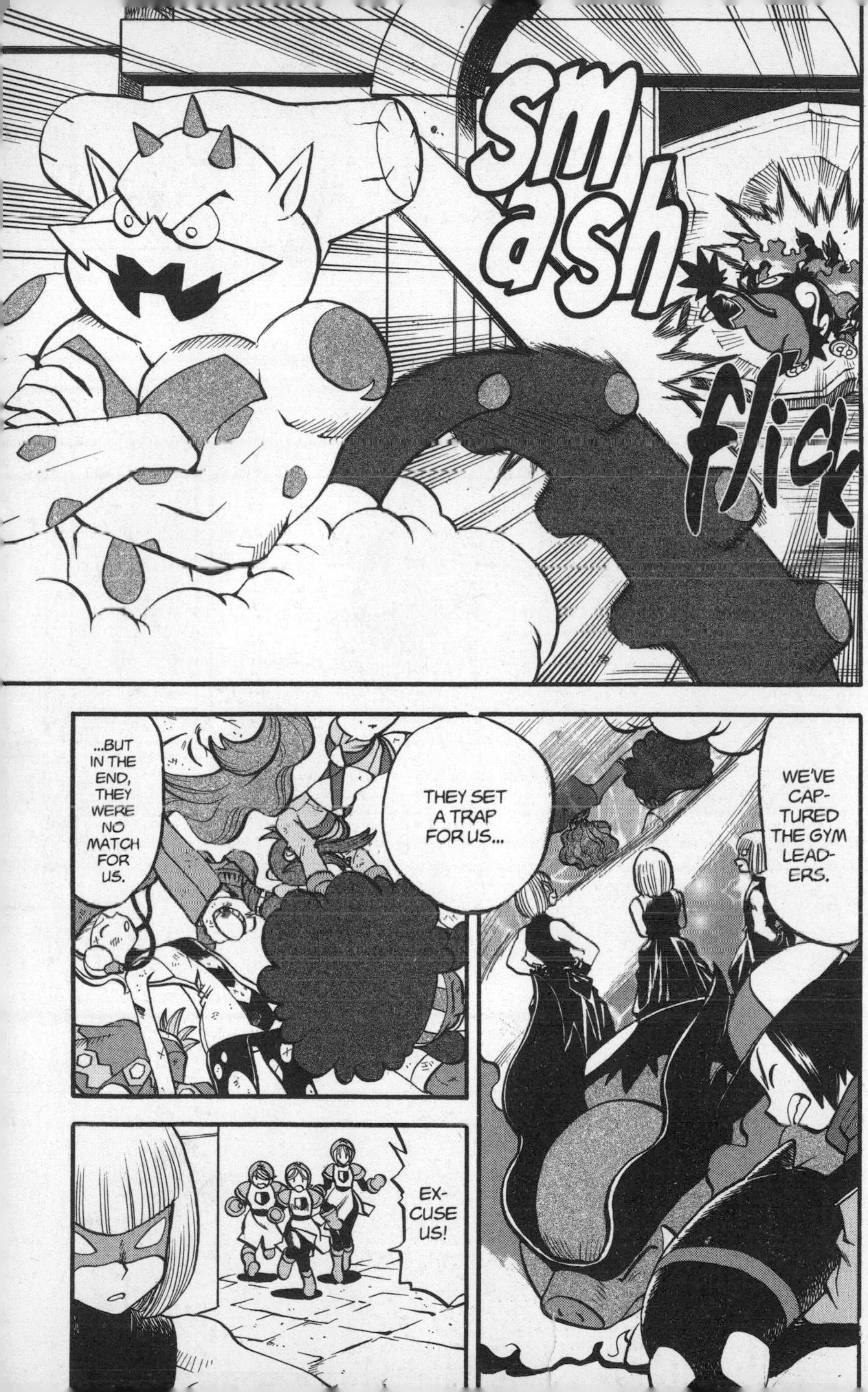
SMASH
FLICK
WE'VE CAPTURED THE GYM LEADERS.
THEY SET A TRAP FOR US...
...BUT IN THE END, THEY WERE NO MATCH FOR US.
EXCUSE US!

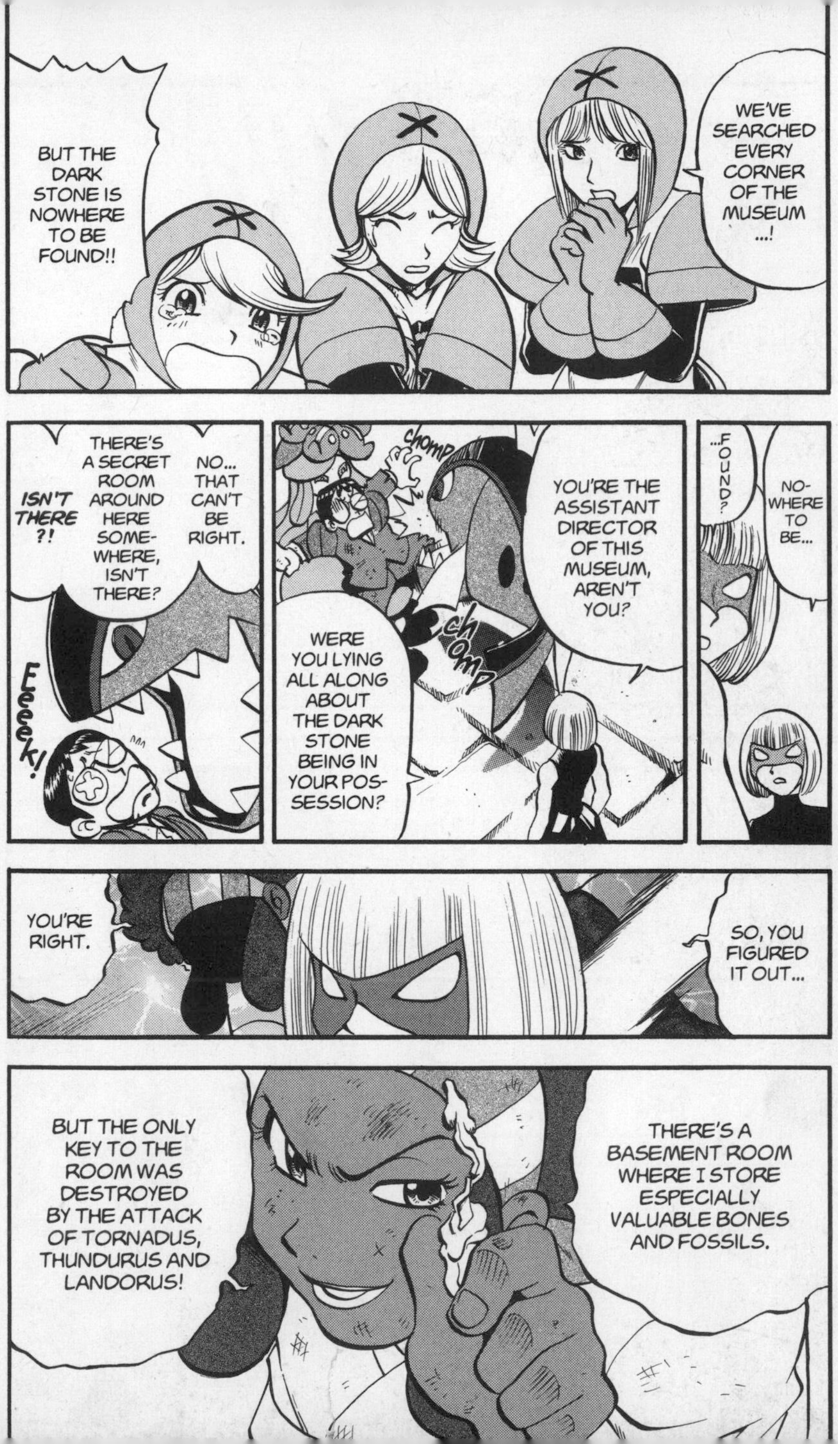
WE'VE SEARCHED EVERY CORNER OF THE MUSEUM ...!
BUT THE DARK STONE IS NOWHERE TO BE FOUND!!
NO-WHERE TO BE...
...FOUND?
YOU'RE THE ASSISTANT DIRECTOR OF THIS MUSEUM, AREN'T YOU?
chomp
chomp
WERE YOU LYING ALL ALONG ABOUT THE DARK STONE BEING IN YOUR POS-SESSION?
NO... THAT CAN'T BE RIGHT.
THERE'S A SECRET ROOM AROUND HERE SOME-WHERE, ISN'T THERE?
ISN'T THERE?!
Eeeek!
SO, YOU FIGURED IT OUT...
YOU'RE RIGHT.
THERE'S A BASEMENT ROOM WHERE I STORE ESPECIALLY VALUABLE BONES AND FOSSILS.
BUT THE ONLY KEY TO THE ROOM WAS DESTROYED BY THE ATTACK OF TORNADUS, THUNDURUS AND LANDORUS!

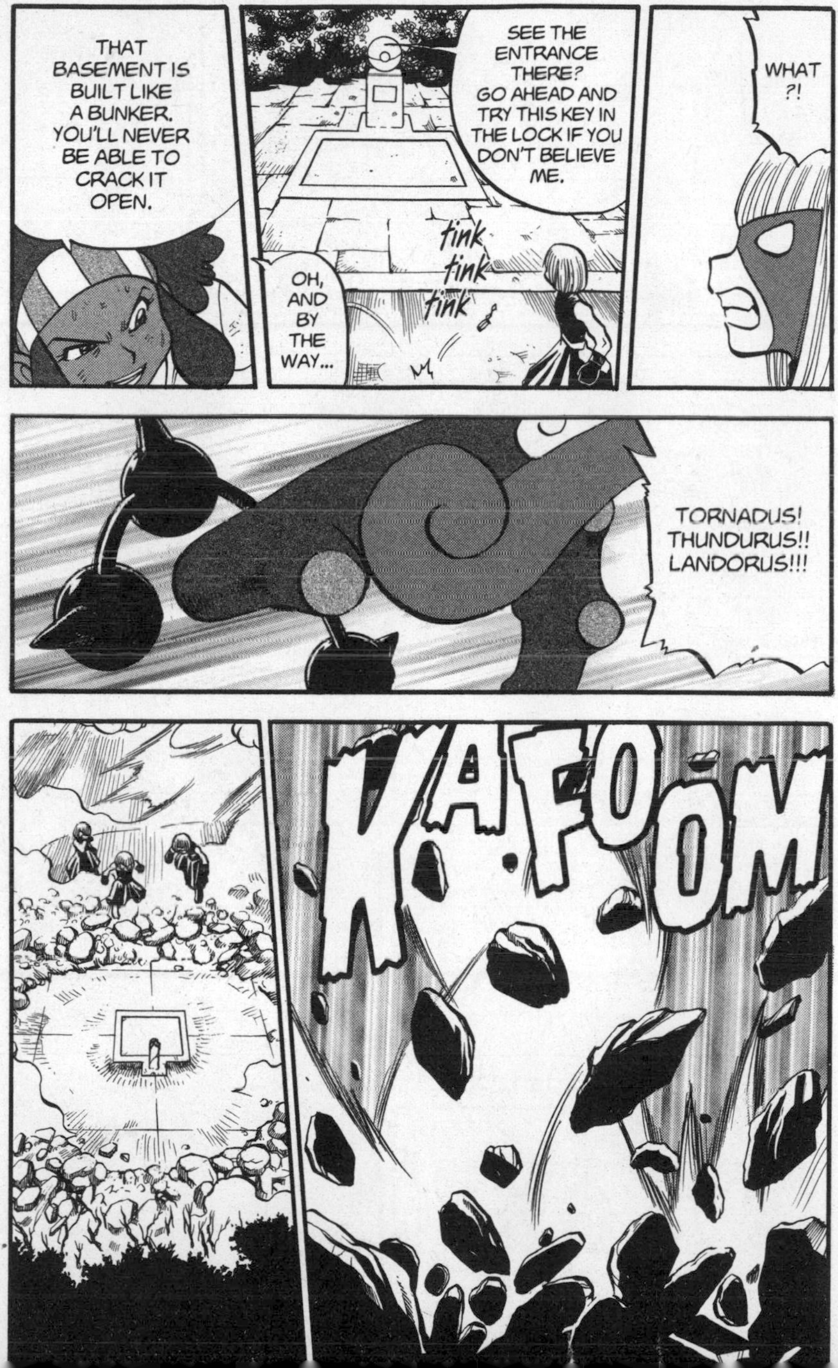
THAT BASEMENT IS BUILT LIKE A BUNKER. YOU'LL NEVER BE ABLE TO CRACK IT OPEN.
SEE THE ENTRANCE THERE? GO AHEAD AND TRY THIS KEY IN THE LOCK IF YOU DON'T BELIEVE ME.
OH, AND BY THE WAY...
tink tink tink
WHAT?!
TORNADUS! THUNDURUS!! LANDORUS!!!
KAFOOM

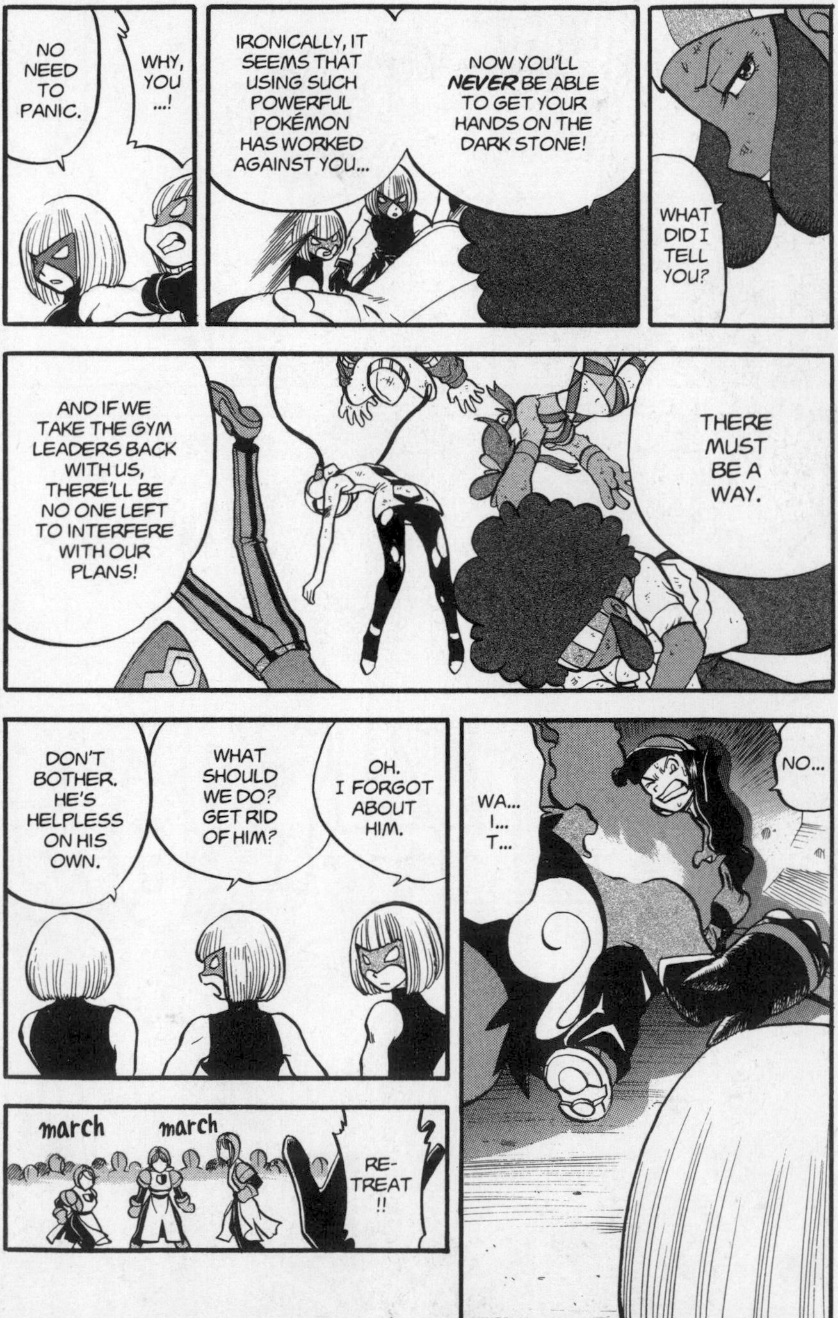
WHAT DID I TELL YOU?
NOW YOU'LL NEVER BE ABLE TO GET YOUR HANDS ON THE DARK STONE!
IRONICALLY, IT SEEMS THAT USING SUCH POWERFUL POKÉMON HAS WORKED AGAINST YOU...
WHY, YOU ...!
NO NEED TO PANIC.
THERE MUST BE A WAY.
AND IF WE TAKE THE GYM LEADERS BACK WITH US, THERE'LL BE NO ONE LEFT TO INTERFERE WITH OUR PLANS!
NO...
WA... I... T...
OH. I FORGOT ABOUT HIM.
WHAT SHOULD WE DO? GET RID OF HIM?
DON'T BOTHER. HE'S HELPLESS ON HIS OWN.
RE-TREAT !!
march
march

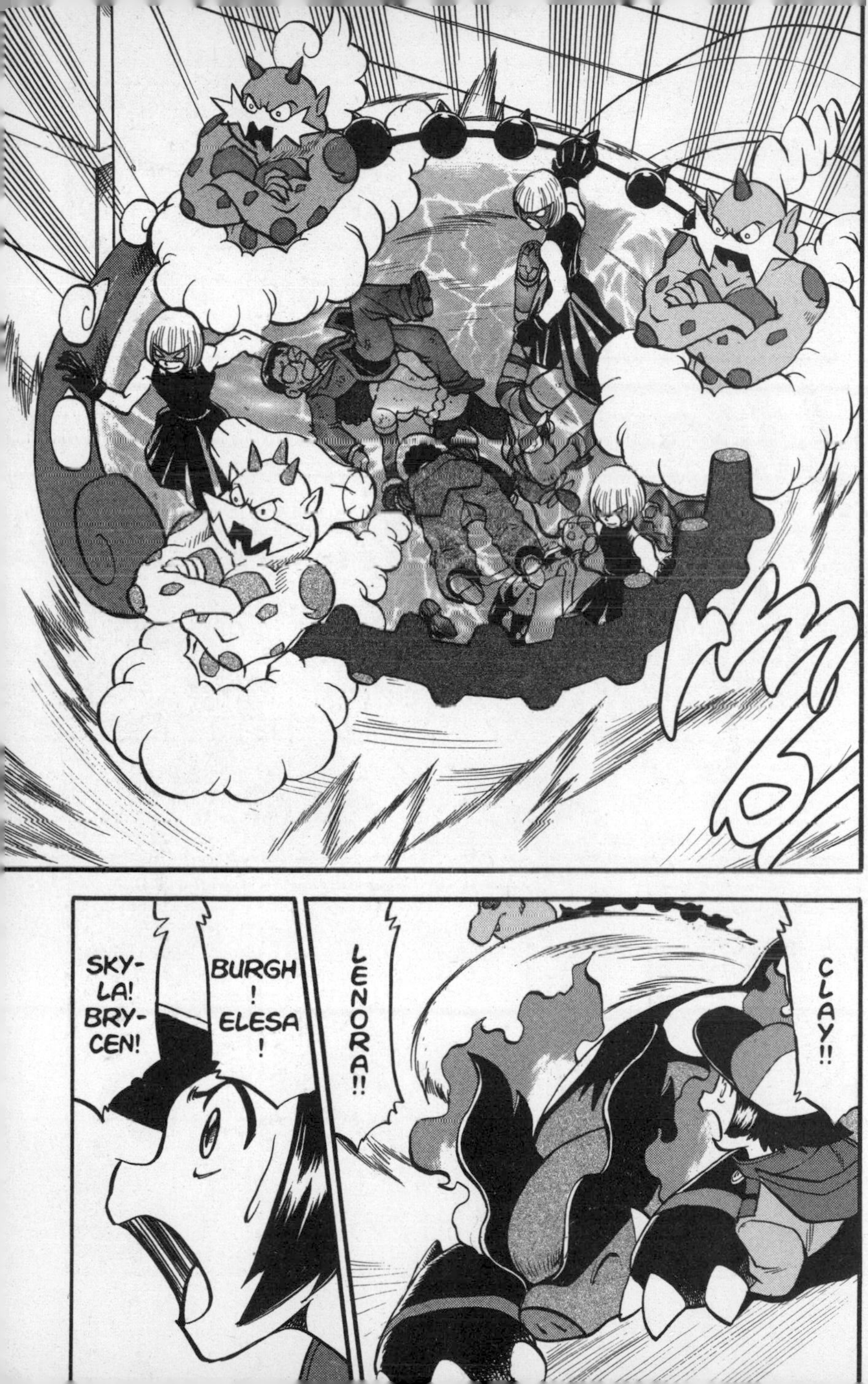
CLAY!!
LENORA!!
BURGH! ELESA!
SKY-LA! BRY-CEN!

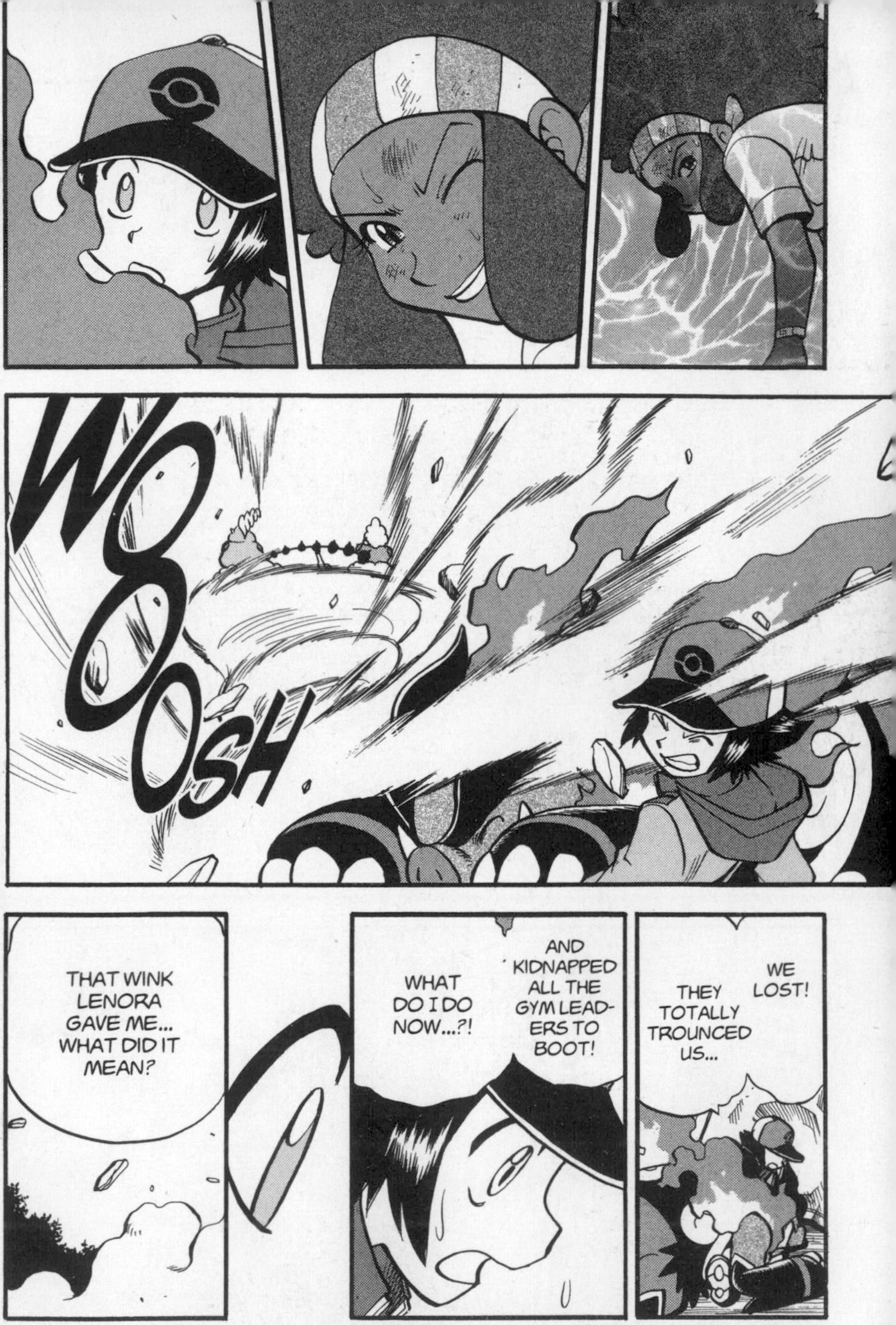
WOOOSH
WE LOST!
THEY TOTALLY TROUNCED US...
AND KIDNAPPED ALL THE GYM LEADERS TO BOOT!
WHAT DO I DO NOW...?!
THAT WINK LENORA GAVE ME... WHAT DID IT MEAN?

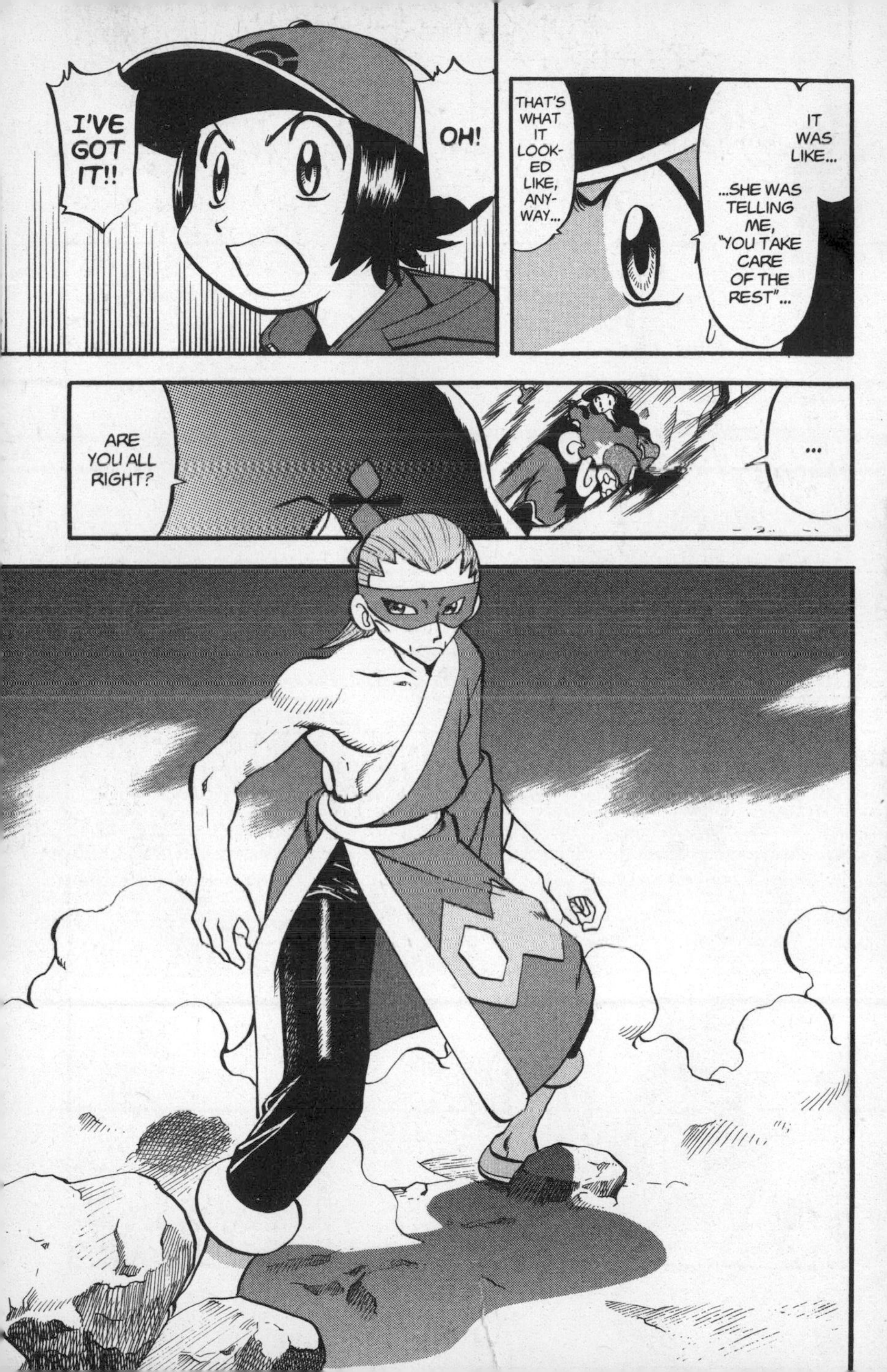
IT WAS LIKE...
...SHE WAS TELLING ME, "YOU TAKE CARE OF THE REST"...
THAT'S WHAT IT LOOKED LIKE, ANYWAY...
OH!
I'VE GOT IT!!
...
ARE YOU ALL RIGHT?

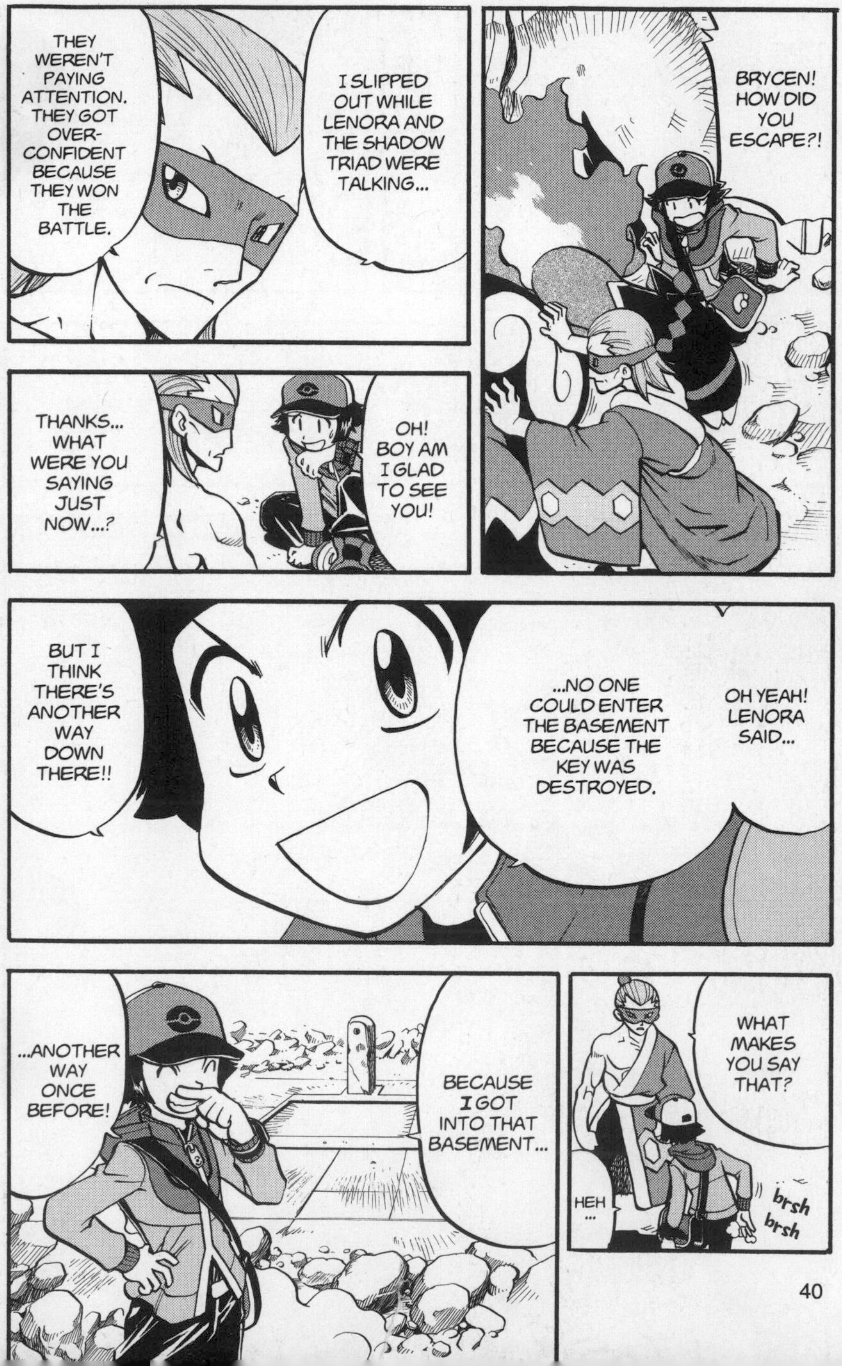

BRYCEN! HOW DID YOU ESCAPE?!
I SLIPPED OUT WHILE LENORA AND THE SHADOW TRIAD WERE TALKING...
THEY WEREN'T PAYING ATTENTION. THEY GOT OVER-CONFIDENT BECAUSE THEY WON THE BATTLE.
OH! BOY AM I GLAD TO SEE YOU!
THANKS... WHAT WERE YOU SAYING JUST NOW...?
OH YEAH! LENORA SAID...
...NO ONE COULD ENTER THE BASEMENT BECAUSE THE KEY WAS DESTROYED.
BUT I THINK THERE'S ANOTHER WAY DOWN THERE!!
WHAT MAKES YOU SAY THAT?
HEH...
brsh brsh
BECAUSE I GOT INTO THAT BASEMENT...
...ANOTHER WAY ONCE BEFORE!

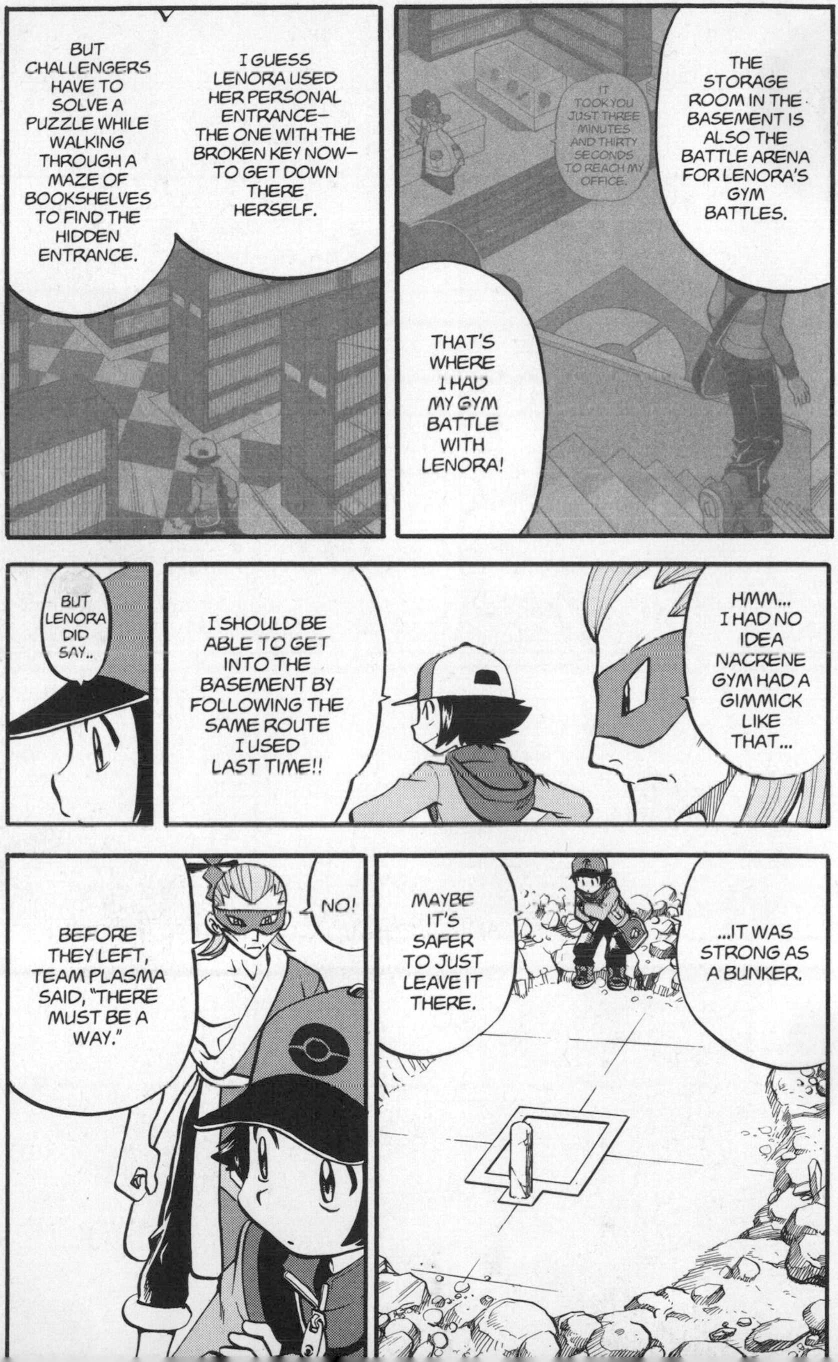
THE STORAGE ROOM IN THE BASEMENT IS ALSO THE BATTLE ARENA FOR LENORA'S GYM BATTLES.
IT TOOK YOU JUST THREE MINUTES AND THIRTY SECONDS TO REACH MY OFFICE.
THAT'S WHERE I HAD MY GYM BATTLE WITH LENORA!
I GUESS LENORA USED HER PERSONAL ENTRANCE— THE ONE WITH THE BROKEN KEY NOW— TO GET DOWN THERE HERSELF.
BUT CHALLENGERS HAVE TO SOLVE A PUZZLE WHILE WALKING THROUGH A MAZE OF BOOKSHELVES TO FIND THE HIDDEN ENTRANCE.
HMM... I HAD NO IDEA NACRENE GYM HAD A GIMMICK LIKE THAT...
I SHOULD BE ABLE TO GET INTO THE BASEMENT BY FOLLOWING THE SAME ROUTE I USED LAST TIME!!
BUT LENORA DID SAY..
...IT WAS STRONG AS A BUNKER.
MAYBE IT'S SAFER TO JUST LEAVE IT THERE.
NO!
BEFORE THEY LEFT, TEAM PLASMA SAID, "THERE MUST BE A WAY."

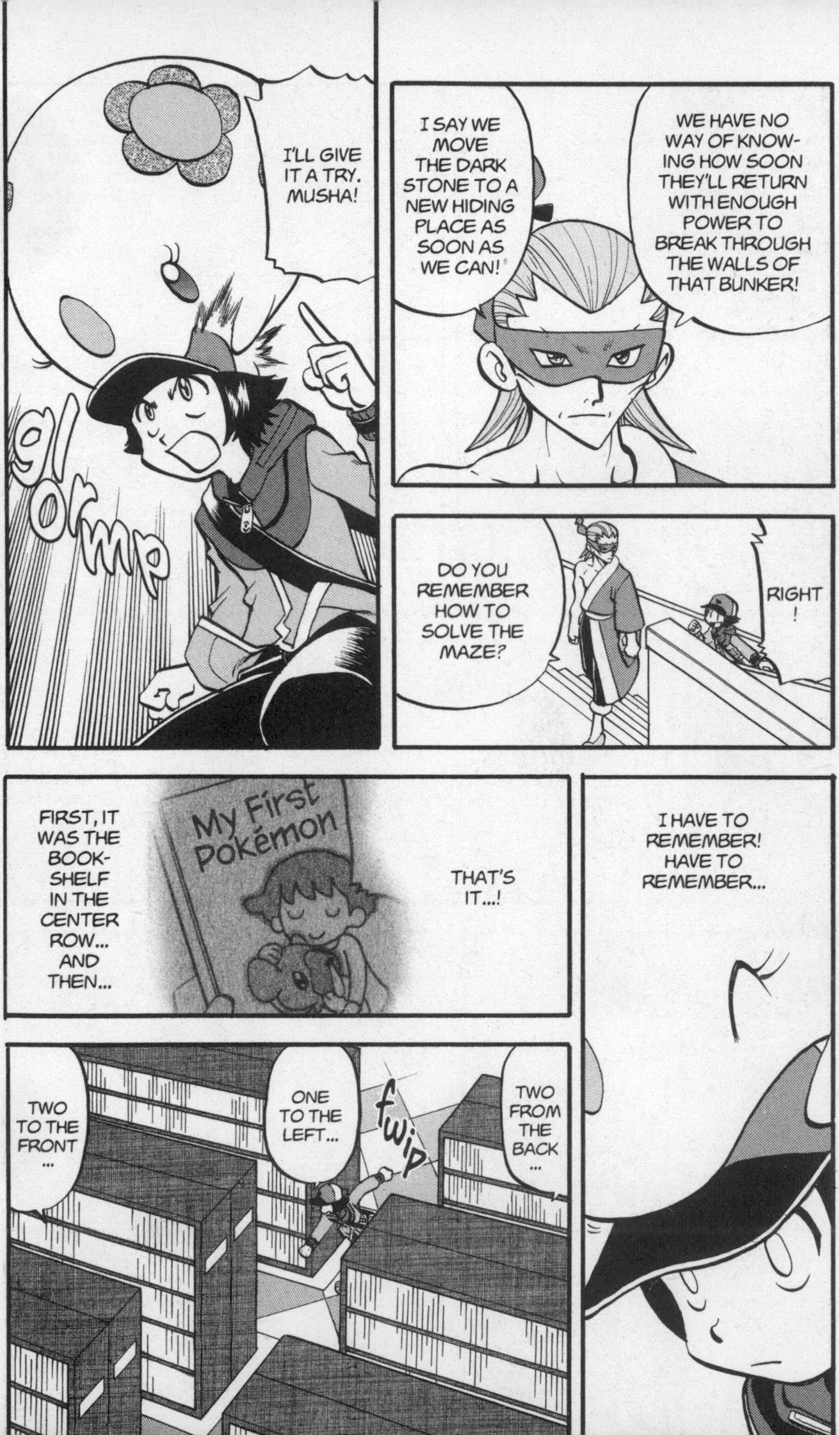

WE HAVE NO WAY OF KNOWING HOW SOON THEY'LL RETURN WITH ENOUGH POWER TO BREAK THROUGH THE WALLS OF THAT BUNKER!
I SAY WE MOVE THE DARK STONE TO A NEW HIDING PLACE AS SOON AS WE CAN!
RIGHT!
DO YOU REMEMBER HOW TO SOLVE THE MAZE?
I'LL GIVE IT A TRY. MUSHA!
glormp
I HAVE TO REMEMBER! HAVE TO REMEMBER...
THAT'S IT...!
My First Pokémon
FIRST, IT WAS THE BOOKSHELF IN THE CENTER ROW... AND THEN...
TWO FROM THE BACK...
fwip
ONE TO THE LEFT...
TWO TO THE FRONT...

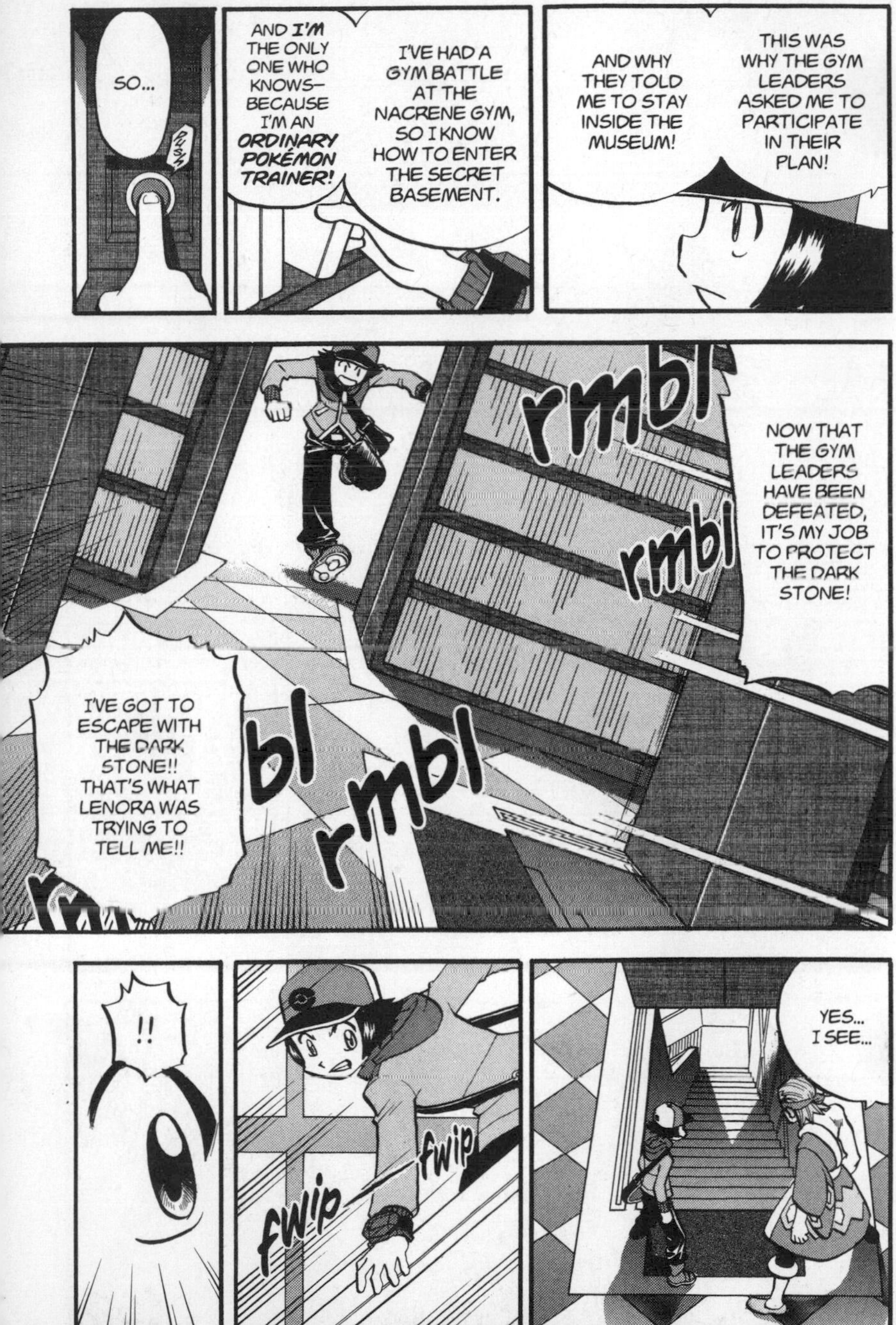
THIS WAS WHY THE GYM LEADERS ASKED ME TO PARTICIPATE IN THEIR PLAN!
AND WHY THEY TOLD ME TO STAY INSIDE THE MUSEUM!
I'VE HAD A GYM BATTLE AT THE NACRENE GYM, SO I KNOW HOW TO ENTER THE SECRET BASEMENT.
AND **I'M** THE ONLY ONE WHO KNOWS— BECAUSE I'M AN ***ORDINARY POKÉMON TRAINER!***
PUSH
SO...
NOW THAT THE GYM LEADERS HAVE BEEN DEFEATED, IT'S MY JOB TO PROTECT THE DARK STONE!
rmbl
rmbl
bl
rmbl
I'VE GOT TO ESCAPE WITH THE DARK STONE!! THAT'S WHAT LENORA WAS TRYING TO TELL ME!!
YES... I SEE...
fwip
fwip
!!

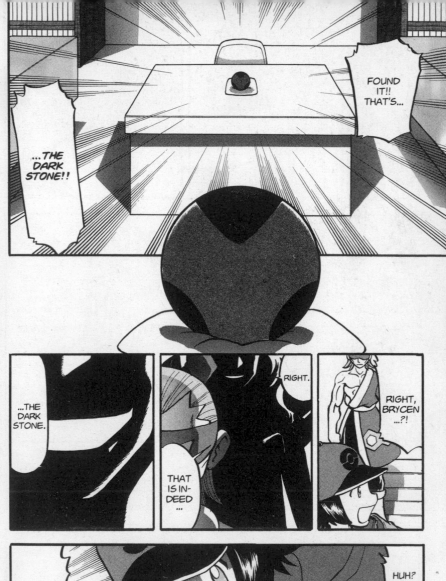

FOUND IT!! THAT'S...

...*THE DARK STONE!!*

...THE DARK STONE.

RIGHT.

THAT IS INDEED...

RIGHT, BRYCEN ...?!

WHO'S THERE?!

HUH?

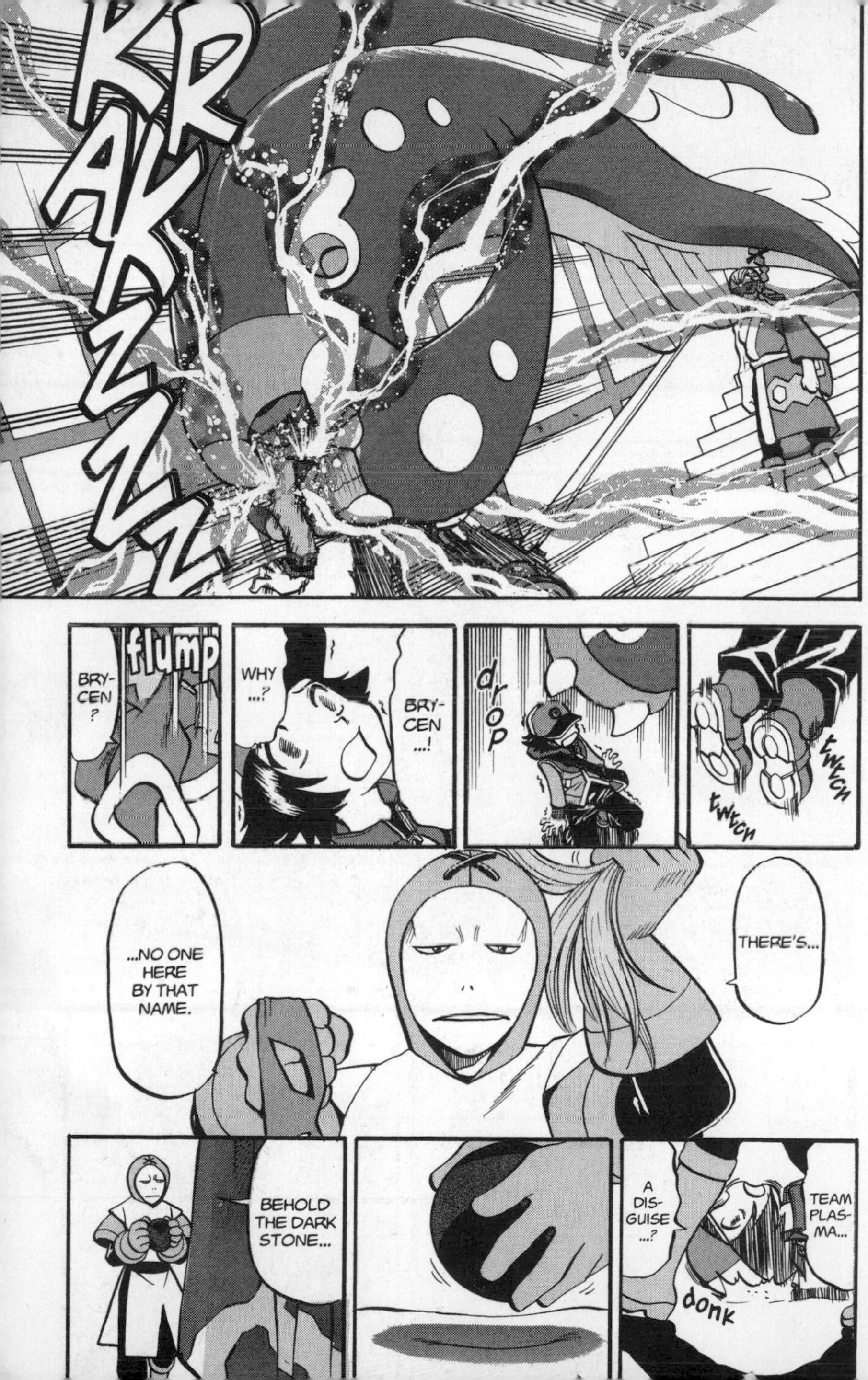
KRAKDZZZZ
twitch
twitch
drop
BRY-CEN...!
WHY...?
flump
BRY-CEN?
THERE'S...
...NO ONE HERE BY THAT NAME.
TEAM PLASMA...
A DISGUISE...?
donk
BEHOLD THE DARK STONE...

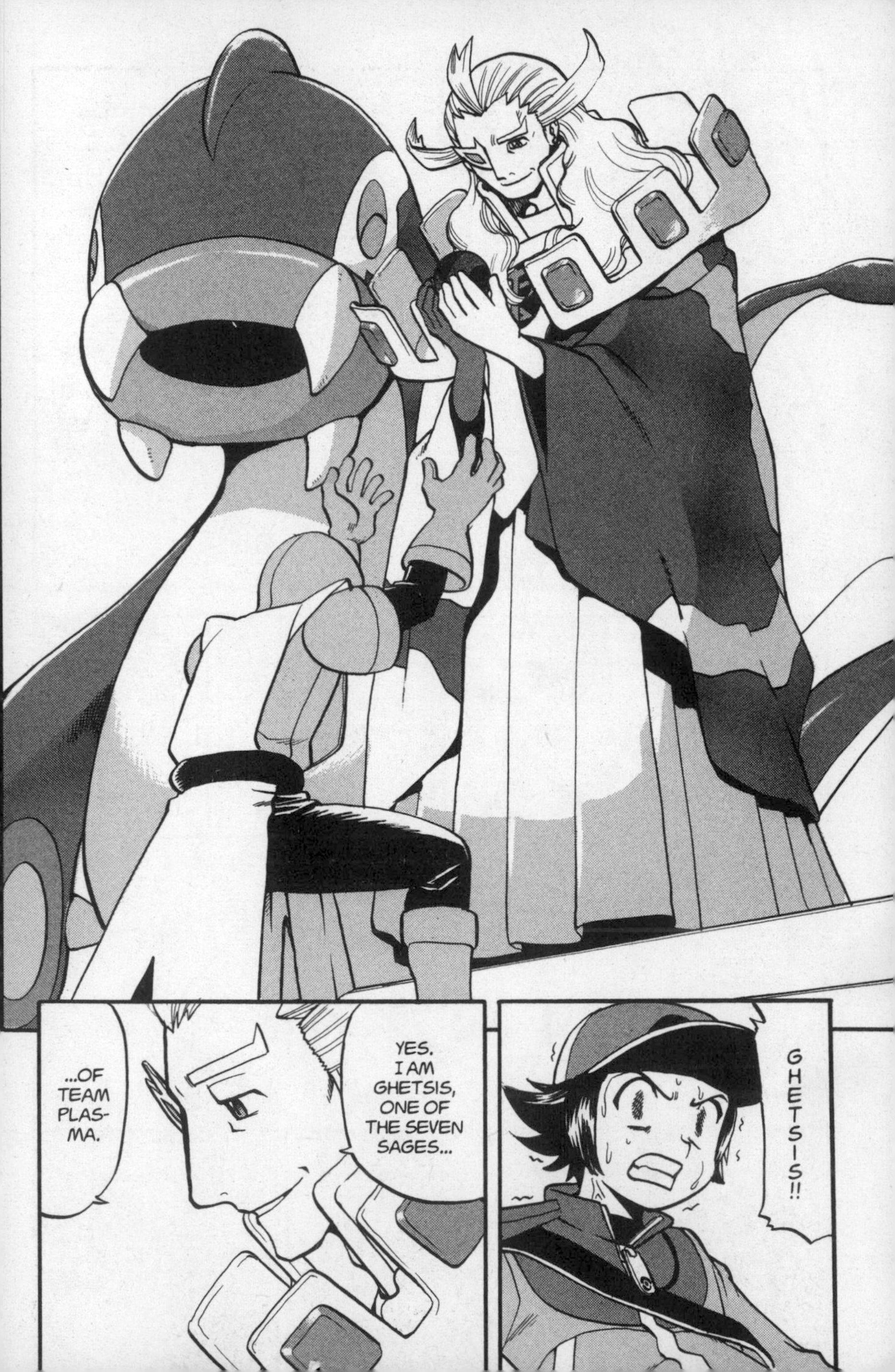
GHETSIS!!
YES. I AM GHETSIS, ONE OF THE SEVEN SAGES...
...OF TEAM PLAS-MA.

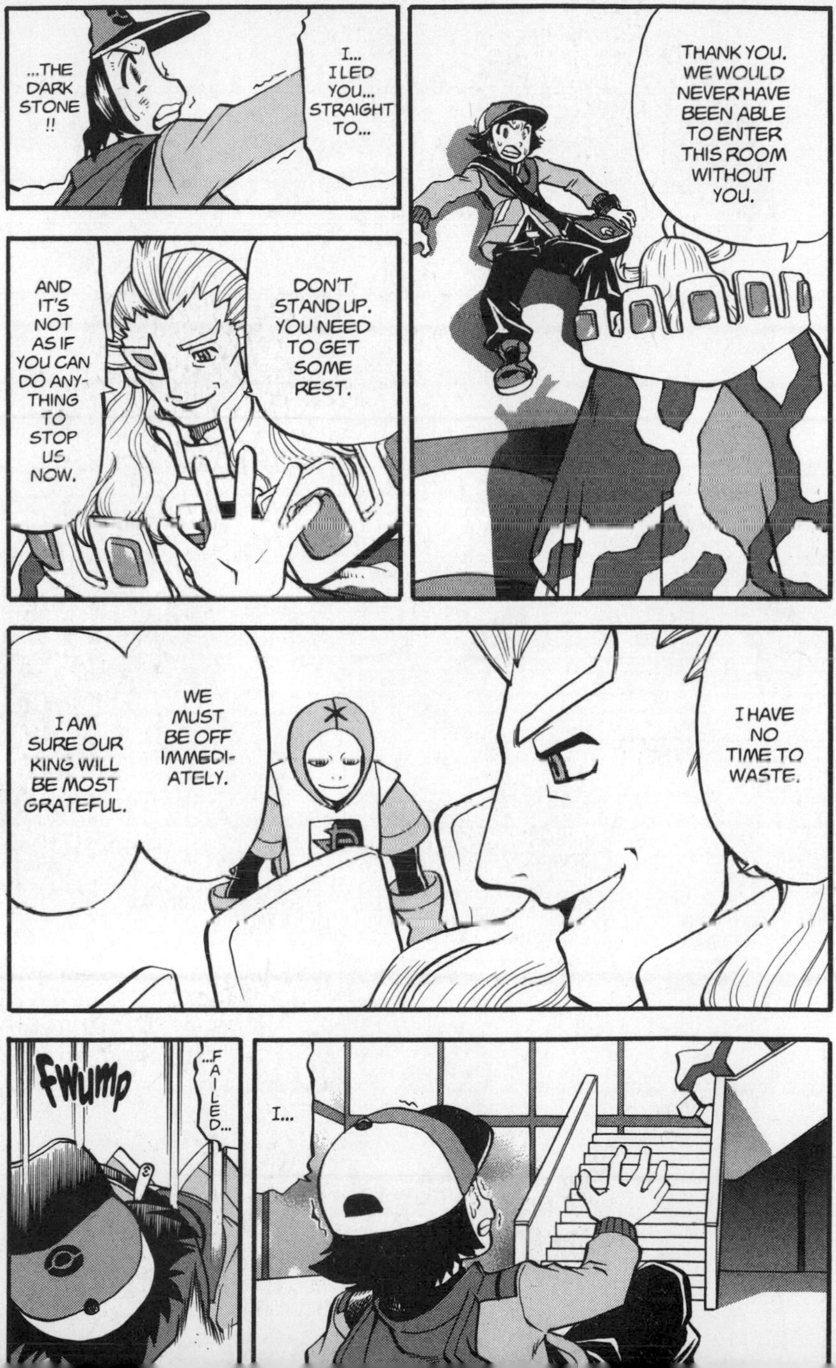
THANK YOU. WE WOULD NEVER HAVE BEEN ABLE TO ENTER THIS ROOM WITHOUT YOU.
I... I LED YOU... STRAIGHT TO...
...THE DARK STONE !!
DON'T STAND UP. YOU NEED TO GET SOME REST.
AND IT'S NOT AS IF YOU CAN DO ANYTHING TO STOP US NOW.
I HAVE NO TIME TO WASTE.
WE MUST BE OFF IMMEDIATELY.
I AM SURE OUR KING WILL BE MOST GRATEFUL.
I...
...FAILED...
FWUMP

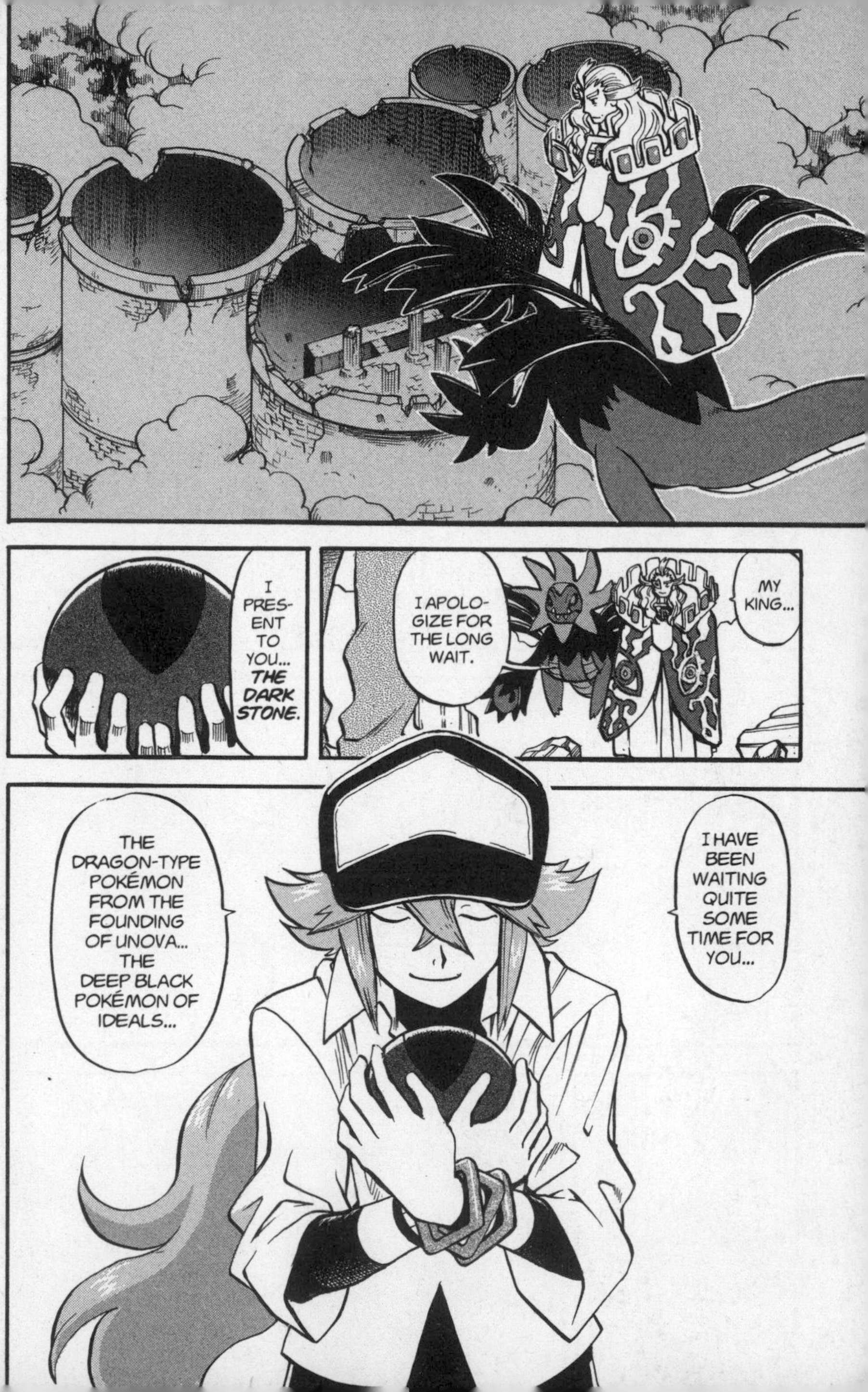
MY KING...
I APOLOGIZE FOR THE LONG WAIT.
I PRESENT TO YOU... ***THE DARK STONE.***
I HAVE BEEN WAITING QUITE SOME TIME FOR YOU...
THE DRAGON-TYPE POKÉMON FROM THE FOUNDING OF UNOVA... THE DEEP BLACK POKÉMON OF IDEALS...

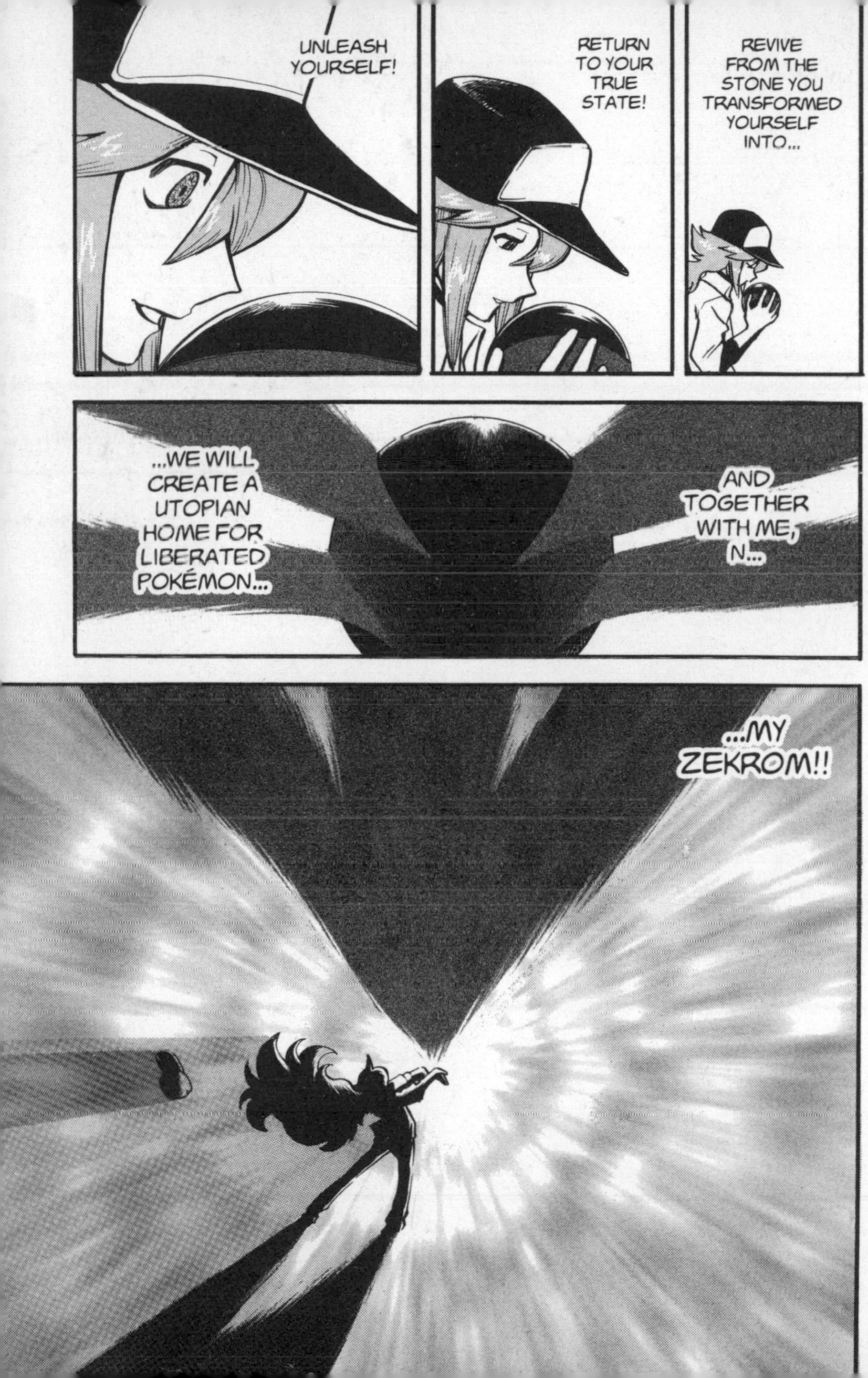
REVIVE FROM THE STONE YOU TRANSFORMED YOURSELF INTO...
RETURN TO YOUR TRUE STATE!
UNLEASH YOURSELF!
AND TOGETHER WITH ME, N...
...WE WILL CREATE A UTOPIAN HOME FOR LIBERATED POKÉMON...
...MY ZEKROM!!

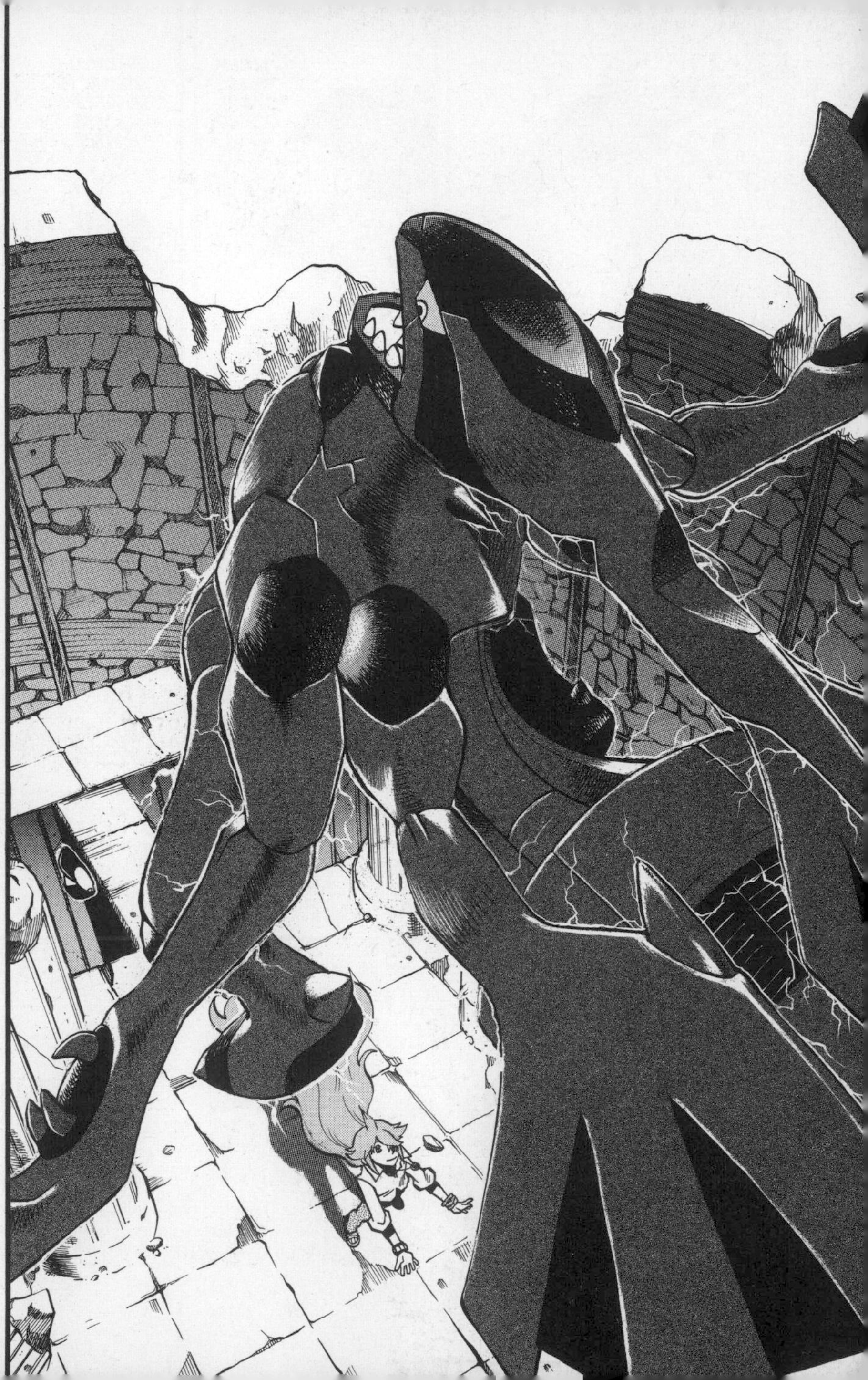

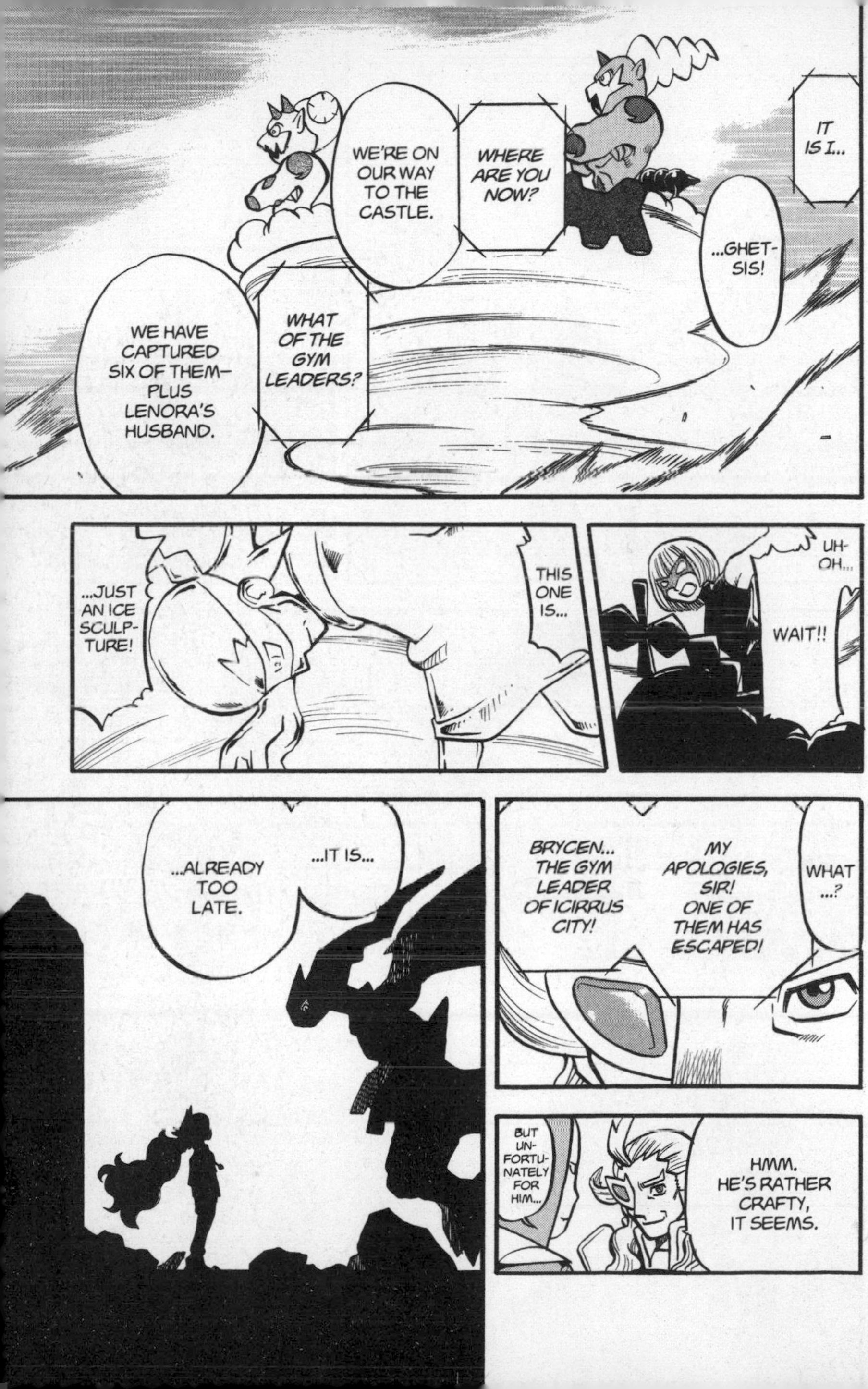
IT IS I...
...GHETSIS!
WHERE ARE YOU NOW?
WE'RE ON OUR WAY TO THE CASTLE.
WHAT OF THE GYM LEADERS?
WE HAVE CAPTURED SIX OF THEM— PLUS LENORA'S HUSBAND.
UH-OH...
WAIT!!
THIS ONE IS...
...JUST AN ICE SCULPTURE!
WHAT...?
MY APOLOGIES, SIR! ONE OF THEM HAS ESCAPED!
BRYCEN... THE GYM LEADER OF ICIRRUS CITY!
HMM. HE'S RATHER CRAFTY, IT SEEMS.
BUT UNFORTUNATELY FOR HIM...
...IT IS...
...ALREADY TOO LATE.

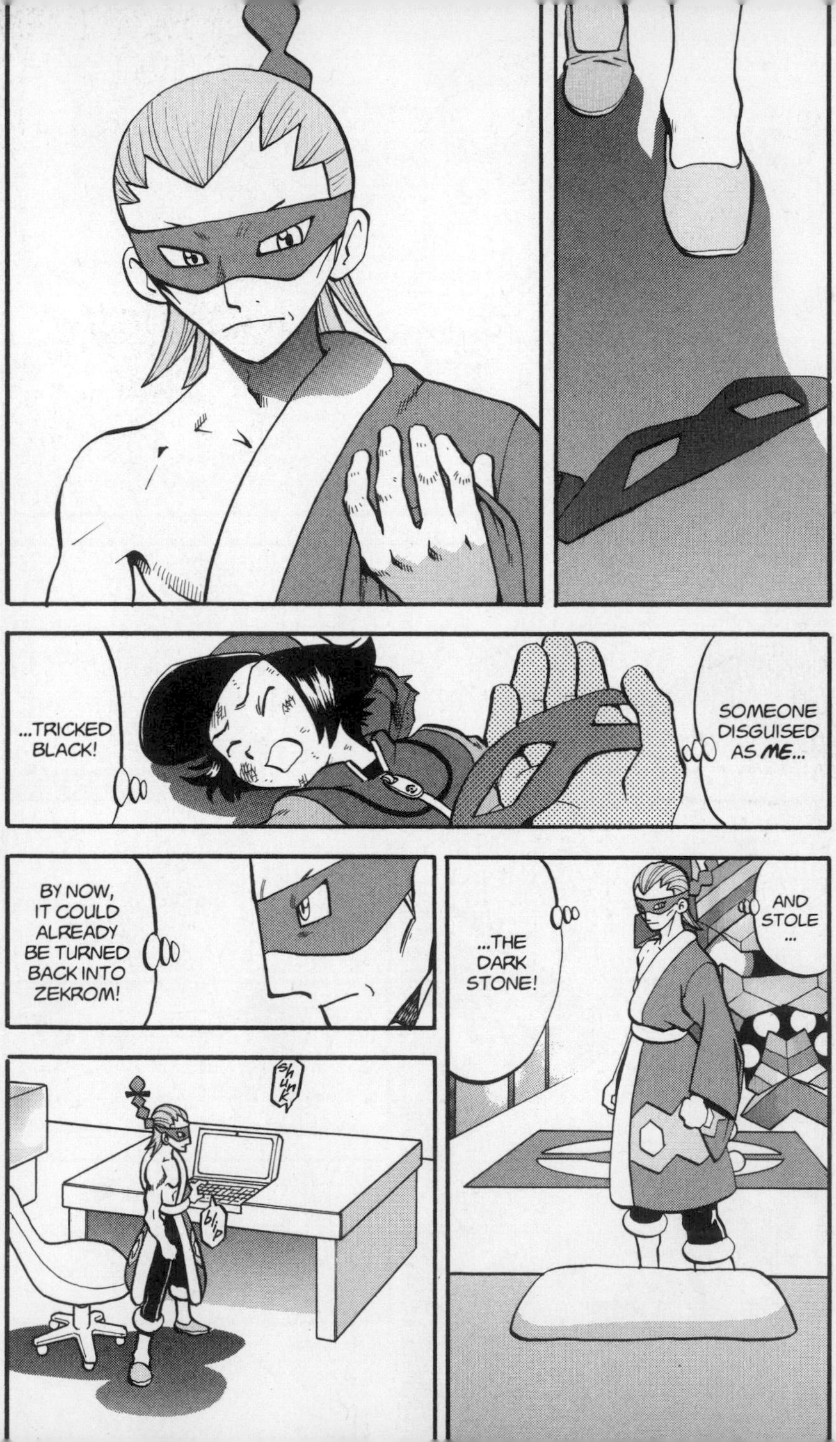
SOMEONE DISGUISED AS ME...
...TRICKED BLACK!
AND STOLE ...
...THE DARK STONE!
BY NOW, IT COULD ALREADY BE TURNED BACK INTO ZEKROM!
shunk
blip

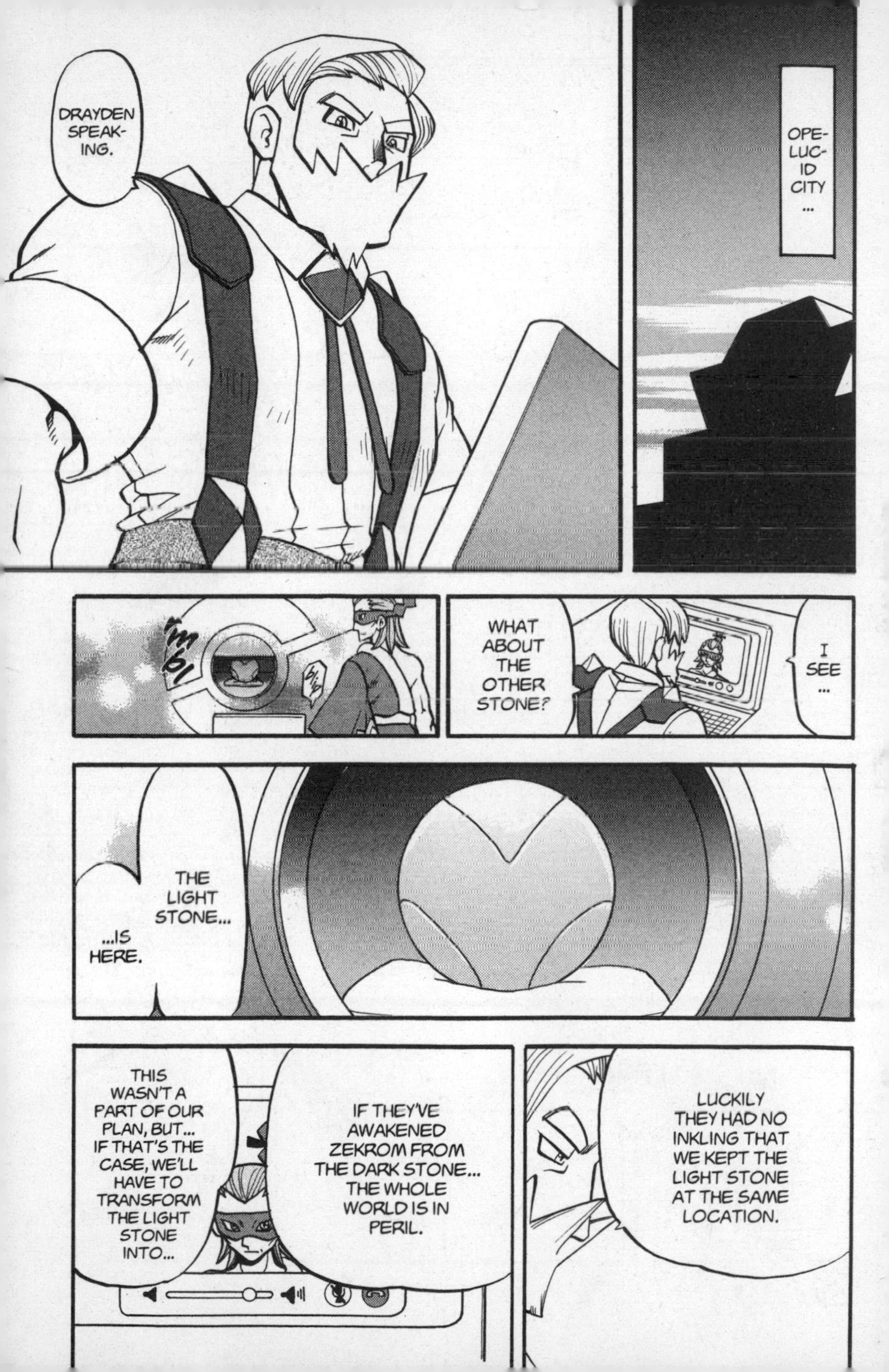
OPE-LUC-ID CITY ...
DRAYDEN SPEAK-ING.
I SEE ...
WHAT ABOUT THE OTHER STONE?
THE LIGHT STONE...
...IS HERE.
LUCKILY THEY HAD NO INKLING THAT WE KEPT THE LIGHT STONE AT THE SAME LOCATION.
IF THEY'VE AWAKENED ZEKROM FROM THE DARK STONE... THE WHOLE WORLD IS IN PERIL.
THIS WASN'T A PART OF OUR PLAN, BUT... IF THAT'S THE CASE, WE'LL HAVE TO TRANSFORM THE LIGHT STONE INTO...

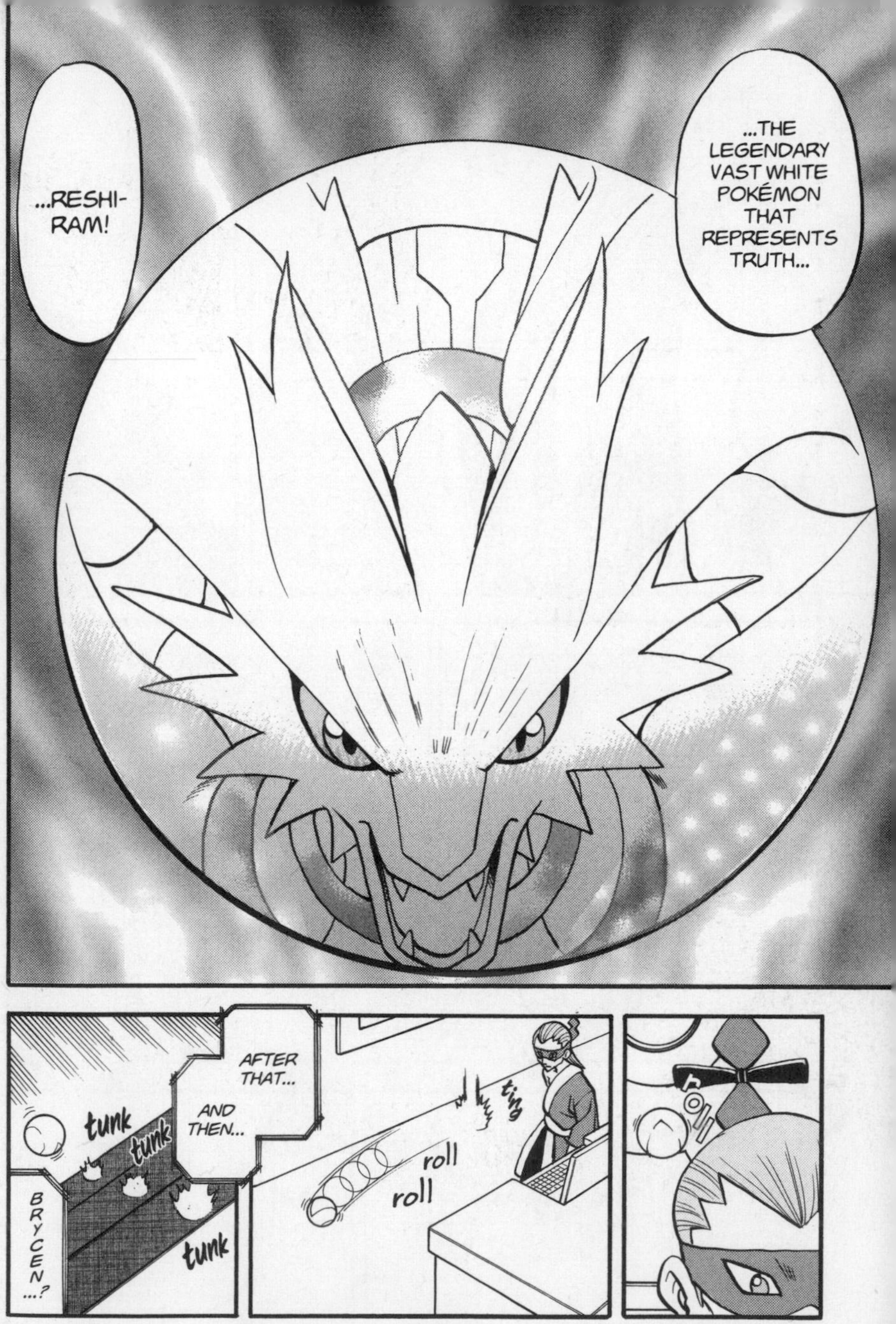
...THE LEGENDARY VAST WHITE POKÉMON THAT REPRESENTS TRUTH...
...RESHIRAM!
roll
ting
roll
roll
AFTER THAT...
AND THEN...
tunk
tunk
tunk
BRYCEN...?

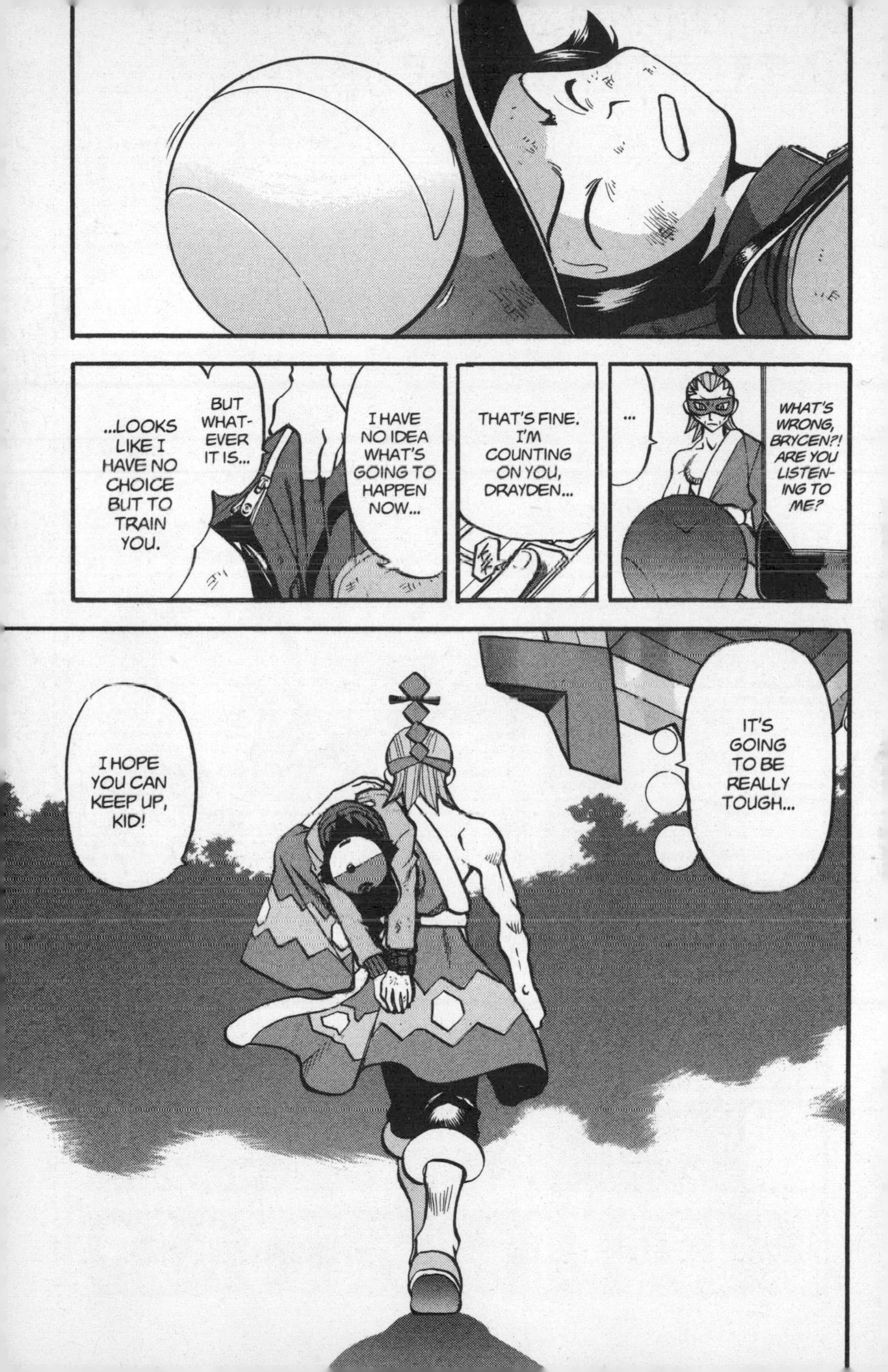
WHAT'S WRONG, BRYCEN?! ARE YOU LISTENING TO ME?
...
THAT'S FINE. I'M COUNTING ON YOU, DRAYDEN...
I HAVE NO IDEA WHAT'S GOING TO HAPPEN NOW...
BUT WHAT-EVER IT IS...
...LOOKS LIKE I HAVE NO CHOICE BUT TO TRAIN YOU.
IT'S GOING TO BE REALLY TOUGH...
I HOPE YOU CAN KEEP UP, KID!

ADVENTURE MAP

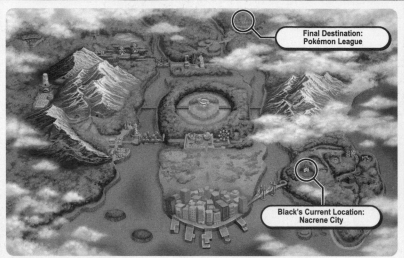

Final Destination:
Pokémon League
Black's Current Location:
Nacrene City

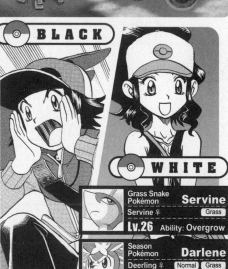

BLACK
WHITE

BLACK

Nite — Mega Fire Pig Pokémon
Emboar ♂ | Fire | Fighting
Lv.36 | Ability: Blaze

Musha — Dream Eater Pokémon
Munna ♂ | Psychic
Lv.52 | Ability: Forewarn

Tula — EleSpider Pokémon
Galvantula ♂ | Bug | Electric
Lv.53 | Ability: Unnerve

Costa — Prototurtle Pokémon
Tirtouga ♂ | Water | Rock
Lv.34 | Ability: Solid Rock

WHITE

Servine — Grass Snake Pokémon
Servine ♀ | Grass
Lv.26 | Ability: Overgrow

Darlene — Season Pokémon
Deerling ♀ | Normal | Grass
Lv.24 | Ability: Chlorophyll

Brav — Valiant Pokémon
Braviary ♂ | Normal | Flying
Lv.54 | Ability: Sheer Force

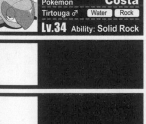

TRIO BADGE | BASIC BADGE | INSECT BADGE | BOLT BADGE | QUAKE BADGE | JET BADGE | ? | ?

Pokémon Adventures Black & White

CRYOGONAL

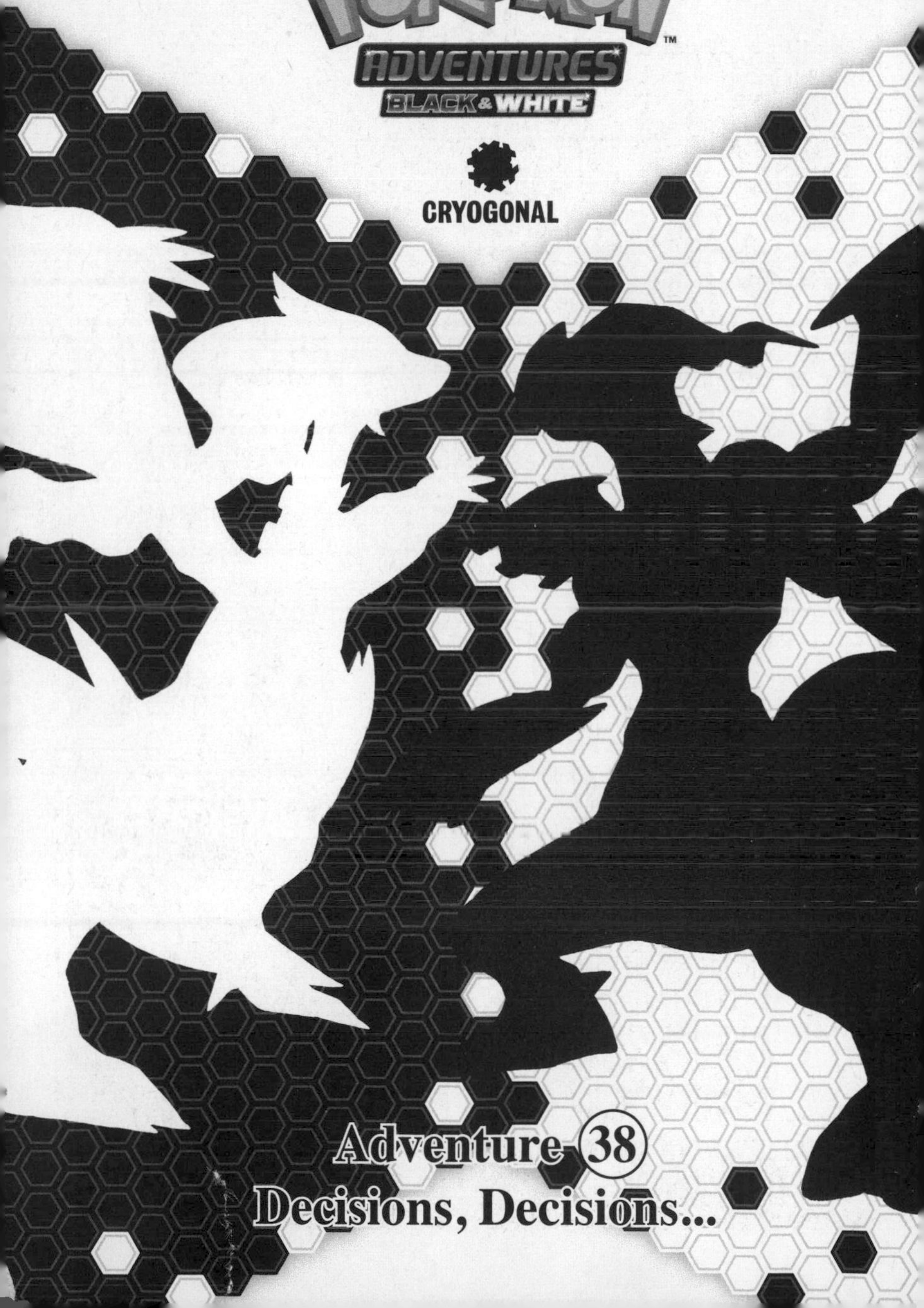

Adventure 38
Decisions, Decisions...

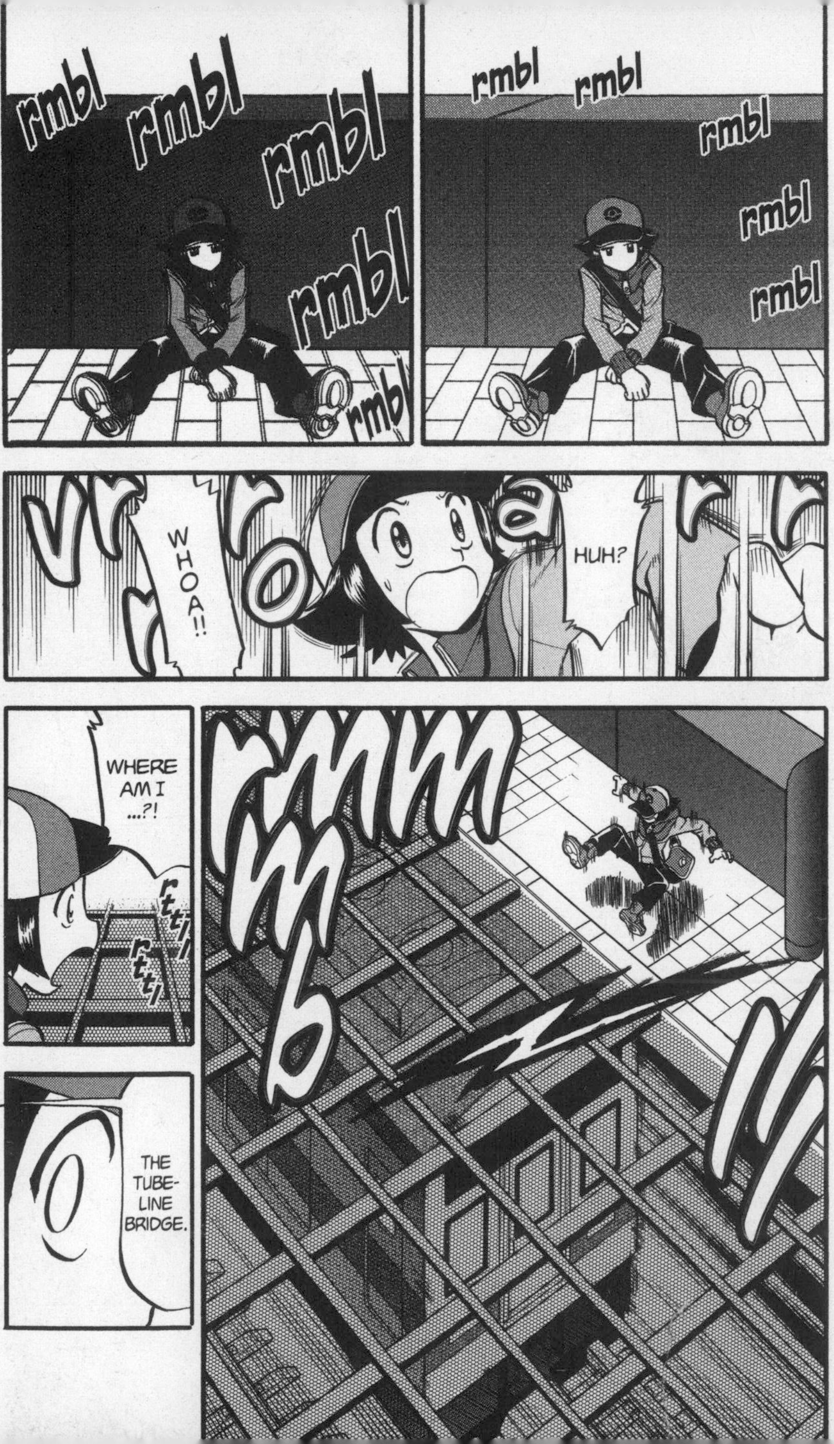
rmbl
rmbl
rmbl
rmbl
rmbl
rmbl
rmbl
rmbl
rmbl
rmbl
rmbl
HUH?
WHOA!!
WHERE AM I ...?!
rttl
rttl
THE TUBE-LINE BRIDGE.

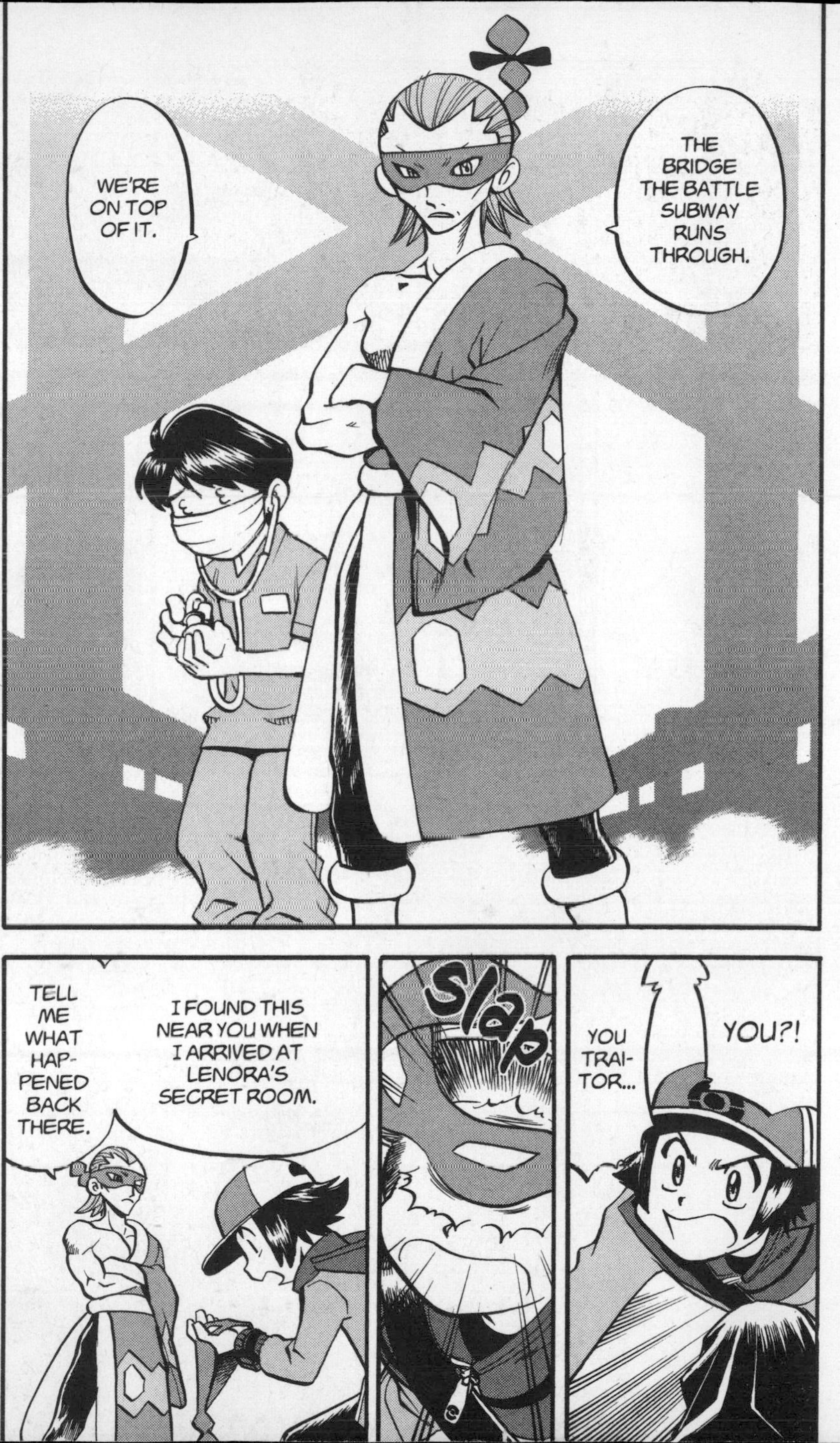
THE BRIDGE THE BATTLE SUBWAY RUNS THROUGH.
WE'RE ON TOP OF IT.
YOU?!
YOU TRAI- TOR...
Slap
I FOUND THIS NEAR YOU WHEN I ARRIVED AT LENORA'S SECRET ROOM.
TELL ME WHAT HAP- PENED BACK THERE.

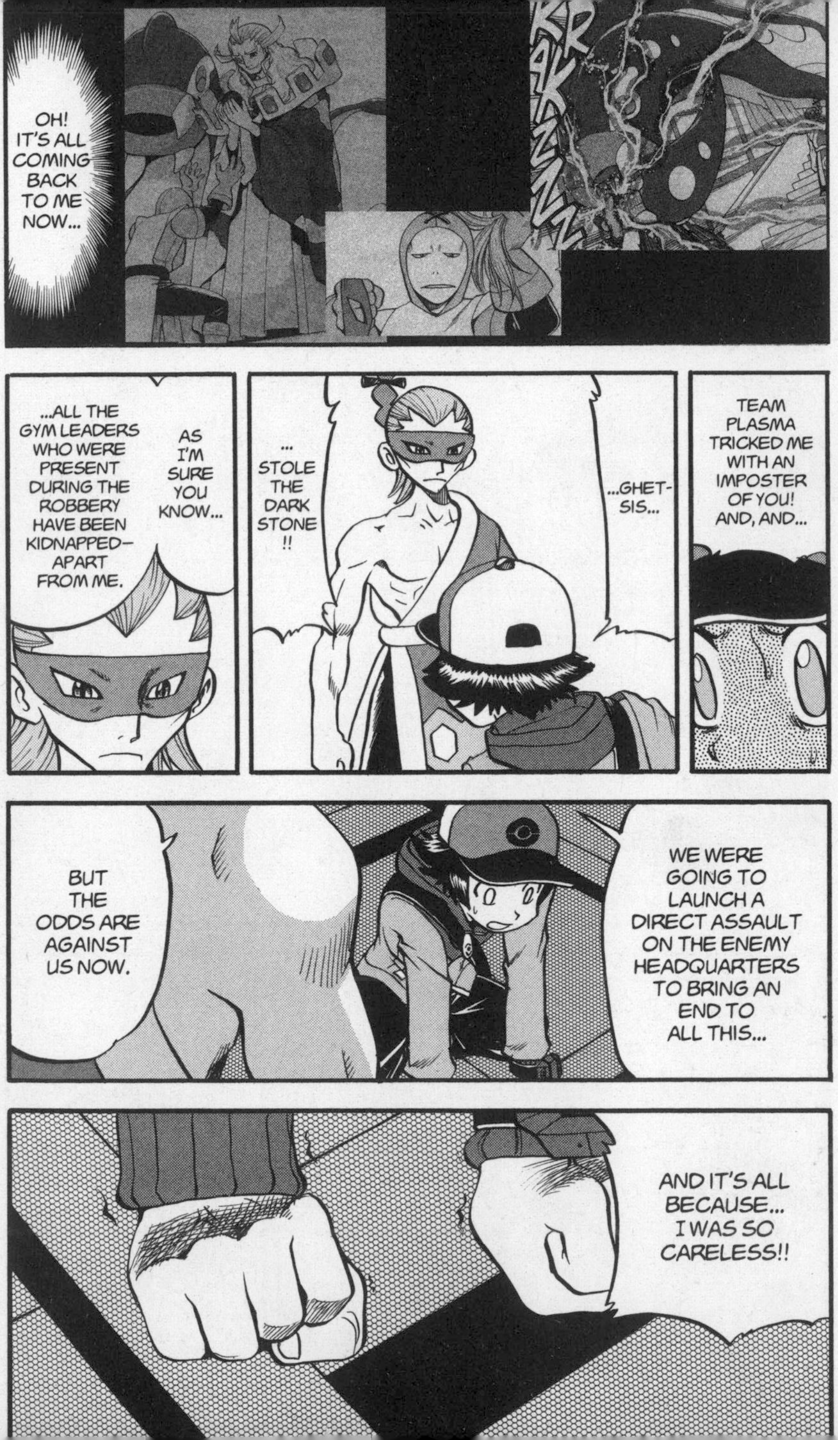
OH! IT'S ALL COMING BACK TO ME NOW...
TEAM PLASMA TRICKED ME WITH AN IMPOSTER OF YOU! AND, AND...
...GHET-SIS...
...STOLE THE DARK STONE!!
AS I'M SURE YOU KNOW...
...ALL THE GYM LEADERS WHO WERE PRESENT DURING THE ROBBERY HAVE BEEN KIDNAPPED—APART FROM ME.
WE WERE GOING TO LAUNCH A DIRECT ASSAULT ON THE ENEMY HEADQUARTERS TO BRING AN END TO ALL THIS...
BUT THE ODDS ARE AGAINST US NOW.
AND IT'S ALL BECAUSE... I WAS SO CARELESS!!

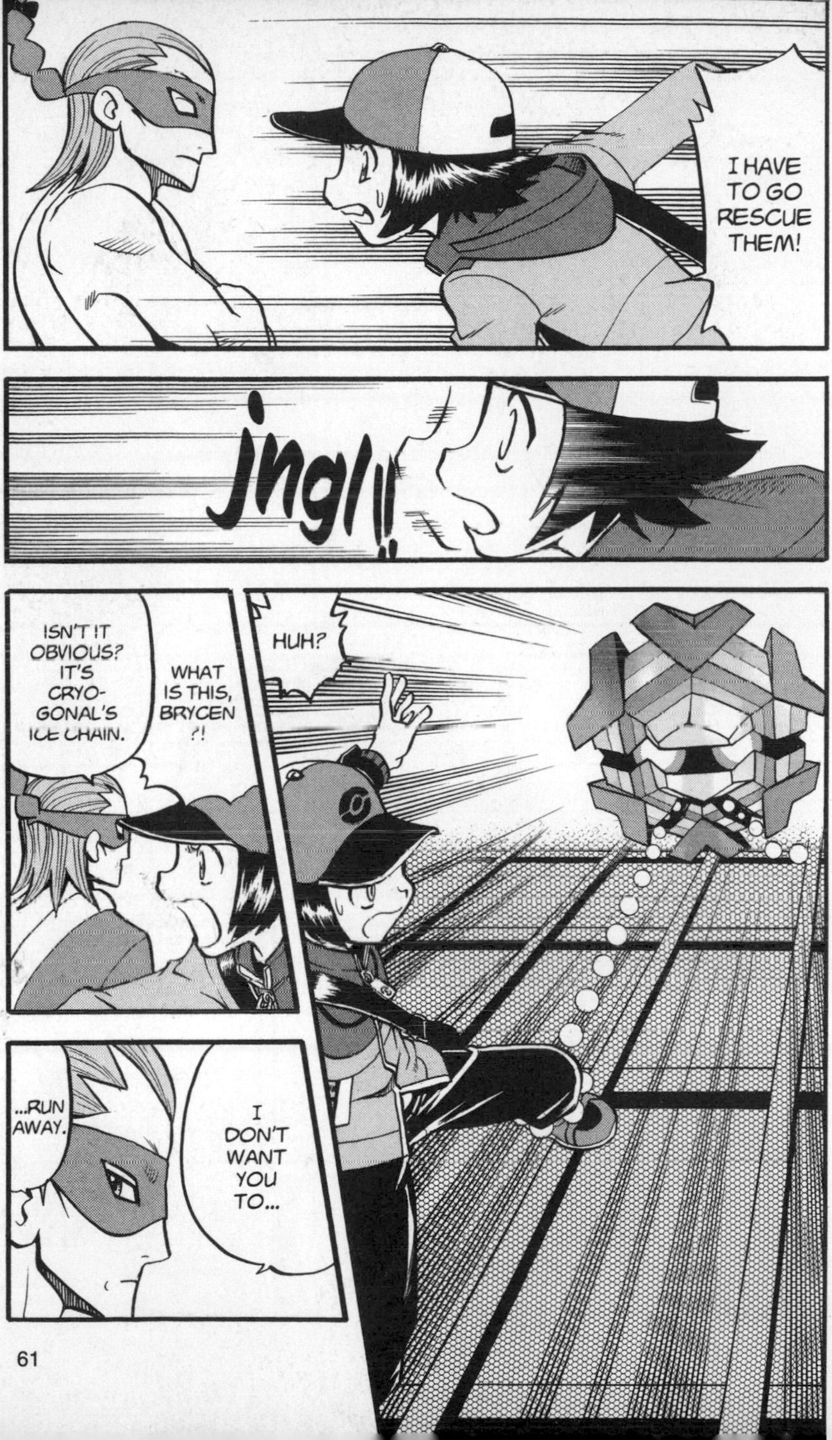
I HAVE TO GO RESCUE THEM!
jngl!!
HUH?
WHAT IS THIS, BRYCEN?!
ISN'T IT OBVIOUS? IT'S CRYOGONAL'S ICE CHAIN.
I DON'T WANT YOU TO...
...RUN AWAY.

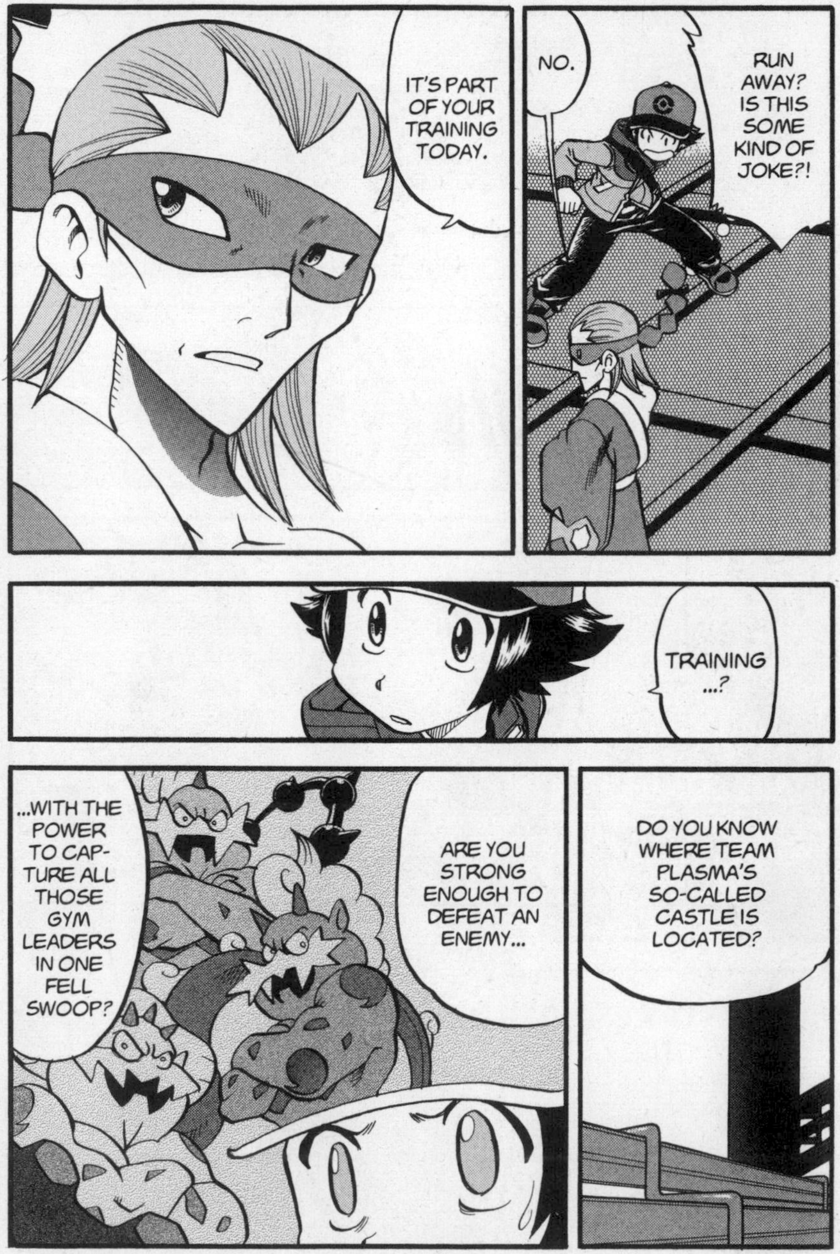
RUN AWAY? IS THIS SOME KIND OF JOKE?!
NO.
IT'S PART OF YOUR TRAINING TODAY.
TRAINING ...?
DO YOU KNOW WHERE TEAM PLASMA'S SO-CALLED CASTLE IS LOCATED?
ARE YOU STRONG ENOUGH TO DEFEAT AN ENEMY...
...WITH THE POWER TO CAPTURE ALL THOSE GYM LEADERS IN ONE FELL SWOOP?

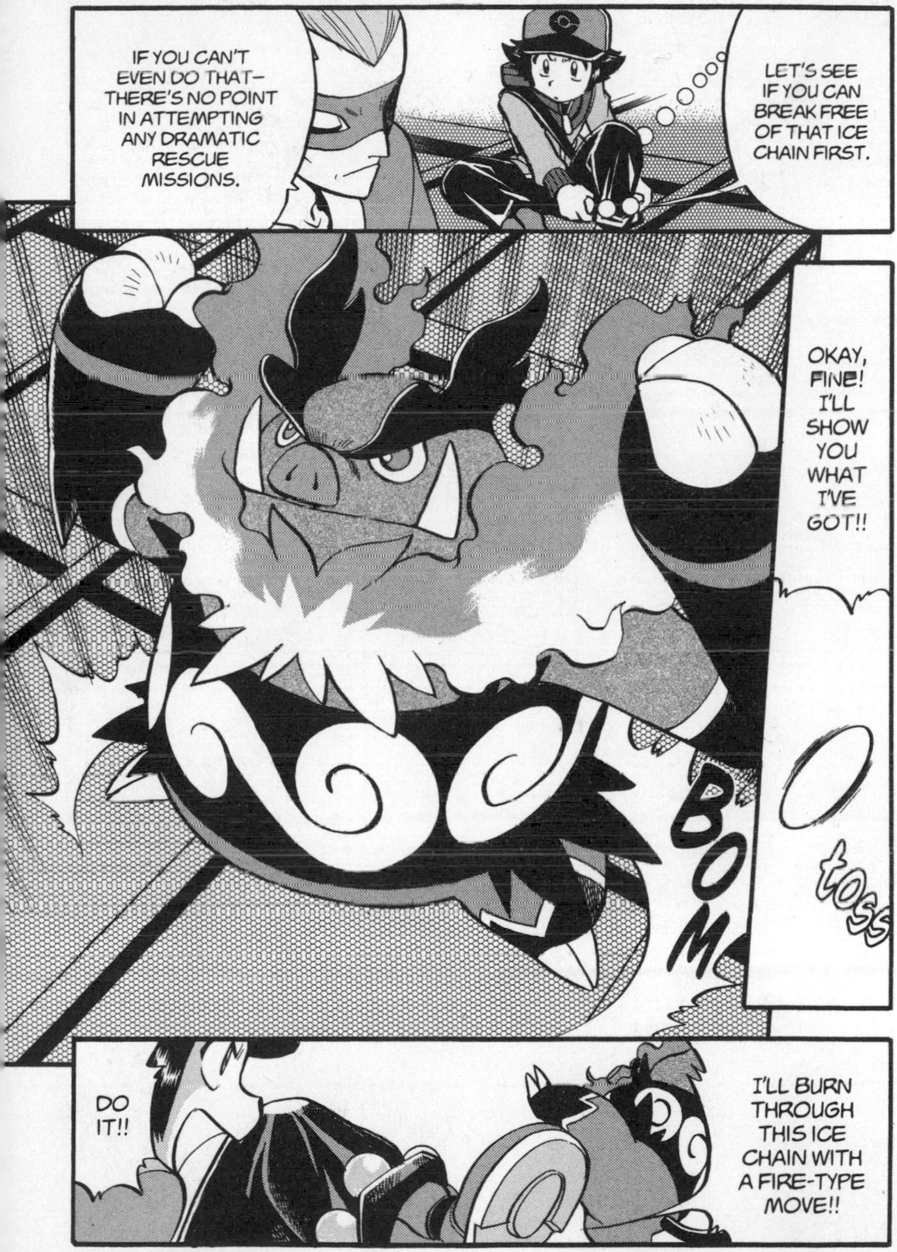
LET'S SEE IF YOU CAN BREAK FREE OF THAT ICE CHAIN FIRST.
IF YOU CAN'T EVEN DO THAT— THERE'S NO POINT IN ATTEMPTING ANY DRAMATIC RESCUE MISSIONS.
OKAY, FINE! I'LL SHOW YOU WHAT I'VE GOT!!
toss
BOOM
I'LL BURN THROUGH THIS ICE CHAIN WITH A FIRE-TYPE MOVE!!
DO IT!!

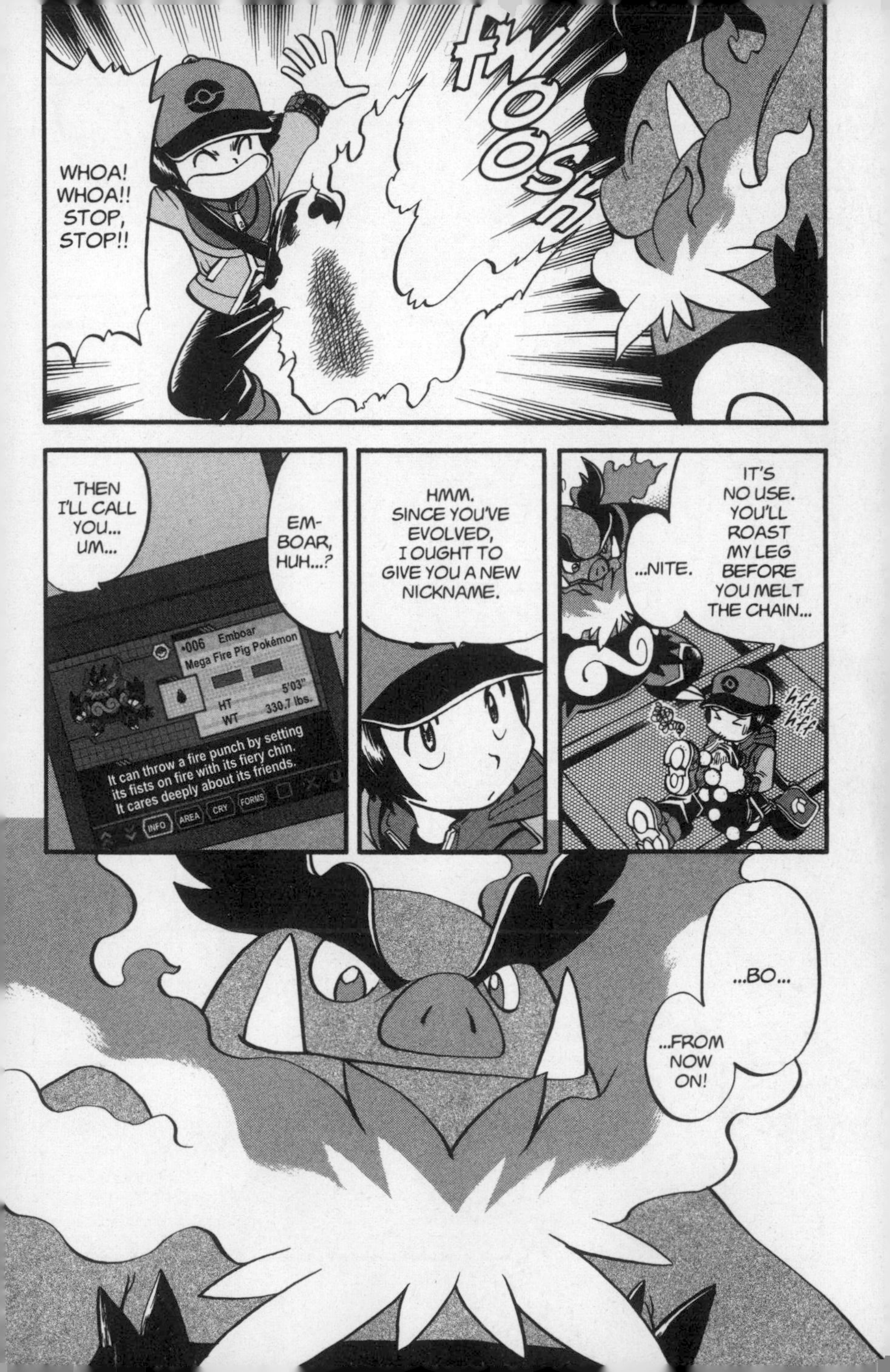
FWOOSH
WHOA! WHOA!! STOP, STOP!!
IT'S NO USE. YOU'LL ROAST MY LEG BEFORE YOU MELT THE CHAIN...
...NITE.
hff hff
HMM. SINCE YOU'VE EVOLVED, I OUGHT TO GIVE YOU A NEW NICKNAME.
EM-BOAR, HUH...?
THEN I'LL CALL YOU... UM...
•006 Emboar
Mega Fire Pig Pokémon
HT 5'03"
WT 330.7 lbs.
It can throw a fire punch by setting its fists on fire with its fiery chin. It cares deeply about its friends.
INFO
AREA
CRY
FORMS
...BO...
...FROM NOW ON!

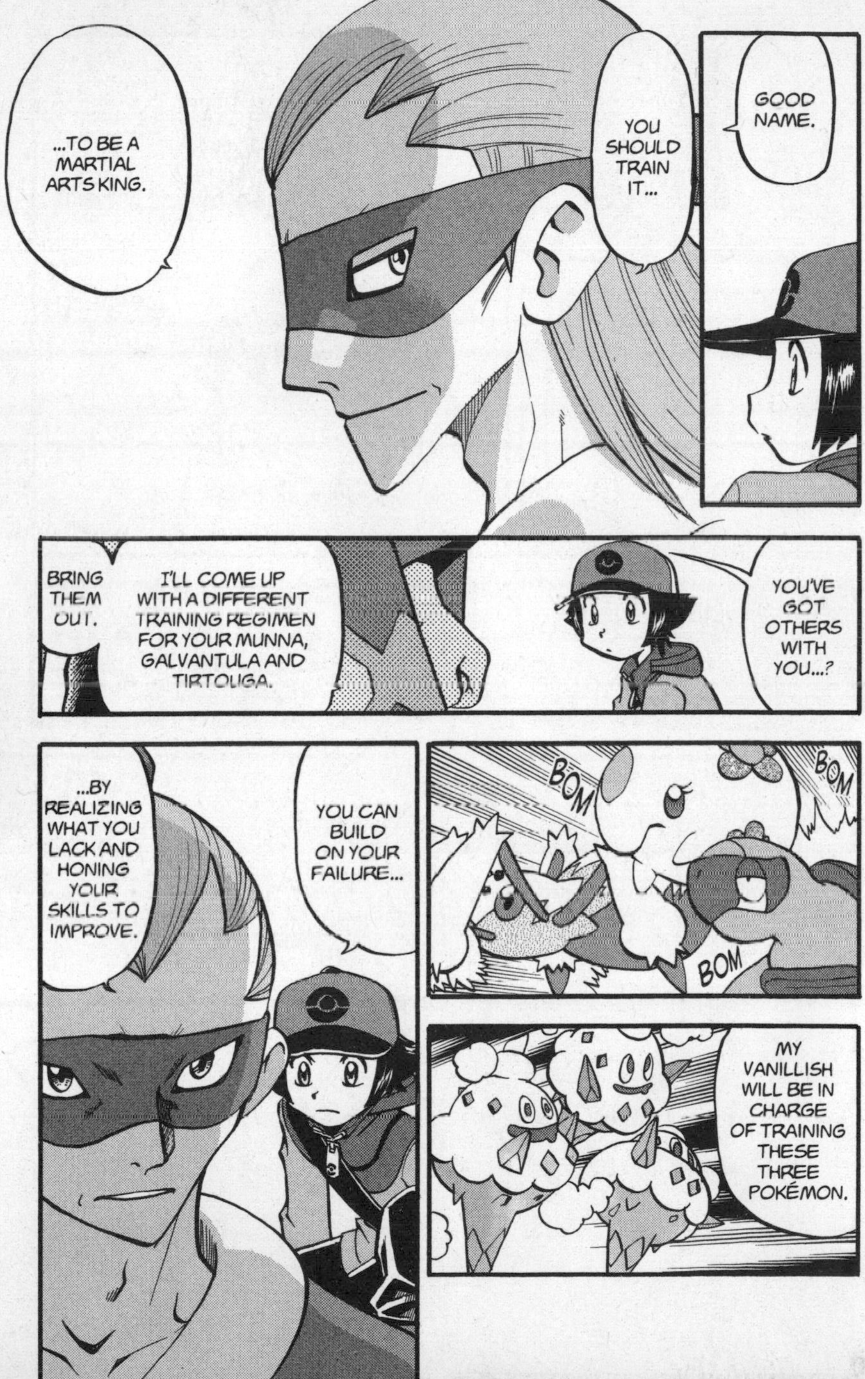
GOOD NAME.
YOU SHOULD TRAIN IT...
...TO BE A MARTIAL ARTS KING.
YOU'VE GOT OTHERS WITH YOU...?
I'LL COME UP WITH A DIFFERENT TRAINING REGIMEN FOR YOUR MUNNA, GALVANTULA AND TIRTOUGA.
BRING THEM OUT.
BOM
BOM
BOM
MY VANILLISH WILL BE IN CHARGE OF TRAINING THESE THREE POKÉMON.
YOU CAN BUILD ON YOUR FAILURE...
...BY REALIZING WHAT YOU LACK AND HONING YOUR SKILLS TO IMPROVE.

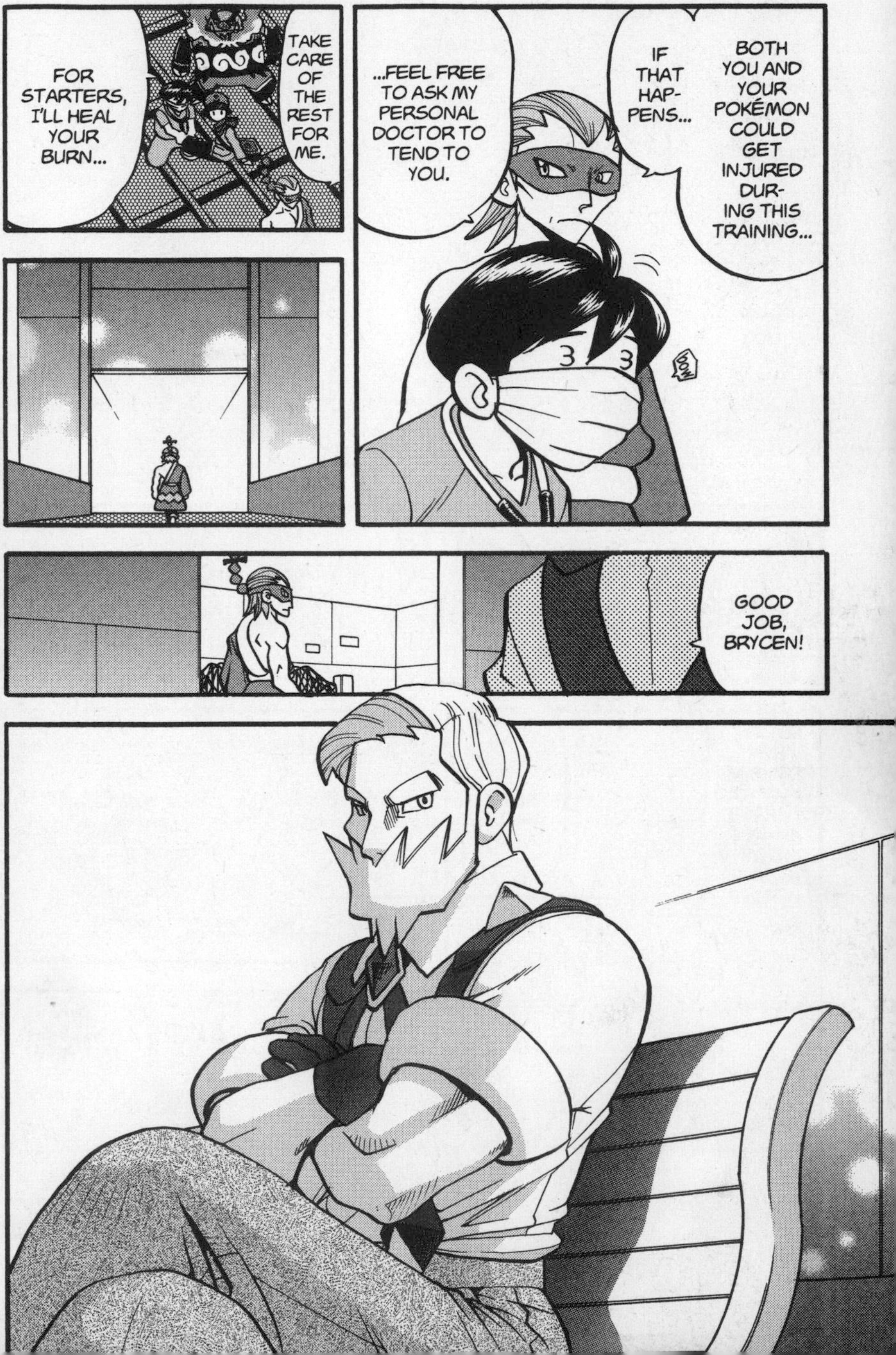
BOTH YOU AND YOUR POKÉMON COULD GET INJURED DUR-ING THIS TRAINING...
IF THAT HAP-PENS...
...FEEL FREE TO ASK MY PERSONAL DOCTOR TO TEND TO YOU.
BOW
TAKE CARE OF THE REST FOR ME.
FOR STARTERS, I'LL HEAL YOUR BURN...
GOOD JOB, BRYCEN!

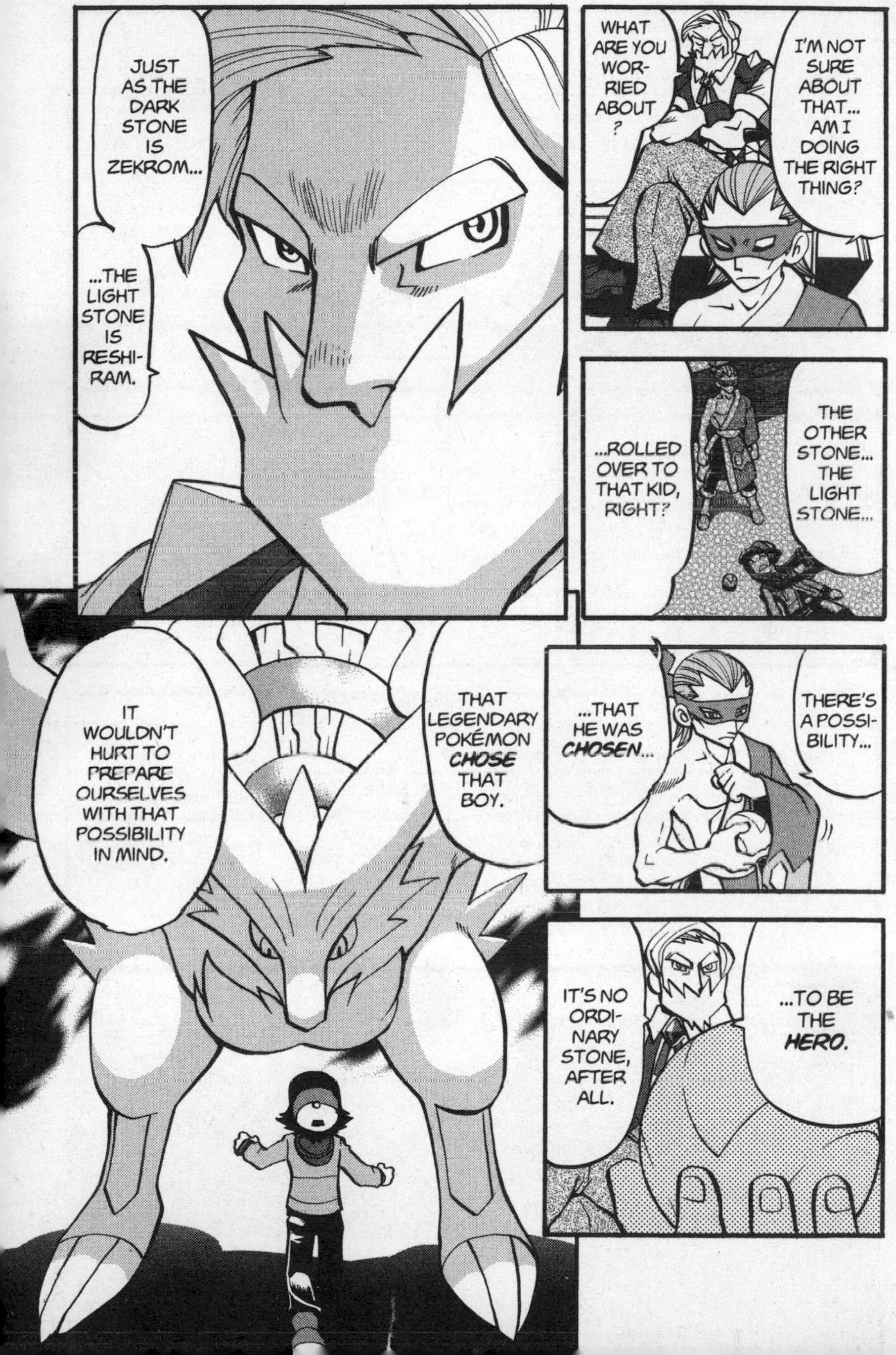
I'M NOT SURE ABOUT THAT... AM I DOING THE RIGHT THING?
WHAT ARE YOU WORRIED ABOUT?
THE OTHER STONE... THE LIGHT STONE...
...ROLLED OVER TO THAT KID, RIGHT?
JUST AS THE DARK STONE IS ZEKROM...
...THE LIGHT STONE IS RESHIRAM.
THERE'S A POSSIBILITY...
...THAT HE WAS *CHOSEN*...
...TO BE THE *HERO*.
IT'S NO ORDINARY STONE, AFTER ALL.
THAT LEGENDARY POKÉMON *CHOSE* THAT BOY.
IT WOULDN'T HURT TO PREPARE OURSELVES WITH THAT POSSIBILITY IN MIND.

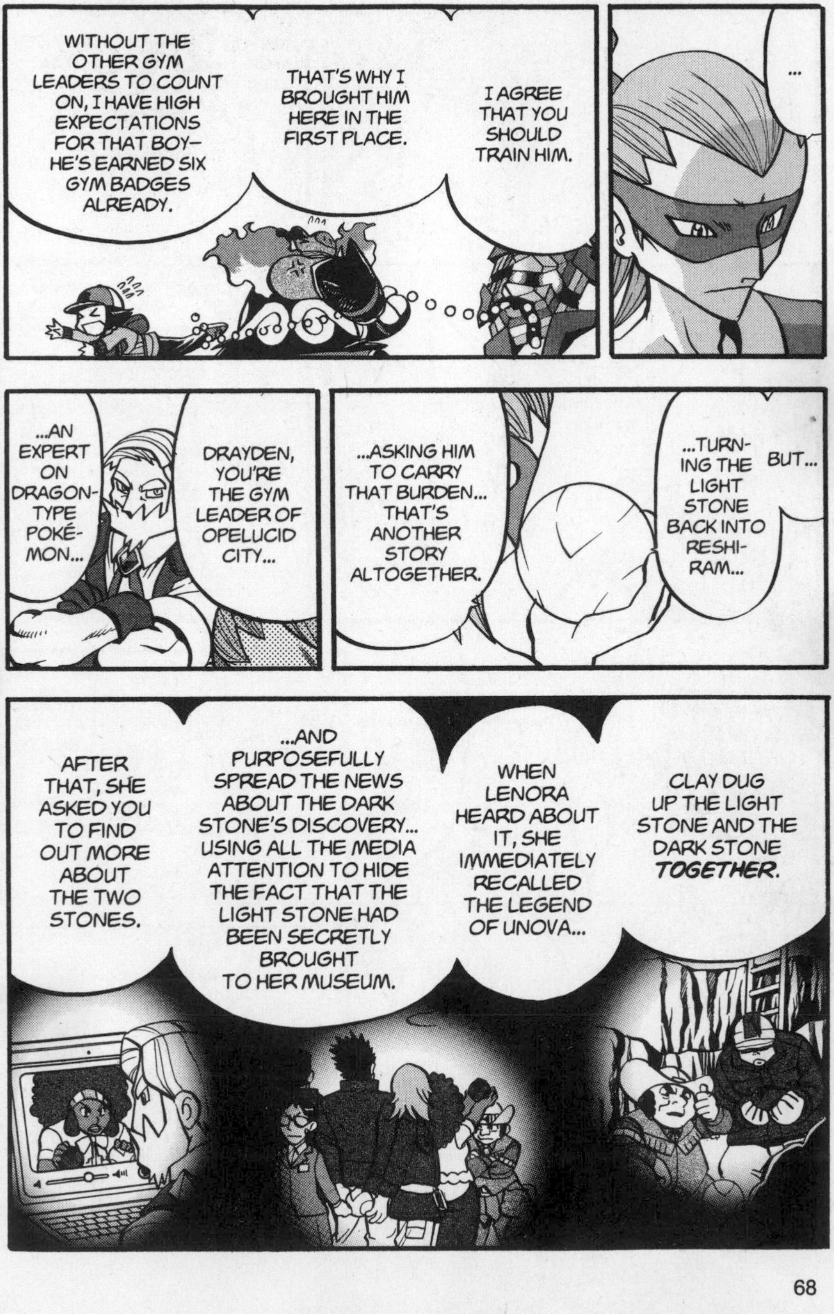
...
I AGREE THAT YOU SHOULD TRAIN HIM.
THAT'S WHY I BROUGHT HIM HERE IN THE FIRST PLACE.
WITHOUT THE OTHER GYM LEADERS TO COUNT ON, I HAVE HIGH EXPECTATIONS FOR THAT BOY— HE'S EARNED SIX GYM BADGES ALREADY.
BUT...
...TURNING THE LIGHT STONE BACK INTO RESHIRAM...
...ASKING HIM TO CARRY THAT BURDEN... THAT'S ANOTHER STORY ALTOGETHER.
DRAYDEN, YOU'RE THE GYM LEADER OF OPELUCID CITY...
...AN EXPERT ON DRAGON-TYPE POKÉMON...
CLAY DUG UP THE LIGHT STONE AND THE DARK STONE *TOGETHER*.
WHEN LENORA HEARD ABOUT IT, SHE IMMEDIATELY RECALLED THE LEGEND OF UNOVA...
...AND PURPOSEFULLY SPREAD THE NEWS ABOUT THE DARK STONE'S DISCOVERY... USING ALL THE MEDIA ATTENTION TO HIDE THE FACT THAT THE LIGHT STONE HAD BEEN SECRETLY BROUGHT TO HER MUSEUM.
AFTER THAT, SHE ASKED YOU TO FIND OUT MORE ABOUT THE TWO STONES.

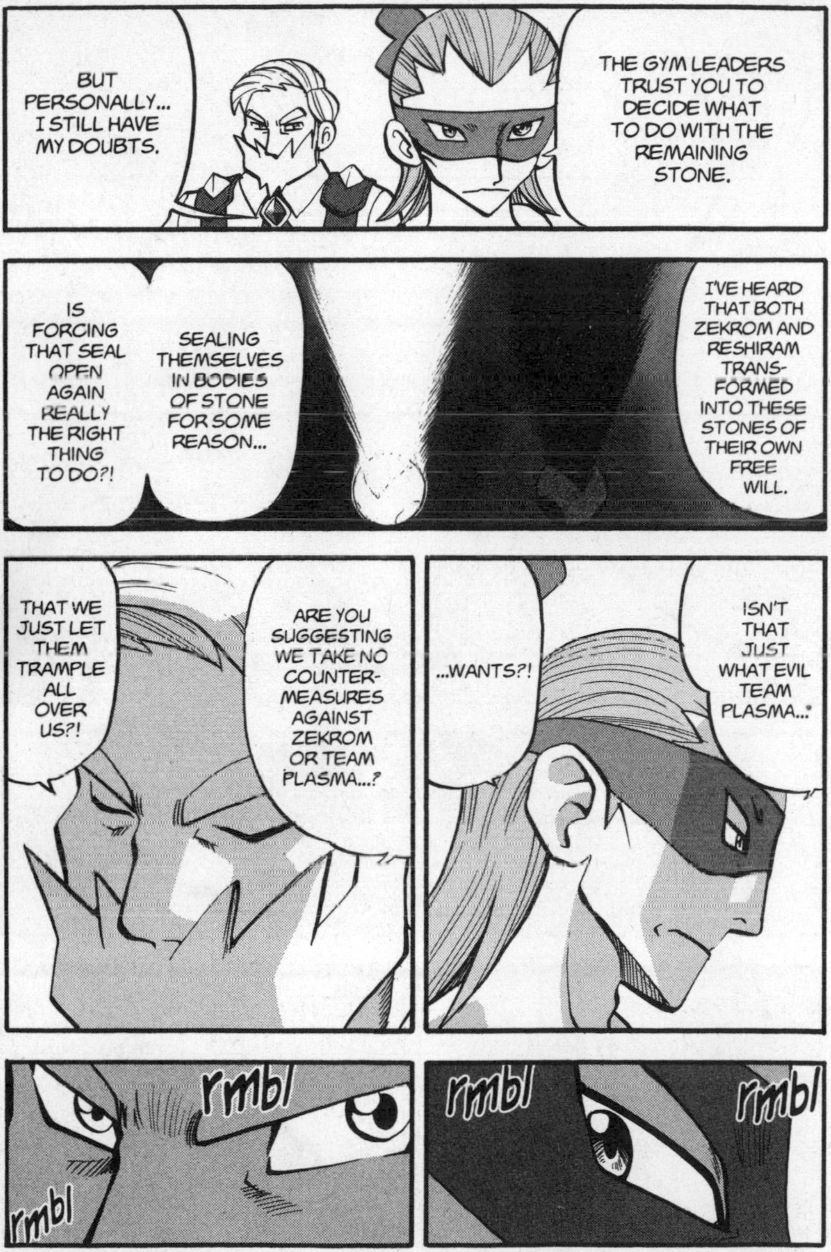
THE GYM LEADERS TRUST YOU TO DECIDE WHAT TO DO WITH THE REMAINING STONE.
BUT PERSONALLY... I STILL HAVE MY DOUBTS.
I'VE HEARD THAT BOTH ZEKROM AND RESHIRAM TRANS-FORMED INTO THESE STONES OF THEIR OWN FREE WILL.
SEALING THEMSELVES IN BODIES OF STONE FOR SOME REASON...
IS FORCING THAT SEAL OPEN AGAIN REALLY THE RIGHT THING TO DO?!
ISN'T THAT JUST WHAT EVIL TEAM PLASMA...?
...WANTS?!
ARE YOU SUGGESTING WE TAKE NO COUNTER-MEASURES AGAINST ZEKROM OR TEAM PLASMA...?
THAT WE JUST LET THEM TRAMPLE ALL OVER US?!
rmbl
rmbl
rmbl
rmbl

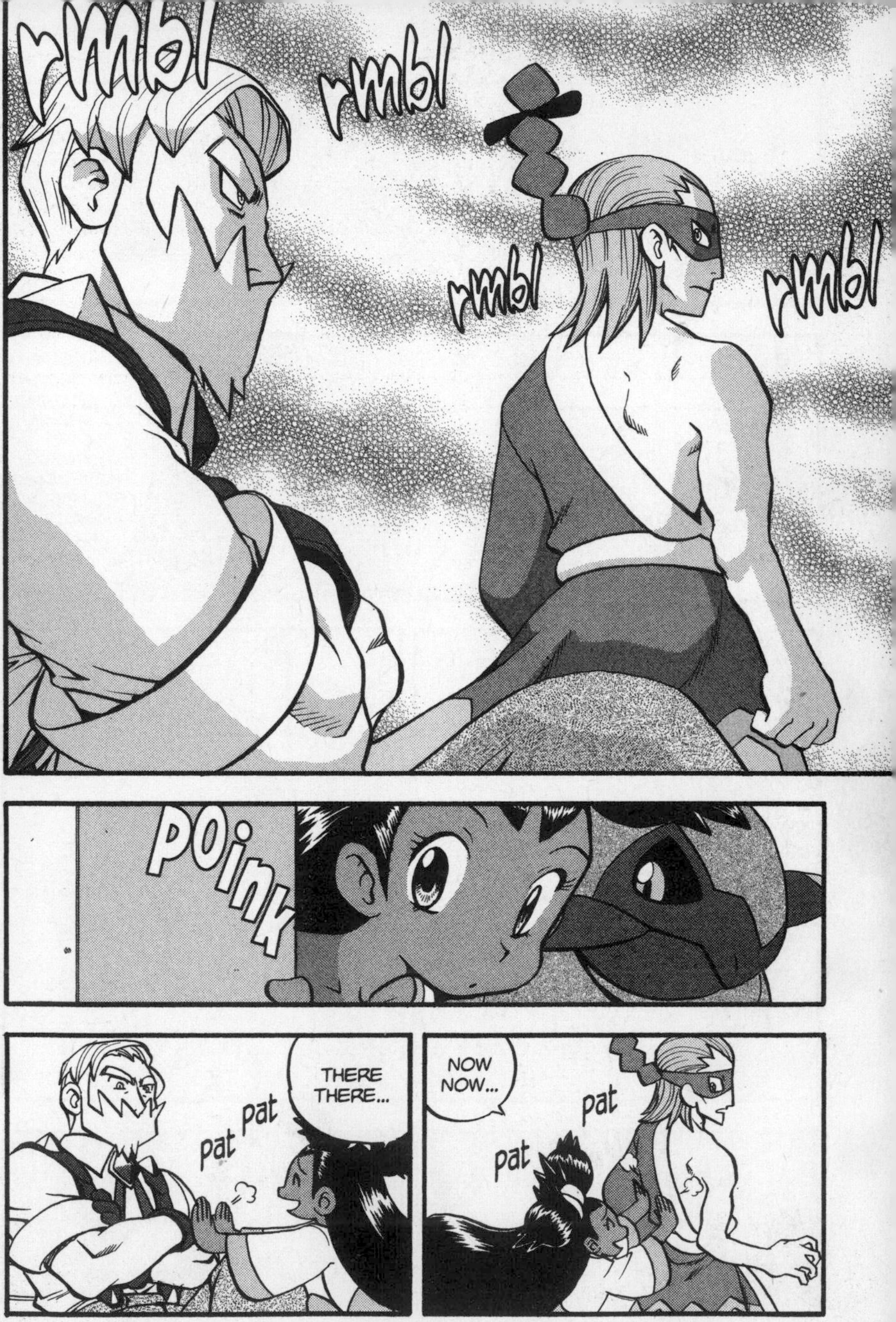
rmbl
rmbl
rmbl
rmbl
poink
NOW NOW...
pat
pat
THERE THERE...
pat
pat

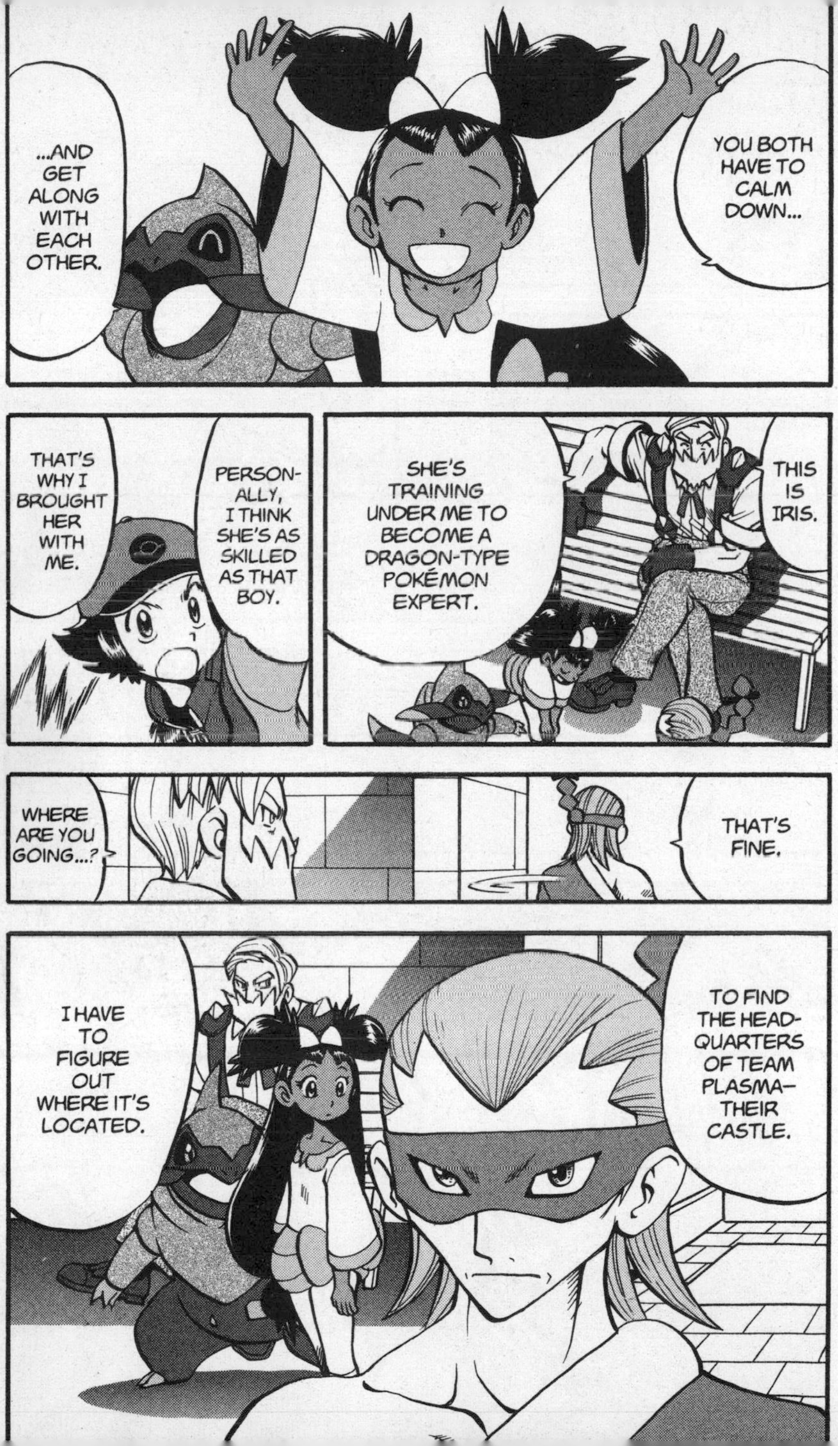
YOU BOTH HAVE TO CALM DOWN...
...AND GET ALONG WITH EACH OTHER.
THIS IS IRIS.
SHE'S TRAINING UNDER ME TO BECOME A DRAGON-TYPE POKÉMON EXPERT.
PERSONALLY, I THINK SHE'S AS SKILLED AS THAT BOY.
THAT'S WHY I BROUGHT HER WITH ME.
THAT'S FINE.
WHERE ARE YOU GOING...?
TO FIND THE HEADQUARTERS OF TEAM PLASMA— THEIR CASTLE.
I HAVE TO FIGURE OUT WHERE IT'S LOCATED.

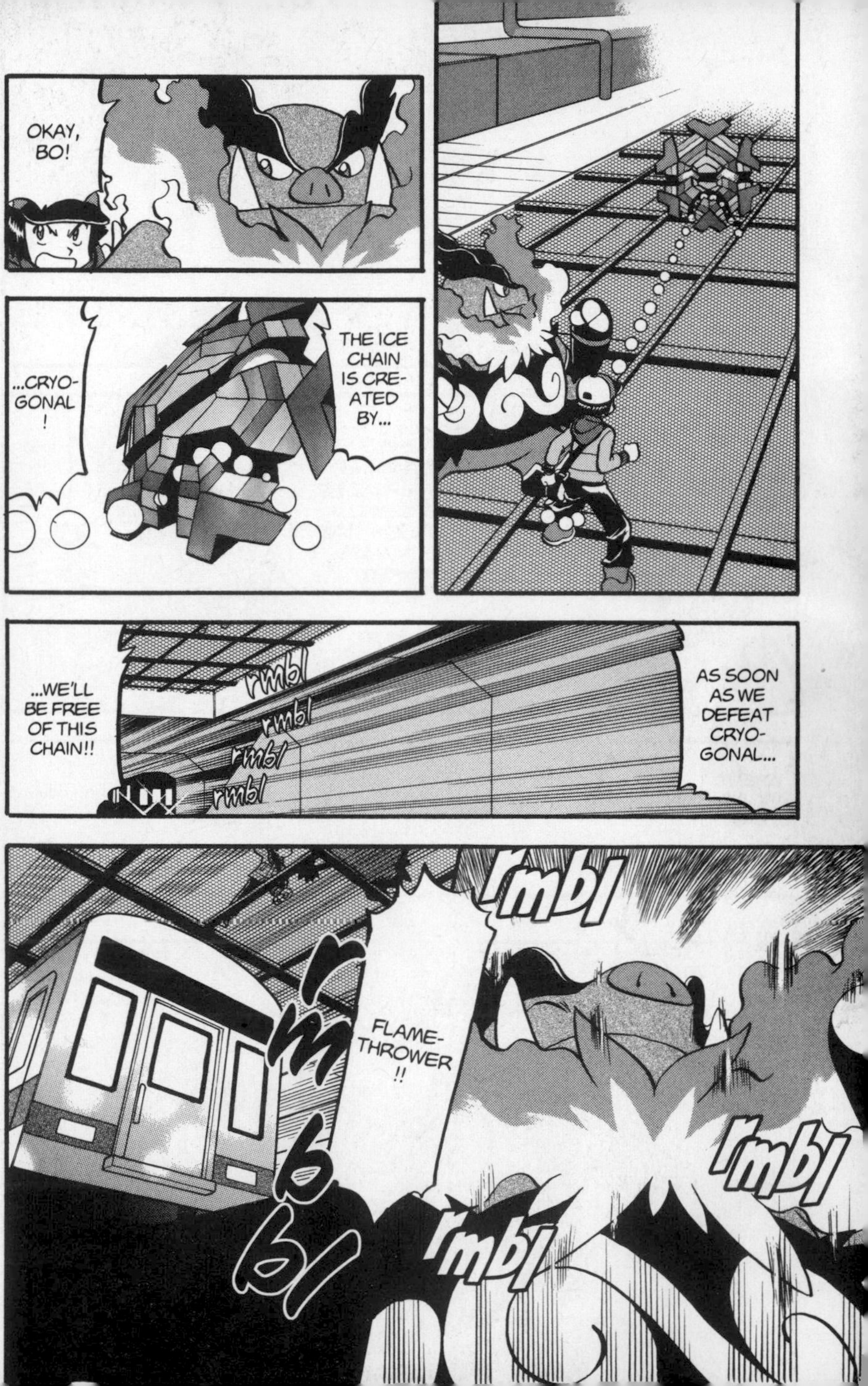
OKAY, BO!
THE ICE CHAIN IS CRE-ATED BY...
...CRYO-GONAL!
AS SOON AS WE DEFEAT CRYO-GONAL...
rmbl
rmbl
rmbl
rmbl
...WE'LL BE FREE OF THIS CHAIN!!
rmbl
FLAME-THROWER!!
rmbl
rmbl
rmbl

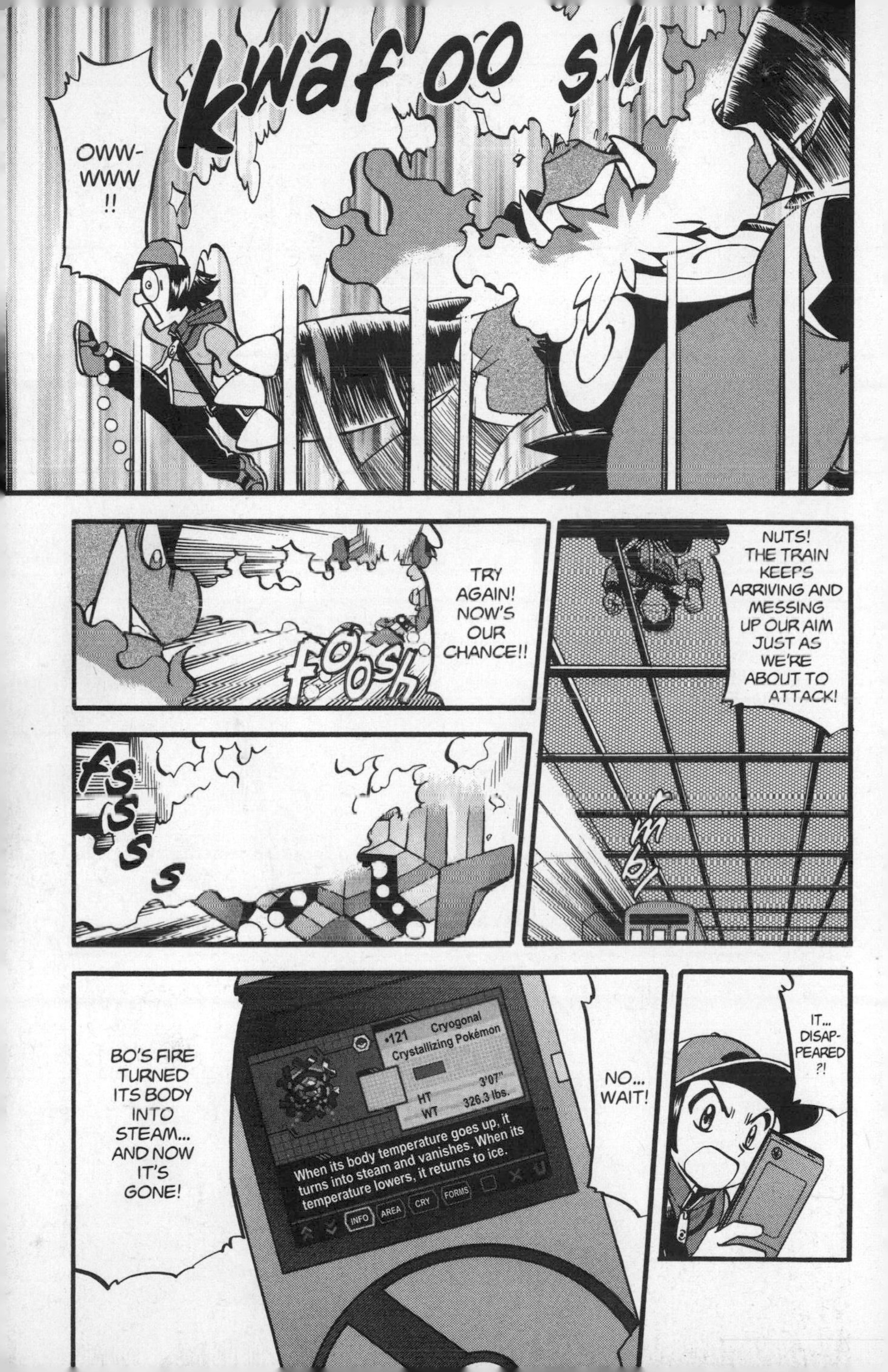
kwafoosh
OWW-WWW!!
NUTS! THE TRAIN KEEPS ARRIVING AND MESSING UP OUR AIM JUST AS WE'RE ABOUT TO ATTACK!
rmbl
TRY AGAIN! NOW'S OUR CHANCE!!
foosh
fsssss
IT... DISAP-PEARED?!
NO... WAIT!
•121 Cryogonal
Crystallizing Pokémon
HT 3'07"
WT 326.3 lbs.
When its body temperature goes up, it turns into steam and vanishes. When its temperature lowers, it returns to ice.
INFO AREA CRY FORMS
BO'S FIRE TURNED ITS BODY INTO STEAM... AND NOW IT'S GONE!

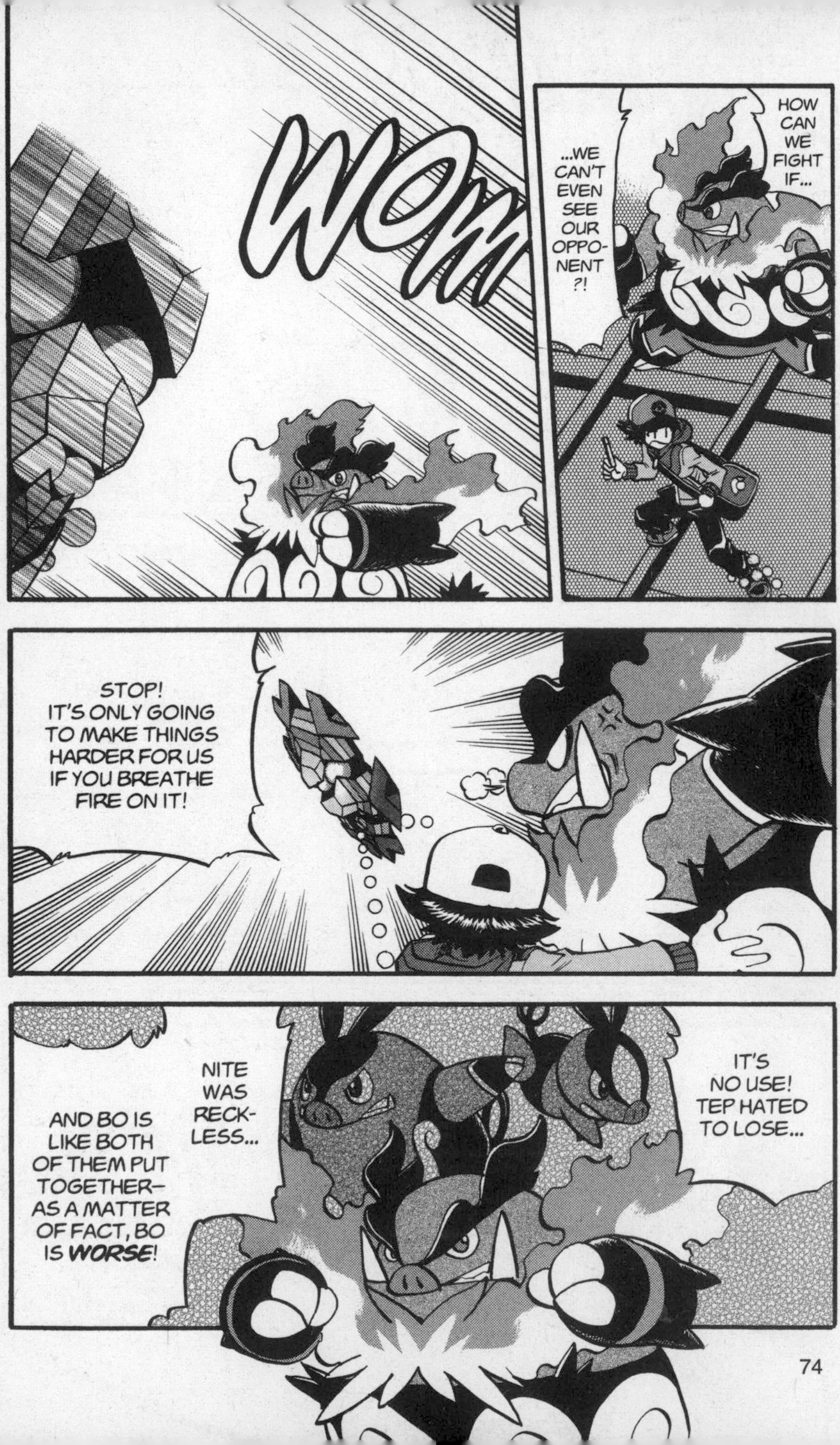
HOW CAN WE FIGHT IF...
...WE CAN'T EVEN SEE OUR OPPONENT?!
WOM
STOP! IT'S ONLY GOING TO MAKE THINGS HARDER FOR US IF YOU BREATHE FIRE ON IT!
IT'S NO USE! TEP HATED TO LOSE...
NITE WAS RECKLESS...
AND BO IS LIKE BOTH OF THEM PUT TOGETHER—AS A MATTER OF FACT, BO IS ***WORSE***!

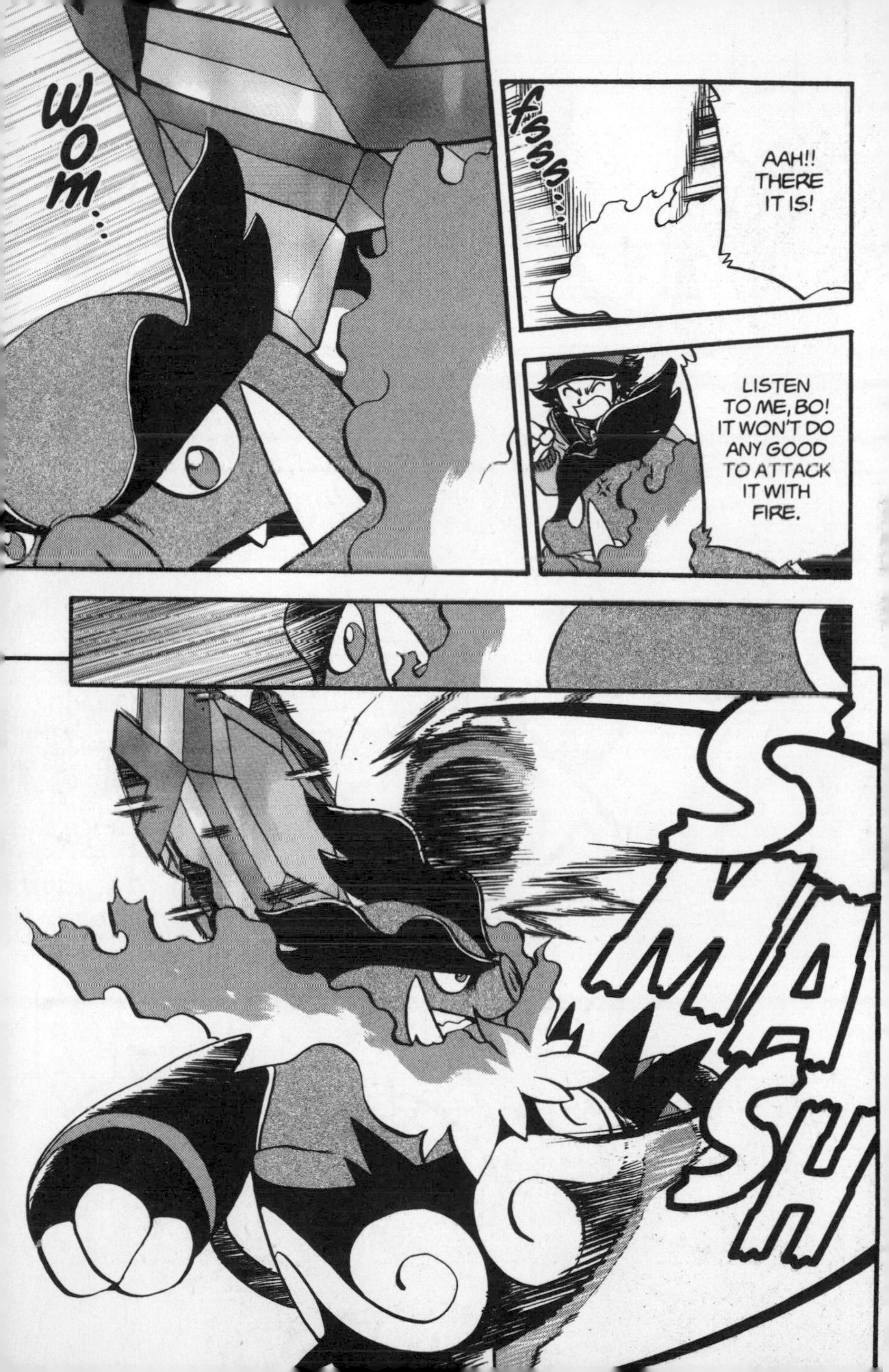

FSSSS...
AAH!! THERE IT IS!
LISTEN TO ME, BO! IT WON'T DO ANY GOOD TO ATTACK IT WITH FIRE.
WOM...
SMASH

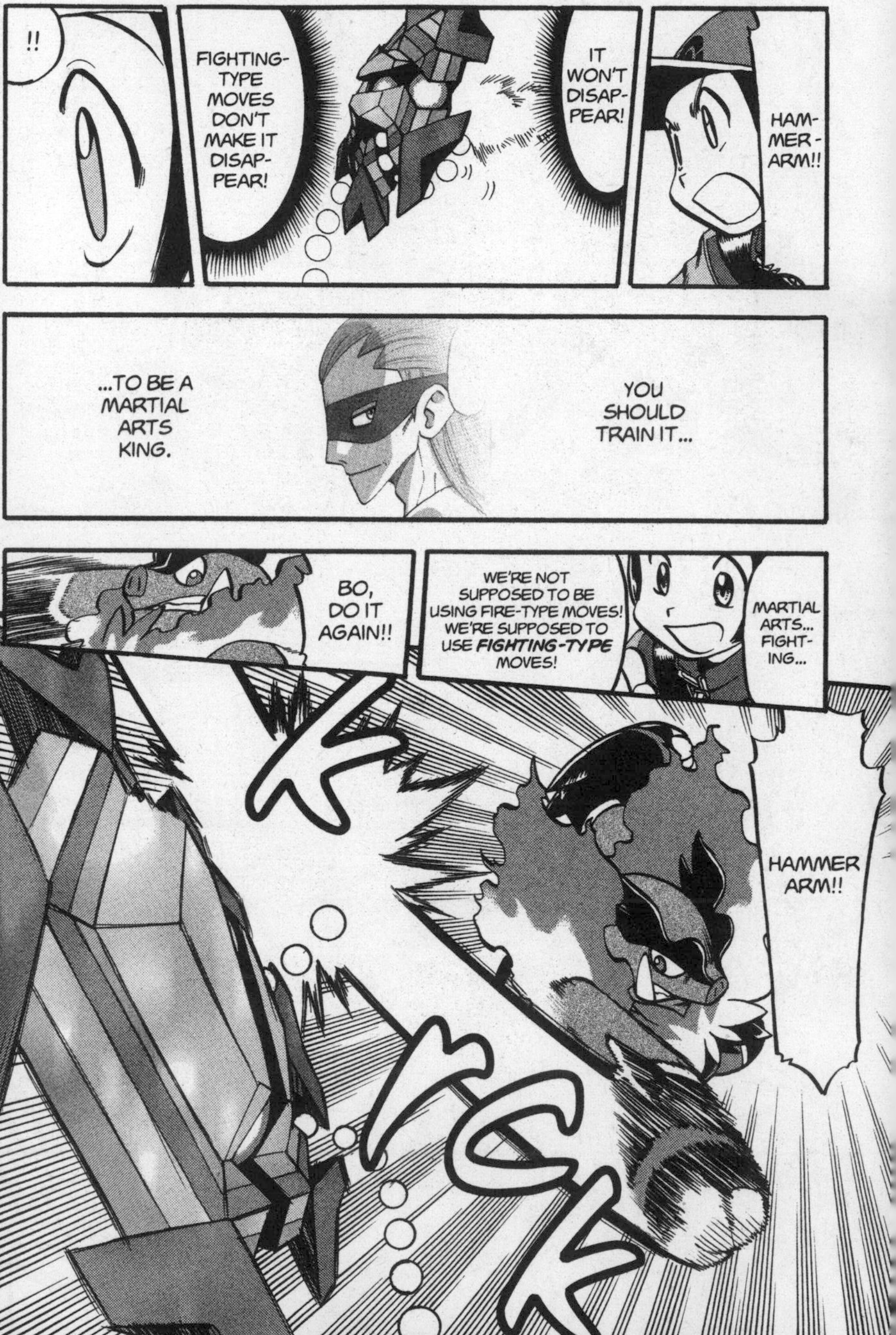
HAM-MER-ARM!!
IT WON'T DISAP-PEAR!
FIGHTING-TYPE MOVES DON'T MAKE IT DISAP-PEAR!
!!
YOU SHOULD TRAIN IT...
...TO BE A MARTIAL ARTS KING.
MARTIAL ARTS... FIGHT-ING...
WE'RE NOT SUPPOSED TO BE USING FIRE-TYPE MOVES! WE'RE SUPPOSED TO USE ***FIGHTING-TYPE*** MOVES!
BO, DO IT AGAIN!!
HAMMER ARM!!

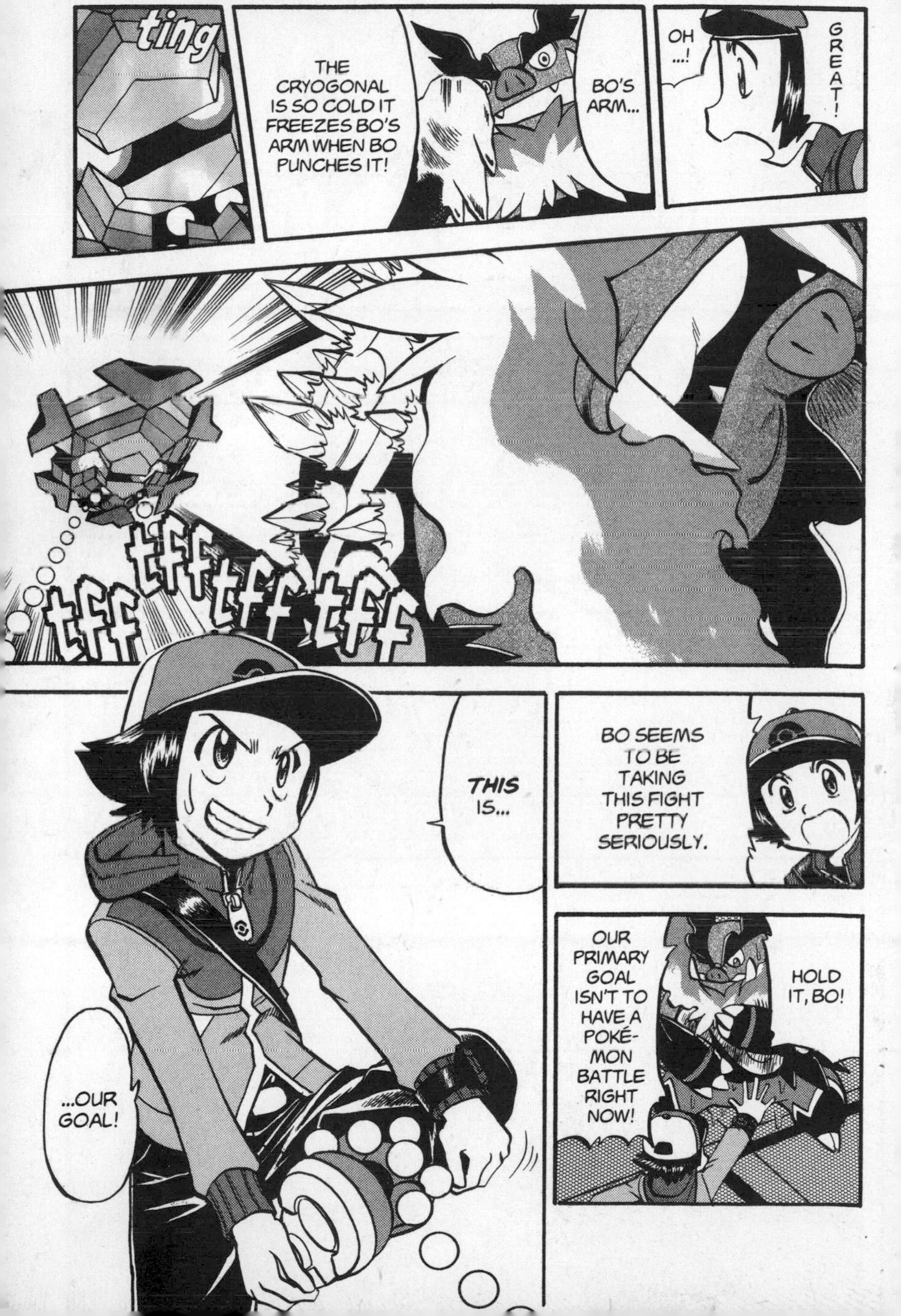
ting
THE CRYOGONAL IS SO COLD IT FREEZES BO'S ARM WHEN BO PUNCHES IT!
BO'S ARM...
OH ...!
GREAT!
tff tff tff tff
THIS IS...
...OUR GOAL!
BO SEEMS TO BE TAKING THIS FIGHT PRETTY SERIOUSLY.
HOLD IT, BO!
OUR PRIMARY GOAL ISN'T TO HAVE A POKÉ-MON BATTLE RIGHT NOW!

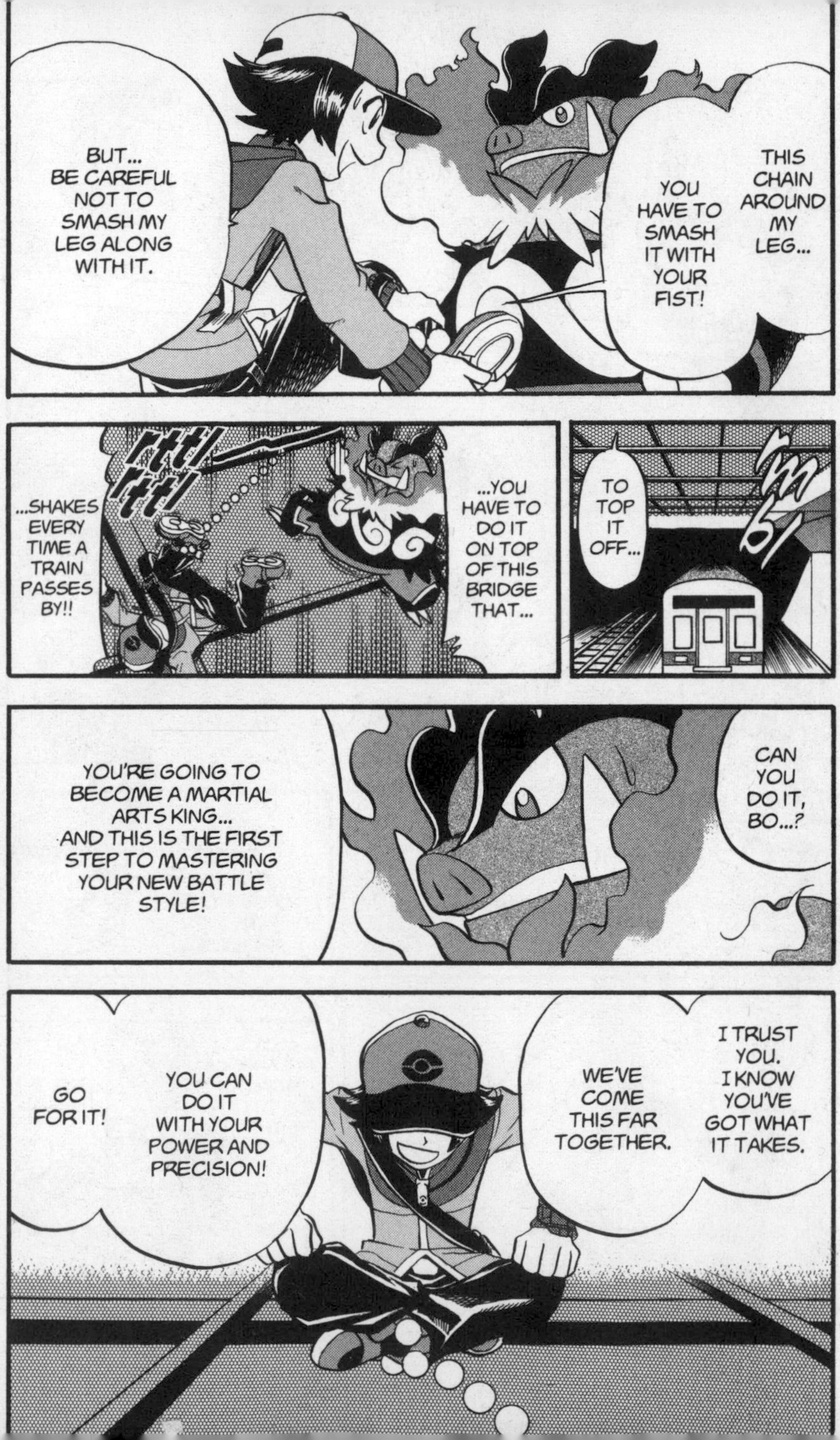
THIS CHAIN AROUND MY LEG...
YOU HAVE TO SMASH IT WITH YOUR FIST!
BUT... BE CAREFUL NOT TO SMASH MY LEG ALONG WITH IT.
rmbl
TO TOP IT OFF...
...YOU HAVE TO DO IT ON TOP OF THIS BRIDGE THAT...
rttl rttl
...SHAKES EVERY TIME A TRAIN PASSES BY!!
CAN YOU DO IT, BO...?
YOU'RE GOING TO BECOME A MARTIAL ARTS KING... AND THIS IS THE FIRST STEP TO MASTERING YOUR NEW BATTLE STYLE!
I TRUST YOU. I KNOW YOU'VE GOT WHAT IT TAKES.
WE'VE COME THIS FAR TOGETHER.
YOU CAN DO IT WITH YOUR POWER AND PRECISION!
GO FOR IT!

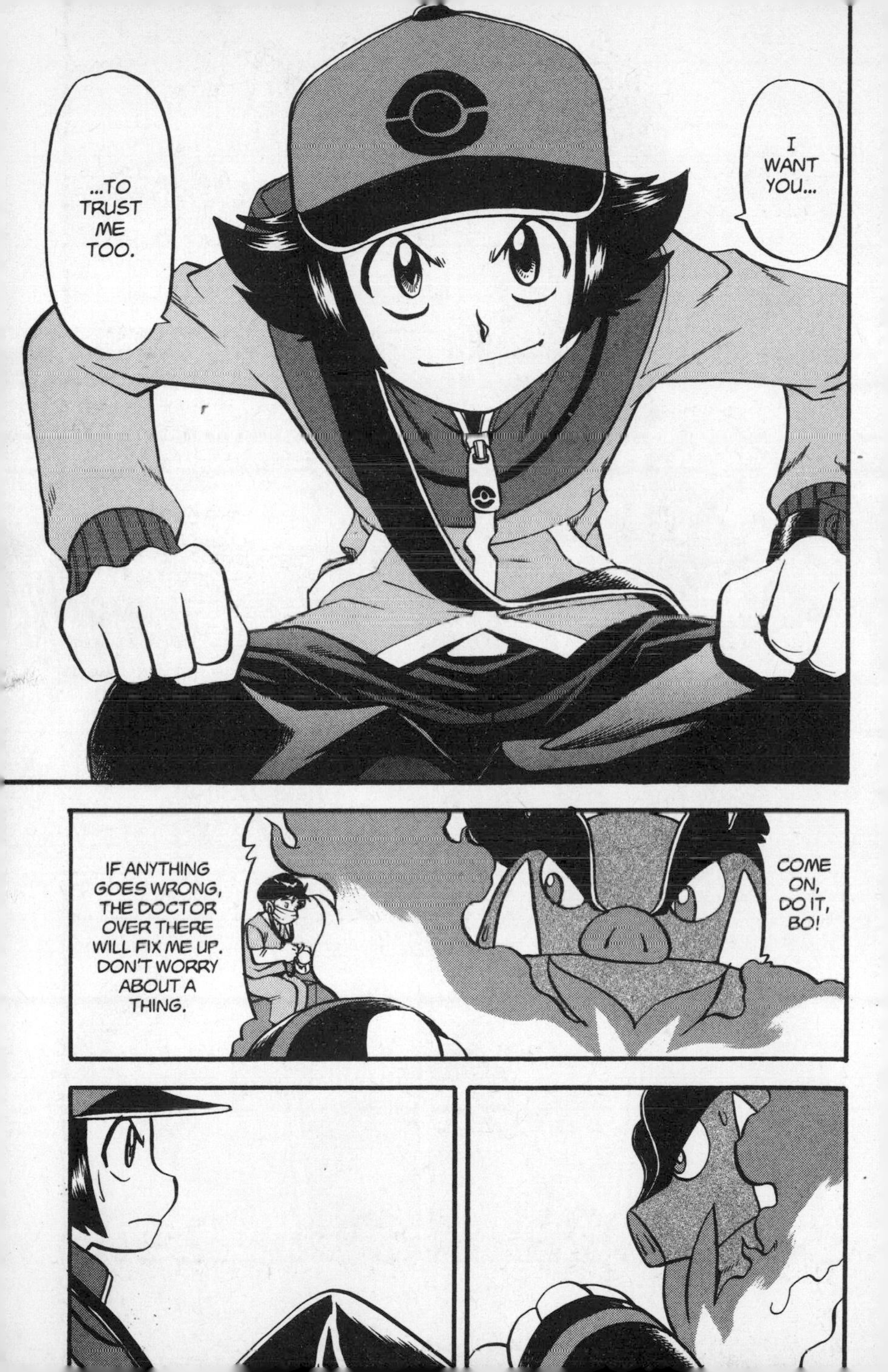
I WANT YOU...
...TO TRUST ME TOO.
COME ON, DO IT, BO!
IF ANYTHING GOES WRONG, THE DOCTOR OVER THERE WILL FIX ME UP. DON'T WORRY ABOUT A THING.

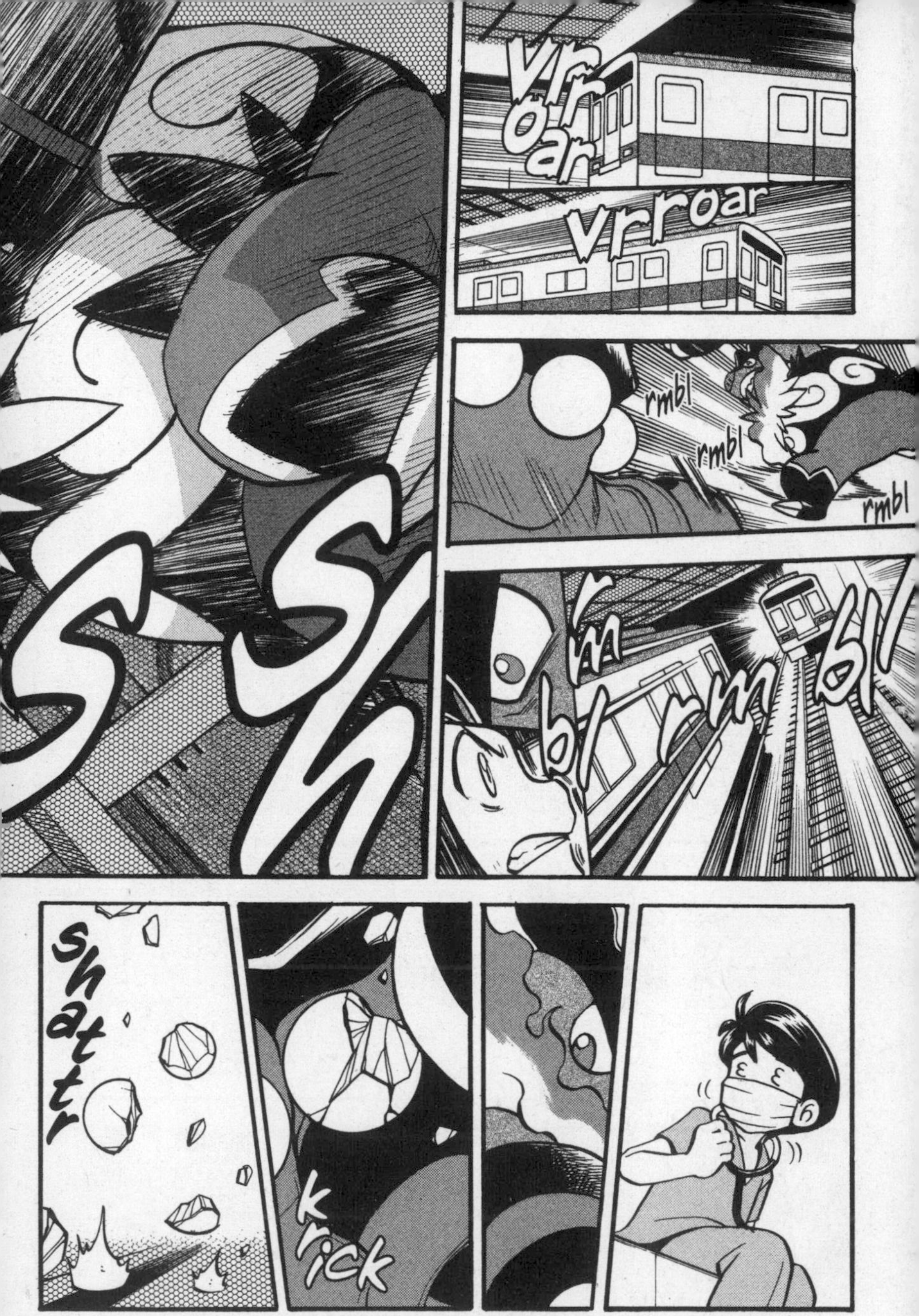
vrroar
vrroar
rmbl
rmbl
rmbl
rmbl rmbl
SSh
krick
shattr

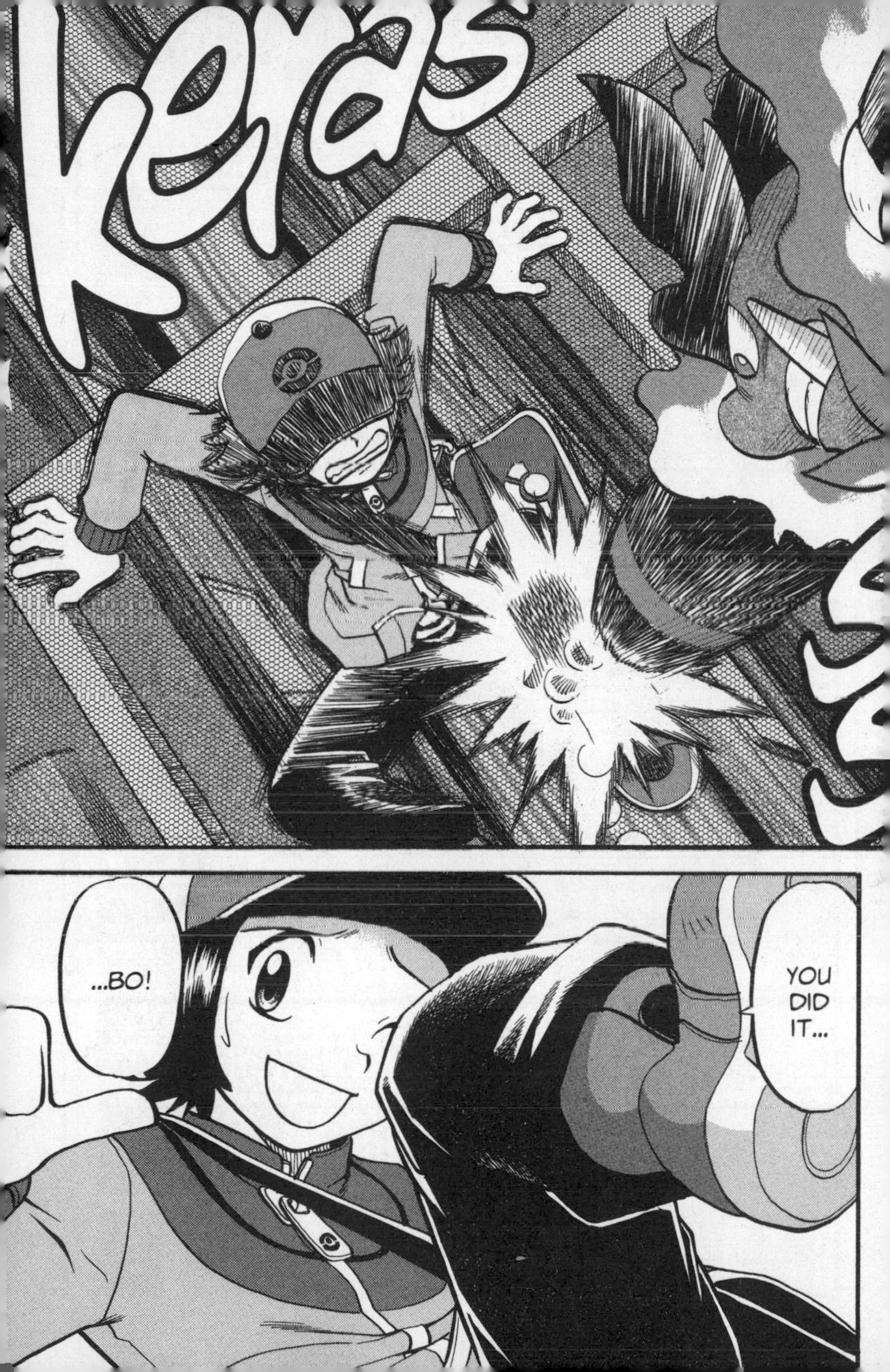
keras
YOU DID IT...
...BO!

Final Destination:
Pokémon League

Black's Current Location:
Tubeline Bridge

○ BLACK

○ WHITE

Mega Fire Pig Pokémon **Bo**
Emboar ♂ | Fire | Fighting |
Lv.38 Ability: Blaze

Dream Eater Pokémon **Musha**
Munna ♂ | Psychic |
Lv.53 Ability: Forewarn

EleSpider Pokémon **Tula**
Galvantula ♂ | Bug | Electric |
Lv.54 Ability: Unnerve

Prototurtle Pokémon **Costa**
Tirtouga ♂ | Water | Rock |
Lv.34 Ability: Solid Rock

Grass Snake Pokémon **Servine**
Servine ♀ | Grass |
Lv.28 Ability: Overgrow

Season Pokémon **Darlene**
Deerling ♀ | Normal | Grass |
Lv.25 Ability: Chlorophyll

Valiant Pokémon **Brav**
Braviary ♂ | Normal | Flying |
Lv.54 Ability: Sheer Force

TRIO BADGE | BASIC BADGE | INSECT BADGE | BOLT BADGE | QUAKE BADGE | JET BADGE | ? | ?

Pokémon Adventures Black & White

TIRTOUGA

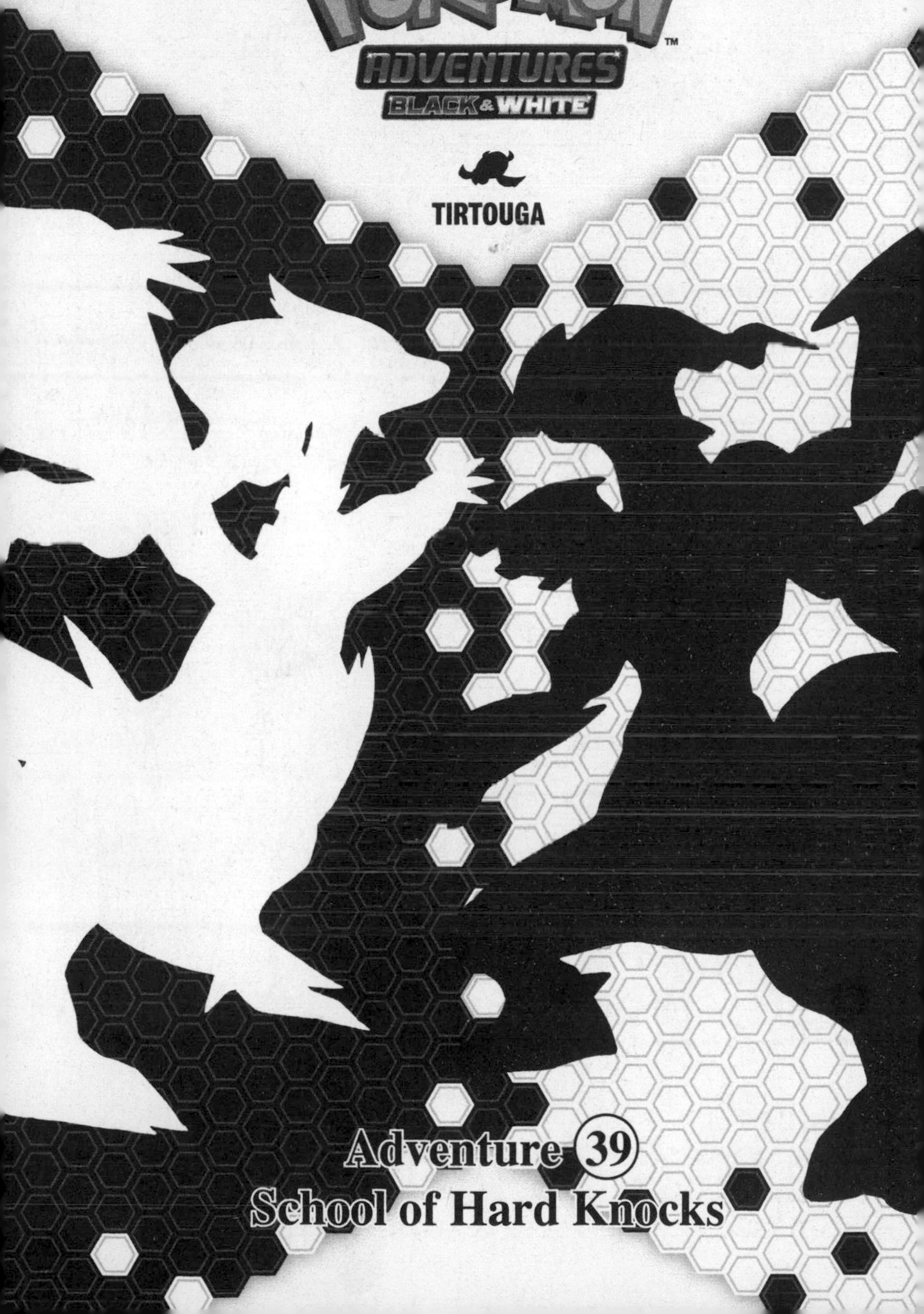

Adventure 39
School of Hard Knocks

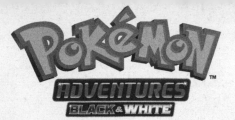

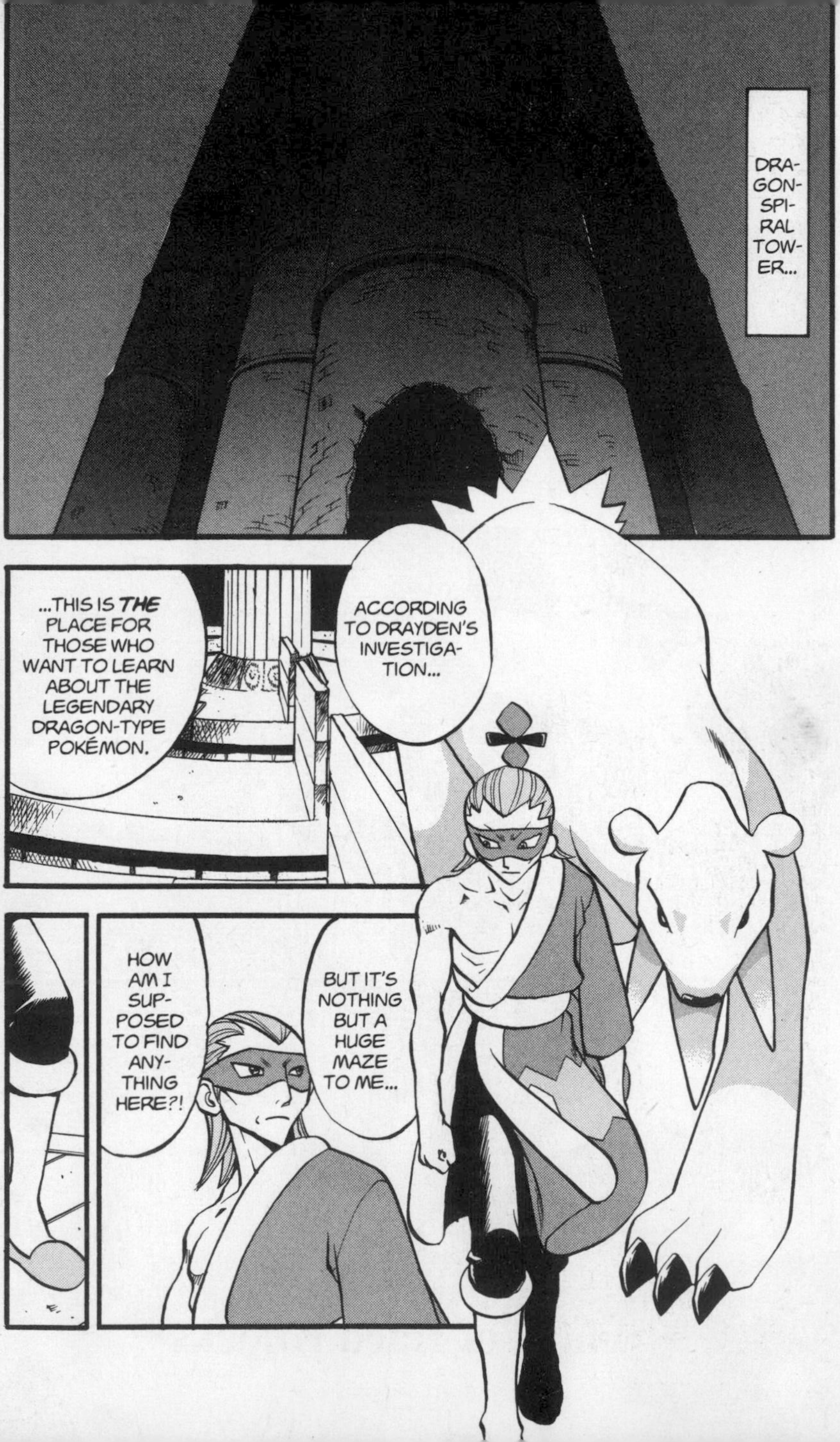
DRAGONSPIRAL TOWER...
ACCORDING TO DRAYDEN'S INVESTIGATION...
...THIS IS *THE* PLACE FOR THOSE WHO WANT TO LEARN ABOUT THE LEGENDARY DRAGON-TYPE POKÉMON.
BUT IT'S NOTHING BUT A HUGE MAZE TO ME...
HOW AM I SUPPOSED TO FIND ANYTHING HERE?!

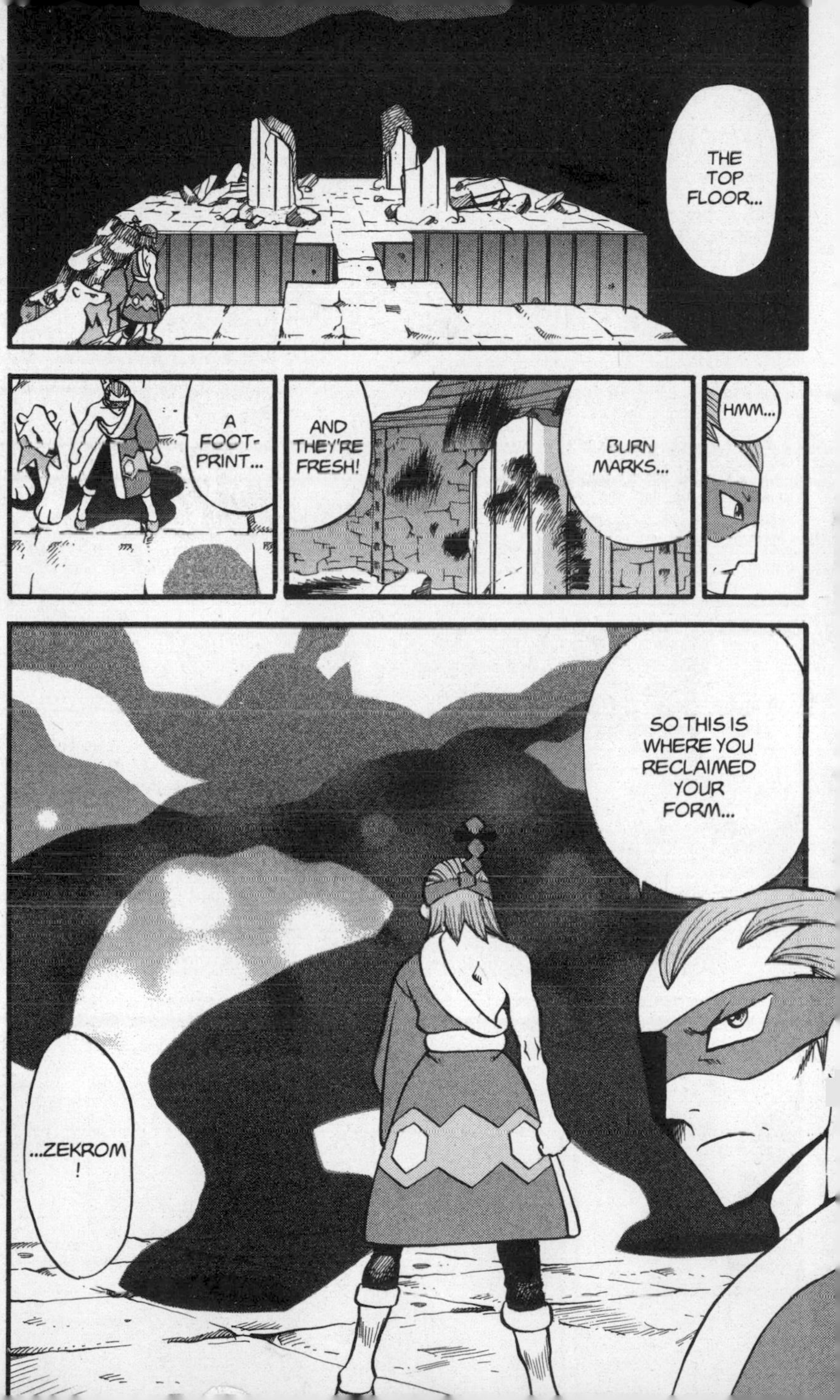
THE TOP FLOOR...
HMM...
BURN MARKS...
AND THEY'RE FRESH!
A FOOT-PRINT...
SO THIS IS WHERE YOU RECLAIMED YOUR FORM...
...ZEKROM!

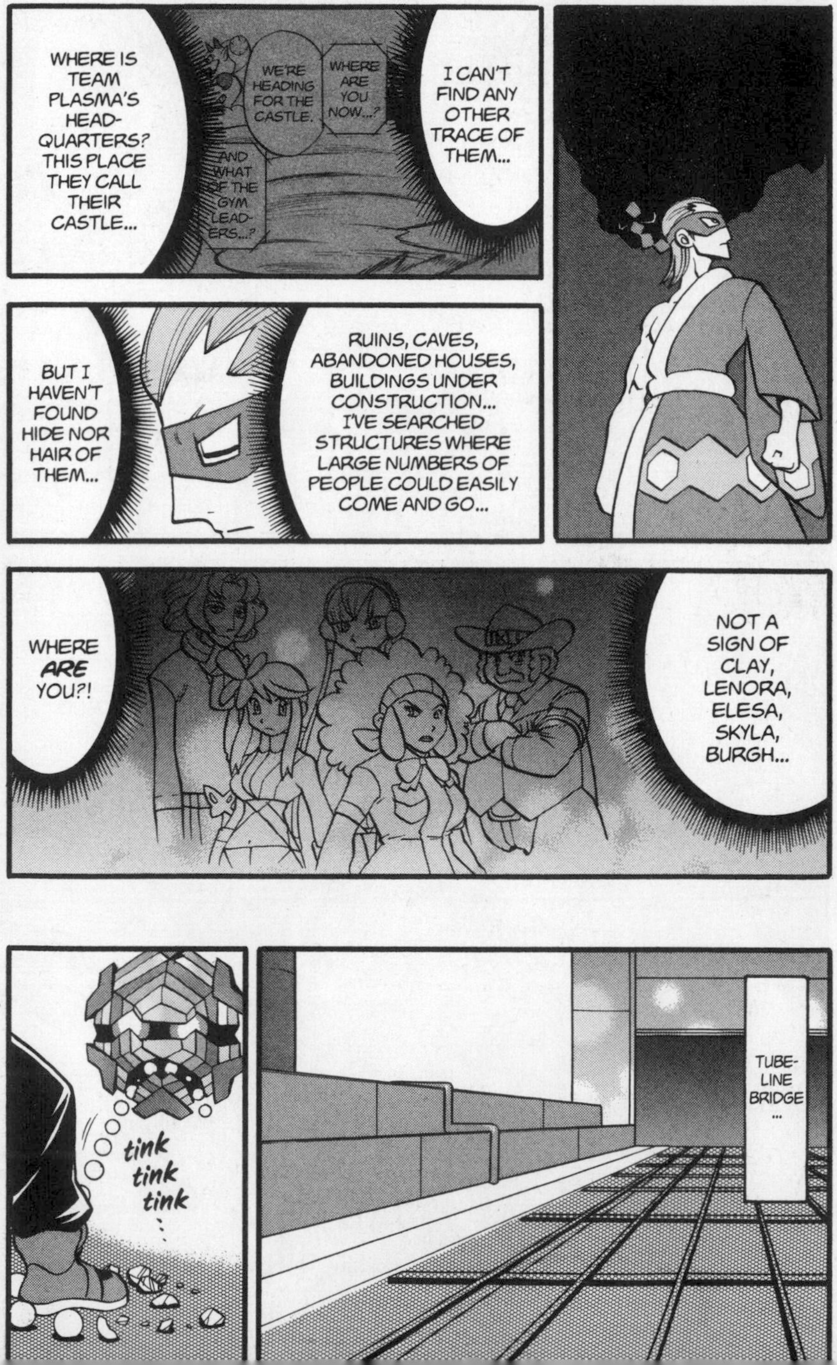
I CAN'T FIND ANY OTHER TRACE OF THEM...
WHERE ARE YOU NOW...?
WE'RE HEADING FOR THE CASTLE.
AND WHAT OF THE GYM LEADERS...?
WHERE IS TEAM PLASMA'S HEAD-QUARTERS? THIS PLACE THEY CALL THEIR CASTLE...
RUINS, CAVES, ABANDONED HOUSES, BUILDINGS UNDER CONSTRUCTION... I'VE SEARCHED STRUCTURES WHERE LARGE NUMBERS OF PEOPLE COULD EASILY COME AND GO...
BUT I HAVEN'T FOUND HIDE NOR HAIR OF THEM...
NOT A SIGN OF CLAY, LENORA, ELESA, SKYLA, BURGH...
WHERE ***ARE*** YOU?!
TUBE-LINE BRIDGE ...
tink tink tink

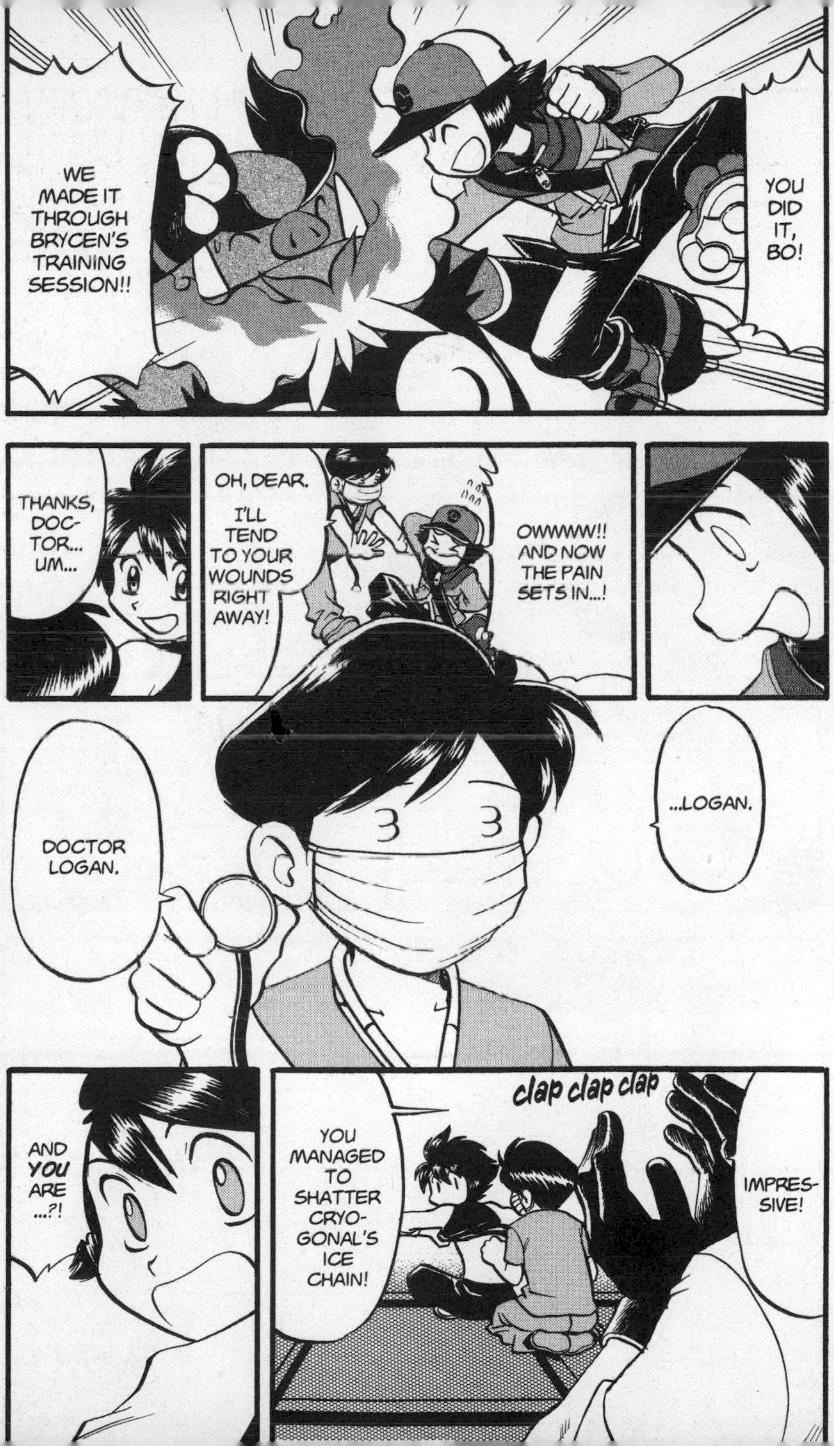
YOU DID IT, BO!
WE MADE IT THROUGH BRYCEN'S TRAINING SESSION!!
OWWWW!! AND NOW THE PAIN SETS IN...!
OH, DEAR. I'LL TEND TO YOUR WOUNDS RIGHT AWAY!
THANKS, DOC-TOR... UM...
...LOGAN.
DOCTOR LOGAN.
clap clap clap
IMPRES-SIVE!
YOU MANAGED TO SHATTER CRYO-GONAL'S ICE CHAIN!
AND YOU ARE ...?!

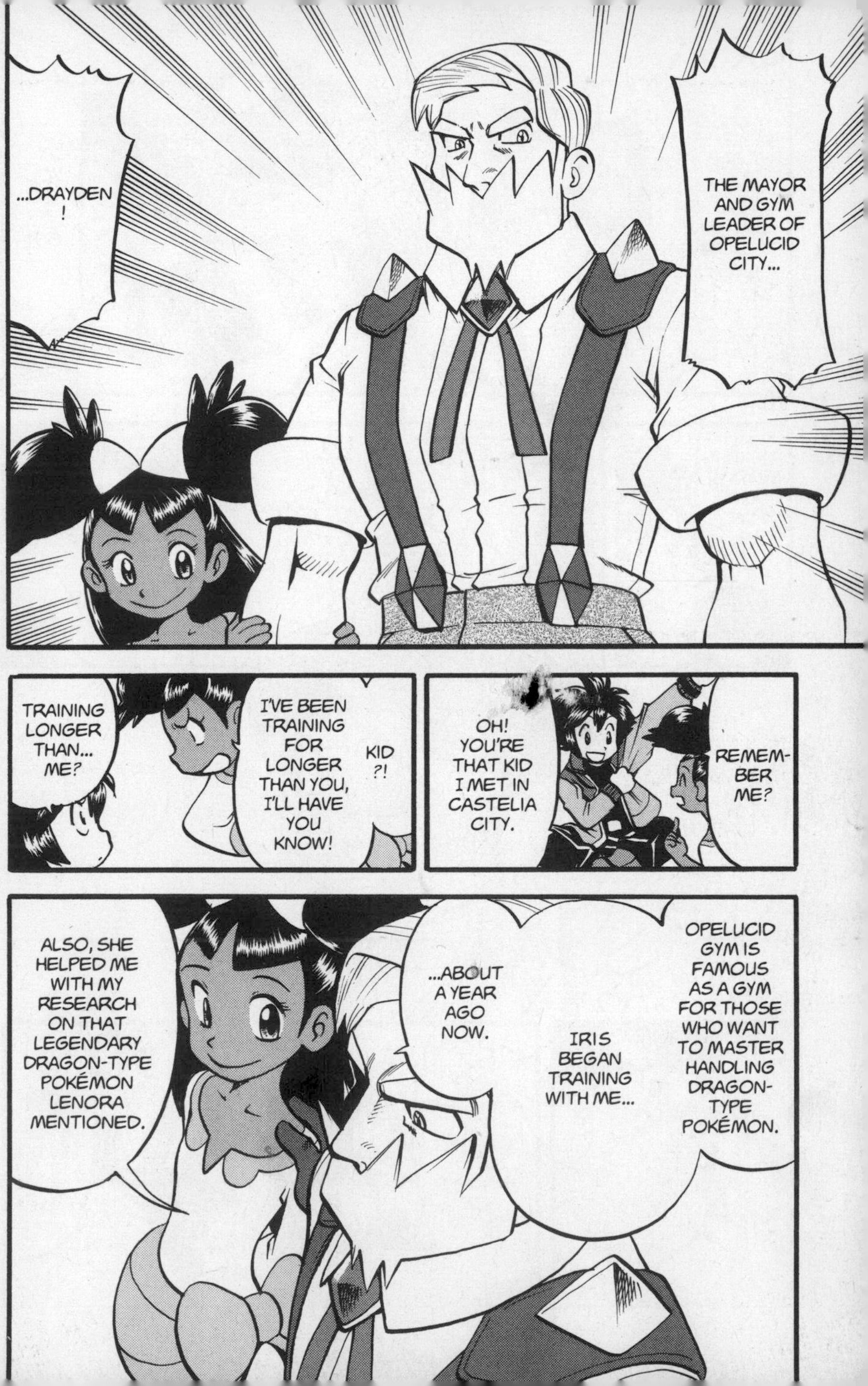
THE MAYOR AND GYM LEADER OF OPELUCID CITY...
...DRAYDEN!
REMEM-BER ME?
OH! YOU'RE THAT KID I MET IN CASTELIA CITY.
KID?!
I'VE BEEN TRAINING FOR LONGER THAN YOU, I'LL HAVE YOU KNOW!
TRAINING LONGER THAN... ME?
OPELUCID GYM IS FAMOUS AS A GYM FOR THOSE WHO WANT TO MASTER HANDLING DRAGON-TYPE POKÉMON.
IRIS BEGAN TRAINING WITH ME...
...ABOUT A YEAR AGO NOW.
ALSO, SHE HELPED ME WITH MY RESEARCH ON THAT LEGENDARY DRAGON-TYPE POKÉMON LENORA MENTIONED.

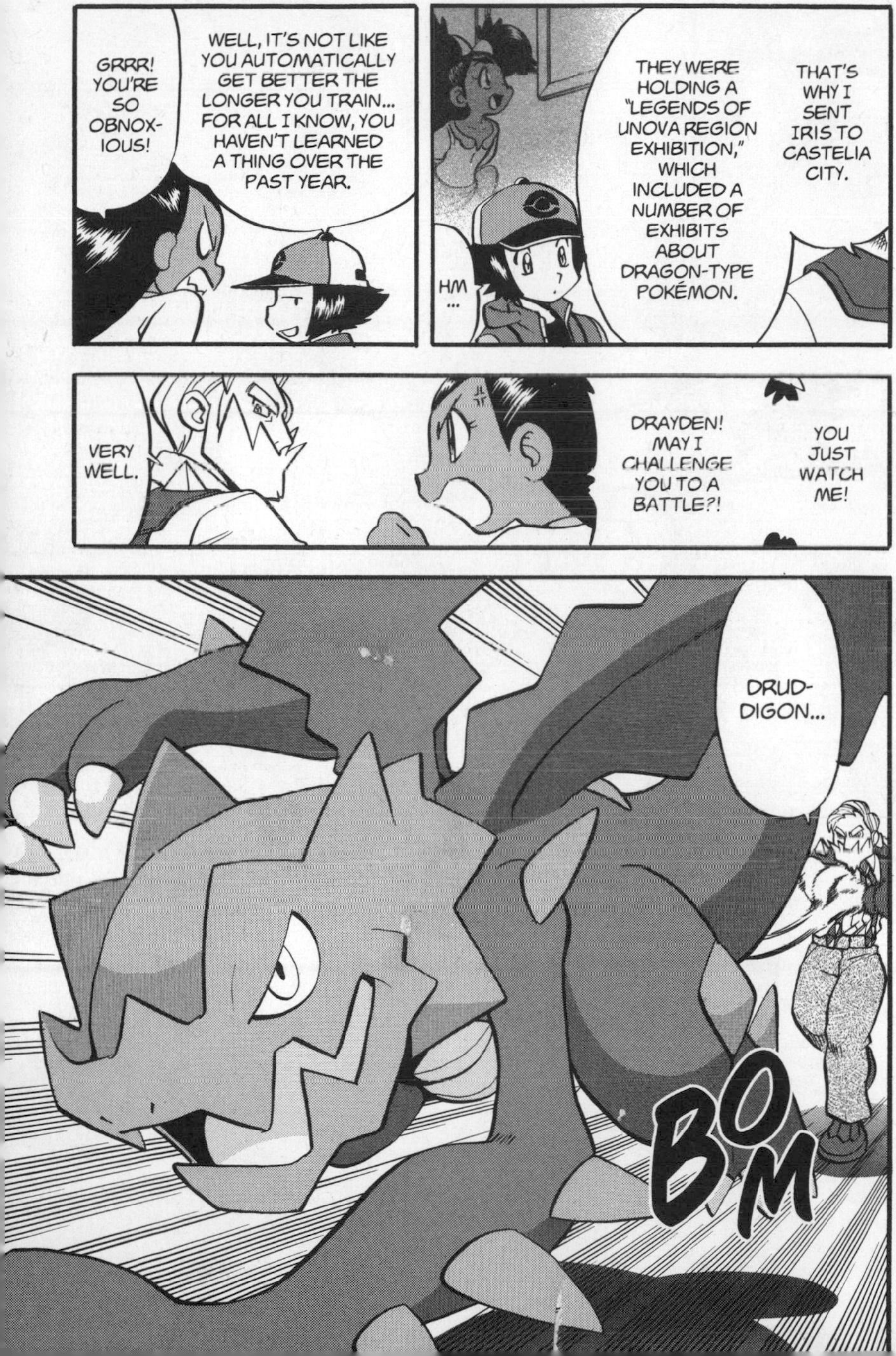
THAT'S WHY I SENT IRIS TO CASTELIA CITY.
THEY WERE HOLDING A "LEGENDS OF UNOVA REGION EXHIBITION," WHICH INCLUDED A NUMBER OF EXHIBITS ABOUT DRAGON-TYPE POKÉMON.
HM...
WELL, IT'S NOT LIKE YOU AUTOMATICALLY GET BETTER THE LONGER YOU TRAIN... FOR ALL I KNOW, YOU HAVEN'T LEARNED A THING OVER THE PAST YEAR.
GRRR! YOU'RE SO OBNOX-IOUS!
YOU JUST WATCH ME!
DRAYDEN! MAY I CHALLENGE YOU TO A BATTLE?!
VERY WELL.
DRUD-DIGON...
BOOM

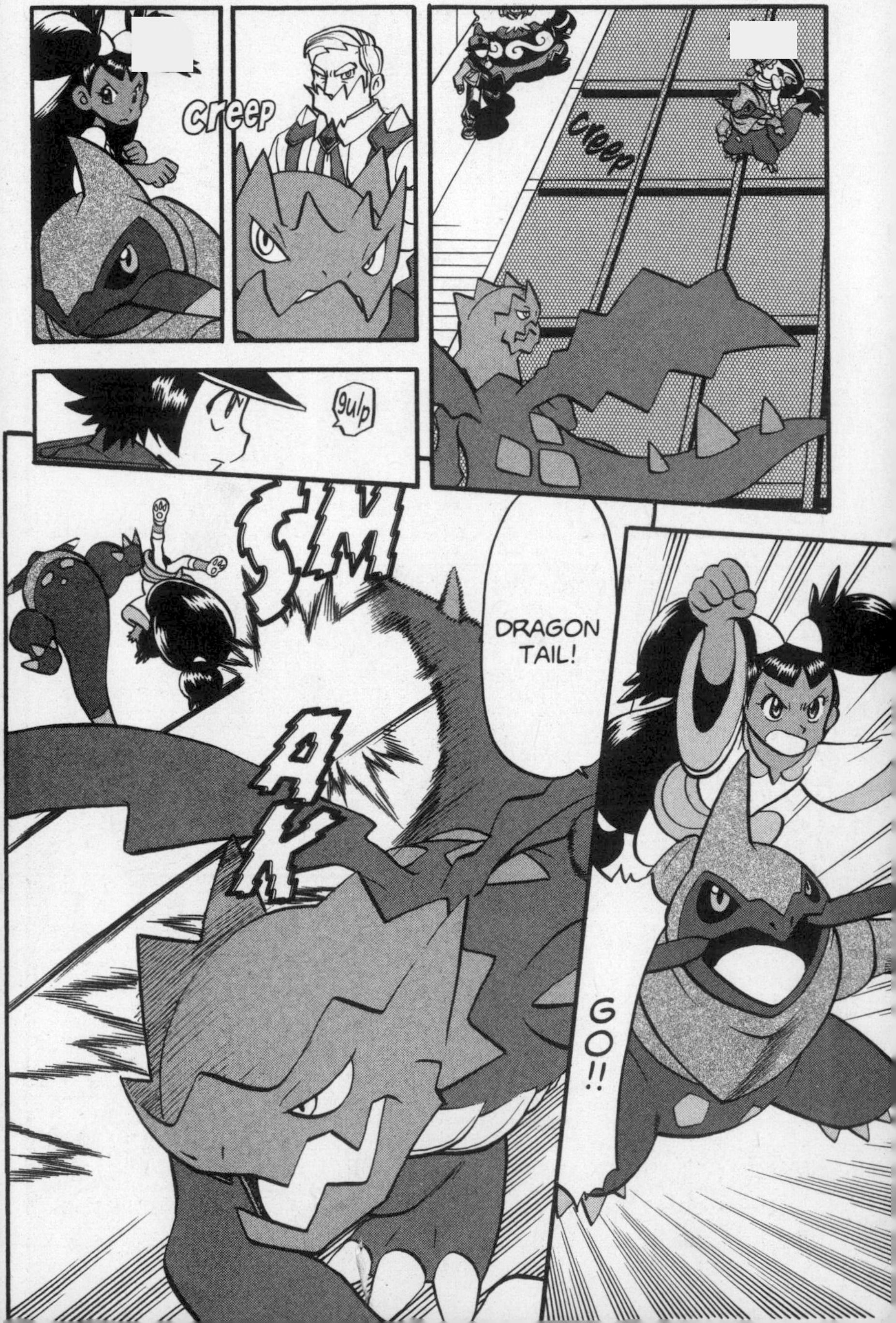
creep
creep
gulp
DRAGON TAIL!
GO!!

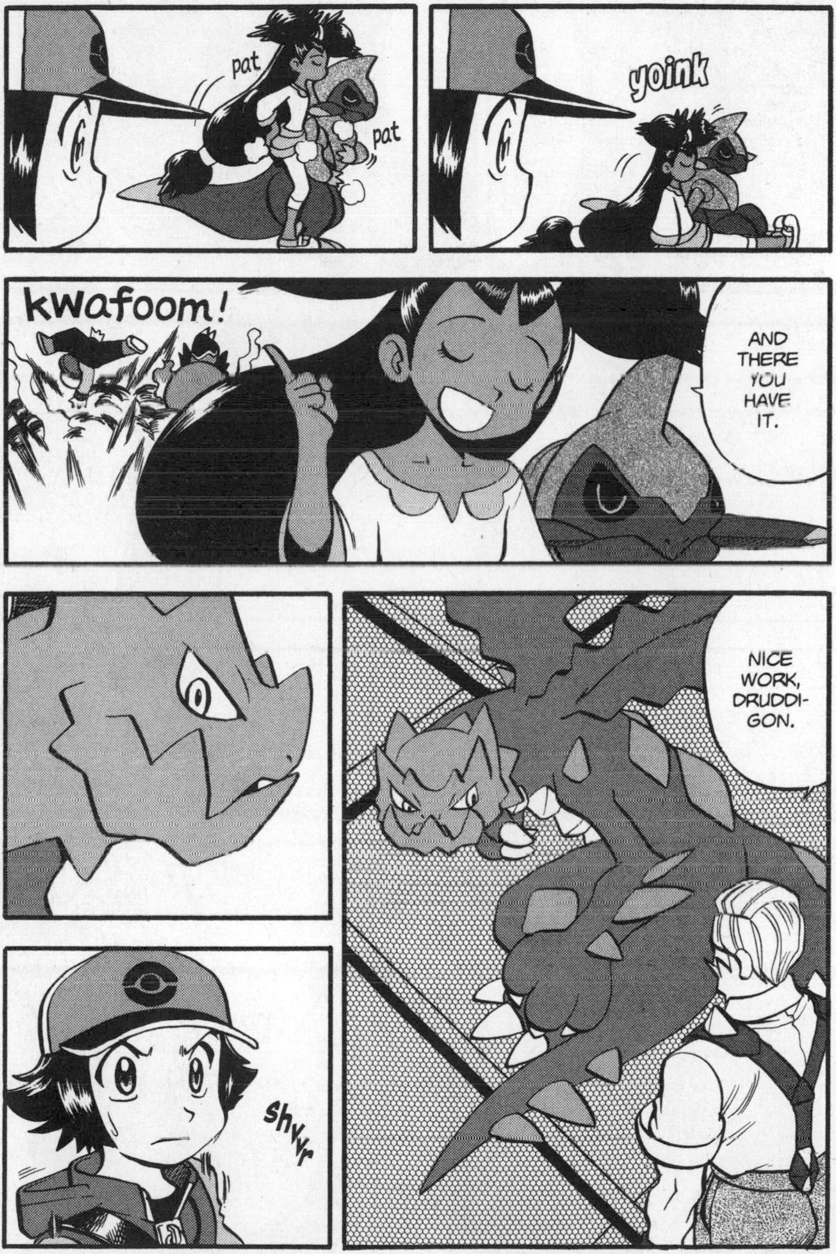
yoink
pat
pat
AND THERE YOU HAVE IT.
kwafoom!
NICE WORK, DRUDDIGON.
shvvr

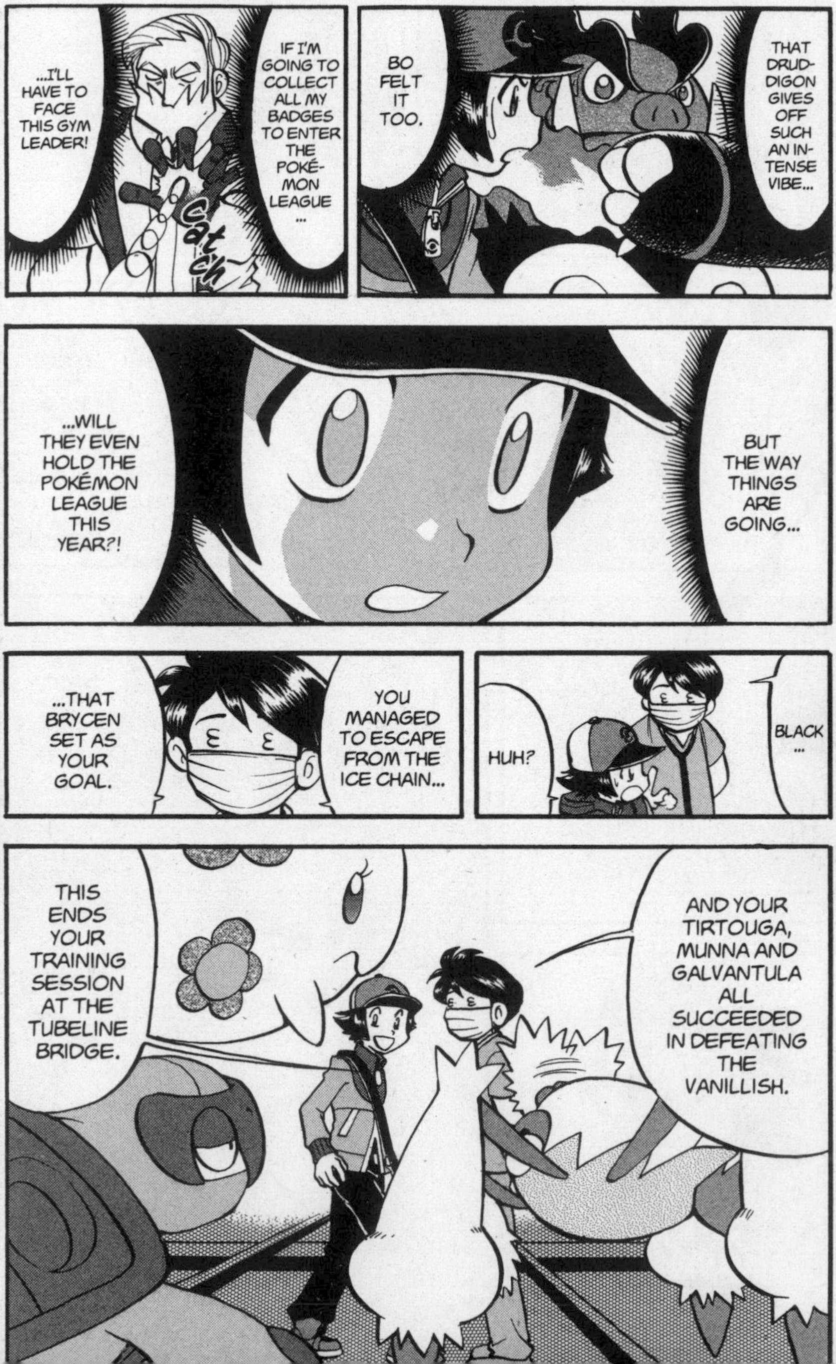
THAT DRUDDIGON GIVES OFF SUCH AN INTENSE VIBE...
BO FELT IT TOO.
IF I'M GOING TO COLLECT ALL MY BADGES TO ENTER THE POKÉMON LEAGUE...
...I'LL HAVE TO FACE THIS GYM LEADER!
catch
BUT THE WAY THINGS ARE GOING...
...WILL THEY EVEN HOLD THE POKÉMON LEAGUE THIS YEAR?!
BLACK...
HUH?
YOU MANAGED TO ESCAPE FROM THE ICE CHAIN...
...THAT BRYCEN SET AS YOUR GOAL.
THIS ENDS YOUR TRAINING SESSION AT THE TUBELINE BRIDGE.
AND YOUR TIRTOUGA, MUNNA AND GALVANTULA ALL SUCCEEDED IN DEFEATING THE VANILLISH.

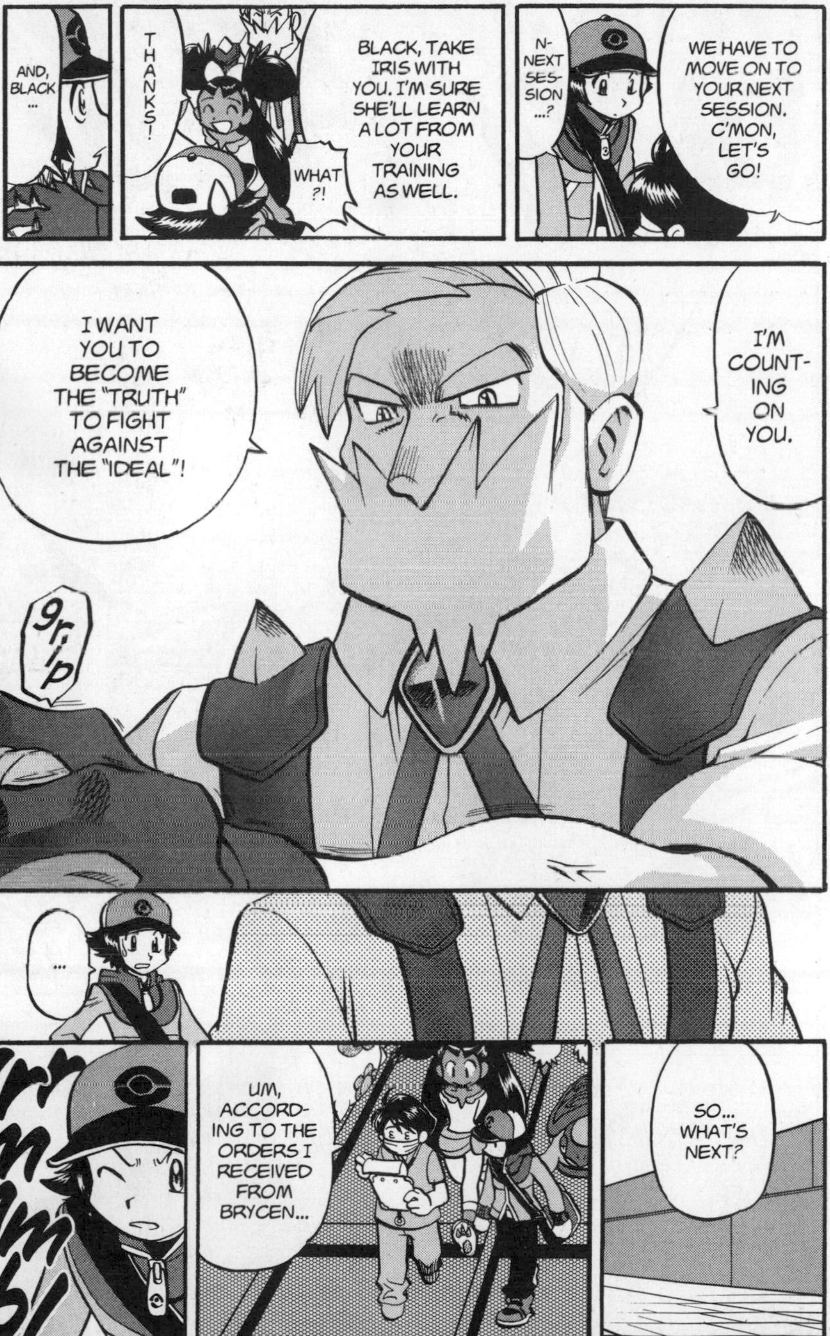
WE HAVE TO MOVE ON TO YOUR NEXT SESSION. C'MON, LET'S GO!
N-NEXT SESSION...?
BLACK, TAKE IRIS WITH YOU. I'M SURE SHE'LL LEARN A LOT FROM YOUR TRAINING AS WELL.
THANKS!
WHAT?!
AND, BLACK...
I'M COUNTING ON YOU.
I WANT YOU TO BECOME THE "TRUTH" TO FIGHT AGAINST THE "IDEAL"!
grip
...
SO... WHAT'S NEXT?
UM, ACCORDING TO THE ORDERS I RECEIVED FROM BRYCEN...
Vrrmmmbl

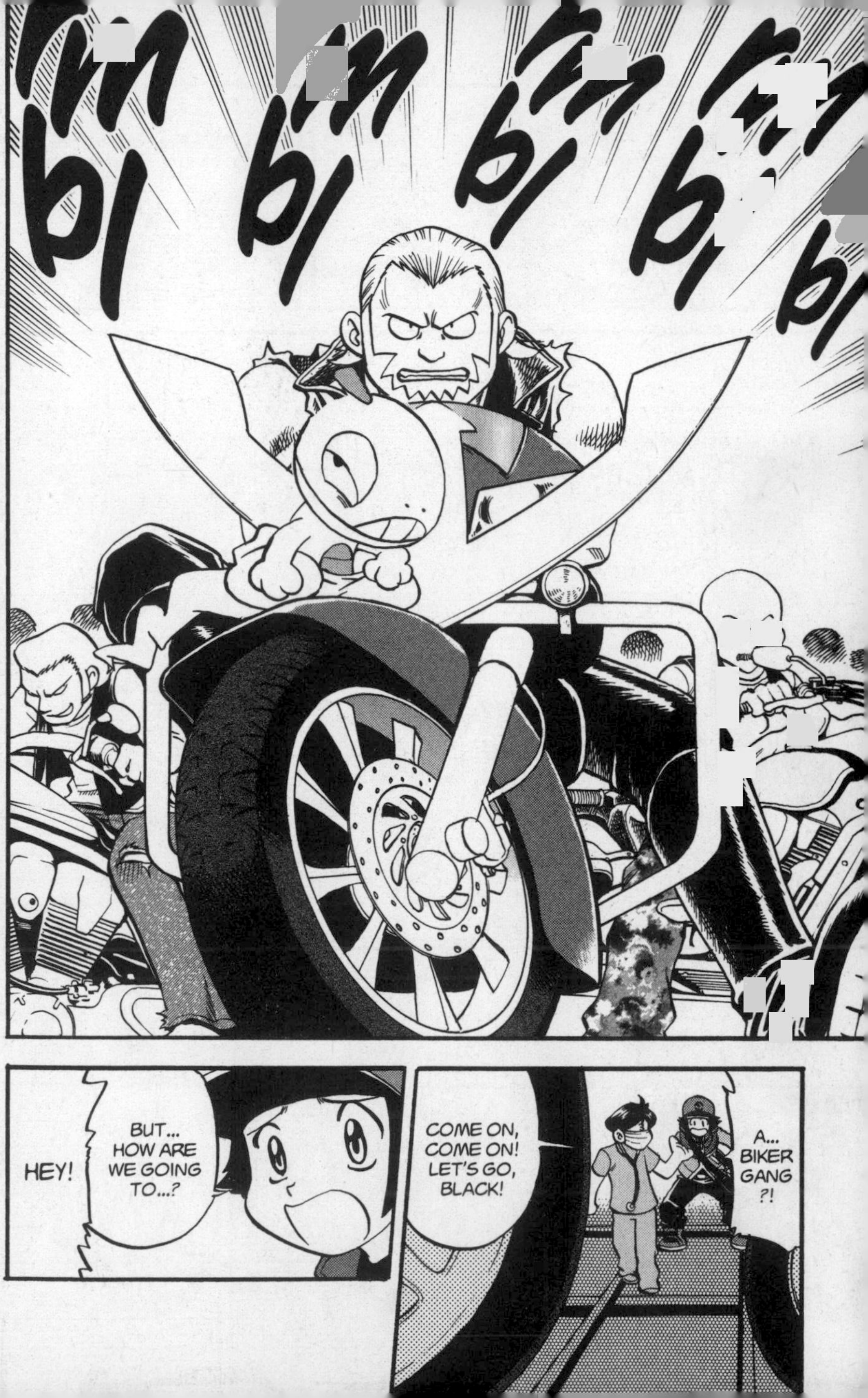
A... BIKER GANG ?!
COME ON, COME ON! LET'S GO, BLACK!
BUT... HOW ARE WE GOING TO...?
HEY!

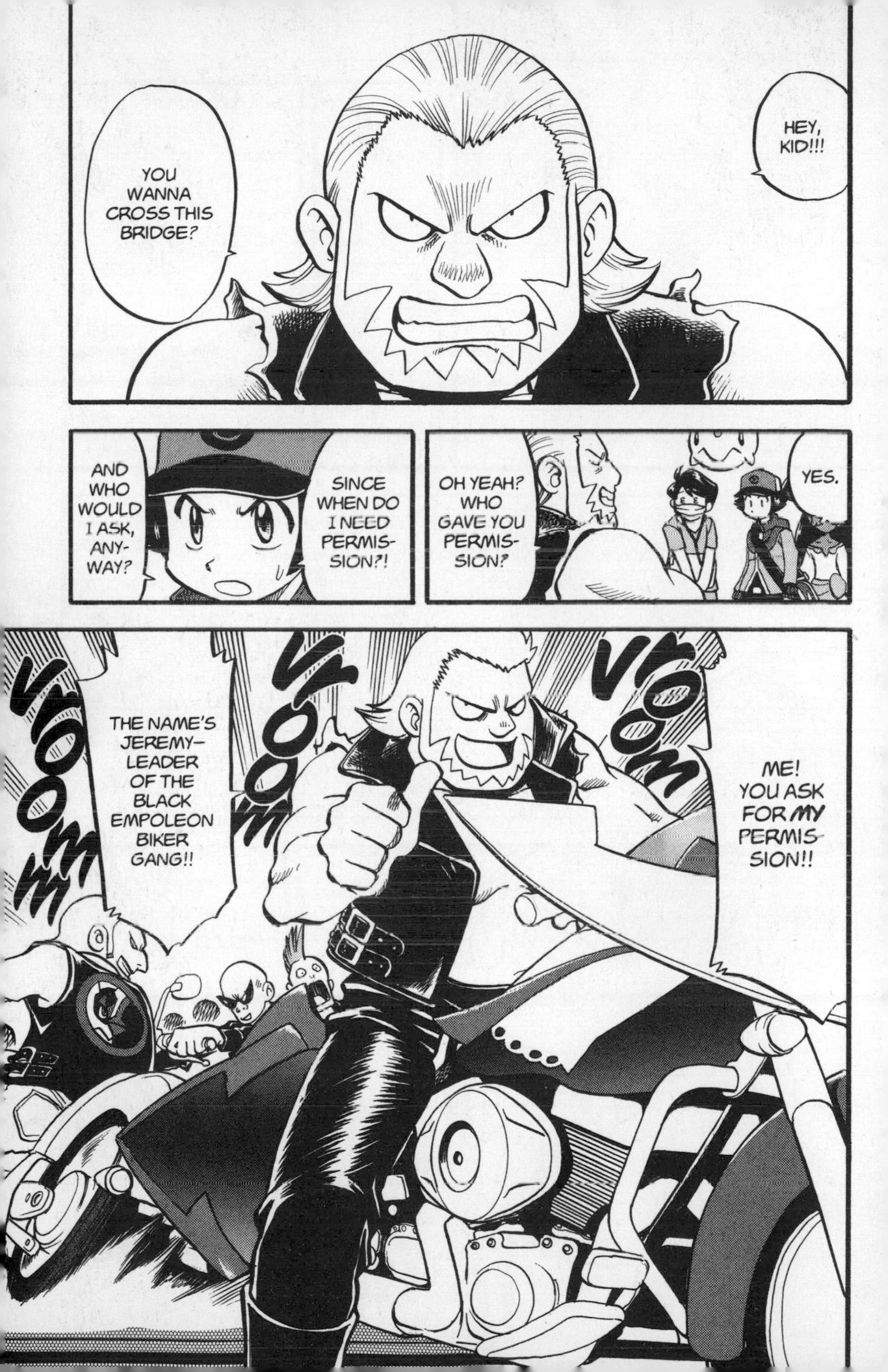
HEY, KID!!!
YOU WANNA CROSS THIS BRIDGE?
YES.
OH YEAH? WHO GAVE YOU PERMISSION?
SINCE WHEN DO I NEED PERMISSION?!
AND WHO WOULD I ASK, ANYWAY?
VROOM
ME! YOU ASK FOR *MY* PERMISSION!!
VROOM
THE NAME'S JEREMY—LEADER OF THE BLACK EMPOLEON BIKER GANG!!
VROOM

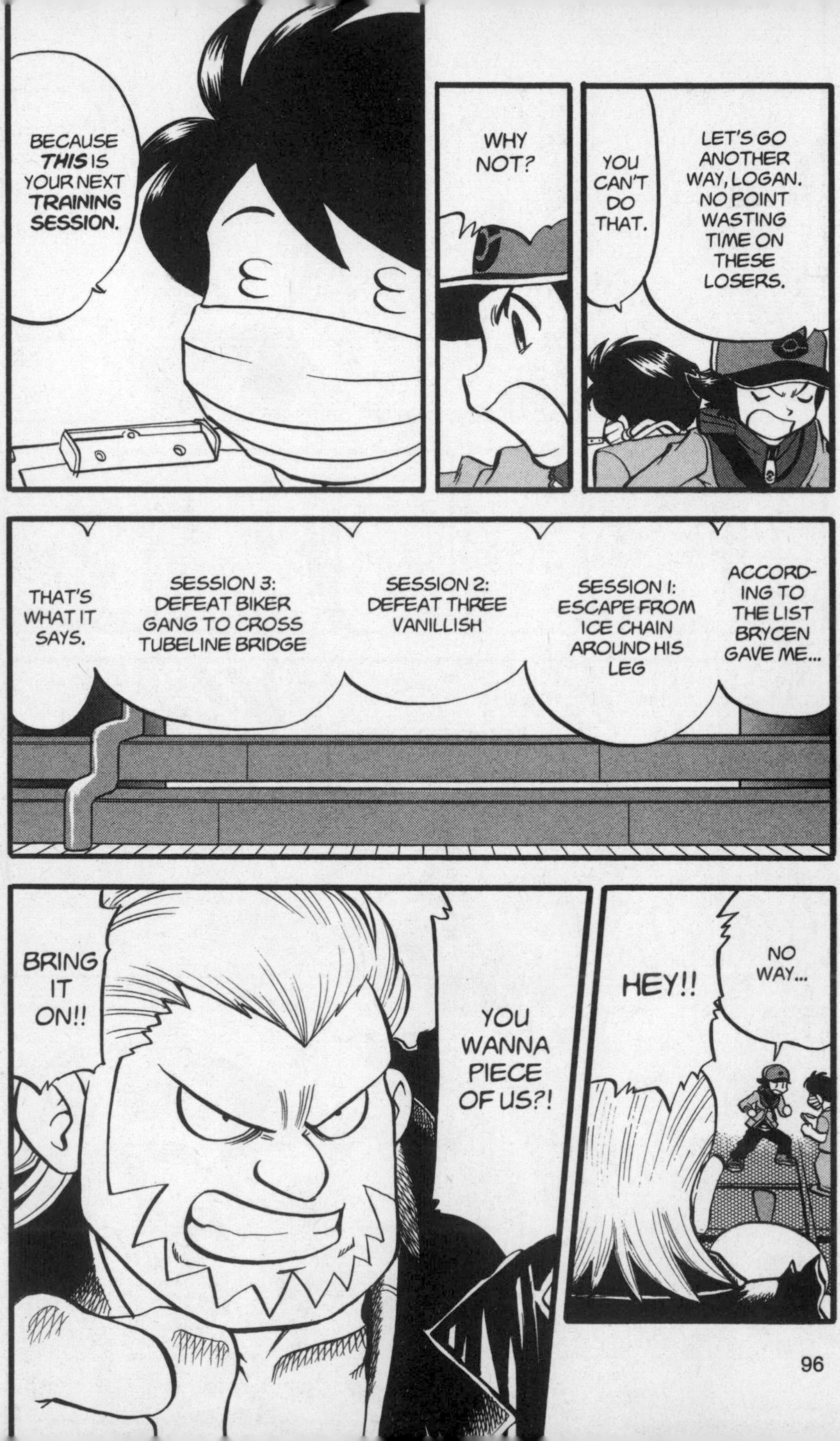
LET'S GO ANOTHER WAY, LOGAN. NO POINT WASTING TIME ON THESE LOSERS.
YOU CAN'T DO THAT.
WHY NOT?
BECAUSE THIS IS YOUR NEXT TRAINING SESSION.
ACCORDING TO THE LIST BRYCEN GAVE ME...
SESSION 1: ESCAPE FROM ICE CHAIN AROUND HIS LEG
SESSION 2: DEFEAT THREE VANILLISH
SESSION 3: DEFEAT BIKER GANG TO CROSS TUBELINE BRIDGE
THAT'S WHAT IT SAYS.
NO WAY...
HEY!!
YOU WANNA PIECE OF US?!
BRING IT ON!!

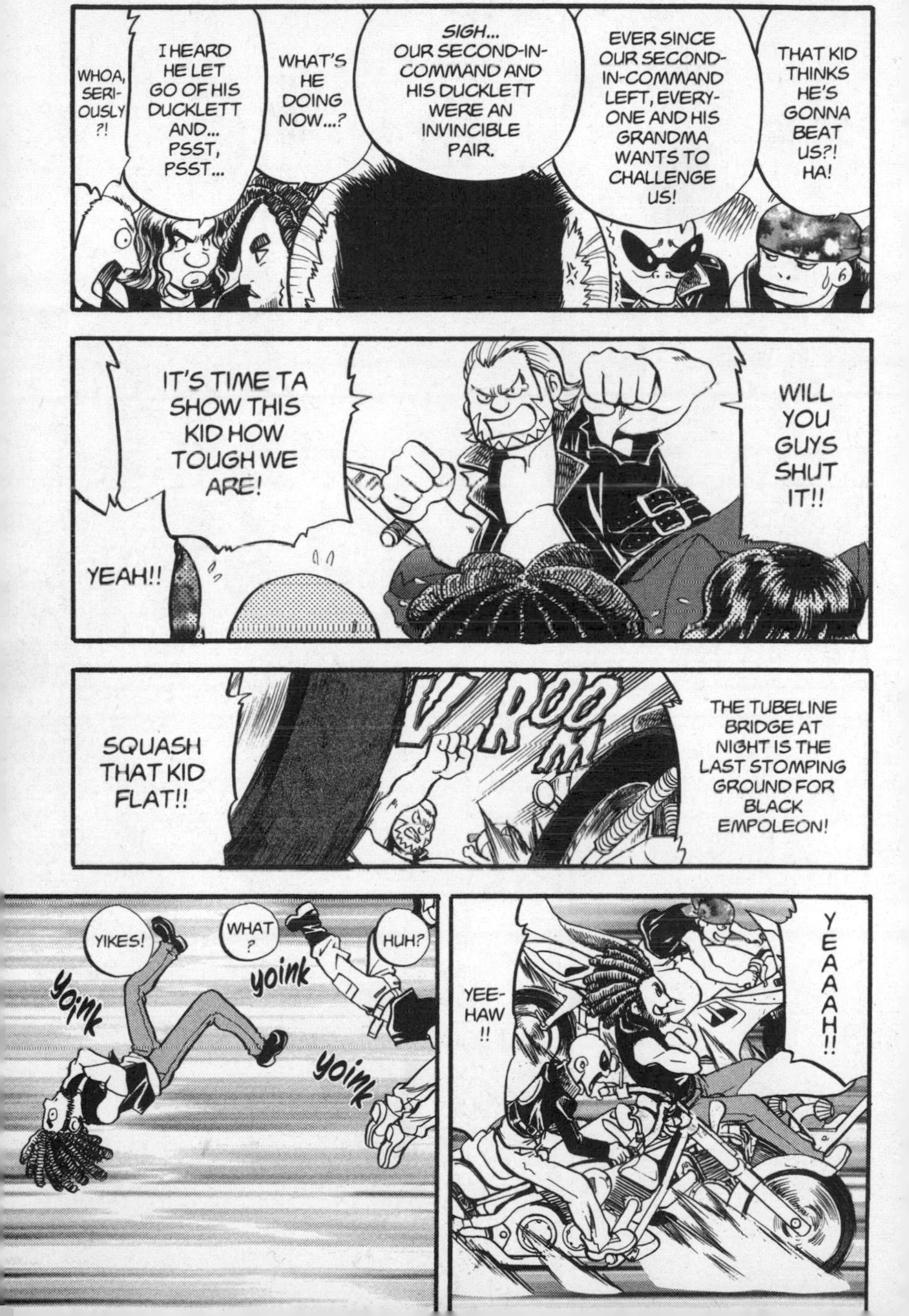
THAT KID THINKS HE'S GONNA BEAT US?! HA!
EVER SINCE OUR SECOND-IN-COMMAND LEFT, EVERY-ONE AND HIS GRANDMA WANTS TO CHALLENGE US!
SIGH... OUR SECOND-IN-COMMAND AND HIS DUCKLETT WERE AN INVINCIBLE PAIR.
WHAT'S HE DOING NOW...?
I HEARD HE LET GO OF HIS DUCKLETT AND... PSST, PSST...
WHOA, SERI-OUSLY ?!
WILL YOU GUYS SHUT IT!!
IT'S TIME TA SHOW THIS KID HOW TOUGH WE ARE!
YEAH!!
THE TUBELINE BRIDGE AT NIGHT IS THE LAST STOMPING GROUND FOR BLACK EMPOLEON!
VROOM
SQUASH THAT KID FLAT!!
YEAAAAH!!
YEE-HAW !!
HUH?
yoink
WHAT ?
yoink
YIKES!
yoink

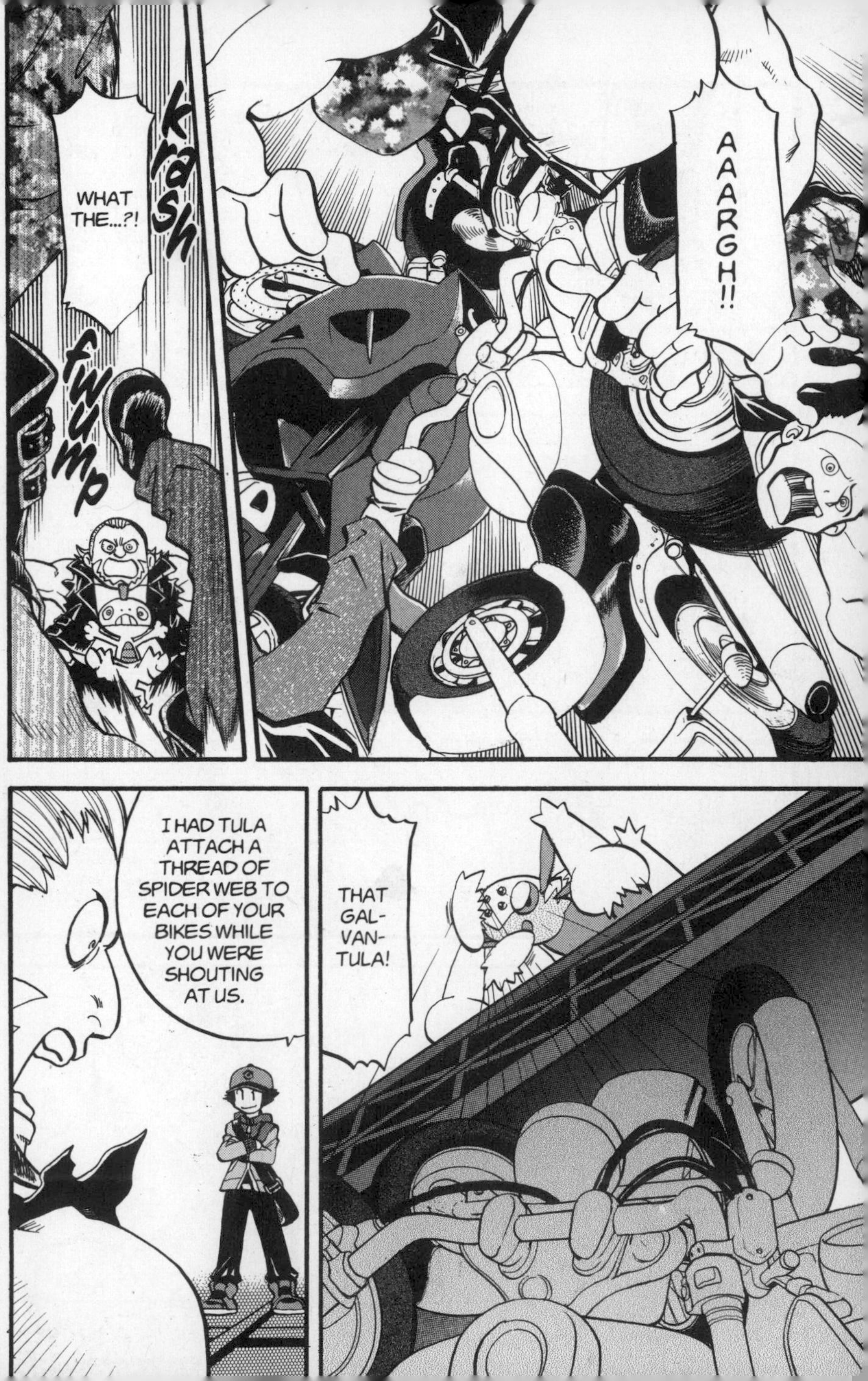
AAAARGH!!
krash
fwump
WHAT THE...?!
THAT GAL-VAN-TULA!
I HAD TULA ATTACH A THREAD OF SPIDER WEB TO EACH OF YOUR BIKES WHILE YOU WERE SHOUTING AT US.

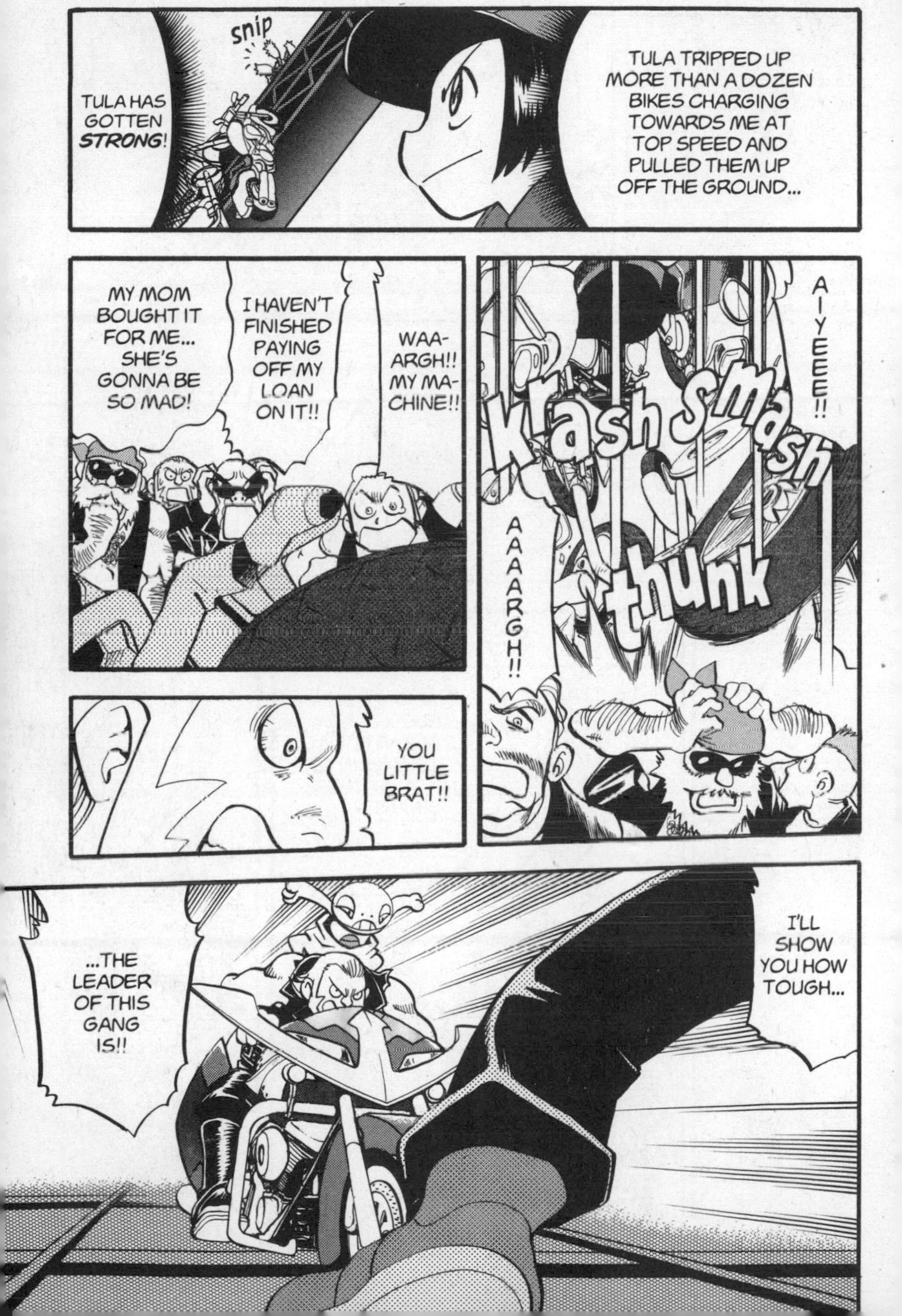
TULA TRIPPED UP MORE THAN A DOZEN BIKES CHARGING TOWARDS ME AT TOP SPEED AND PULLED THEM UP OFF THE GROUND...
snip
TULA HAS GOTTEN **STRONG**!
AIYEEE!!
krash smash
AAAARGH!!
thunk
WAA-ARGH!! MY MA-CHINE!!
I HAVEN'T FINISHED PAYING OFF MY LOAN ON IT!!
MY MOM BOUGHT IT FOR ME... SHE'S GONNA BE SO MAD!
YOU LITTLE BRAT!!
I'LL SHOW YOU HOW TOUGH...
...THE LEADER OF THIS GANG IS!!

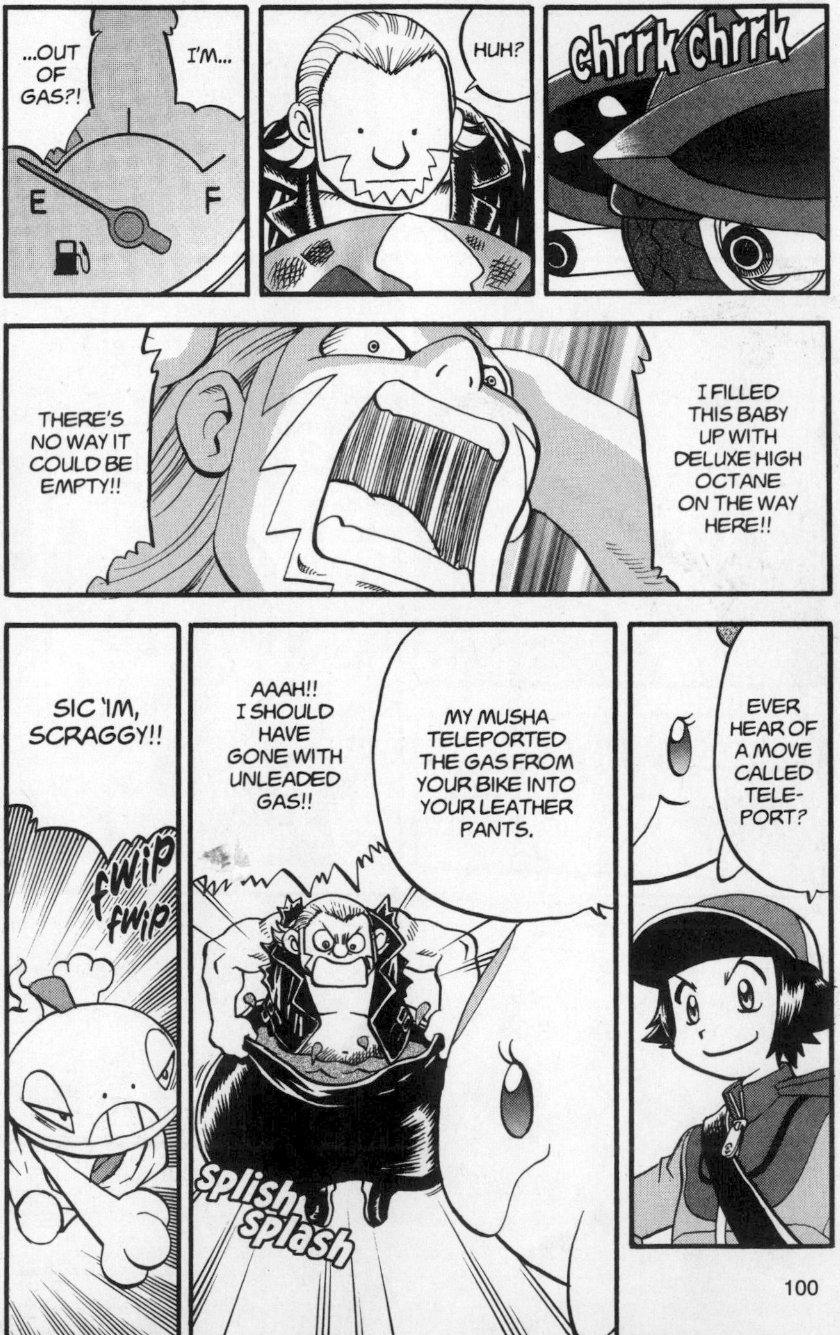
chrrk chrrk
HUH?
I'M...
...OUT OF GAS?!
I FILLED THIS BABY UP WITH DELUXE HIGH OCTANE ON THE WAY HERE!!
THERE'S NO WAY IT COULD BE EMPTY!!
EVER HEAR OF A MOVE CALLED TELE-PORT?
MY MUSHA TELEPORTED THE GAS FROM YOUR BIKE INTO YOUR LEATHER PANTS.
AAAH!! I SHOULD HAVE GONE WITH UNLEADED GAS!!
splish splash
SIC 'IM, SCRAGGY!!
fwip fwip

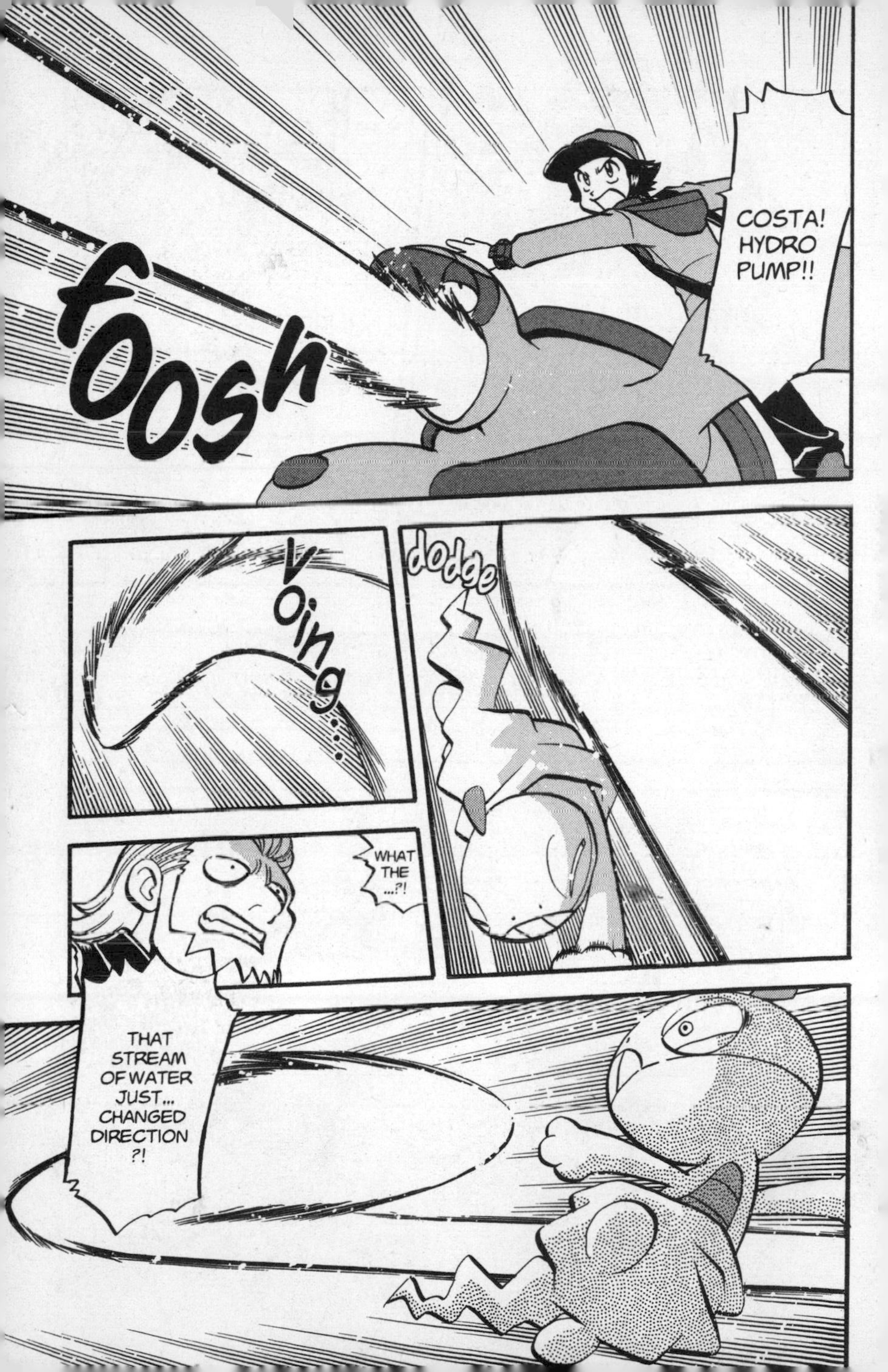
COSTA! HYDRO PUMP!!
foosh
dodge
voing...
WHAT THE ...?!
THAT STREAM OF WATER JUST... CHANGED DIRECTION?!

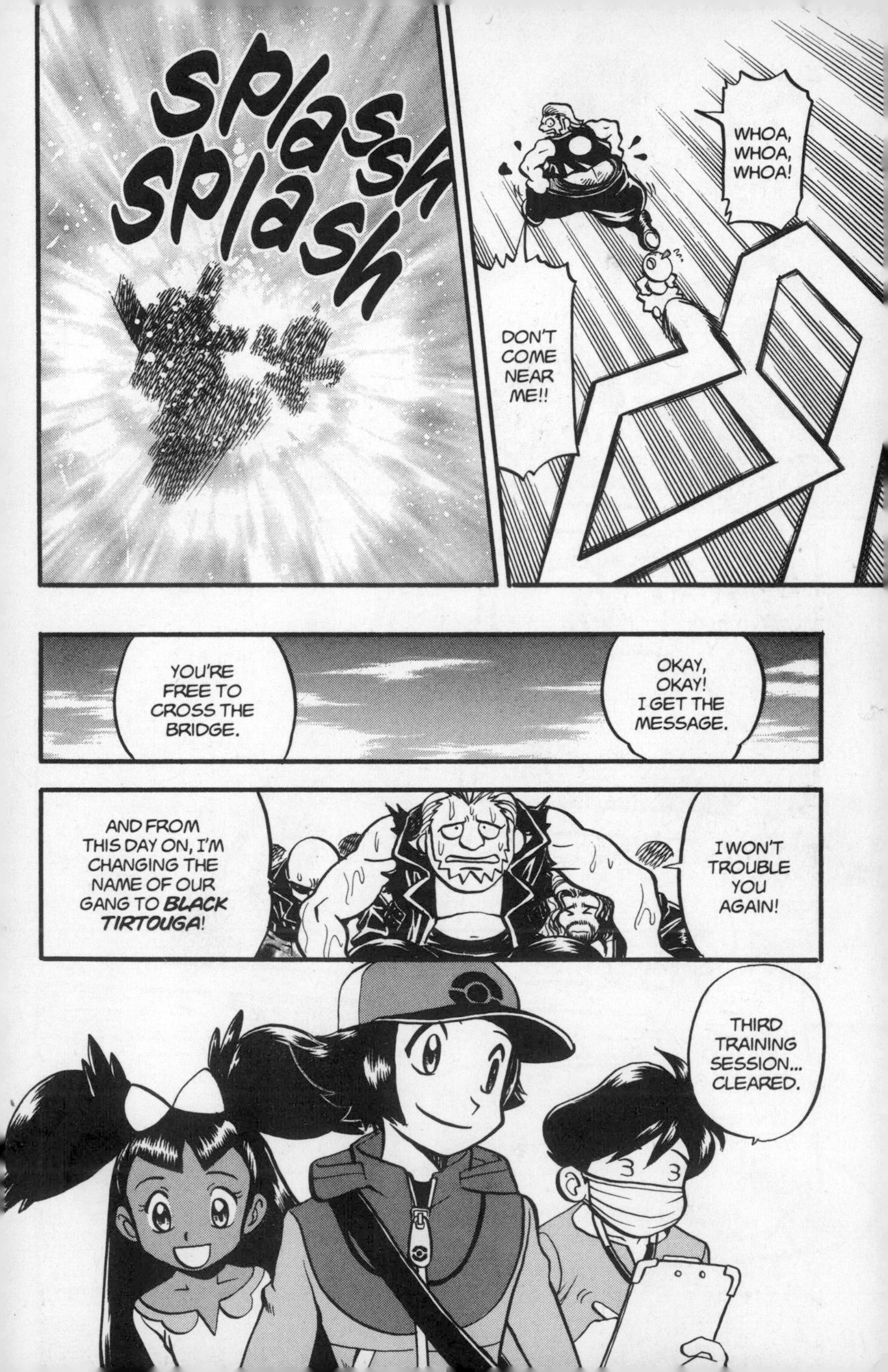
WHOA, WHOA, WHOA!
DON'T COME NEAR ME!!
SPLASH SPLASH
OKAY, OKAY! I GET THE MESSAGE.
YOU'RE FREE TO CROSS THE BRIDGE.
I WON'T TROUBLE YOU AGAIN!
AND FROM THIS DAY ON, I'M CHANGING THE NAME OF OUR GANG TO BLACK TIRTOUGA!
THIRD TRAINING SESSION... CLEARED.

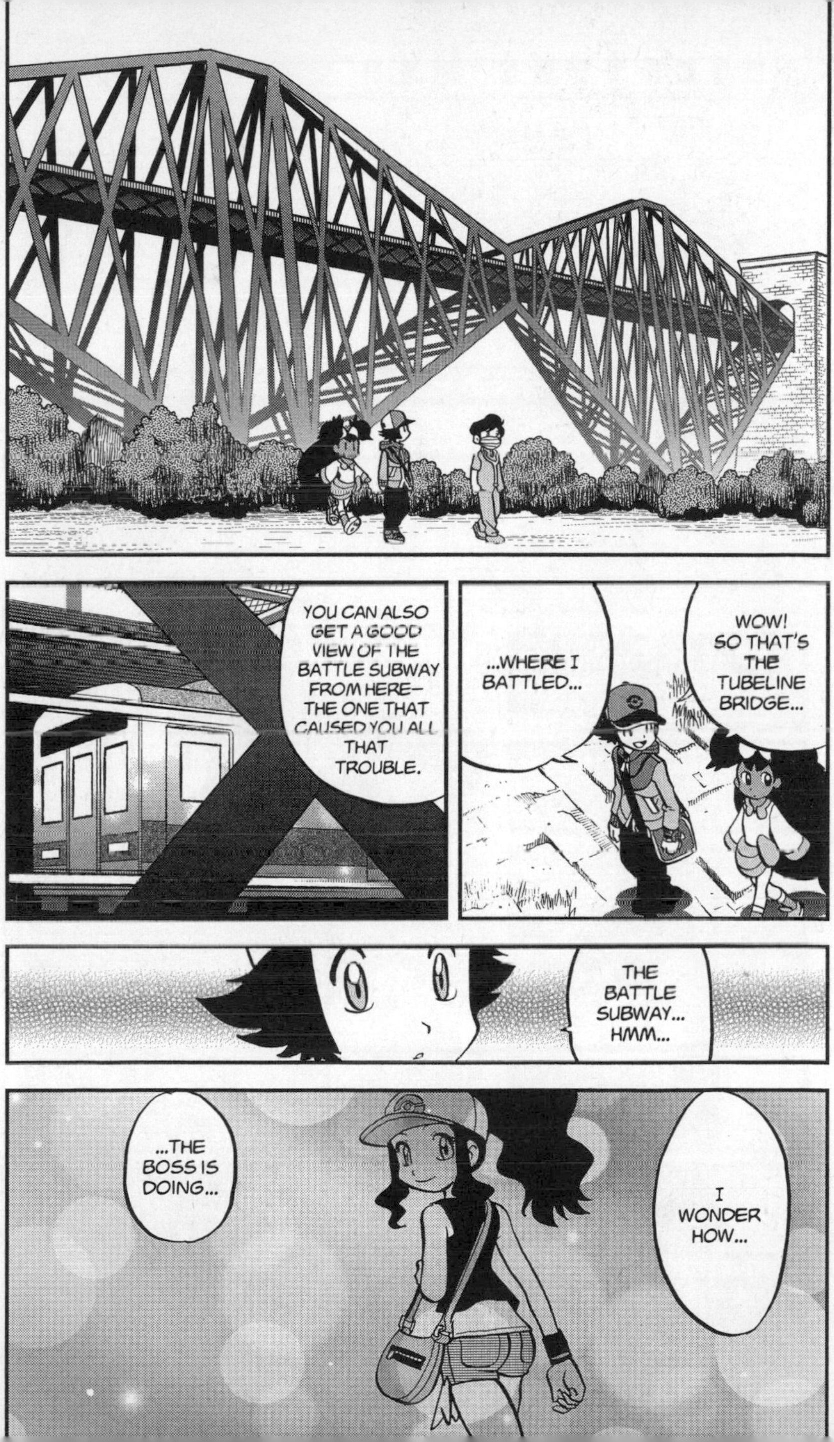
WOW! SO THAT'S THE TUBELINE BRIDGE...
...WHERE I BATTLED...
YOU CAN ALSO GET A GOOD VIEW OF THE BATTLE SUBWAY FROM HERE– THE ONE THAT CAUSED YOU ALL THAT TROUBLE.
THE BATTLE SUBWAY... HMM...
I WONDER HOW...
...THE BOSS IS DOING...

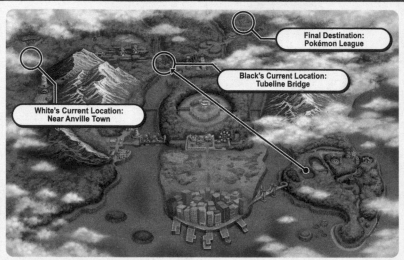

Final Destination:
Pokémon League

Black's Current Location:
Tubeline Bridge

White's Current Location:
Near Anville Town

BLACK

WHITE

 Mega Fire Pig Pokémon **Bo**
Emboar ♂ | Fire | Fighting
Lv.40 Ability: Blaze

Dream Eater Pokémon **Musha**
Munna ♂ | Psychic
Lv.53 Ability: Forewarn

EleSpider Pokémon **Tula**
Galvantula ♂ | Bug | Electric
Lv.54 Ability: Unnerve

Prototurtle Pokémon **Costa**
Tirtouga ♂ | Water | Rock
Lv.35 Ability: Solid Rock

Grass Snake Pokémon **Servine**
Servine ♀ | Grass
Lv.29 Ability: Overgrow

Season Pokémon **Darlene**
Deerling ♀ | Normal | Grass
Lv.26 Ability: Chlorophyll

Valiant Pokémon **Brav**
Braviary ♂ | Normal | Flying
Lv.54 Ability: Sheer Force

 TRIO BADGE BASIC BADGE INSECT BADGE BOLT BADGE QUAKE BADGE JET BADGE ?   ?

Pokémon™ Adventures Black & White

MELOETTA I

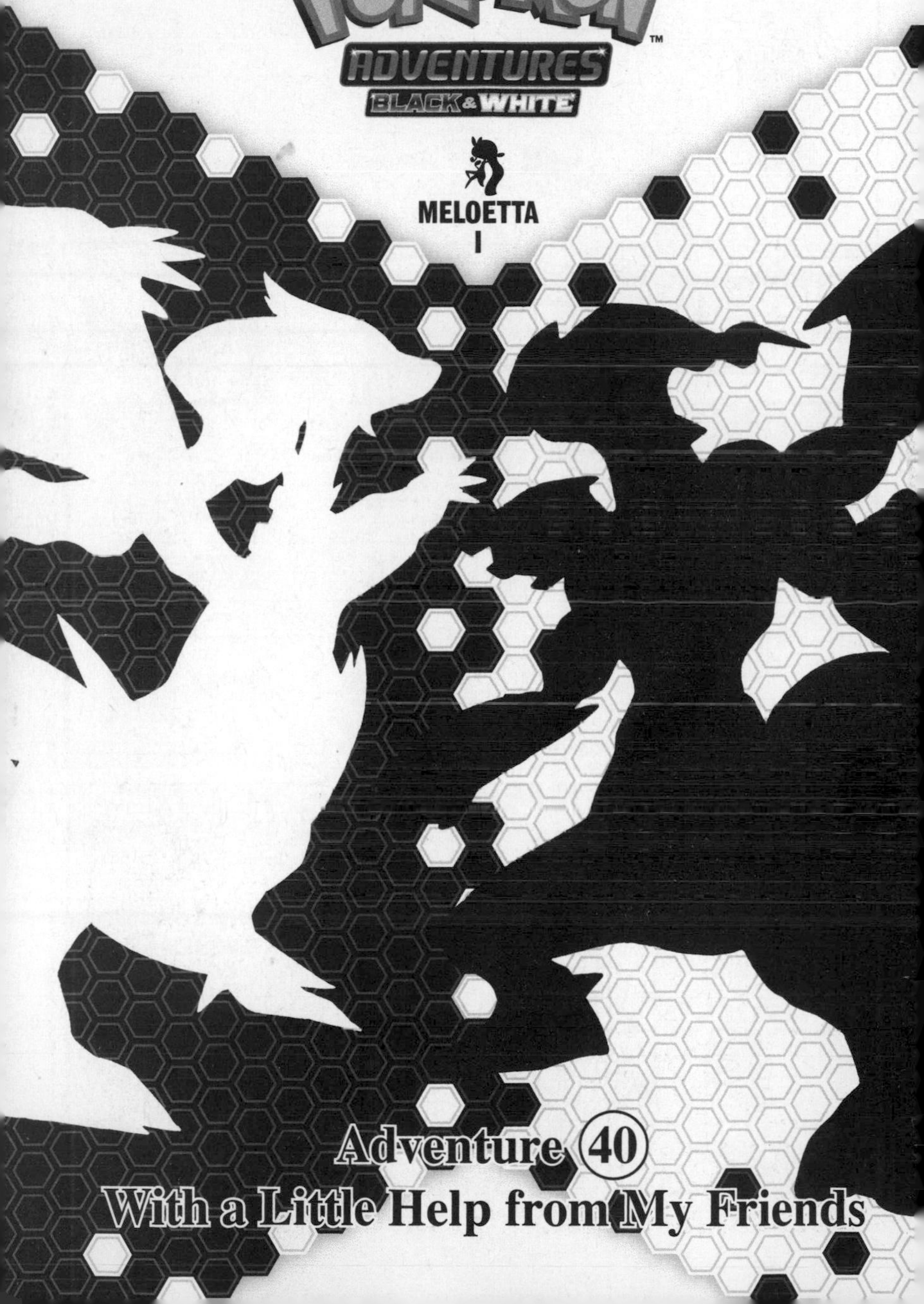

Adventure 40
With a Little Help from My Friends

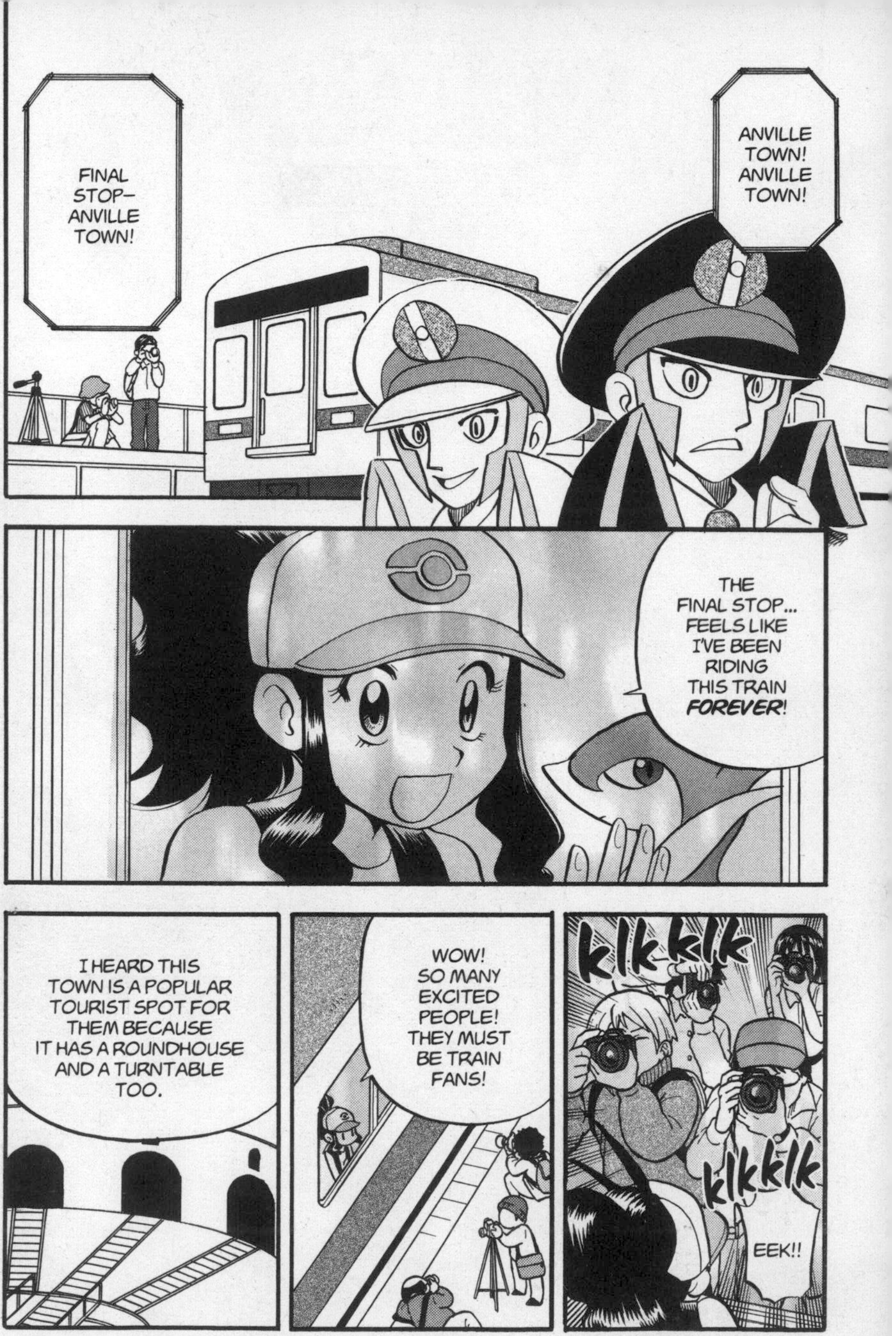
ANVILLE TOWN! ANVILLE TOWN!
FINAL STOP— ANVILLE TOWN!
THE FINAL STOP... FEELS LIKE I'VE BEEN RIDING THIS TRAIN ***FOREVER***!
klk klk
klkklk
EEK!!
WOW! SO MANY EXCITED PEOPLE! THEY MUST BE TRAIN FANS!
I HEARD THIS TOWN IS A POPULAR TOURIST SPOT FOR THEM BECAUSE IT HAS A ROUNDHOUSE AND A TURNTABLE TOO.

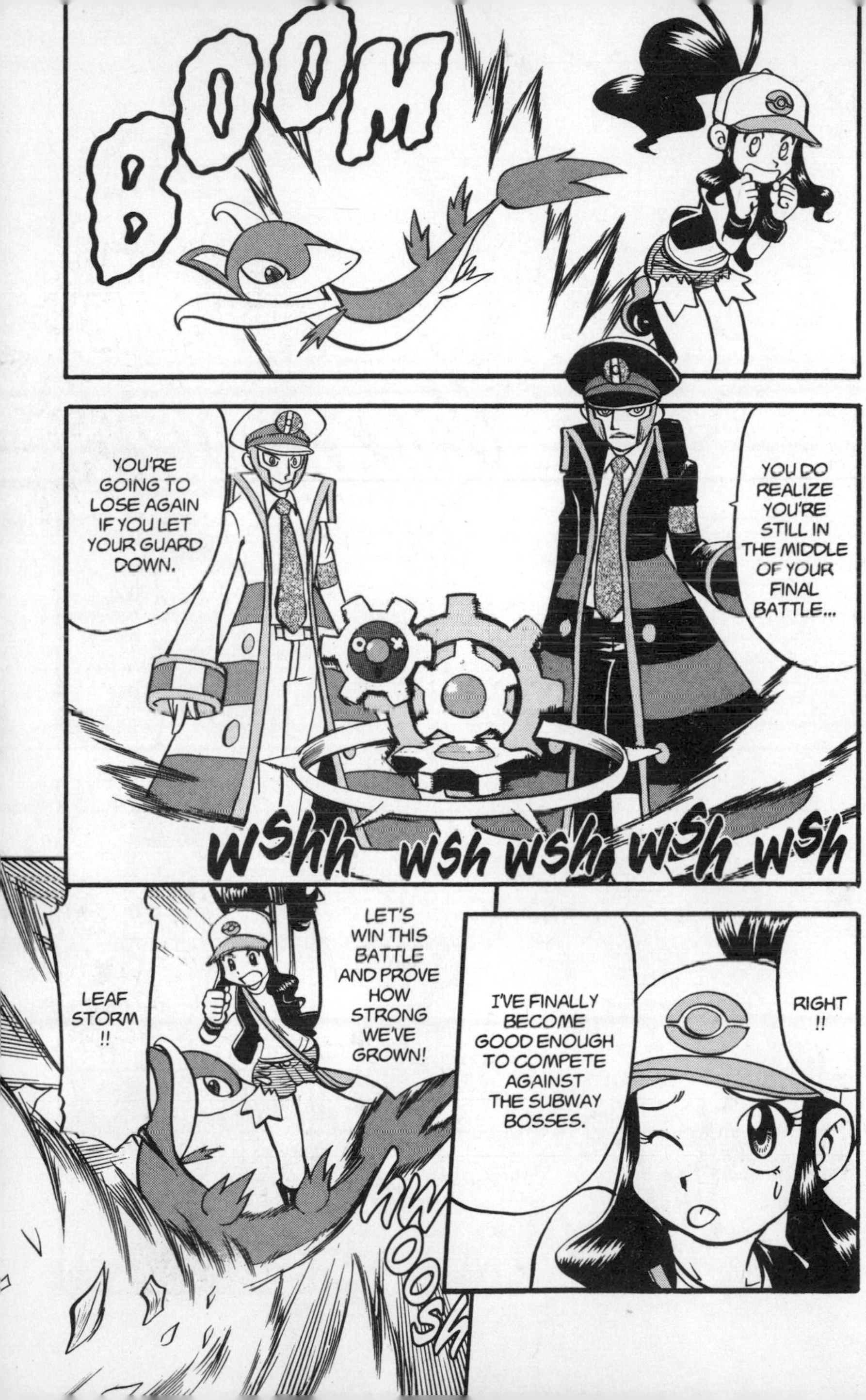
BOOM
YOU DO REALIZE YOU'RE STILL IN THE MIDDLE OF YOUR FINAL BATTLE...
YOU'RE GOING TO LOSE AGAIN IF YOU LET YOUR GUARD DOWN.
WSHH WSH WSH WSH WSH
RIGHT!!
I'VE FINALLY BECOME GOOD ENOUGH TO COMPETE AGAINST THE SUBWAY BOSSES.
LET'S WIN THIS BATTLE AND PROVE HOW STRONG WE'VE GROWN!
LEAF STORM!!
HWOOOSH

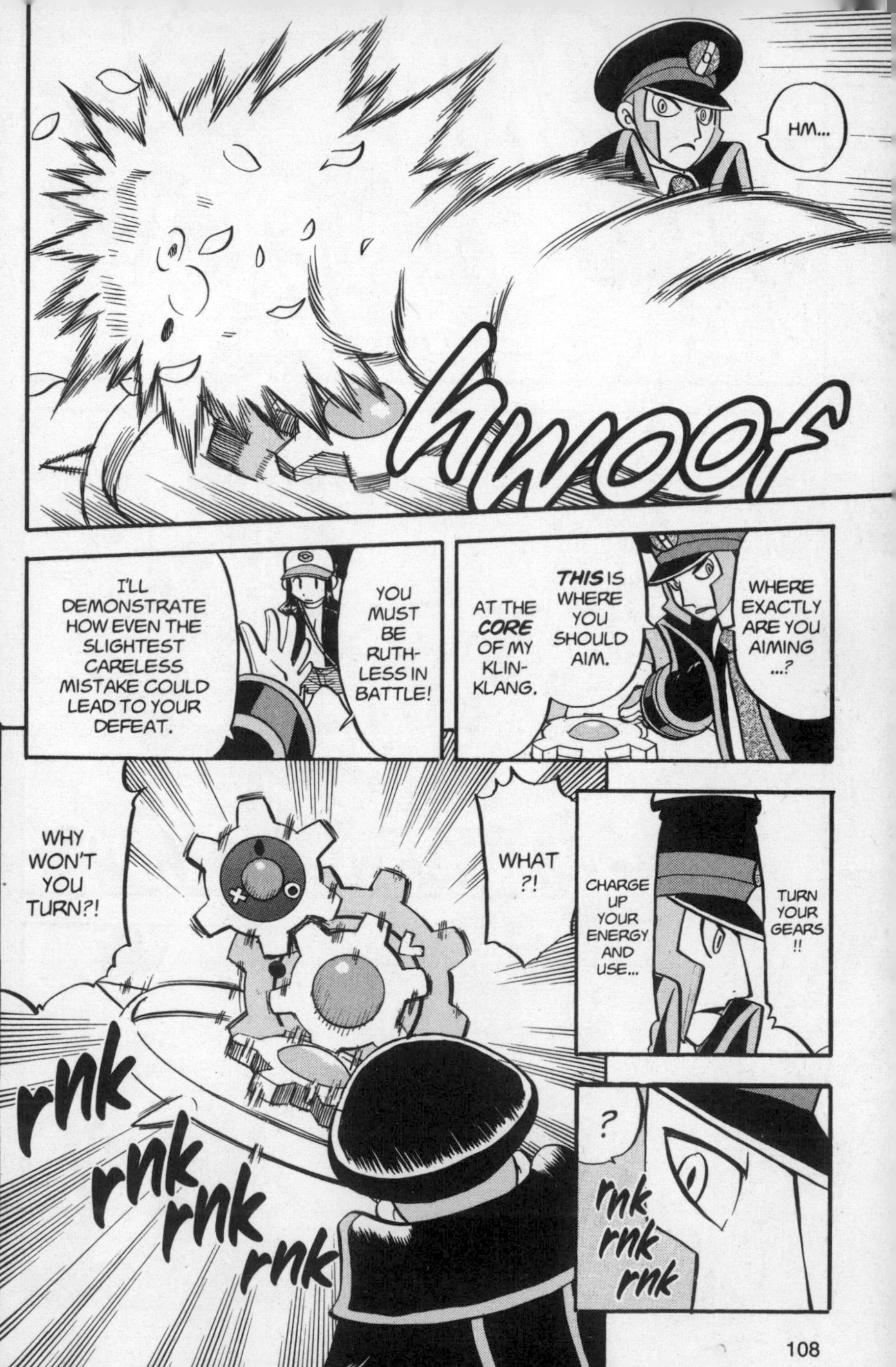
HM...
hwoof
WHERE EXACTLY ARE YOU AIMING ...?
THIS IS WHERE YOU SHOULD AIM.
AT THE CORE OF MY KLIN-KLANG.
YOU MUST BE RUTH-LESS IN BATTLE!
I'LL DEMONSTRATE HOW EVEN THE SLIGHTEST CARELESS MISTAKE COULD LEAD TO YOUR DEFEAT.
TURN YOUR GEARS !!
CHARGE UP YOUR ENERGY AND USE...
?
rnk rnk rnk
WHAT ?!
WHY WON'T YOU TURN?!
rnk rnk rnk rnk

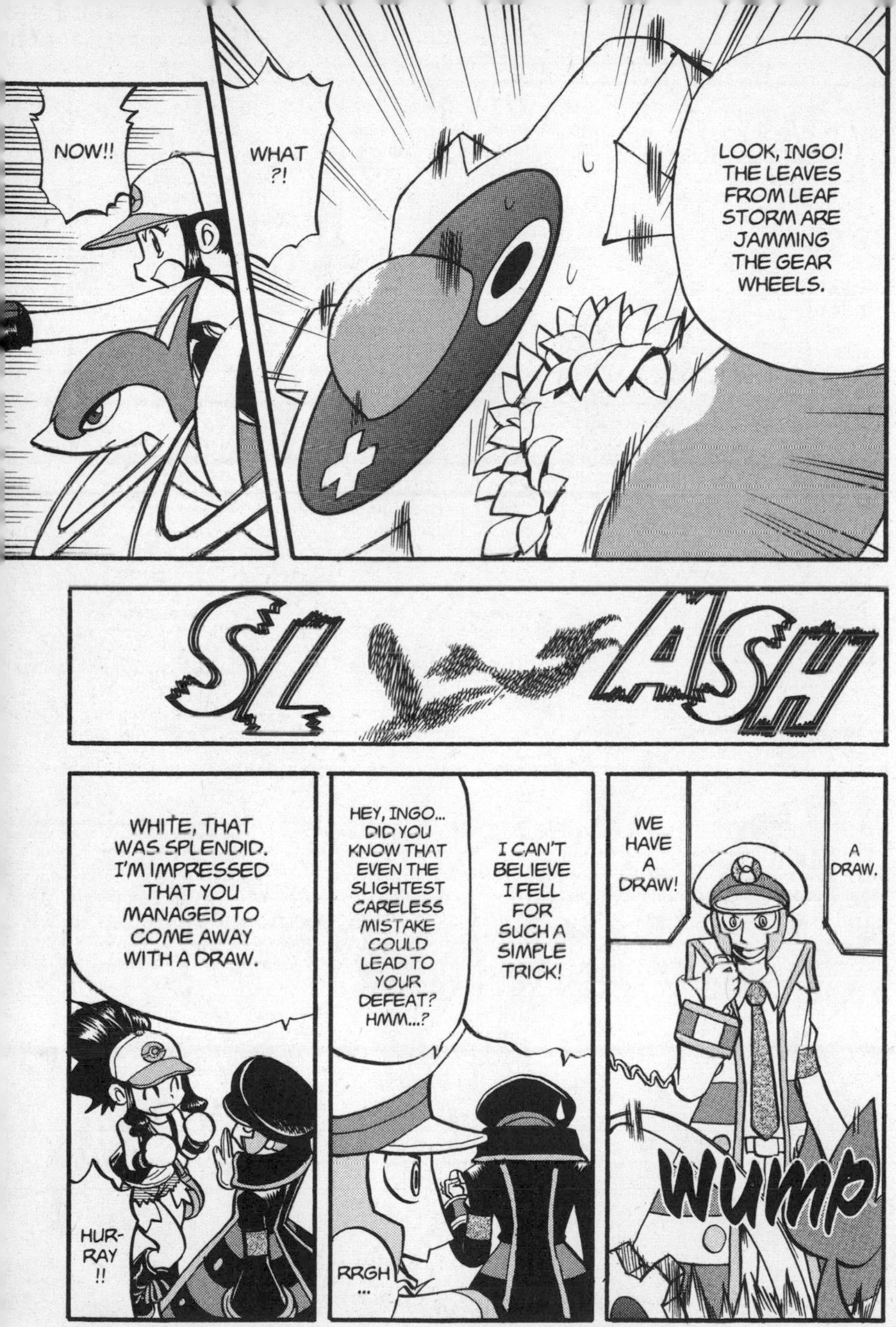
LOOK, INGO! THE LEAVES FROM LEAF STORM ARE JAMMING THE GEAR WHEELS.
WHAT ?!
NOW!!
SLASH
A DRAW.
WE HAVE A DRAW!
WUMP
I CAN'T BELIEVE I FELL FOR SUCH A SIMPLE TRICK!
HEY, INGO... DID YOU KNOW THAT EVEN THE SLIGHTEST CARELESS MISTAKE COULD LEAD TO YOUR DEFEAT? HMM...?
RRGH ...
WHITE, THAT WAS SPLENDID. I'M IMPRESSED THAT YOU MANAGED TO COME AWAY WITH A DRAW.
HUR-RAY !!

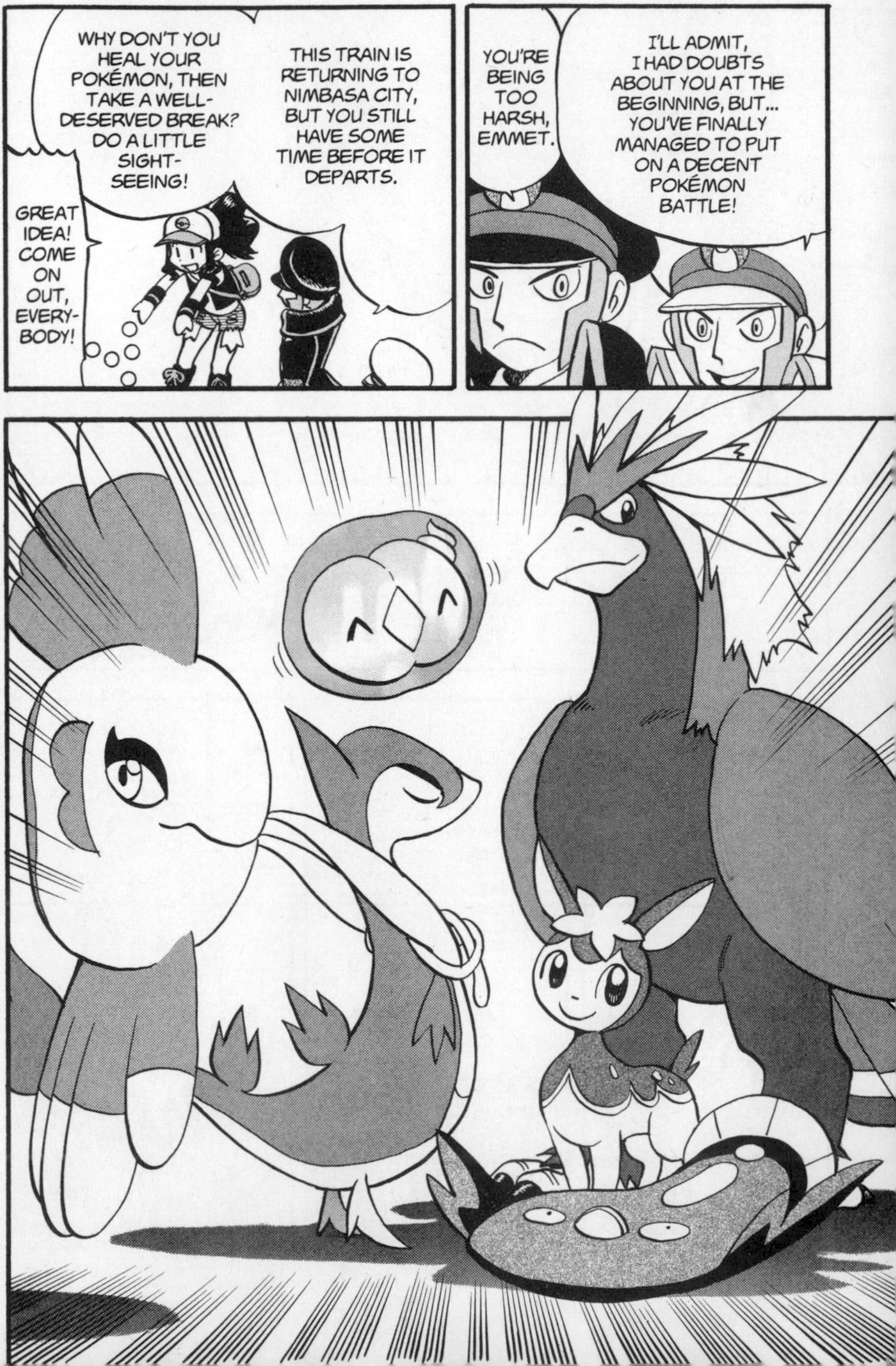
I'LL ADMIT, I HAD DOUBTS ABOUT YOU AT THE BEGINNING, BUT... YOU'VE FINALLY MANAGED TO PUT ON A DECENT POKÉMON BATTLE!
YOU'RE BEING TOO HARSH, EMMET.
THIS TRAIN IS RETURNING TO NIMBASA CITY, BUT YOU STILL HAVE SOME TIME BEFORE IT DEPARTS.
WHY DON'T YOU HEAL YOUR POKÉMON, THEN TAKE A WELL-DESERVED BREAK? DO A LITTLE SIGHT-SEEING!
GREAT IDEA! COME ON OUT, EVERY-BODY!

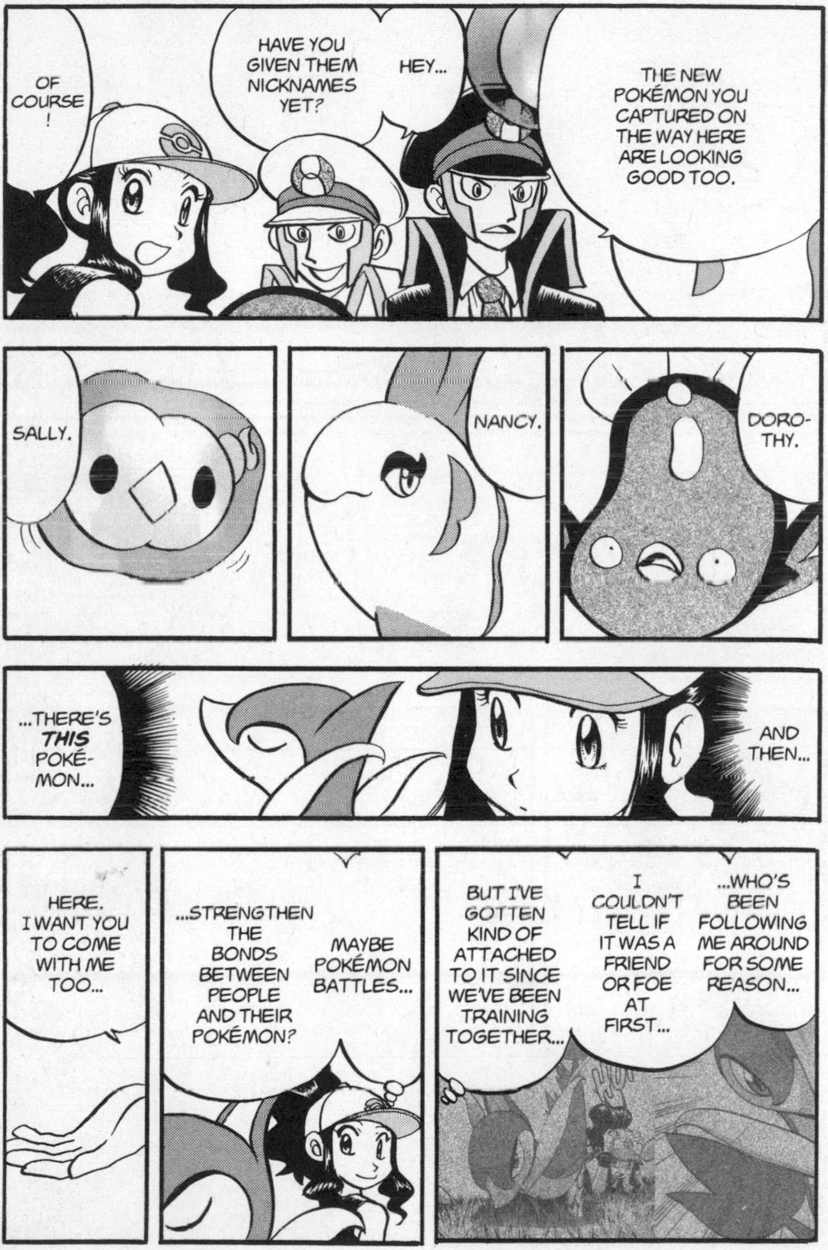
THE NEW POKÉMON YOU CAPTURED ON THE WAY HERE ARE LOOKING GOOD TOO.
HEY...
HAVE YOU GIVEN THEM NICKNAMES YET?
OF COURSE!
DORO-THY.
NANCY.
SALLY.
AND THEN...
...THERE'S **THIS** POKÉ-MON...
...WHO'S BEEN FOLLOWING ME AROUND FOR SOME REASON...
I COULDN'T TELL IF IT WAS A FRIEND OR FOE AT FIRST...
BUT I'VE GOTTEN KIND OF ATTACHED TO IT SINCE WE'VE BEEN TRAINING TOGETHER...
MAYBE POKÉMON BATTLES...
...STRENGTHEN THE BONDS BETWEEN PEOPLE AND THEIR POKÉMON?
HERE. I WANT YOU TO COME WITH ME TOO...

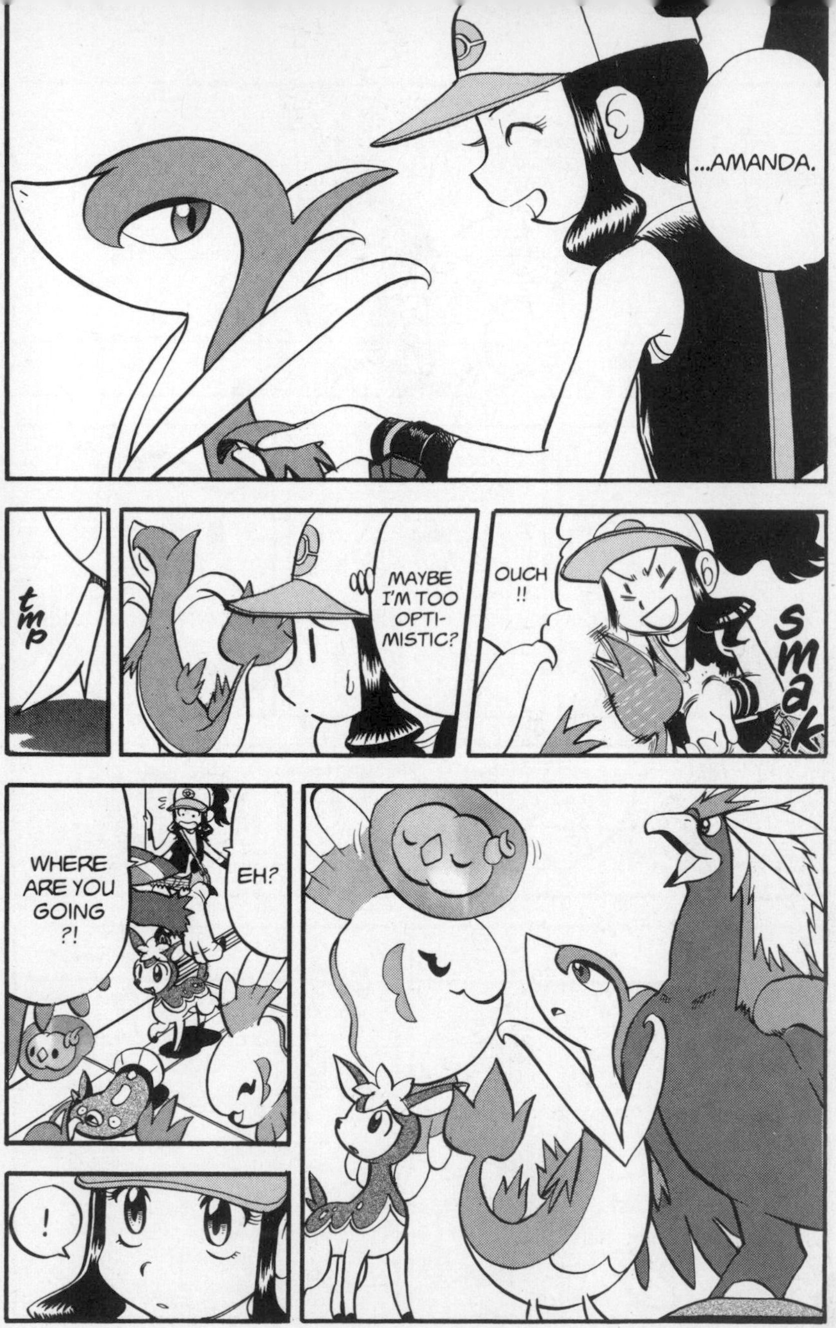
...AMANDA.
OUCH !!
smak
MAYBE I'M TOO OPTI-MISTIC?
tmp
EH?
WHERE ARE YOU GOING ?!
!

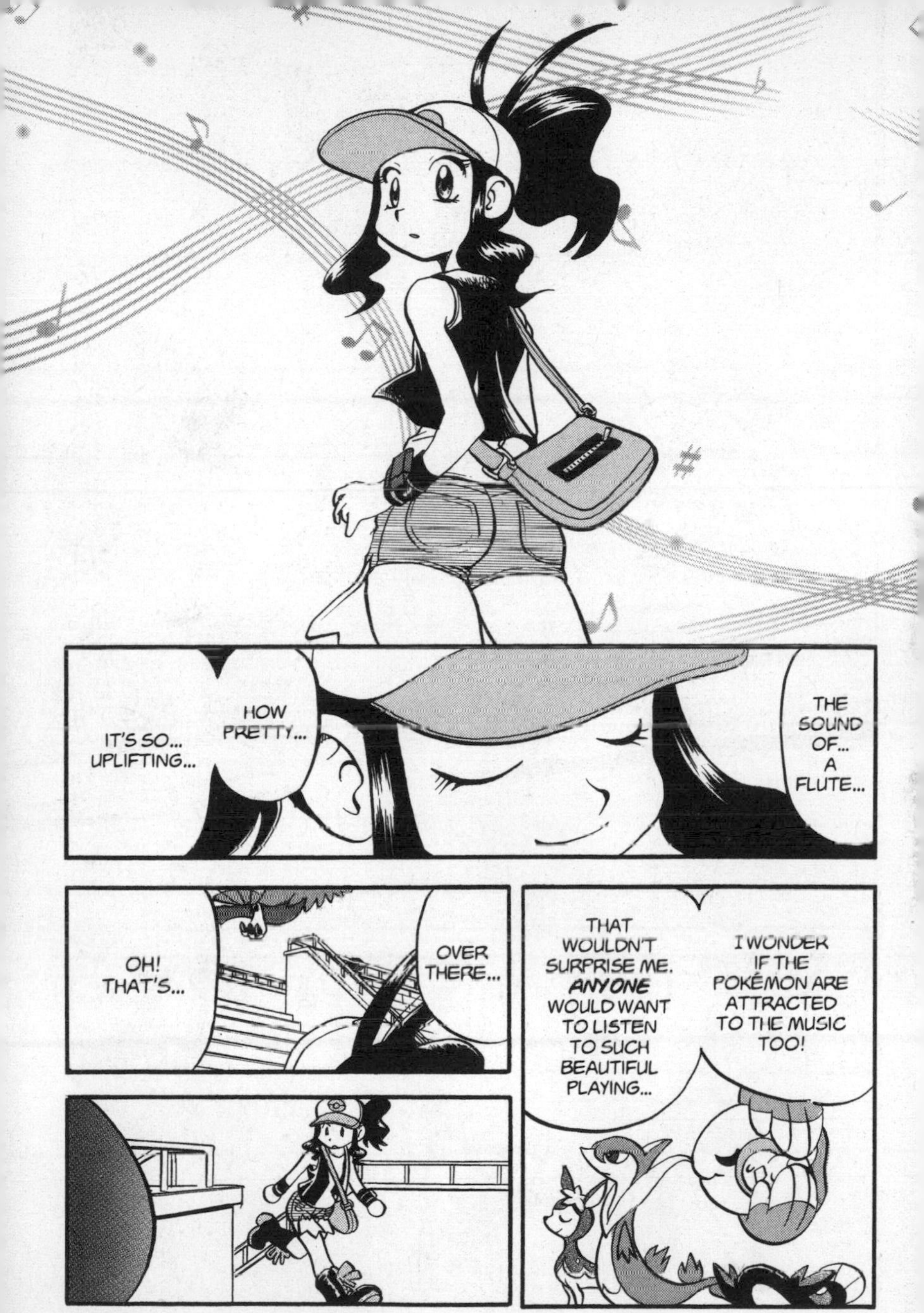
THE SOUND OF... A FLUTE...
HOW PRETTY...
IT'S SO... UPLIFTING...
I WONDER IF THE POKÉMON ARE ATTRACTED TO THE MUSIC TOO!
THAT WOULDN'T SURPRISE ME. ***ANYONE*** WOULD WANT TO LISTEN TO SUCH BEAUTIFUL PLAYING...
OVER THERE...
OH! THAT'S...

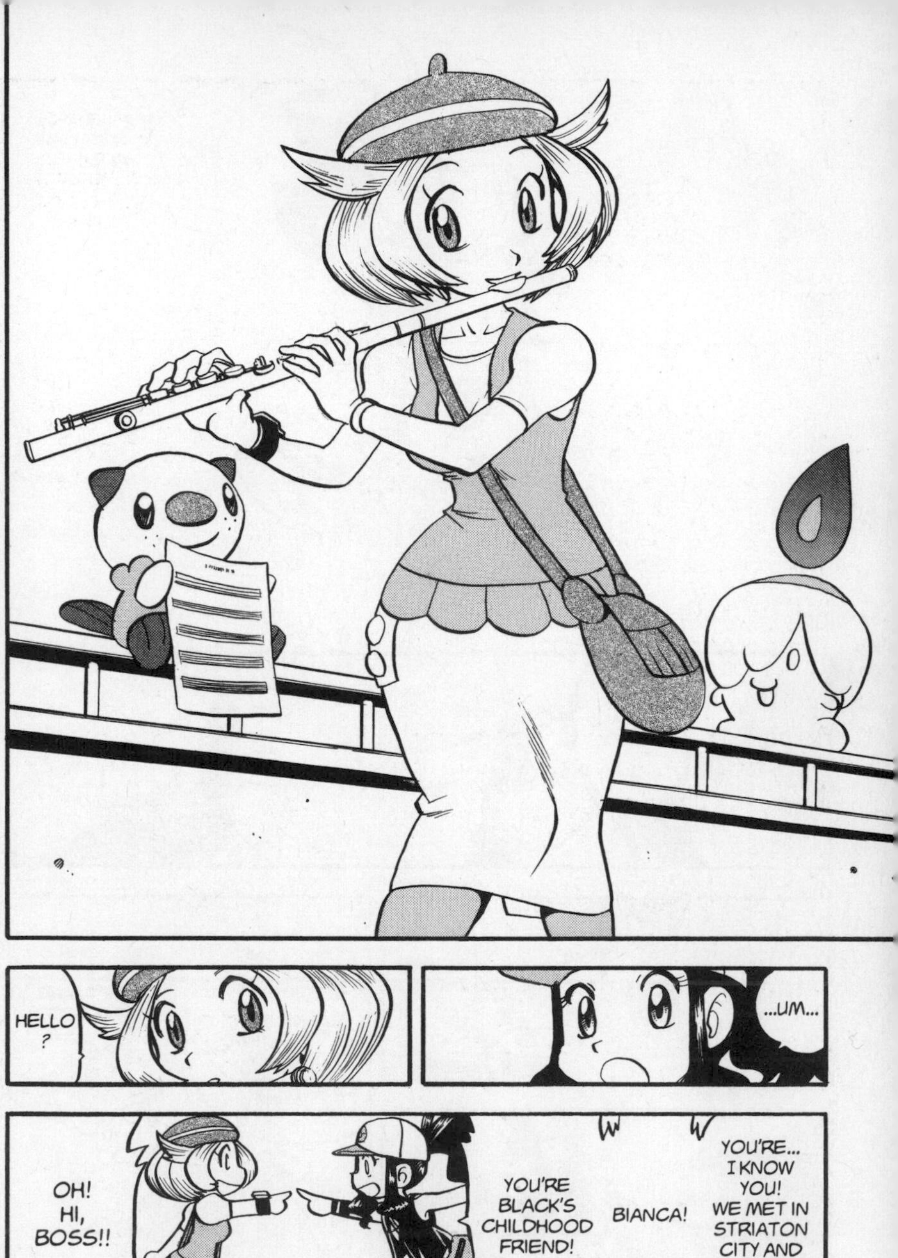
...UM...
HELLO?
YOU'RE... I KNOW YOU! WE MET IN STRIATON CITY AND CASTELIA CITY!
BIANCA!
YOU'RE BLACK'S CHILDHOOD FRIEND!
OH! HI, BOSS!!

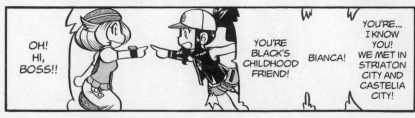

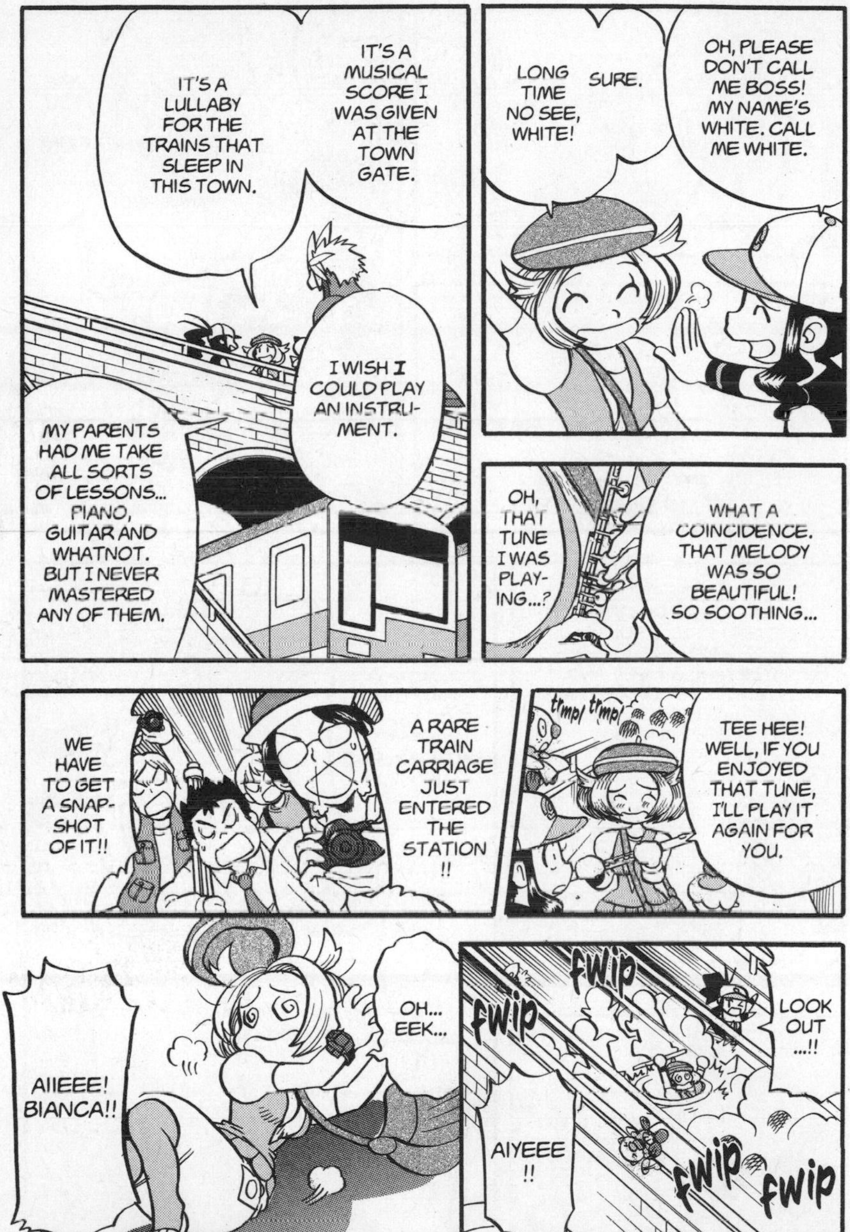
OH, PLEASE DON'T CALL ME BOSS! MY NAME'S WHITE. CALL ME WHITE.
SURE.
LONG TIME NO SEE, WHITE!
WHAT A COINCIDENCE. THAT MELODY WAS SO BEAUTIFUL! SO SOOTHING...
OH, THAT TUNE I WAS PLAYING...?
IT'S A MUSICAL SCORE I WAS GIVEN AT THE TOWN GATE.
IT'S A LULLABY FOR THE TRAINS THAT SLEEP IN THIS TOWN.
I WISH I COULD PLAY AN INSTRUMENT.
MY PARENTS HAD ME TAKE ALL SORTS OF LESSONS... PIANO, GUITAR AND WHATNOT. BUT I NEVER MASTERED ANY OF THEM.
TEE HEE! WELL, IF YOU ENJOYED THAT TUNE, I'LL PLAY IT AGAIN FOR YOU.
trmp! trmp!
A RARE TRAIN CARRIAGE JUST ENTERED THE STATION !!
WE HAVE TO GET A SNAPSHOT OF IT!!
LOOK OUT ...!!
fwip
fwip
AIYEEE !!
fwip
fwip
OH... EEK...
AIIEEE! BIANCA!!

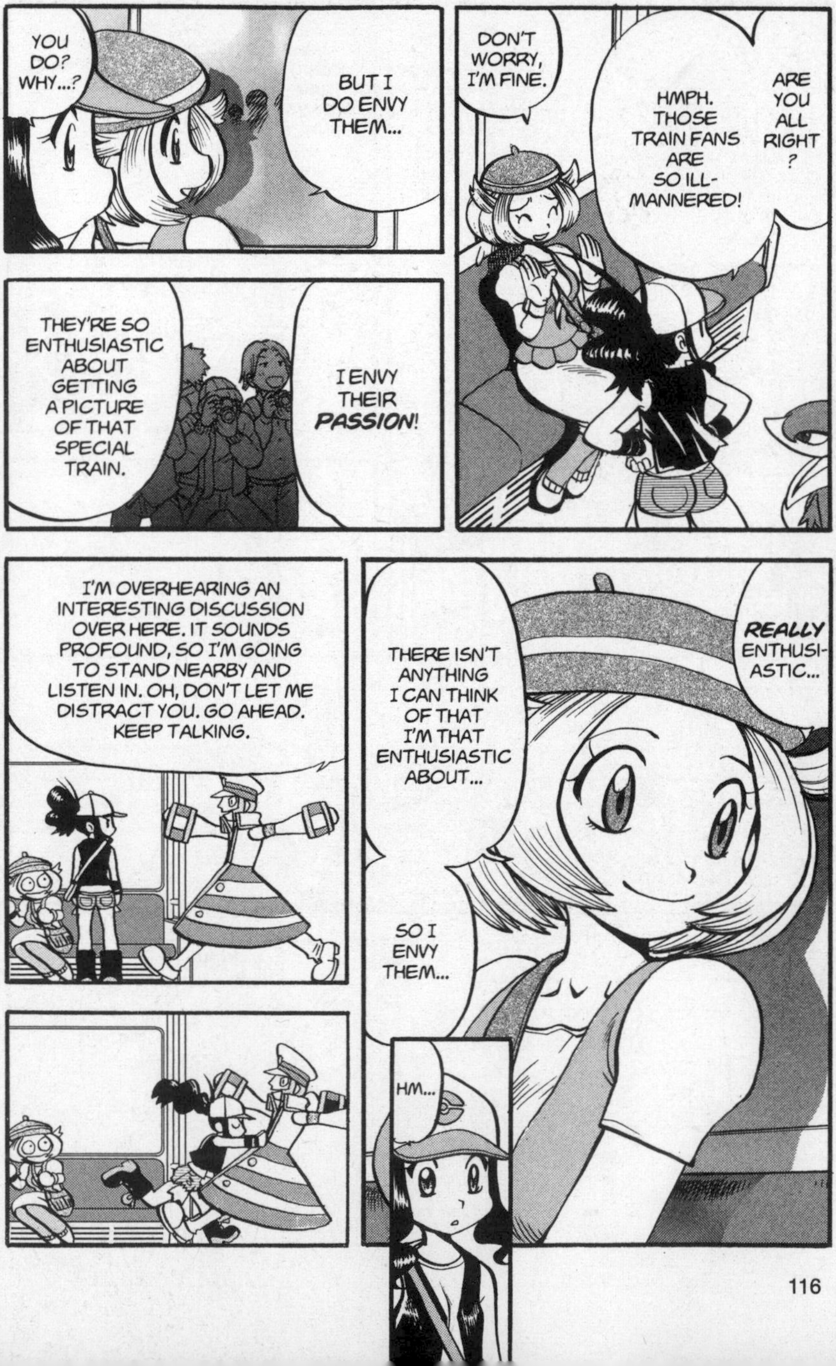

ARE YOU ALL RIGHT?
HMPH. THOSE TRAIN FANS ARE SO ILL-MANNERED!
DON'T WORRY, I'M FINE.
BUT I DO ENVY THEM...
YOU DO? WHY...?
THEY'RE SO ENTHUSIASTIC ABOUT GETTING A PICTURE OF THAT SPECIAL TRAIN.
I ENVY THEIR **PASSION**!
REALLY ENTHUSIASTIC...
THERE ISN'T ANYTHING I CAN THINK OF THAT I'M THAT ENTHUSIASTIC ABOUT...
SO I ENVY THEM...
HM...
I'M OVERHEARING AN INTERESTING DISCUSSION OVER HERE. IT SOUNDS PROFOUND, SO I'M GOING TO STAND NEARBY AND LISTEN IN. OH, DON'T LET ME DISTRACT YOU. GO AHEAD. KEEP TALKING.

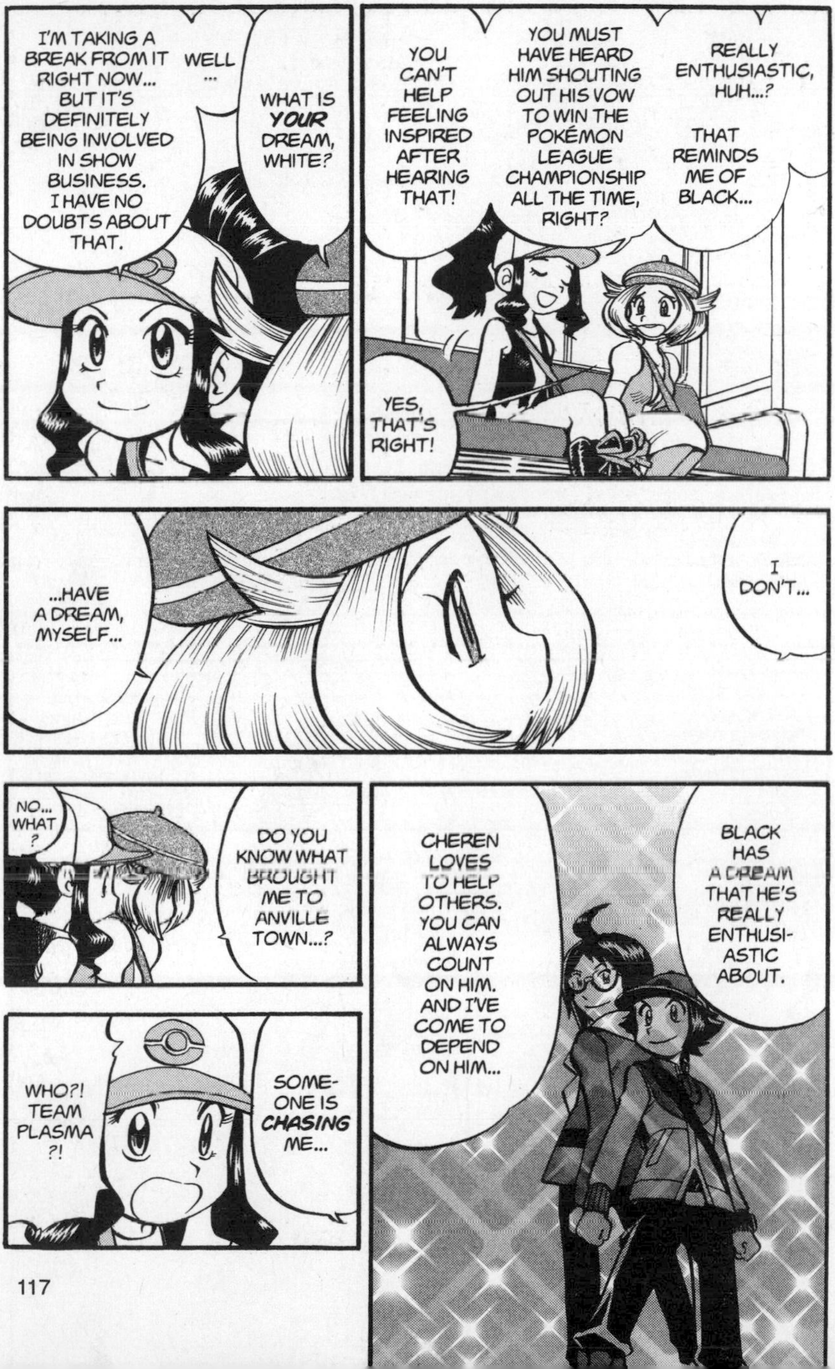
REALLY ENTHUSIASTIC, HUH...?
THAT REMINDS ME OF BLACK...
YOU MUST HAVE HEARD HIM SHOUTING OUT HIS VOW TO WIN THE POKÉMON LEAGUE CHAMPIONSHIP ALL THE TIME, RIGHT?
YOU CAN'T HELP FEELING INSPIRED AFTER HEARING THAT!
YES, THAT'S RIGHT!
WHAT IS *YOUR* DREAM, WHITE?
WELL ...
I'M TAKING A BREAK FROM IT RIGHT NOW... BUT IT'S DEFINITELY BEING INVOLVED IN SHOW BUSINESS. I HAVE NO DOUBTS ABOUT THAT.
I DON'T...
...HAVE A DREAM, MYSELF...
BLACK HAS A DREAM THAT HE'S REALLY ENTHUSI-ASTIC ABOUT.
CHEREN LOVES TO HELP OTHERS. YOU CAN ALWAYS COUNT ON HIM. AND I'VE COME TO DEPEND ON HIM...
DO YOU KNOW WHAT BROUGHT ME TO ANVILLE TOWN...?
NO... WHAT ?
SOME-ONE IS *CHASING* ME...
WHO?! TEAM PLASMA ?!

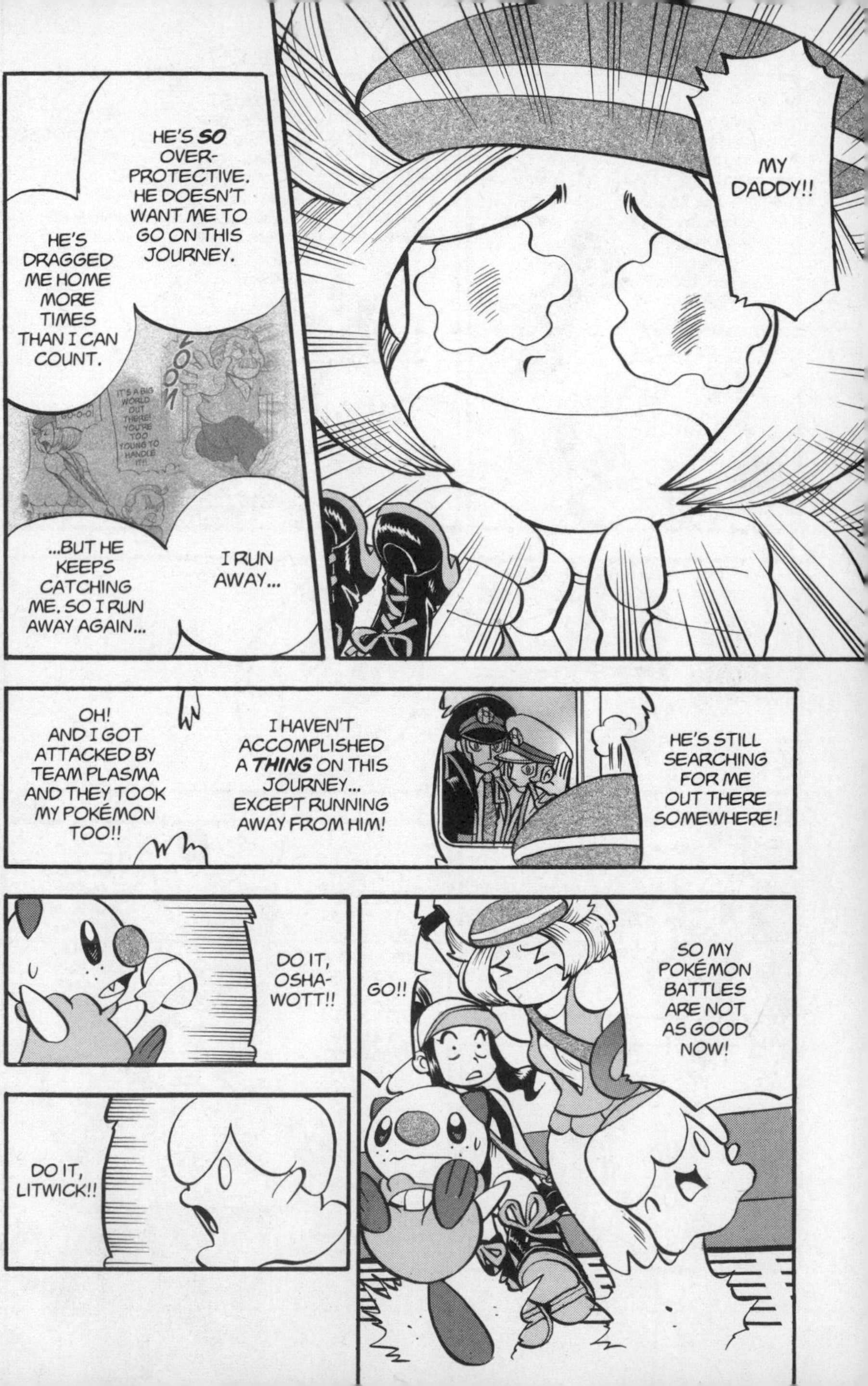
MY DADDY!!
HE'S **SO** OVER-PROTECTIVE. HE DOESN'T WANT ME TO GO ON THIS JOURNEY.
HE'S DRAGGED ME HOME MORE TIMES THAN I CAN COUNT.
ZOOM
IT'S A BIG WORLD OUT THERE! YOU'RE TOO YOUNG TO HANDLE IT!!
I RUN AWAY...
...BUT HE KEEPS CATCHING ME. SO I RUN AWAY AGAIN...
HE'S STILL SEARCHING FOR ME OUT THERE SOMEWHERE!
I HAVEN'T ACCOMPLISHED A ***THING*** ON THIS JOURNEY... EXCEPT RUNNING AWAY FROM HIM!
OH! AND I GOT ATTACKED BY TEAM PLASMA AND THEY TOOK MY POKÉMON TOO!!
SO MY POKÉMON BATTLES ARE NOT AS GOOD NOW!
GO!!
DO IT, OSHAWOTT!!
DO IT, LITWICK!!

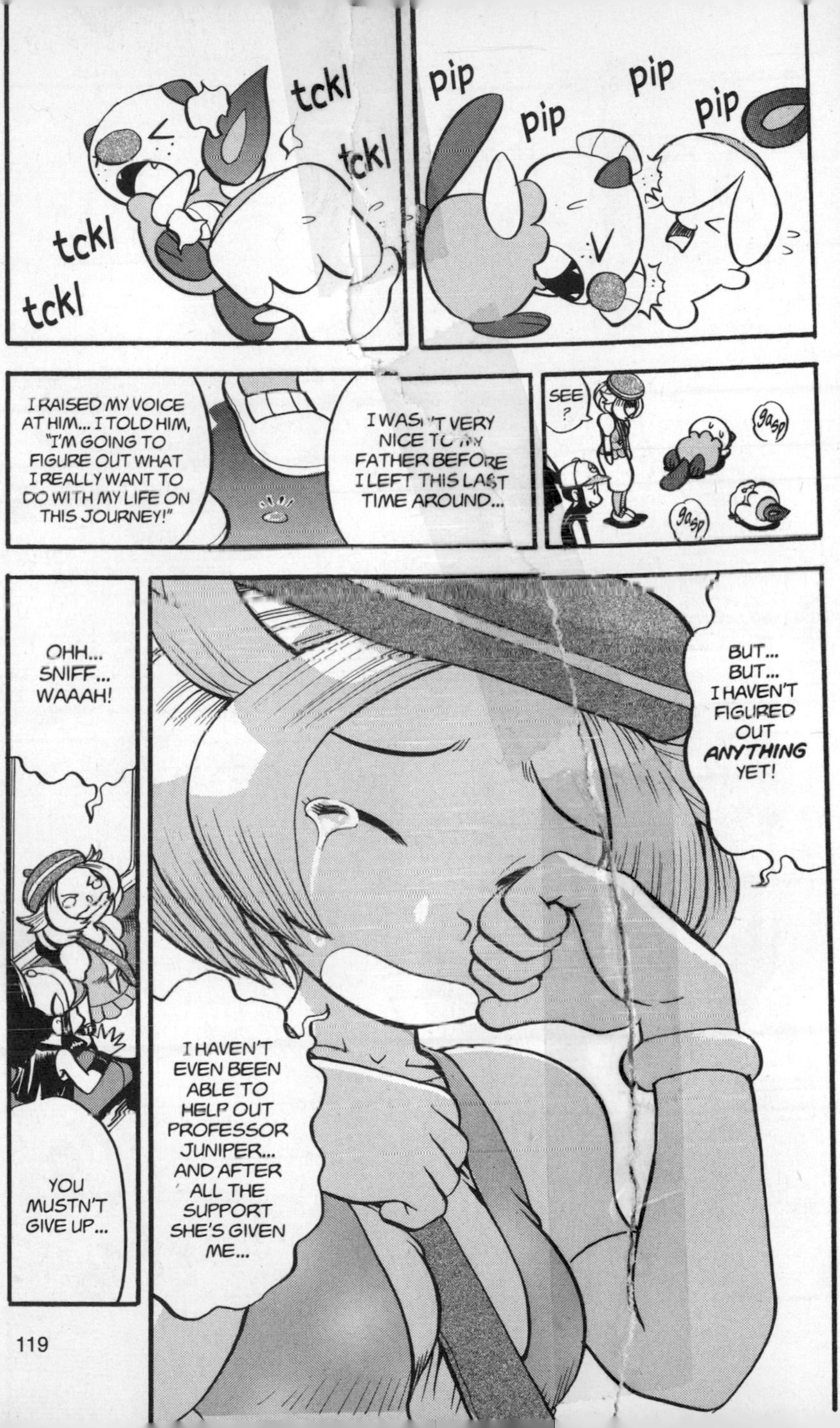
pip
pip
pip
pip
tckl
tckl
tckl
tckl
SEE ?
gasp
gasp
I WASN'T VERY NICE TO MY FATHER BEFORE I LEFT THIS LAST TIME AROUND...
I RAISED MY VOICE AT HIM... I TOLD HIM, "I'M GOING TO FIGURE OUT WHAT I REALLY WANT TO DO WITH MY LIFE ON THIS JOURNEY!"
BUT... BUT... I HAVEN'T FIGURED OUT ANYTHING YET!
I HAVEN'T EVEN BEEN ABLE TO HELP OUT PROFESSOR JUNIPER... AND AFTER ALL THE SUPPORT SHE'S GIVEN ME...
OHH... SNIFF... WAAAH!
YOU MUSTN'T GIVE UP...

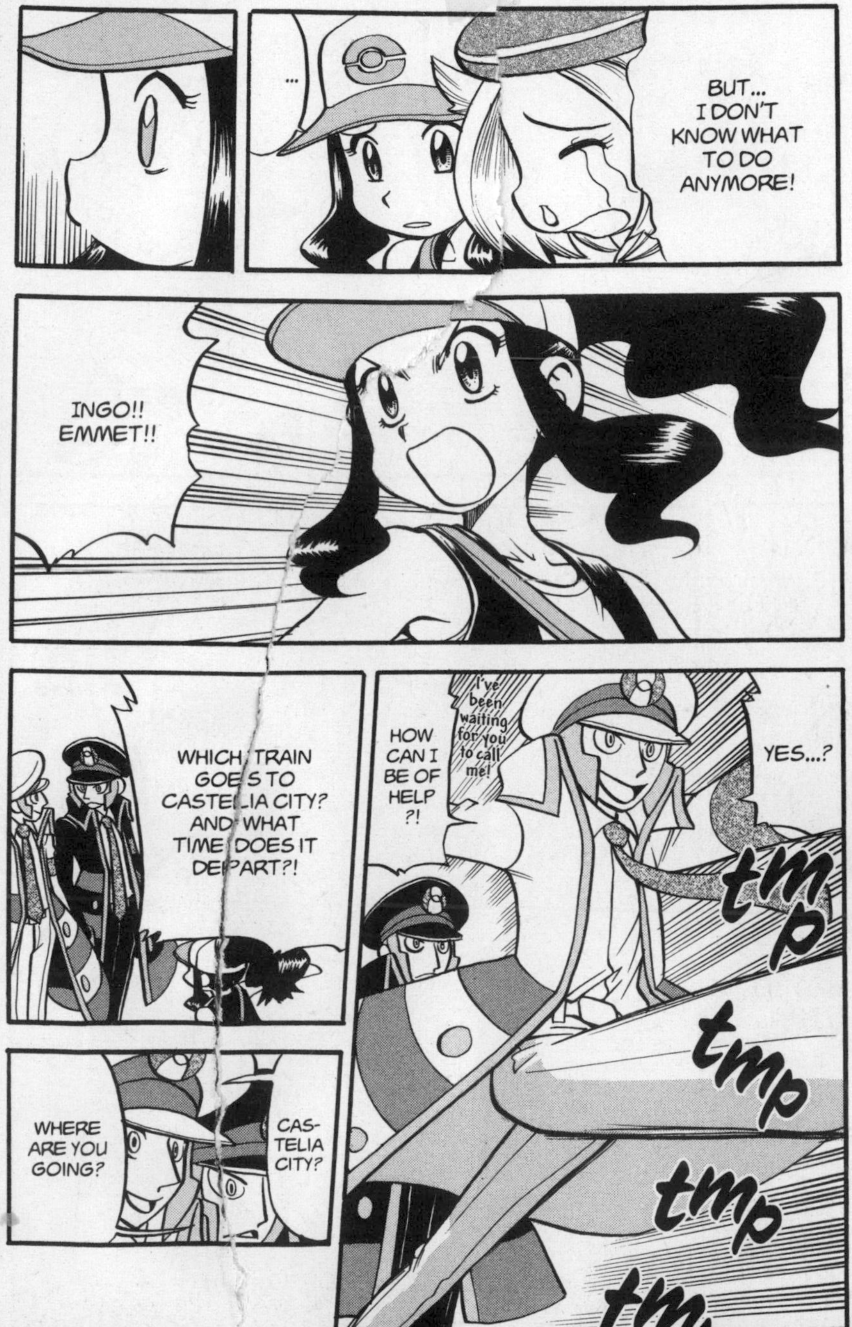
BUT... I DON'T KNOW WHAT TO DO ANYMORE!
...
INGO!! EMMET!!
YES...?
I've been waiting for you to call me!
HOW CAN I BE OF HELP?!
tmp
tmp
tmp
tmp
WHICH TRAIN GOES TO CASTELIA CITY? AND WHAT TIME DOES IT DEPART?!
CAS-TELIA CITY?
WHERE ARE YOU GOING?

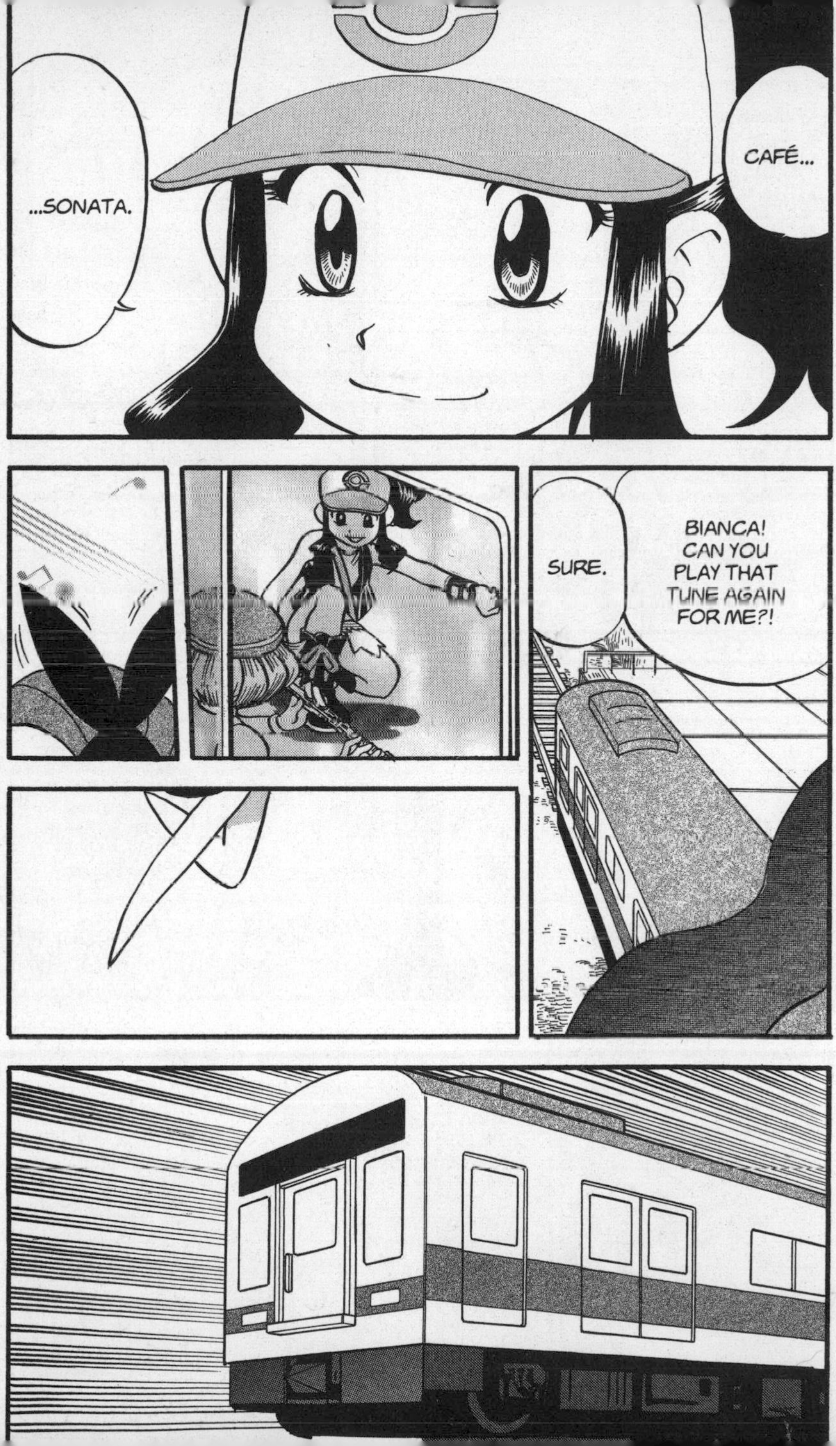
CAFÉ...
...SONATA.
BIANCA! CAN YOU PLAY THAT TUNE AGAIN FOR ME?!
SURE.

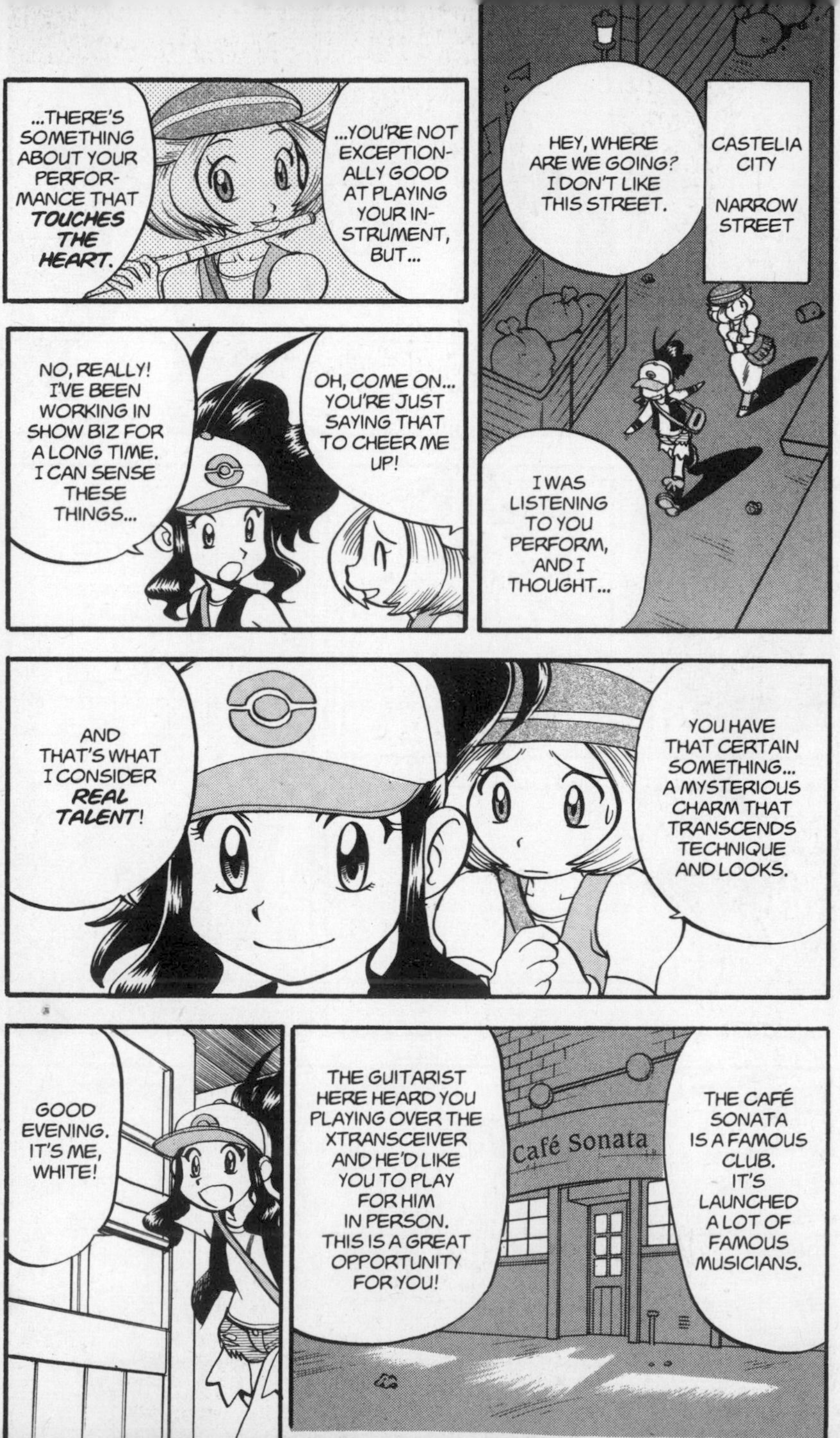
CASTELIA CITY NARROW STREET
HEY, WHERE ARE WE GOING? I DON'T LIKE THIS STREET.
I WAS LISTENING TO YOU PERFORM, AND I THOUGHT...
...YOU'RE NOT EXCEPTIONALLY GOOD AT PLAYING YOUR INSTRUMENT, BUT...
...THERE'S SOMETHING ABOUT YOUR PERFORMANCE THAT TOUCHES THE HEART.
OH, COME ON... YOU'RE JUST SAYING THAT TO CHEER ME UP!
NO, REALLY! I'VE BEEN WORKING IN SHOW BIZ FOR A LONG TIME. I CAN SENSE THESE THINGS...
YOU HAVE THAT CERTAIN SOMETHING... A MYSTERIOUS CHARM THAT TRANSCENDS TECHNIQUE AND LOOKS.
AND THAT'S WHAT I CONSIDER REAL TALENT!
THE CAFÉ SONATA IS A FAMOUS CLUB. IT'S LAUNCHED A LOT OF FAMOUS MUSICIANS.
THE GUITARIST HERE HEARD YOU PLAYING OVER THE XTRANSCEIVER AND HE'D LIKE YOU TO PLAY FOR HIM IN PERSON. THIS IS A GREAT OPPORTUNITY FOR YOU!
Café Sonata
GOOD EVENING. IT'S ME, WHITE!

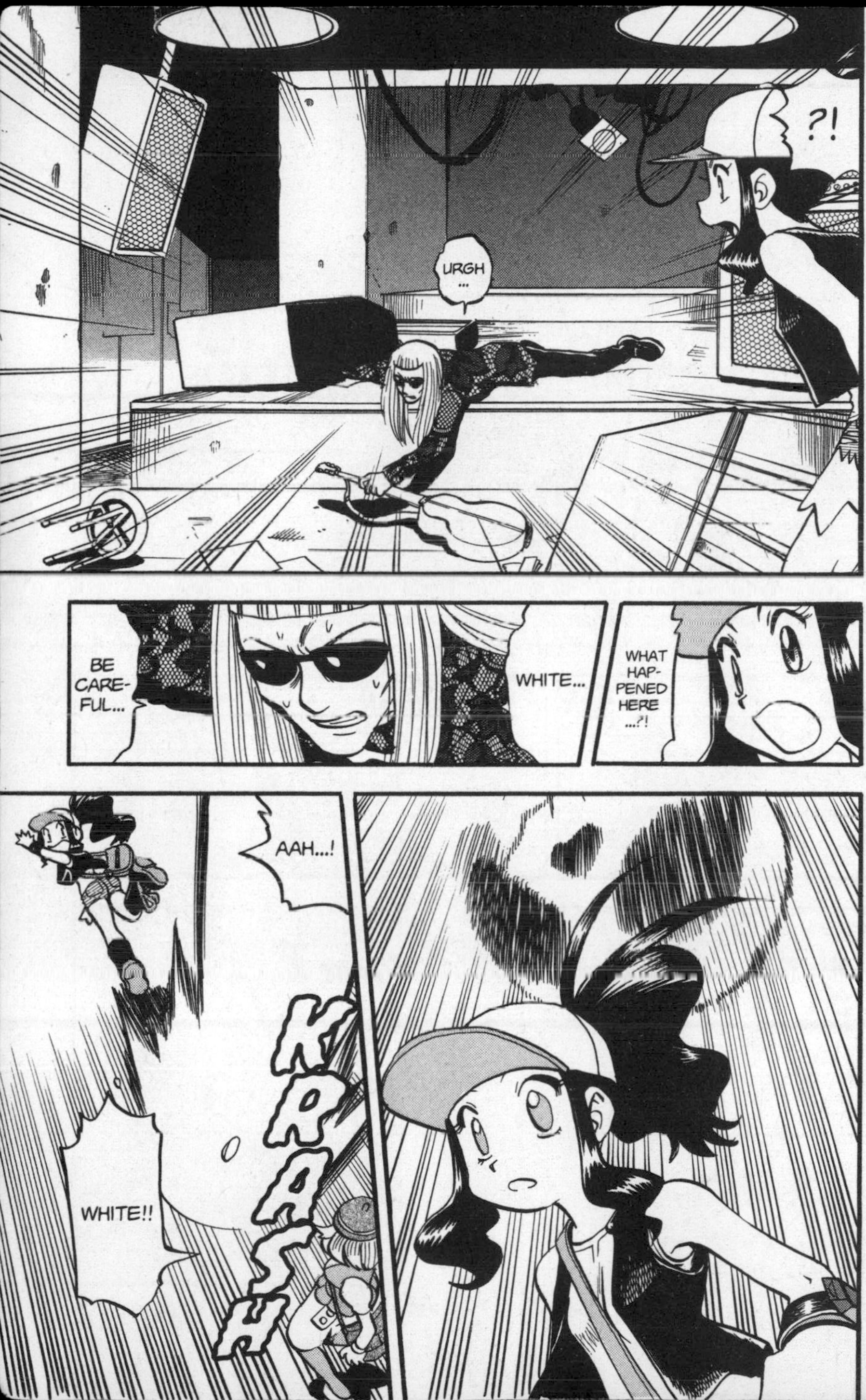
?!
URGH...
WHAT HAP-PENED HERE...?!
WHITE...
BE CARE-FUL...
AAH...!
KRAASH
WHITE!!

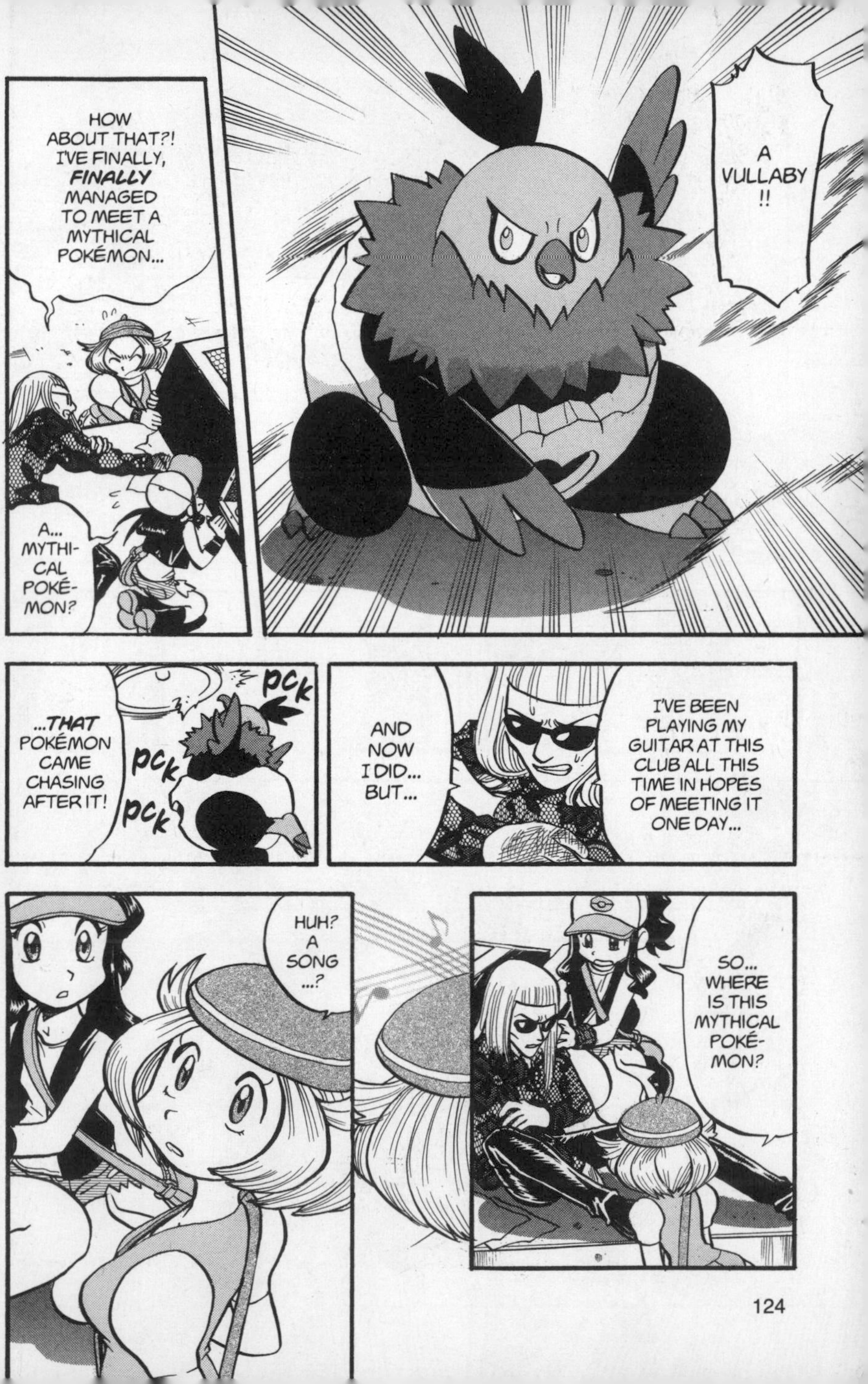
A VULLABY !!
HOW ABOUT THAT?! I'VE FINALLY, FINALLY MANAGED TO MEET A MYTHICAL POKÉMON...
A... MYTHI- CAL POKÉ- MON?
I'VE BEEN PLAYING MY GUITAR AT THIS CLUB ALL THIS TIME IN HOPES OF MEETING IT ONE DAY...
AND NOW I DID... BUT...
...THAT POKÉMON CAME CHASING AFTER IT!
pck
pck
pck
SO... WHERE IS THIS MYTHICAL POKÉ- MON?
HUH? A SONG ...?

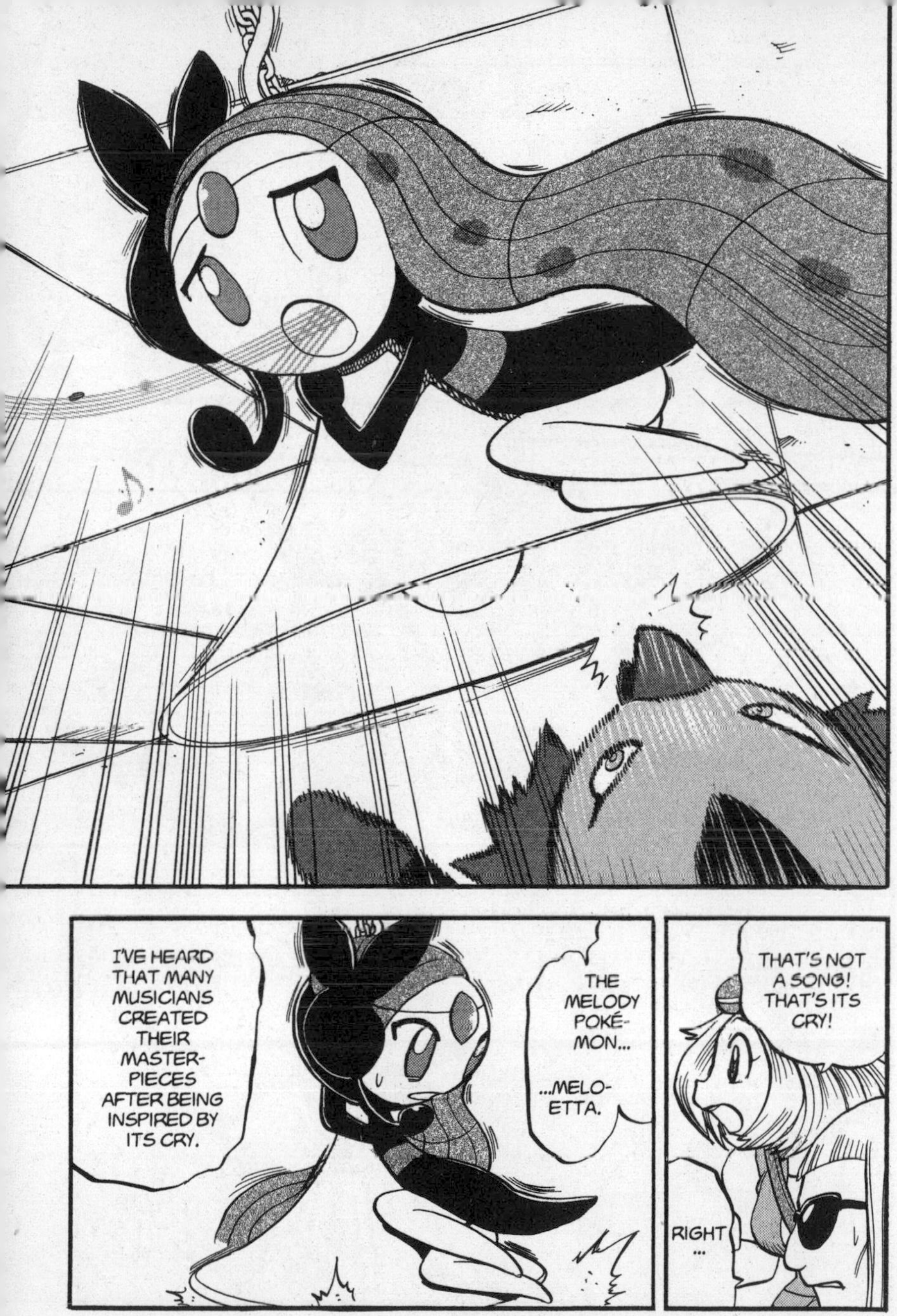
THAT'S NOT A SONG! THAT'S ITS CRY!
RIGHT...
THE MELODY POKÉMON...
...MELOETTA.
I'VE HEARD THAT MANY MUSICIANS CREATED THEIR MASTERPIECES AFTER BEING INSPIRED BY ITS CRY.

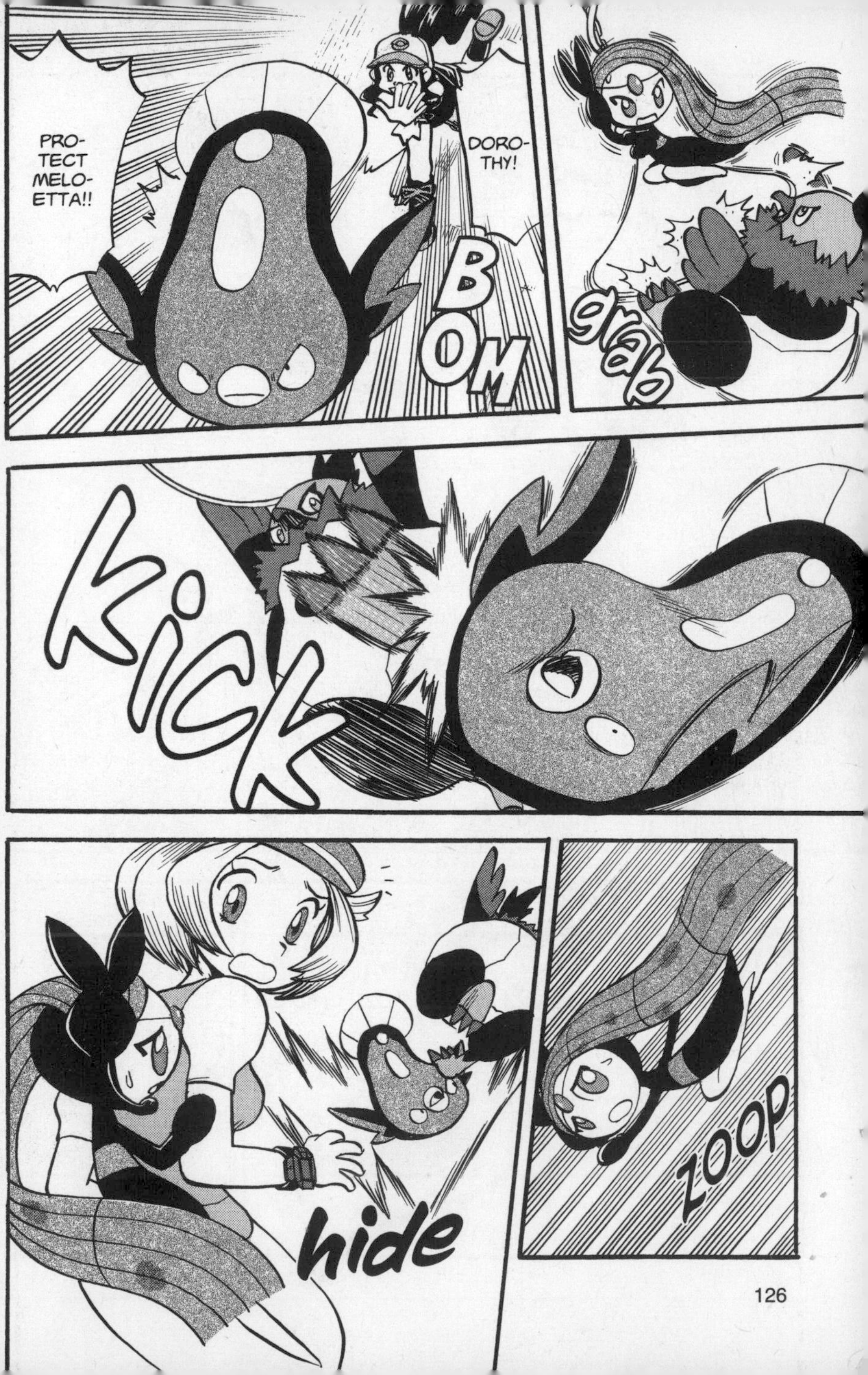
grab
DORO-THY!
PRO-TECT MELO-ETTA!!
BOM
kick
ZOOP
hide

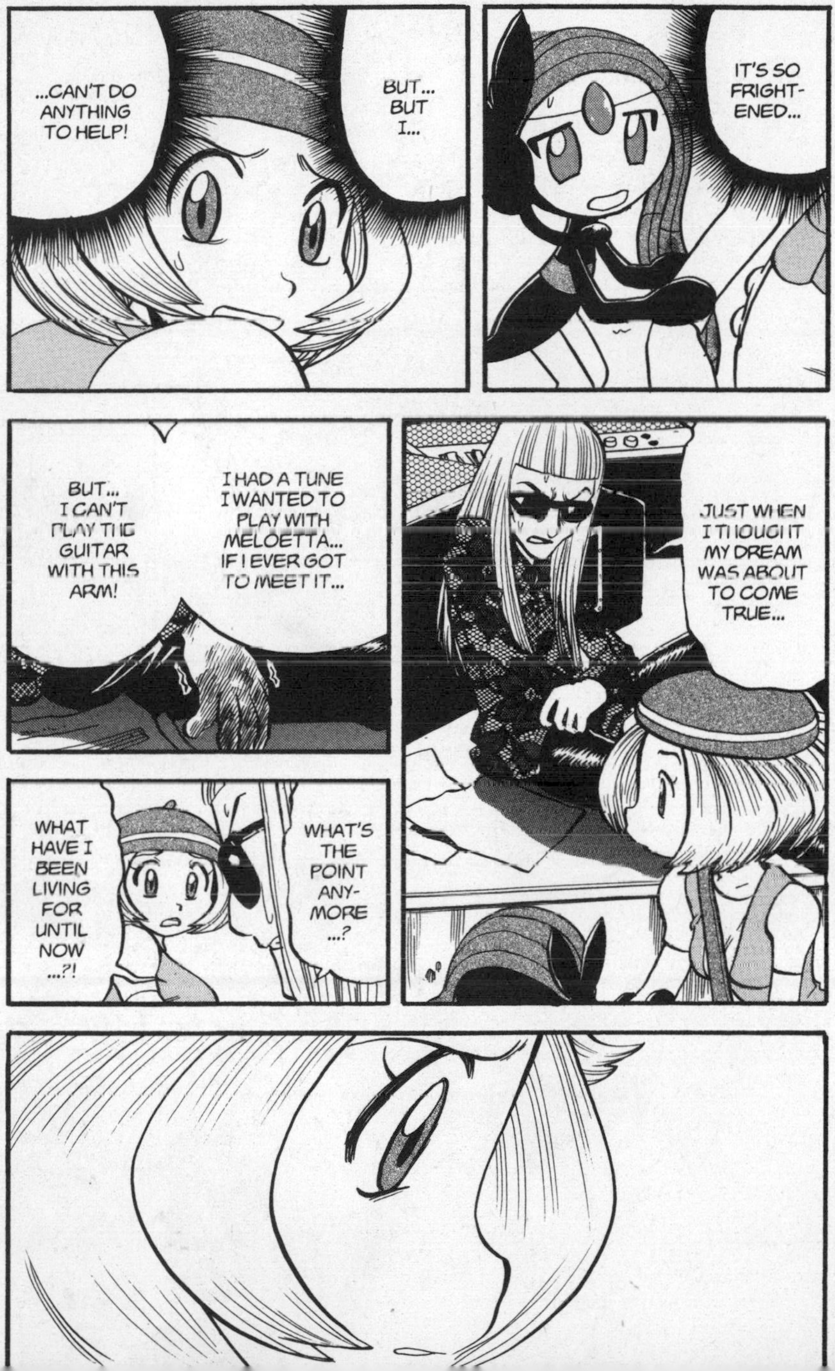
IT'S SO FRIGHT-ENED...
BUT... BUT I...
...CAN'T DO ANYTHING TO HELP!
JUST WHEN I THOUGHT MY DREAM WAS ABOUT TO COME TRUE...
I HAD A TUNE I WANTED TO PLAY WITH MELOETTA... IF I EVER GOT TO MEET IT...
BUT... I CAN'T PLAY THE GUITAR WITH THIS ARM!
WHAT'S THE POINT ANYMORE ...?
WHAT HAVE I BEEN LIVING FOR UNTIL NOW ...?!

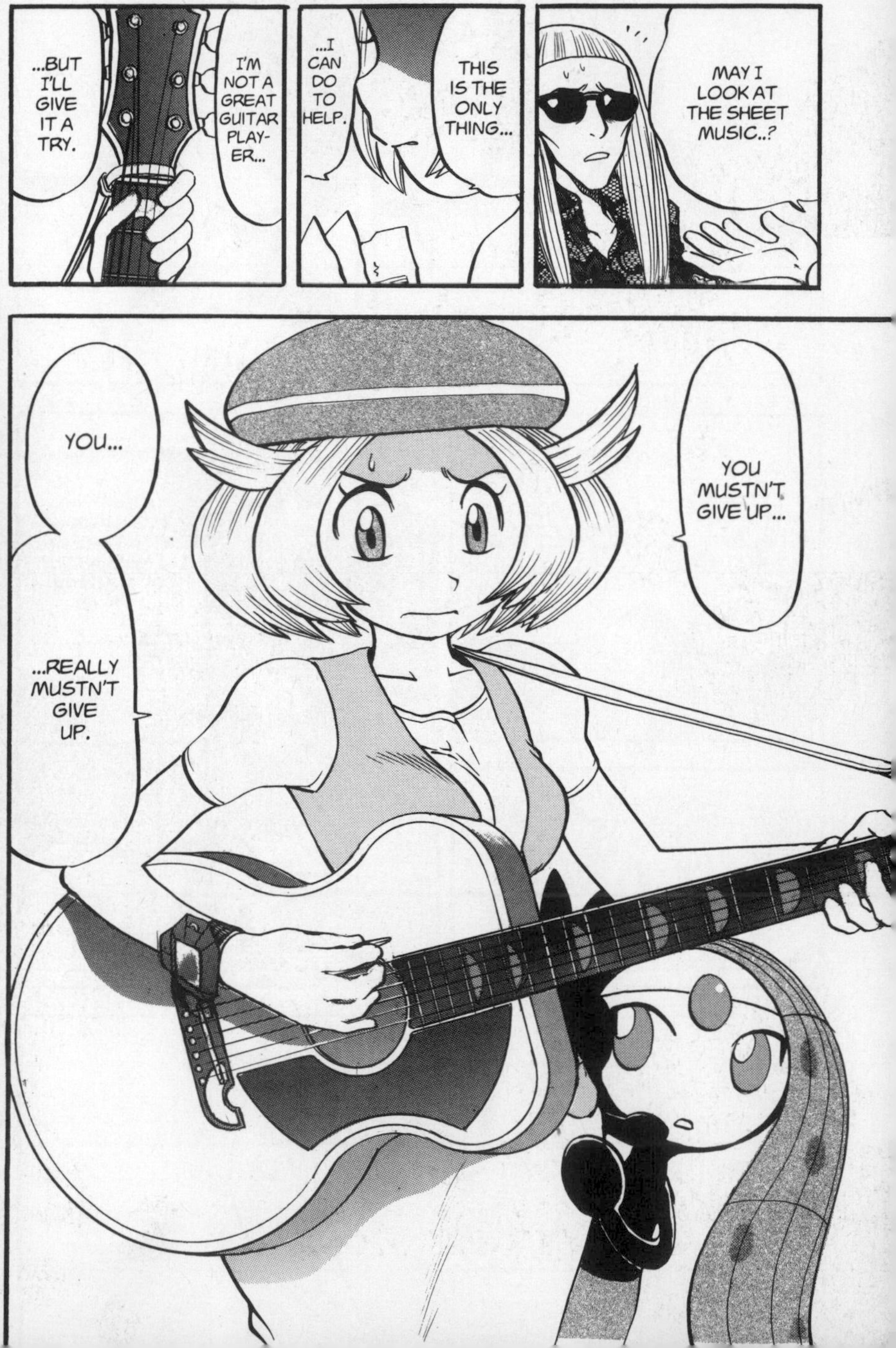
MAY I LOOK AT THE SHEET MUSIC..?
THIS IS THE ONLY THING...
...I CAN DO TO HELP.
I'M NOT A GREAT GUITAR PLAYER...
...BUT I'LL GIVE IT A TRY.
YOU MUSTN'T GIVE UP...
YOU...
...REALLY MUSTN'T GIVE UP.

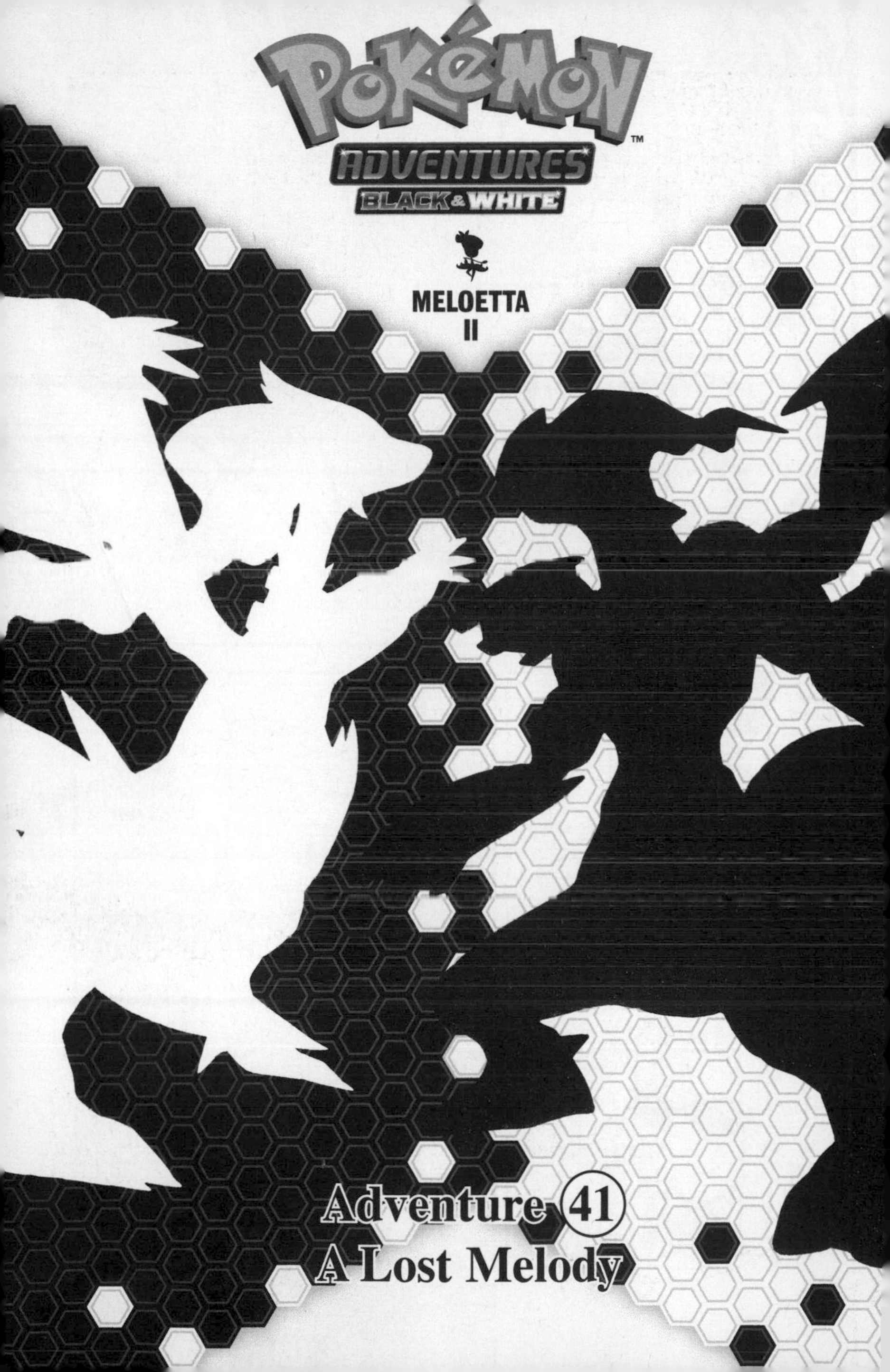
Pokémon™
Adventures
Black & White
MELOETTA
II
Adventure 41
A Lost Melody

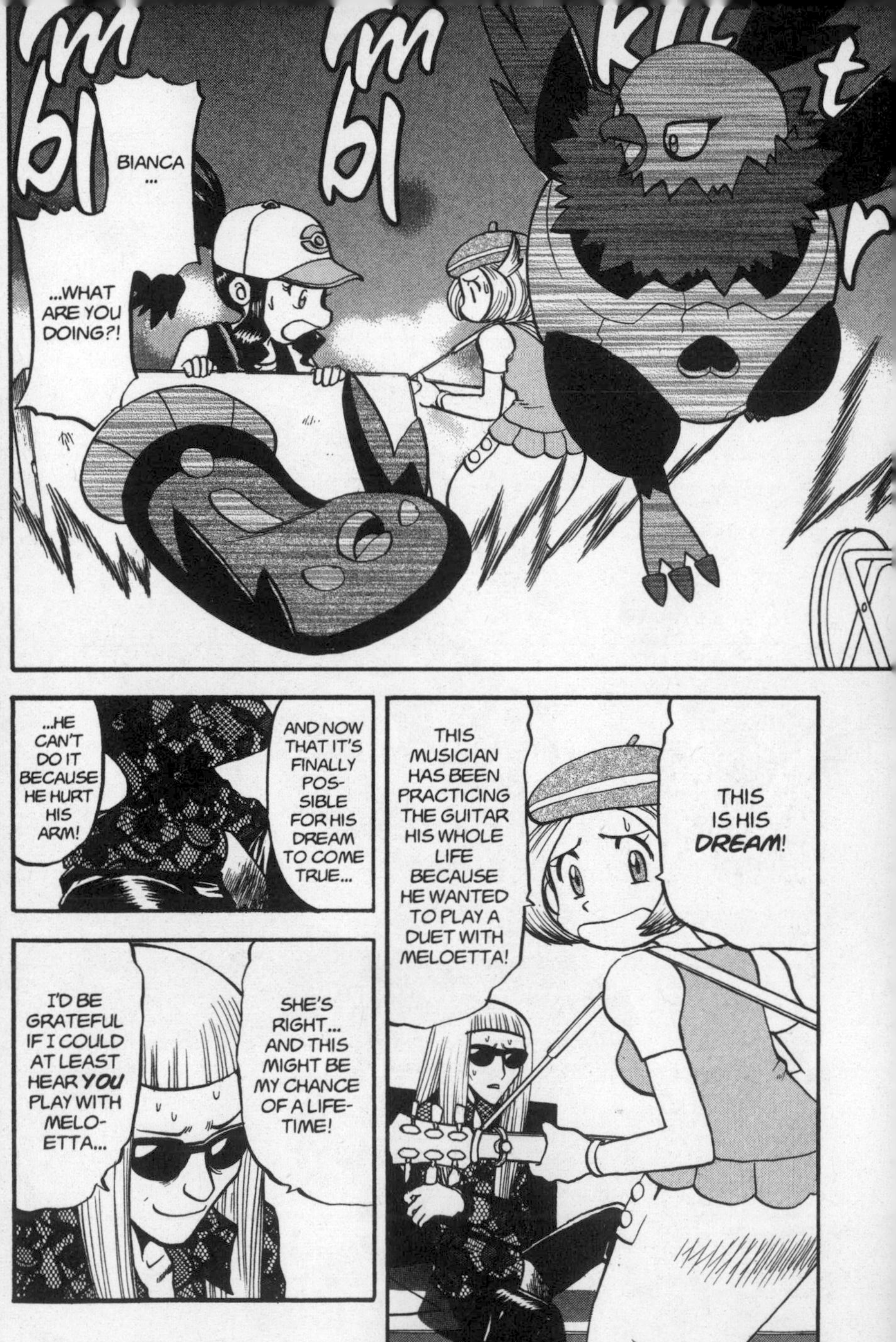
BIANCA...
...WHAT ARE YOU DOING?!
THIS IS HIS **DREAM**!
THIS MUSICIAN HAS BEEN PRACTICING THE GUITAR HIS WHOLE LIFE BECAUSE HE WANTED TO PLAY A DUET WITH MELOETTA!
AND NOW THAT IT'S FINALLY POSSIBLE FOR HIS DREAM TO COME TRUE...
...HE CAN'T DO IT BECAUSE HE HURT HIS ARM!
SHE'S RIGHT... AND THIS MIGHT BE MY CHANCE OF A LIFETIME!
I'D BE GRATEFUL IF I COULD AT LEAST HEAR ***YOU*** PLAY WITH MELOETTA...

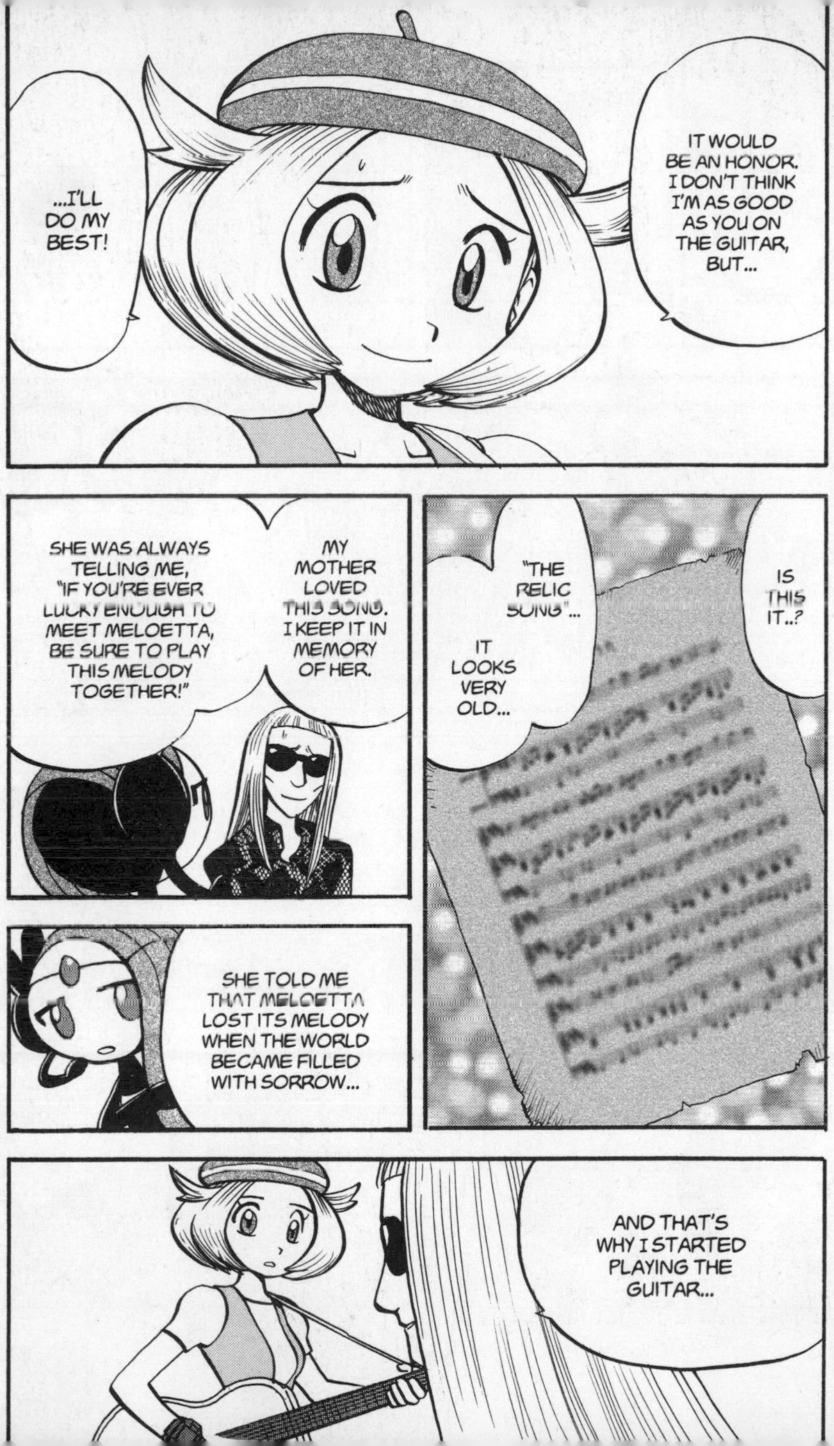
IT WOULD BE AN HONOR. I DON'T THINK I'M AS GOOD AS YOU ON THE GUITAR, BUT...
...I'LL DO MY BEST!
IS THIS IT..?
"THE RELIC SONG"...
IT LOOKS VERY OLD...
MY MOTHER LOVED THIS SONG. I KEEP IT IN MEMORY OF HER.
SHE WAS ALWAYS TELLING ME, "IF YOU'RE EVER LUCKY ENOUGH TO MEET MELOETTA, BE SURE TO PLAY THIS MELODY TOGETHER!"
SHE TOLD ME THAT MELOETTA LOST ITS MELODY WHEN THE WORLD BECAME FILLED WITH SORROW...
AND THAT'S WHY I STARTED PLAYING THE GUITAR...

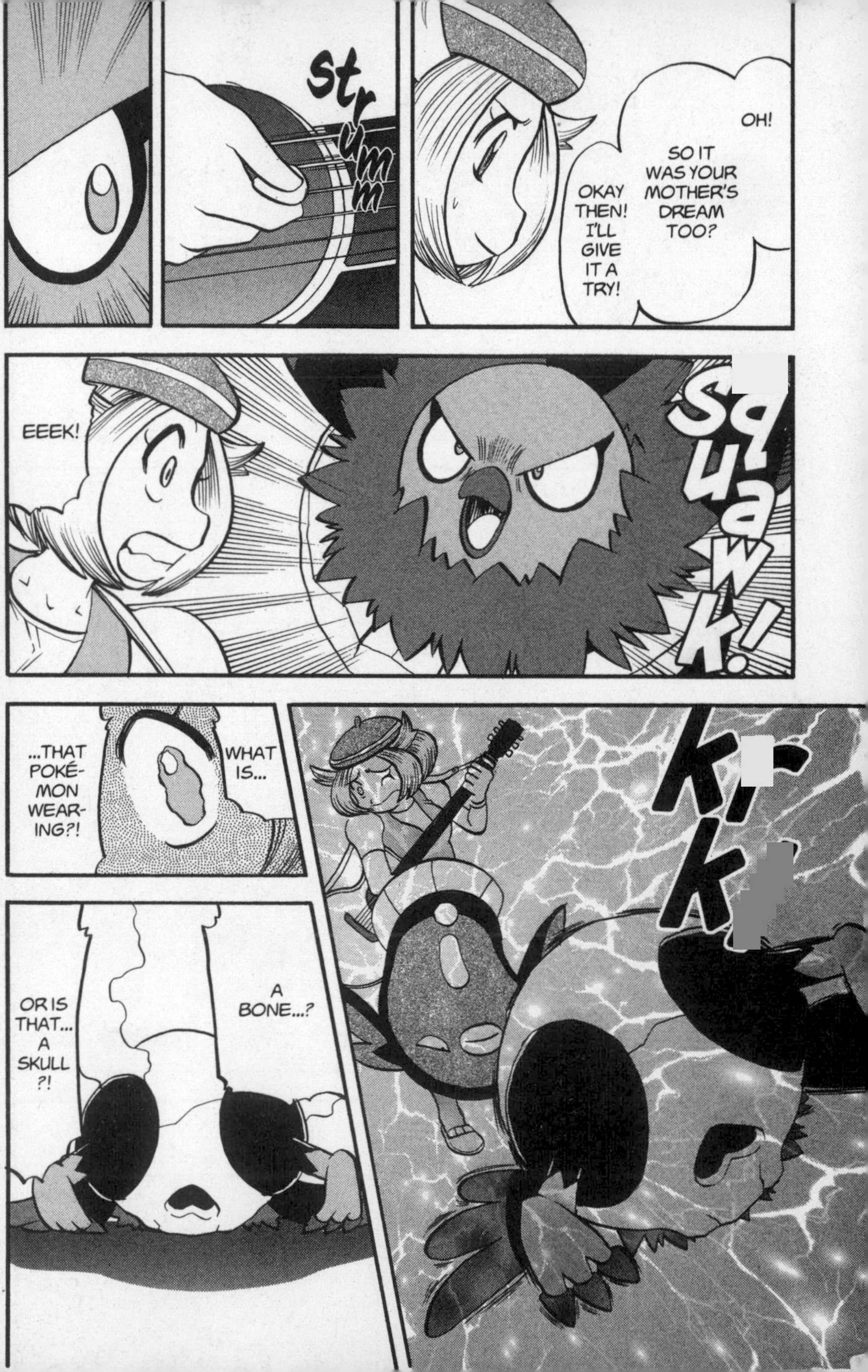
OH!
SO IT WAS YOUR MOTHER'S DREAM TOO?
OKAY THEN! I'LL GIVE IT A TRY!
strumm
Squawk!
EEEK!
WHAT IS...
...THAT POKÉMON WEARING?!
A BONE...?
OR IS THAT... A SKULL?!

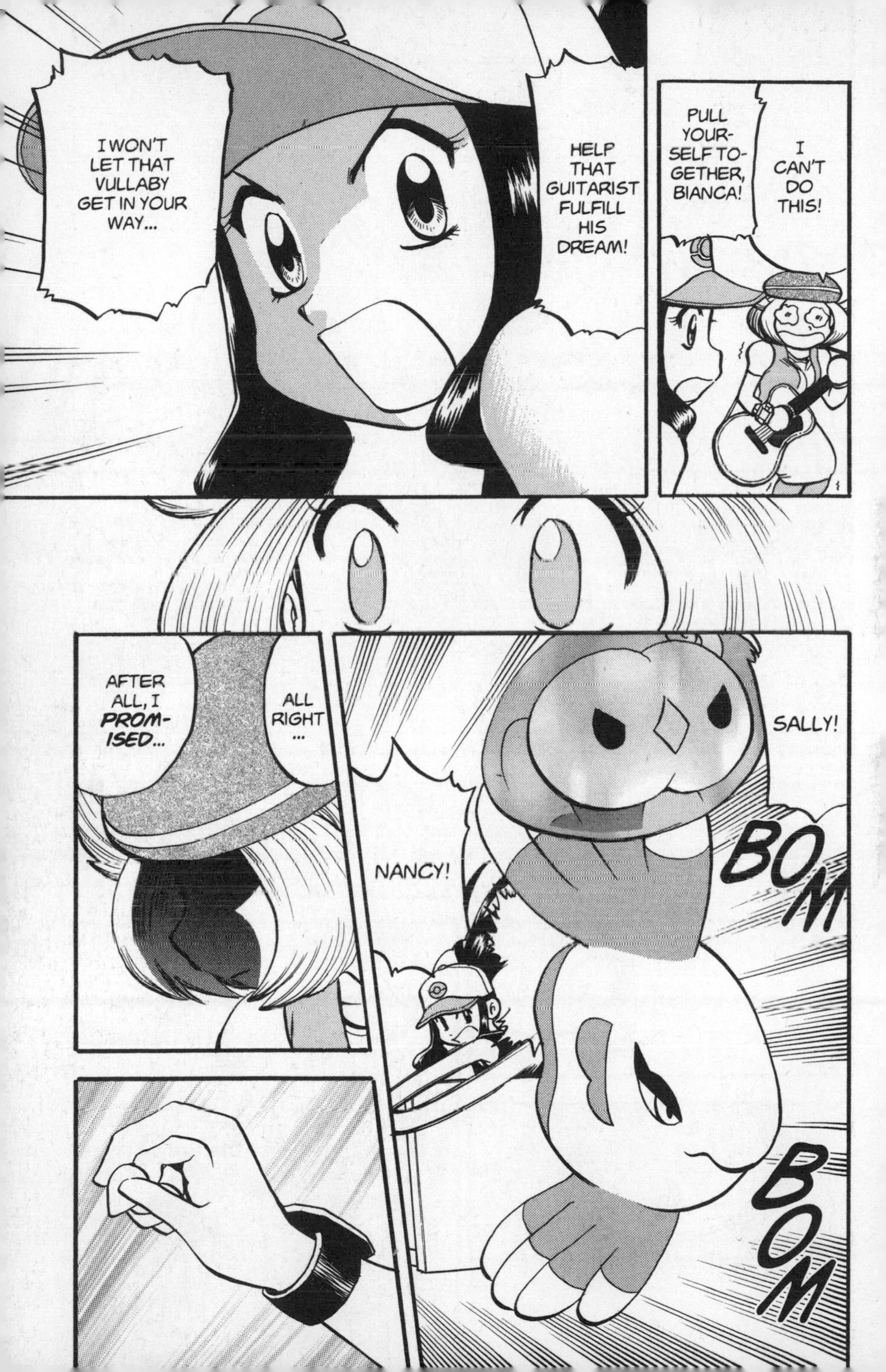
I CAN'T DO THIS!
PULL YOURSELF TOGETHER, BIANCA!
HELP THAT GUITARIST FULFILL HIS DREAM!
I WON'T LET THAT VULLABY GET IN YOUR WAY...
SALLY!
BOM
NANCY!
BOM
ALL RIGHT...
AFTER ALL, I PROMISED...

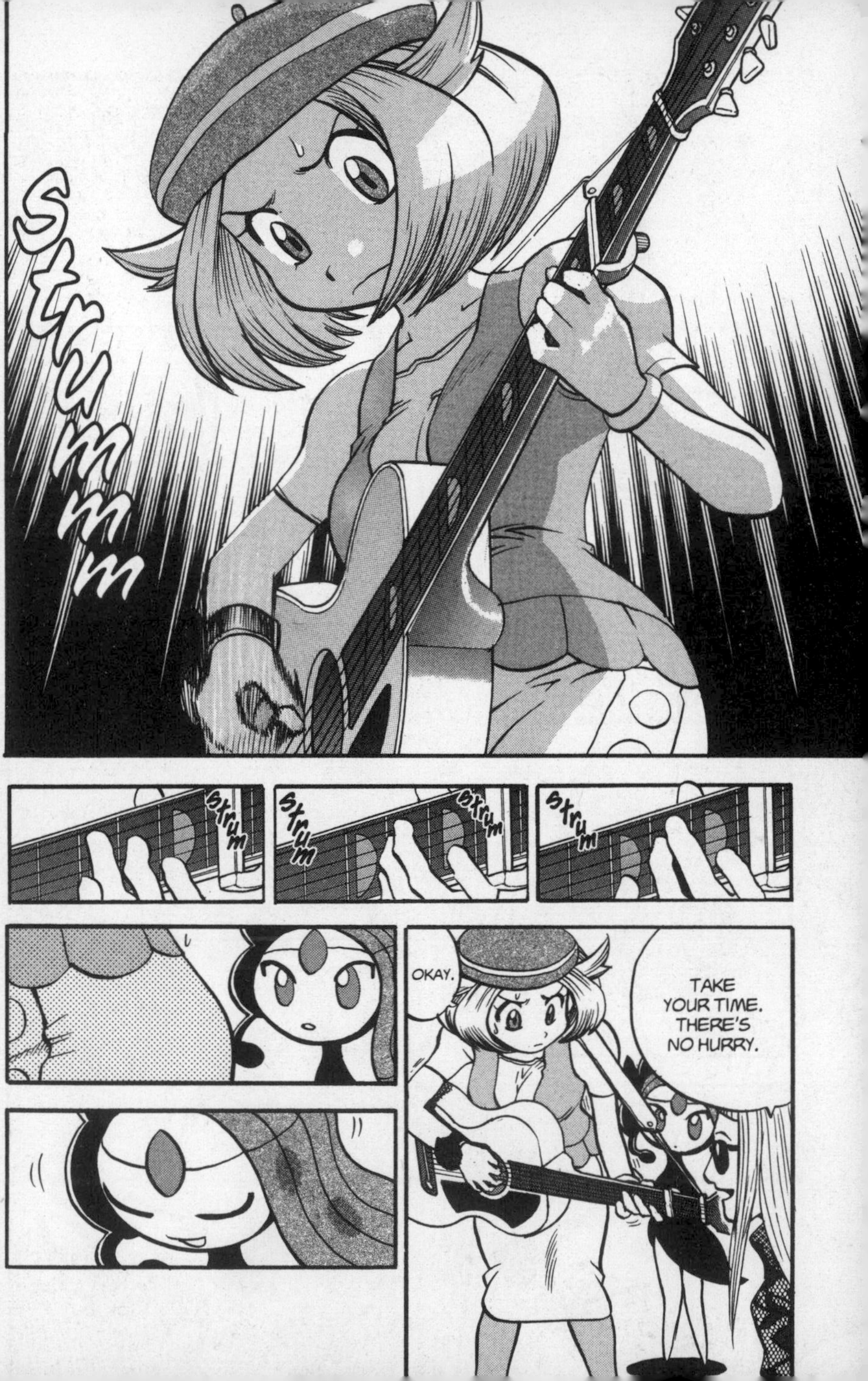
Strummm
strum
strum
strum
strum
TAKE YOUR TIME. THERE'S NO HURRY.
OKAY.

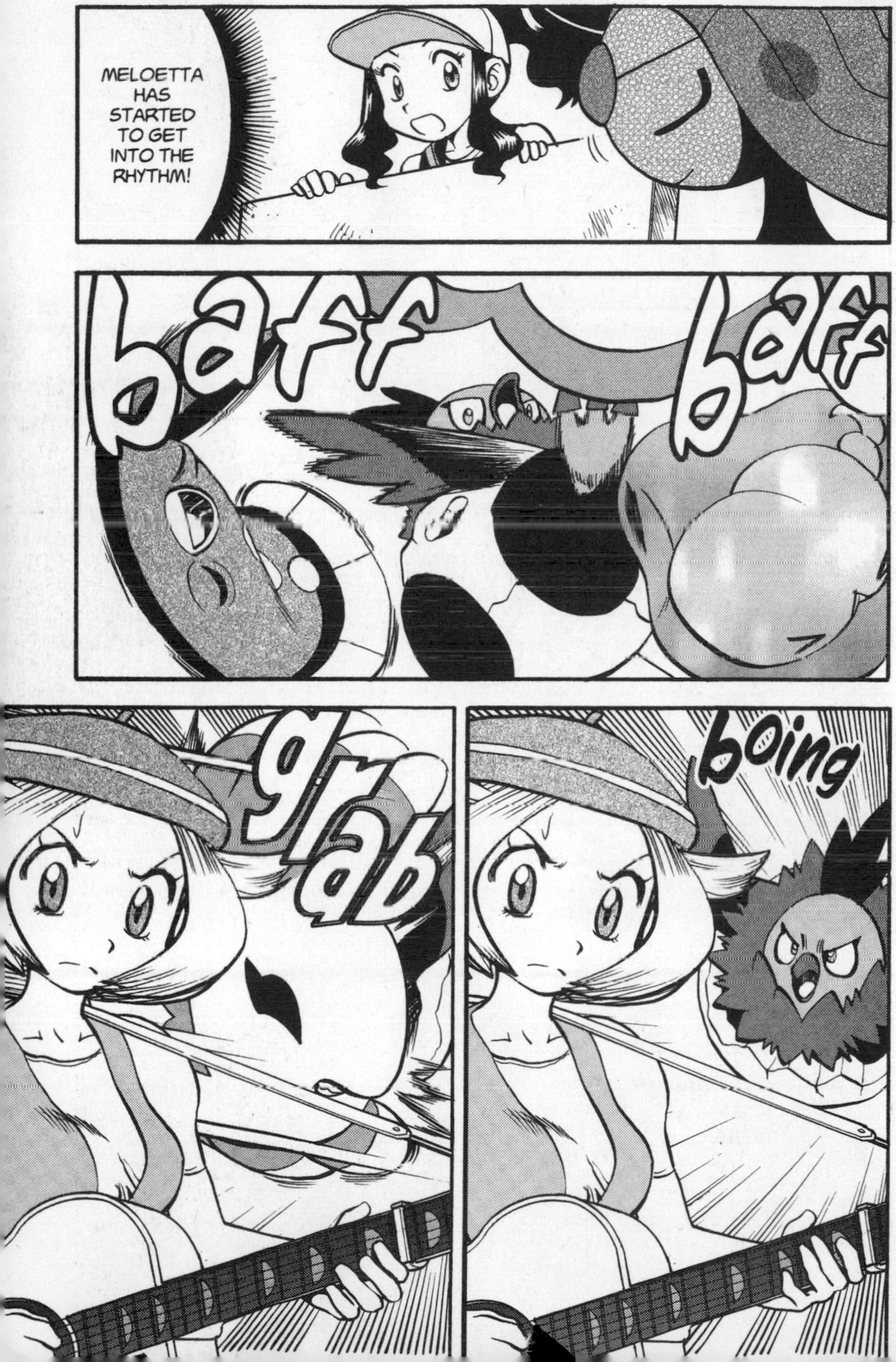
MELOETTA HAS STARTED TO GET INTO THE RHYTHM!
baff
baff
boing
grab

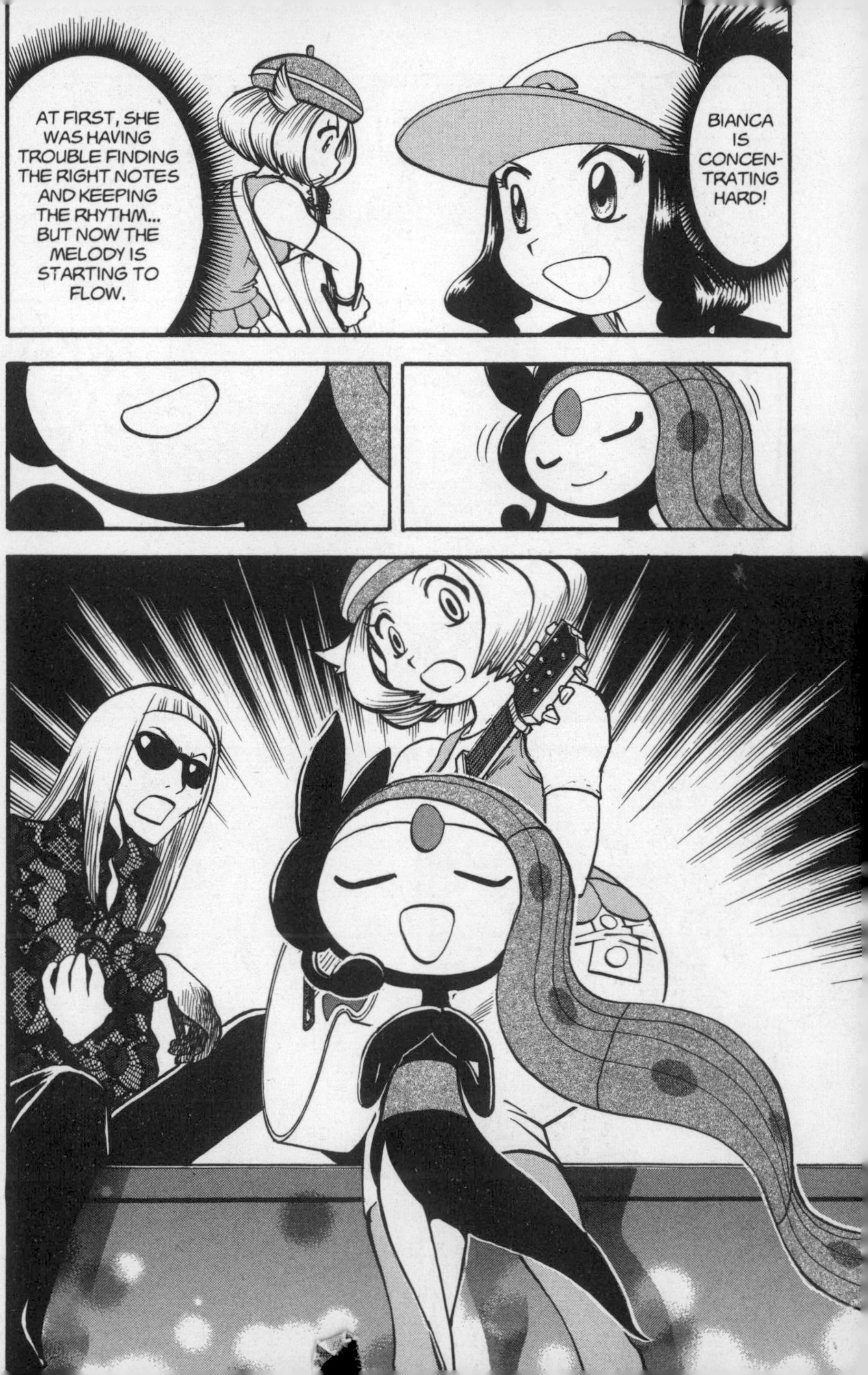
BIANCA IS CONCEN-TRATING HARD!
AT FIRST, SHE WAS HAVING TROUBLE FINDING THE RIGHT NOTES AND KEEPING THE RHYTHM... BUT NOW THE MELODY IS STARTING TO FLOW.

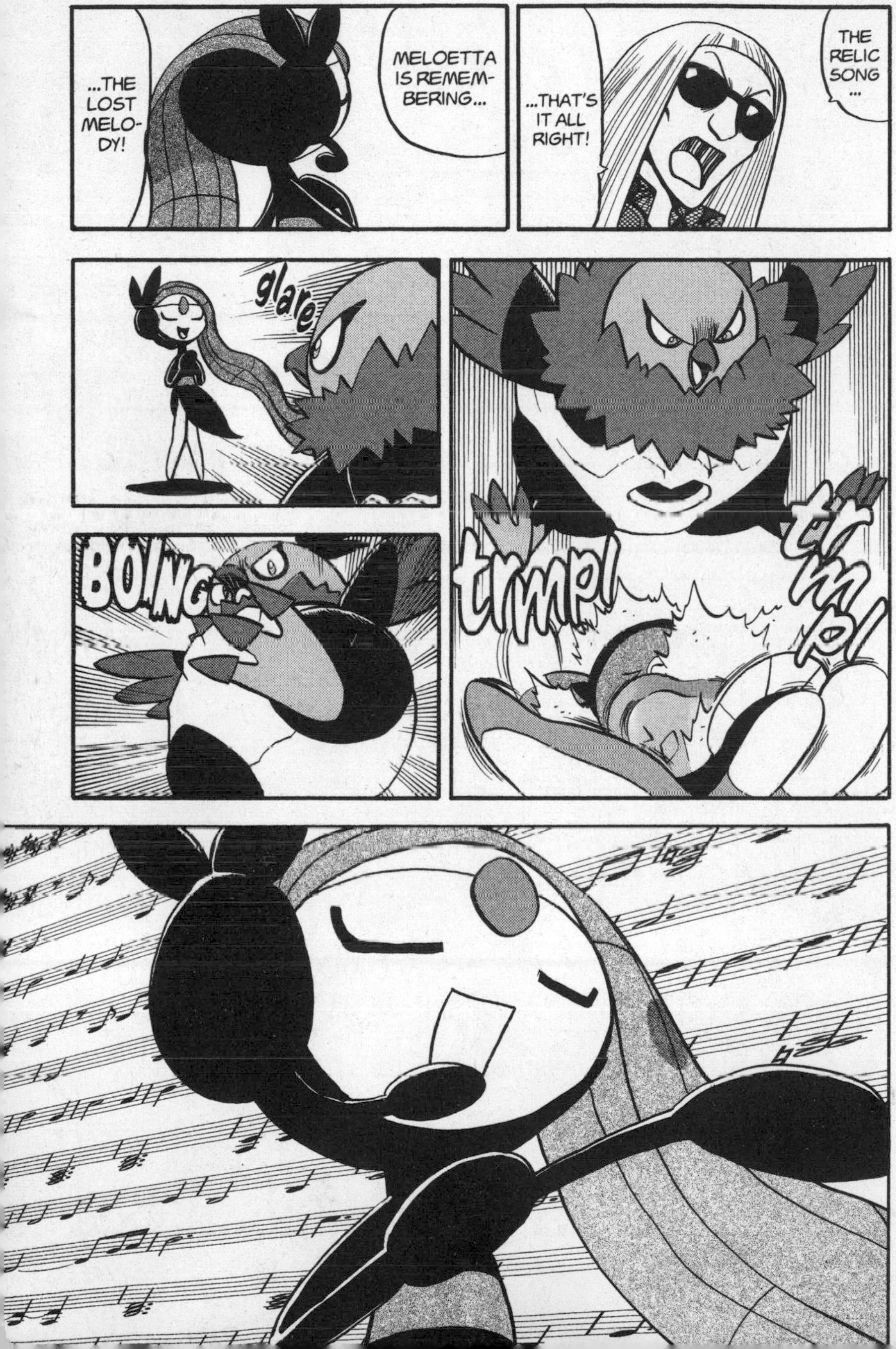
THE RELIC SONG...
...THAT'S IT ALL RIGHT!
MELOETTA IS REMEM-BERING...
...THE LOST MELO-DY!
trmpl!
trmpl!
glare
BOING

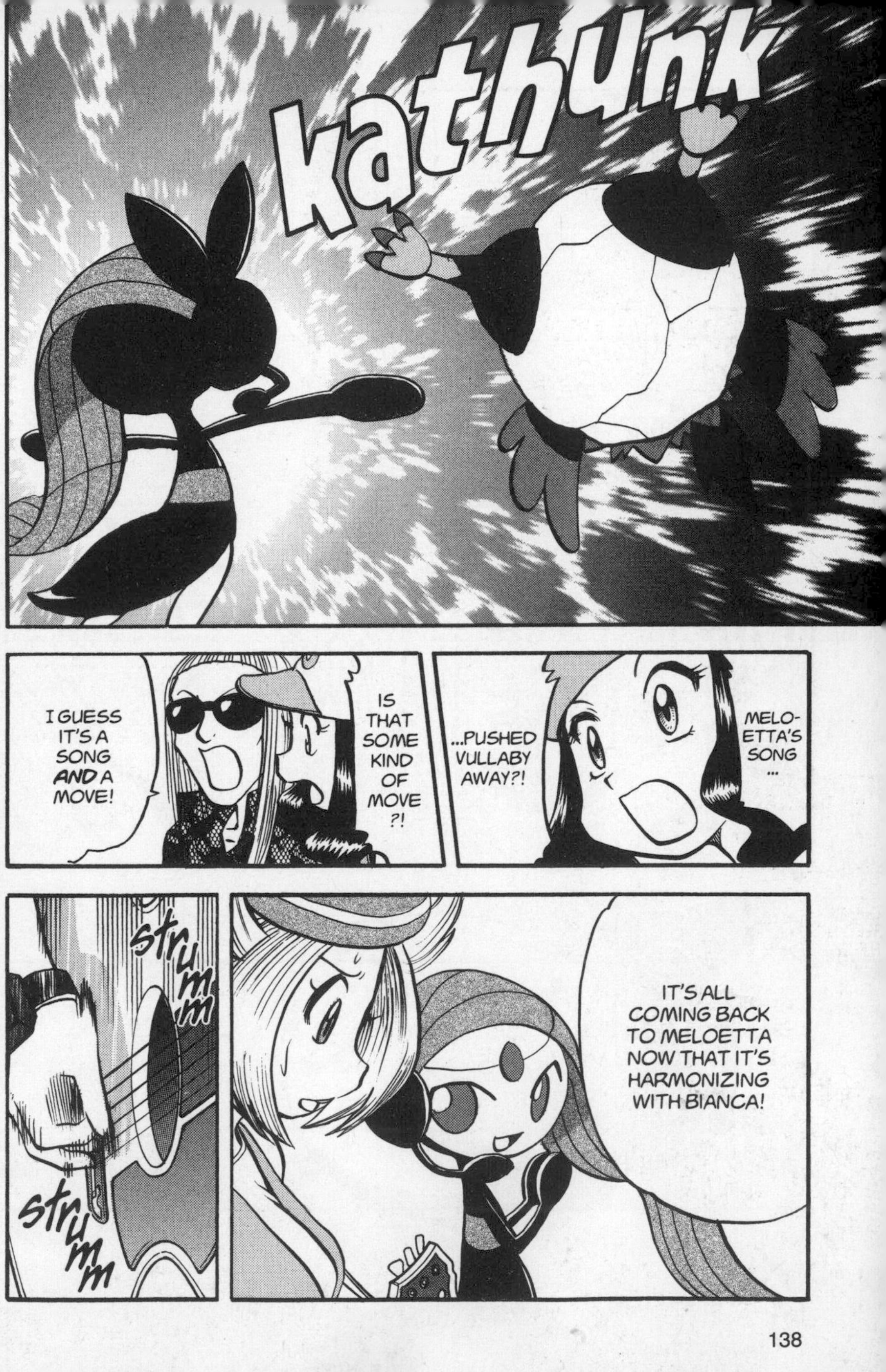
kathunk
MELOETTA'S SONG ...
...PUSHED VULLABY AWAY?!
IS THAT SOME KIND OF MOVE ?!
I GUESS IT'S A SONG **AND** A MOVE!
IT'S ALL COMING BACK TO MELOETTA NOW THAT IT'S HARMONIZING WITH BIANCA!
strumm
strumm

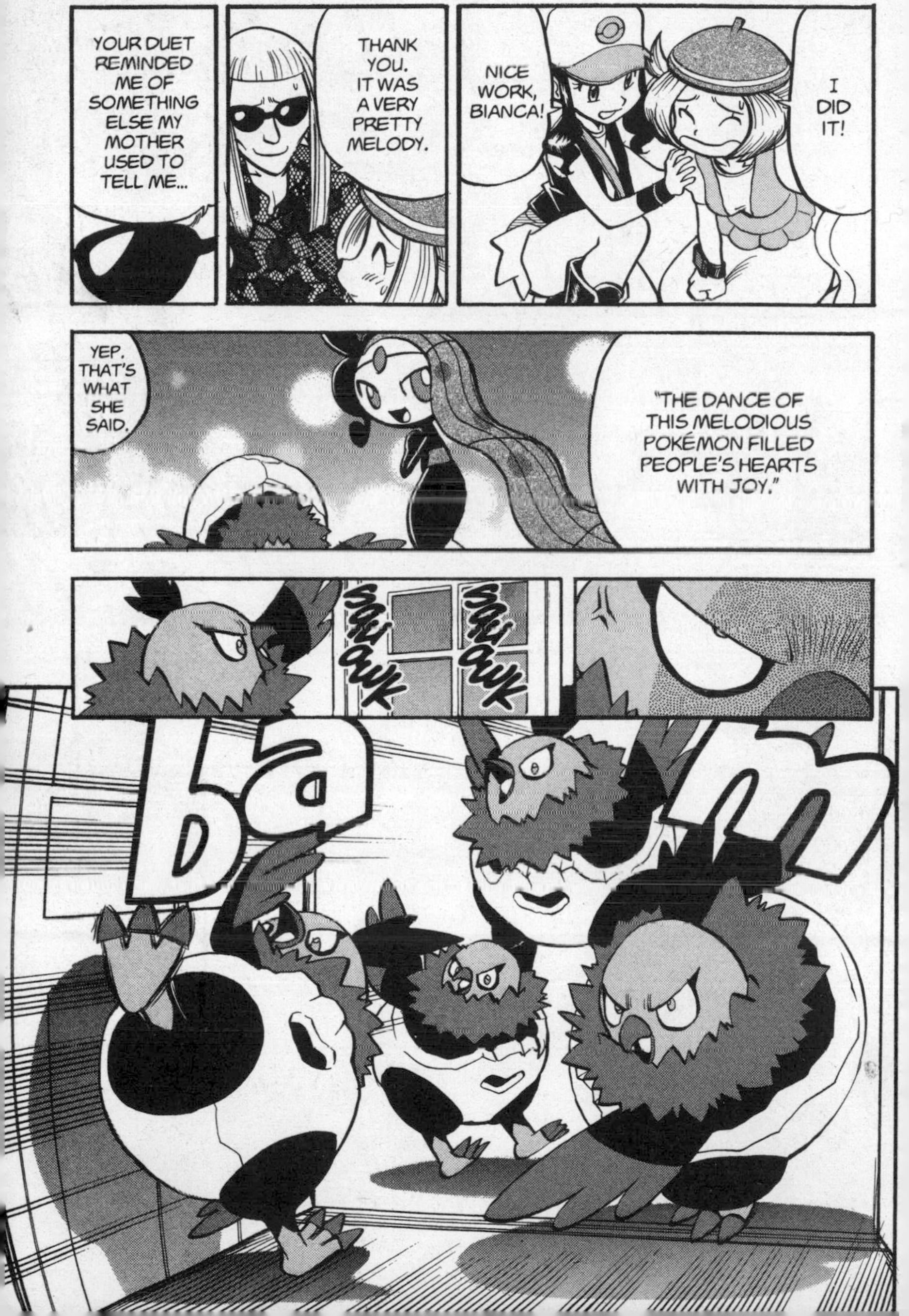
I DID IT!
NICE WORK, BIANCA!
THANK YOU. IT WAS A VERY PRETTY MELODY.
YOUR DUET REMINDED ME OF SOMETHING ELSE MY MOTHER USED TO TELL ME...
"THE DANCE OF THIS MELODIOUS POKÉMON FILLED PEOPLE'S HEARTS WITH JOY."
YEP. THAT'S WHAT SHE SAID.
SQUAWK
SQUAWK
BAM

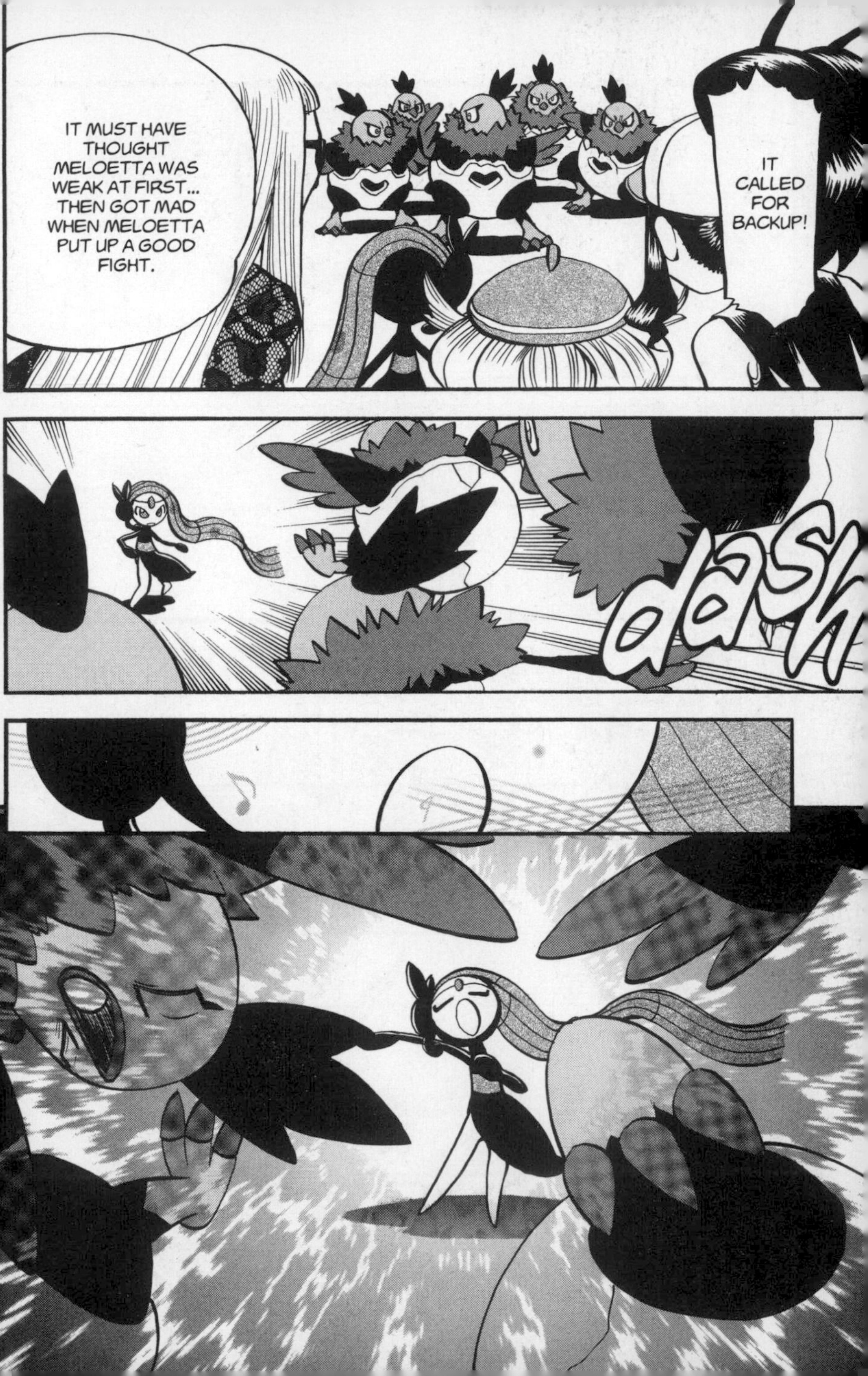
IT CALLED FOR BACKUP!
IT MUST HAVE THOUGHT MELOETTA WAS WEAK AT FIRST... THEN GOT MAD WHEN MELOETTA PUT UP A GOOD FIGHT.
dash

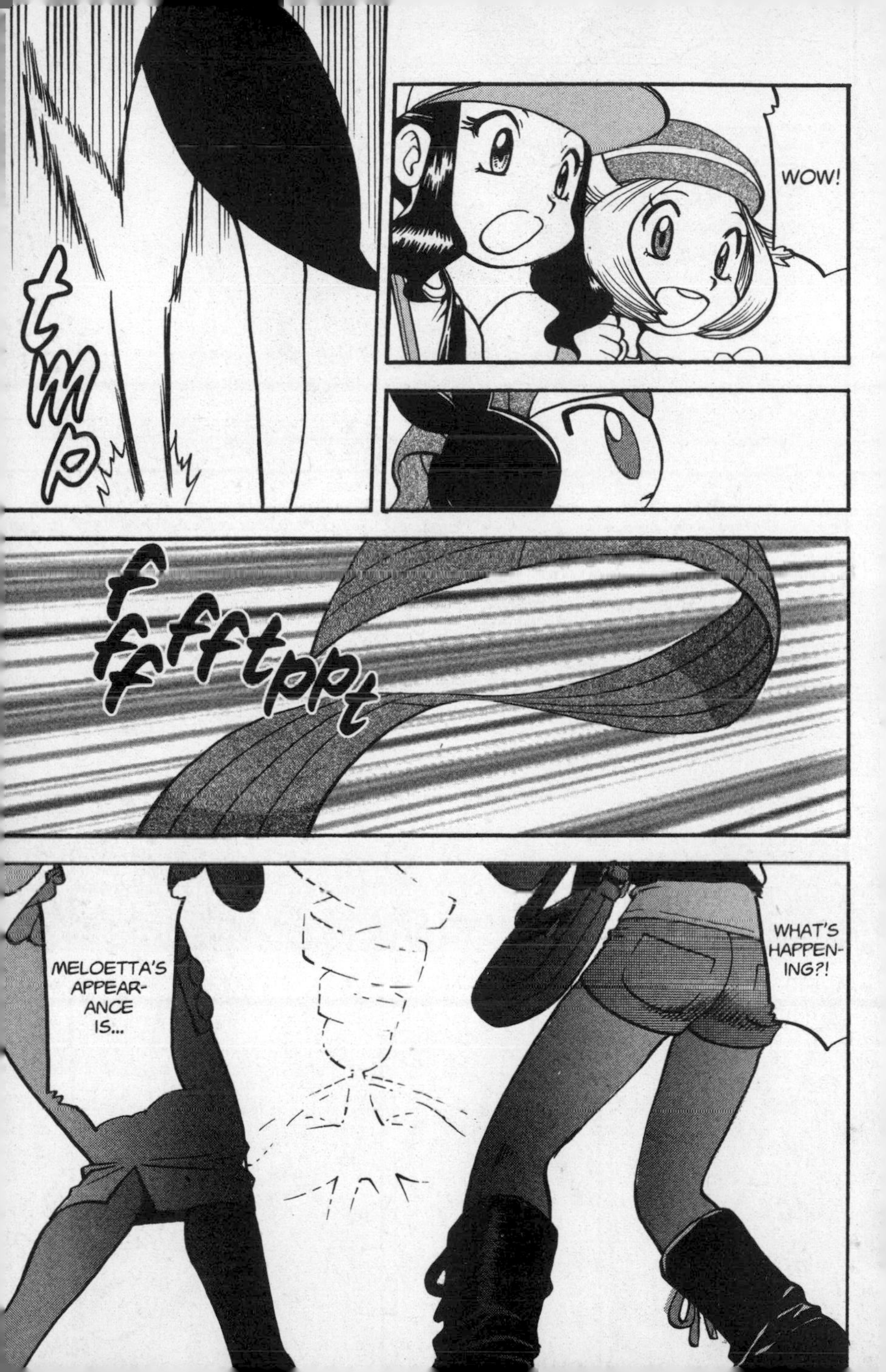
WOW!
tmp
fffftppt
WHAT'S HAPPEN-ING?!
MELOETTA'S APPEAR-ANCE IS...

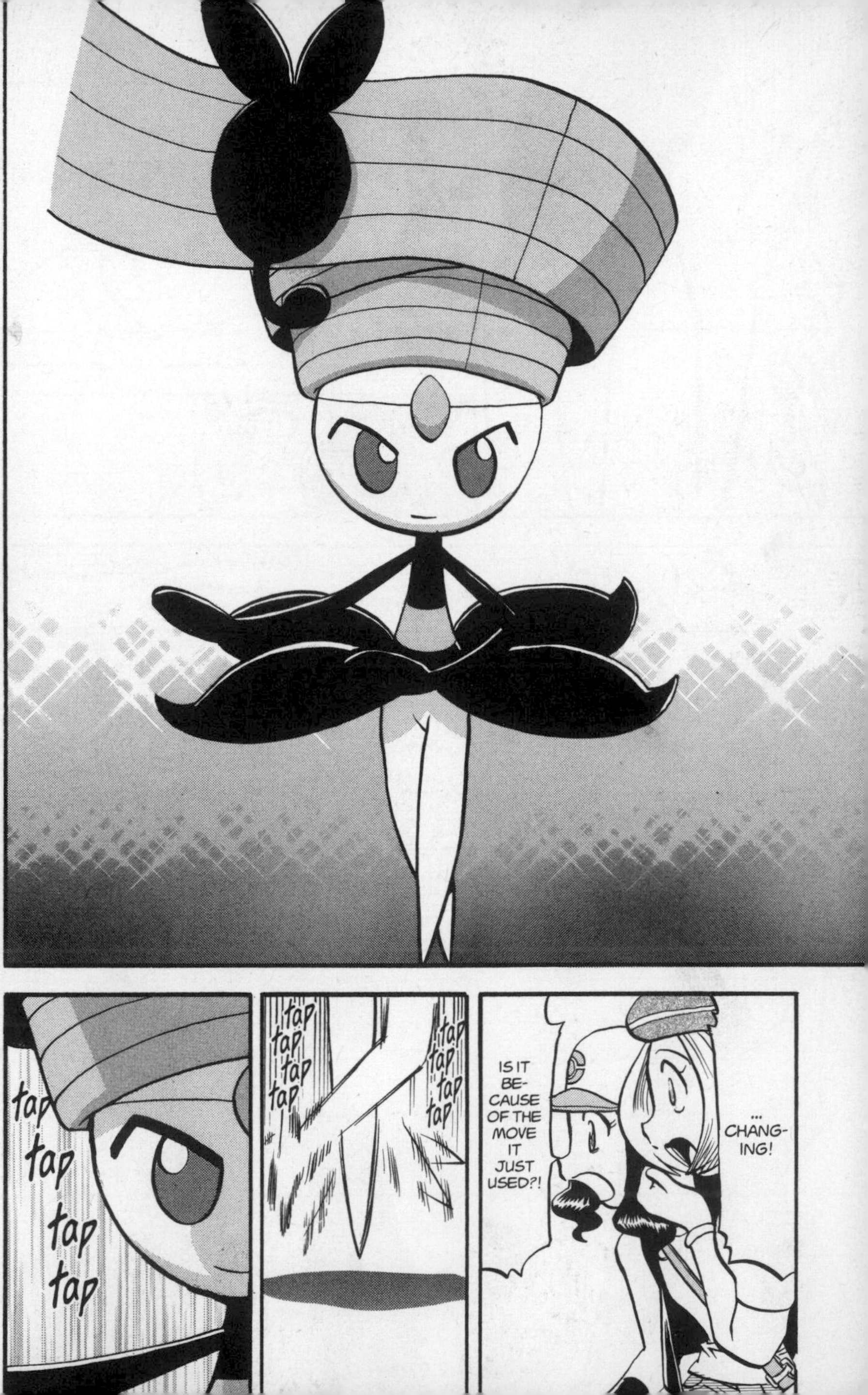
...CHANG-ING!
IS IT BE-CAUSE OF THE MOVE IT JUST USED?!
tap tap tap tap
tap tap tap tap
tap tap tap tap

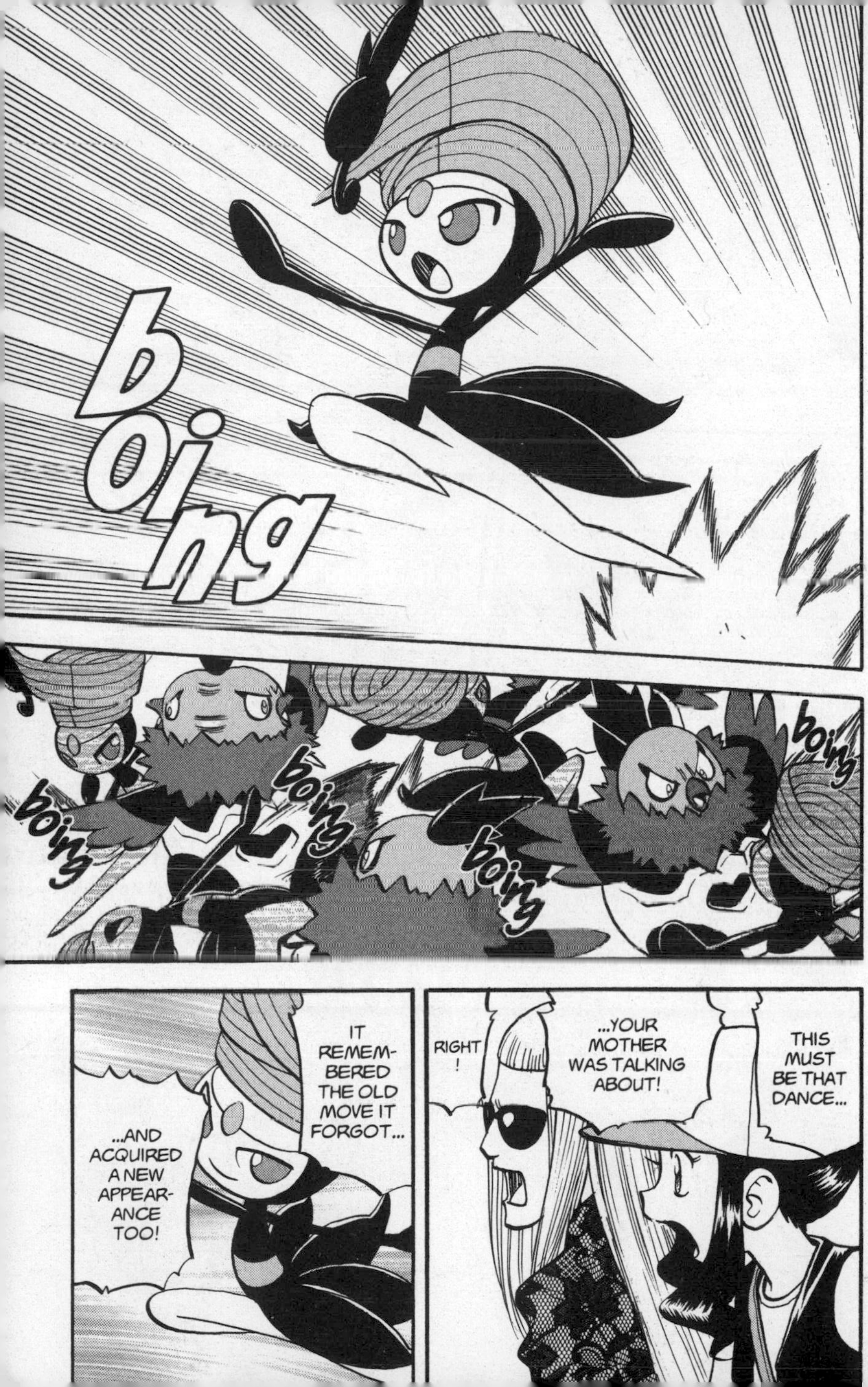
boing
boing
boing
boing
boing
THIS MUST BE THAT DANCE...
...YOUR MOTHER WAS TALKING ABOUT!
RIGHT!
IT REMEMBERED THE OLD MOVE IT FORGOT...
...AND ACQUIRED A NEW APPEARANCE TOO!

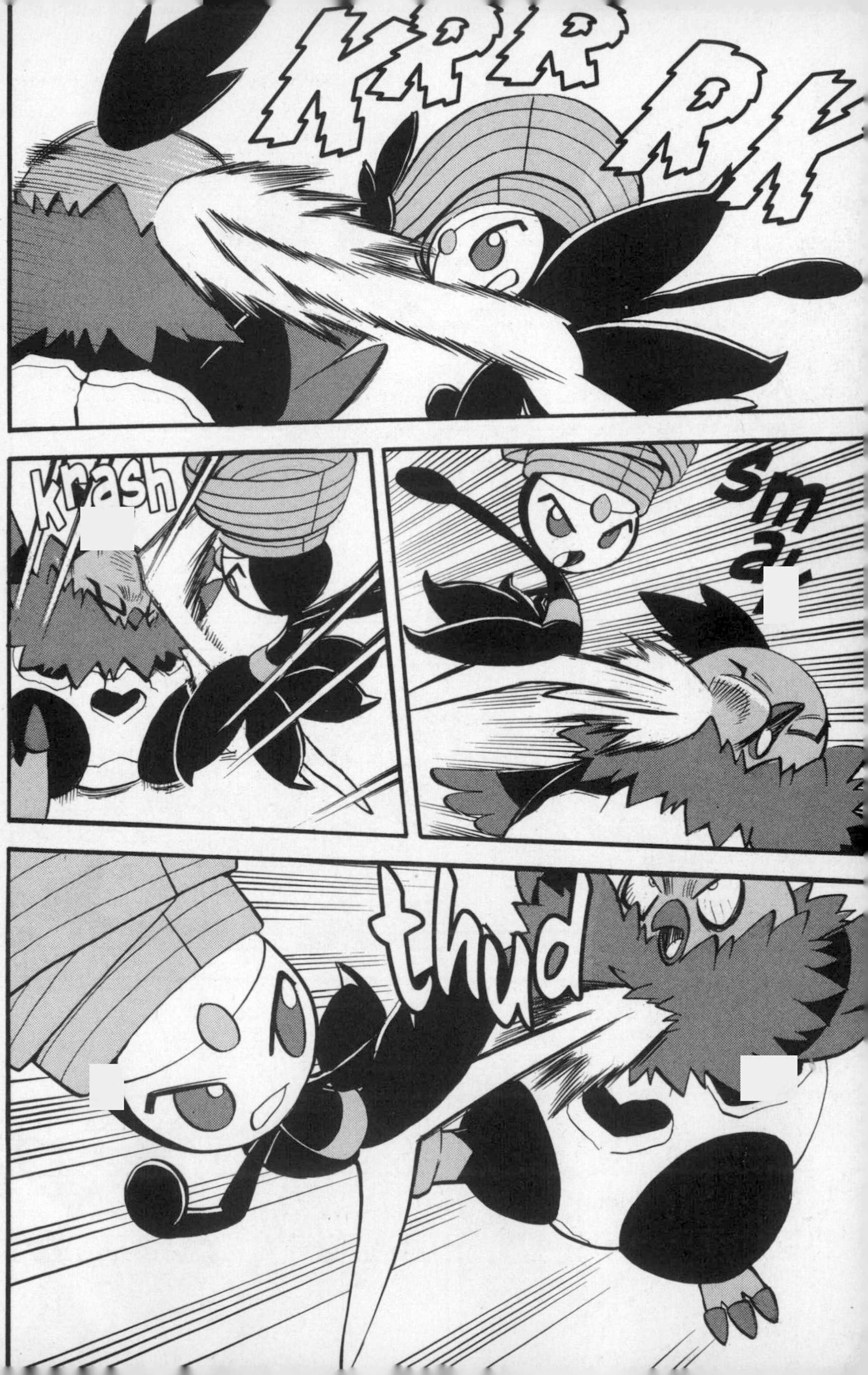
KRRRI
sma
krash
thud

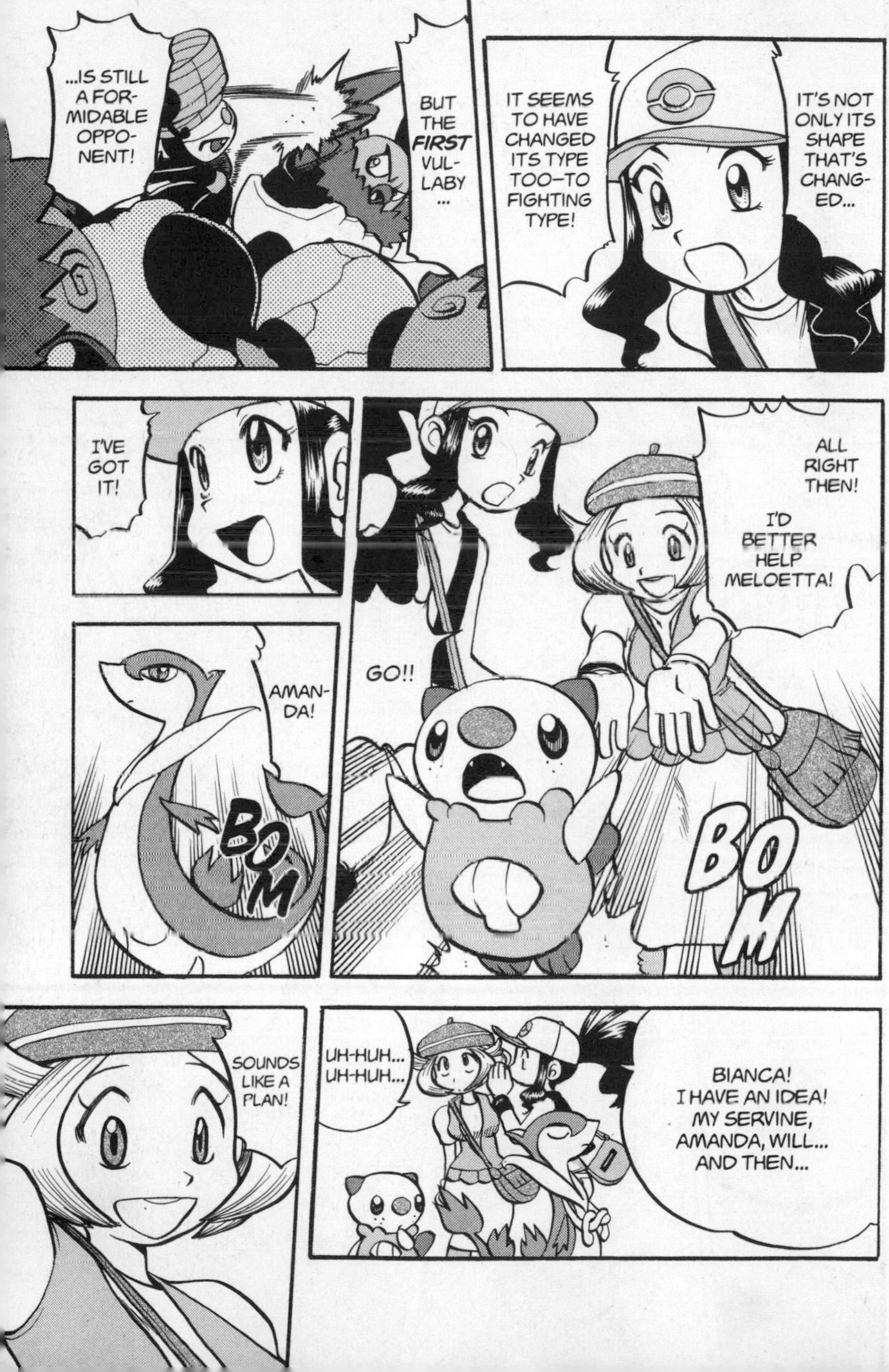

IT'S NOT ONLY ITS SHAPE THAT'S CHANGED...
IT SEEMS TO HAVE CHANGED ITS TYPE TOO—TO FIGHTING TYPE!
BUT THE FIRST VULLABY...
...IS STILL A FORMIDABLE OPPONENT!
ALL RIGHT THEN!
I'D BETTER HELP MELOETTA!
GO!!
BOM
I'VE GOT IT!
AMANDA!
BOM
BIANCA! I HAVE AN IDEA! MY SERVINE, AMANDA, WILL... AND THEN...
UH-HUH... UH-HUH...
SOUNDS LIKE A PLAN!

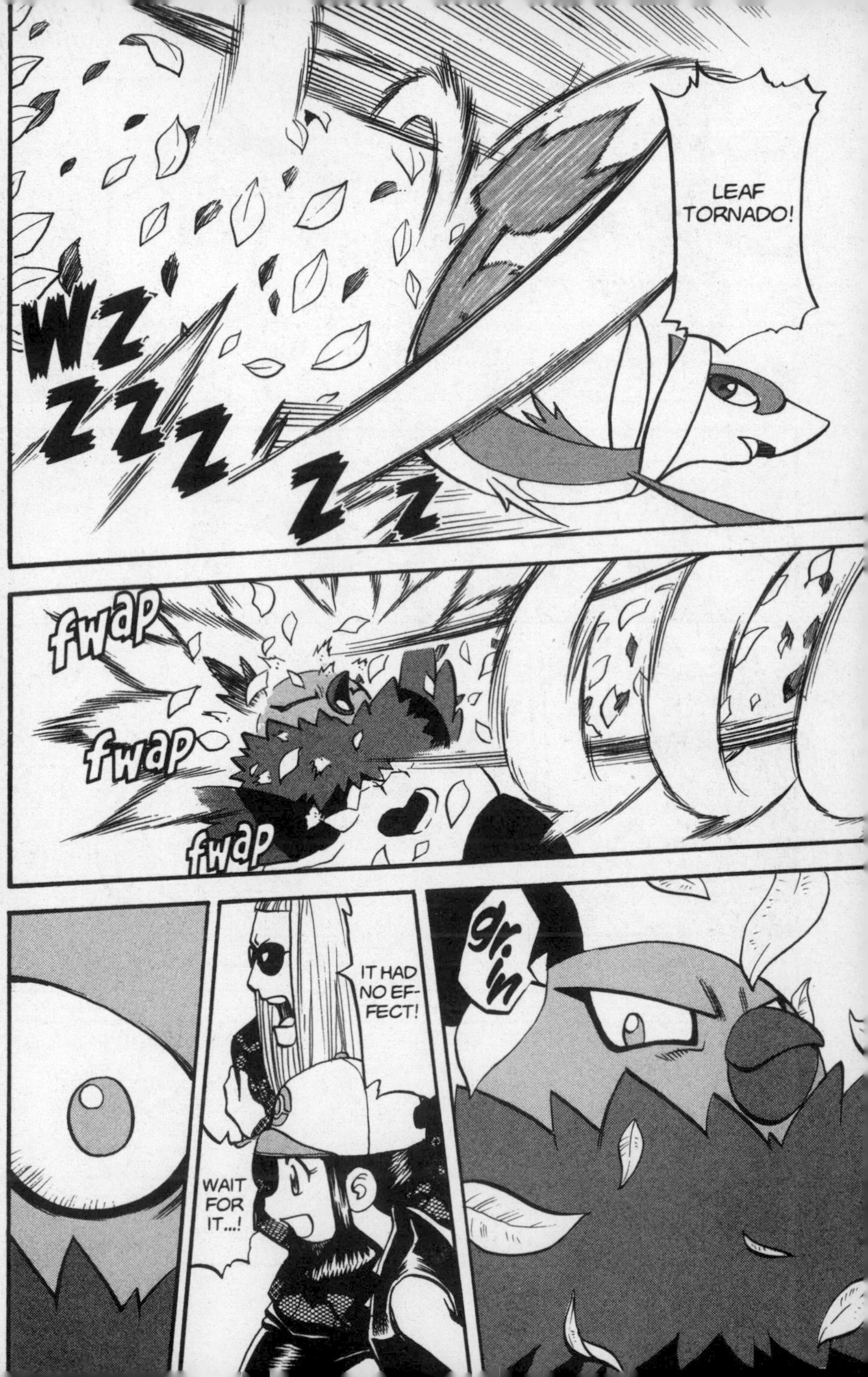
LEAF TORNADO!
WZZZZZZ
fwap
fwap
fwap
grin
IT HAD NO EF-FECT!
WAIT FOR IT...!

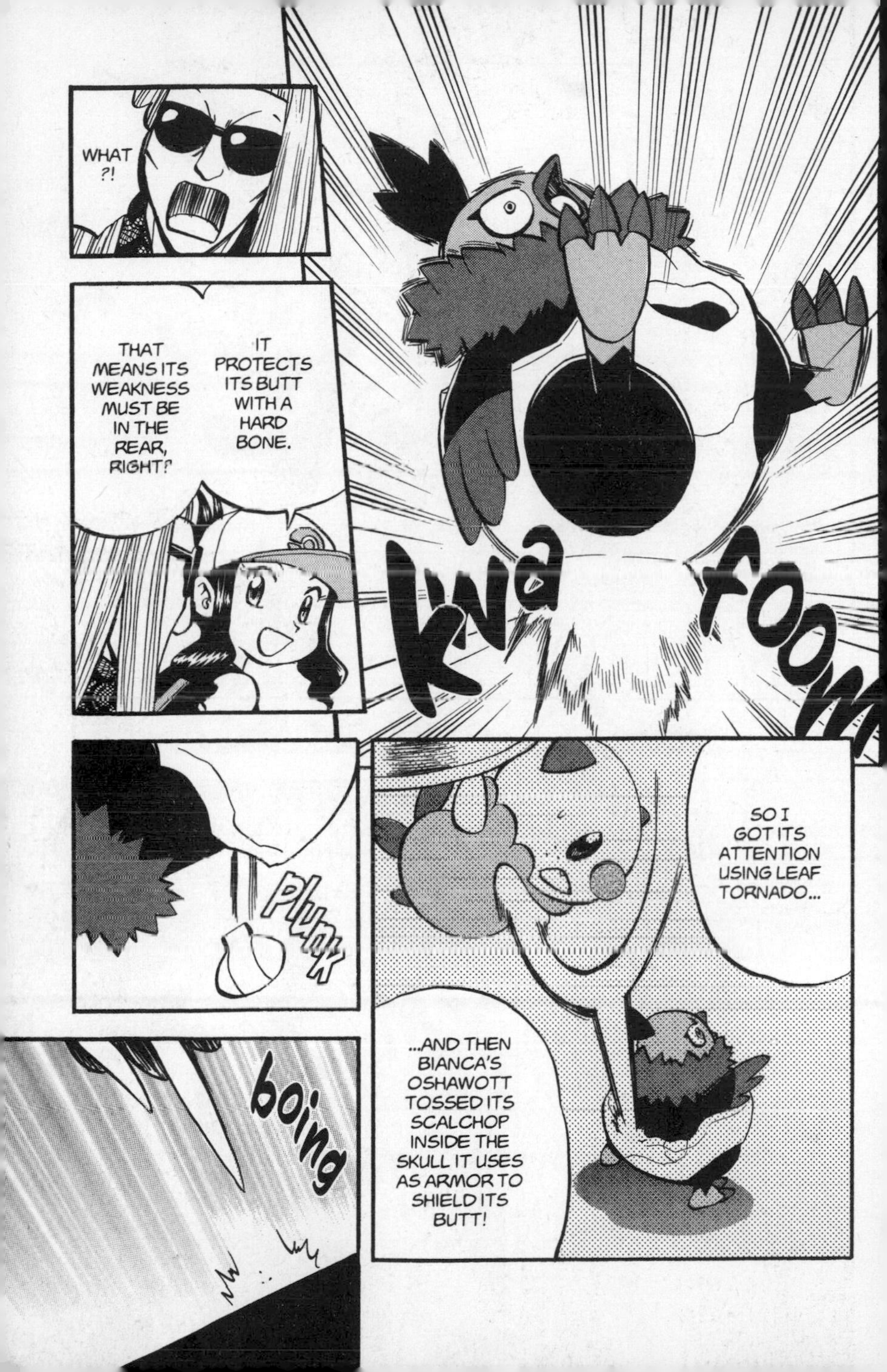
kwa
foom
WHAT ?!
IT PROTECTS ITS BUTT WITH A HARD BONE.
THAT MEANS ITS WEAKNESS MUST BE IN THE REAR, RIGHT?
SO I GOT ITS ATTENTION USING LEAF TORNADO...
...AND THEN BIANCA'S OSHAWOTT TOSSED ITS SCALCHOP INSIDE THE SKULL IT USES AS ARMOR TO SHIELD ITS BUTT!
plunk
boing

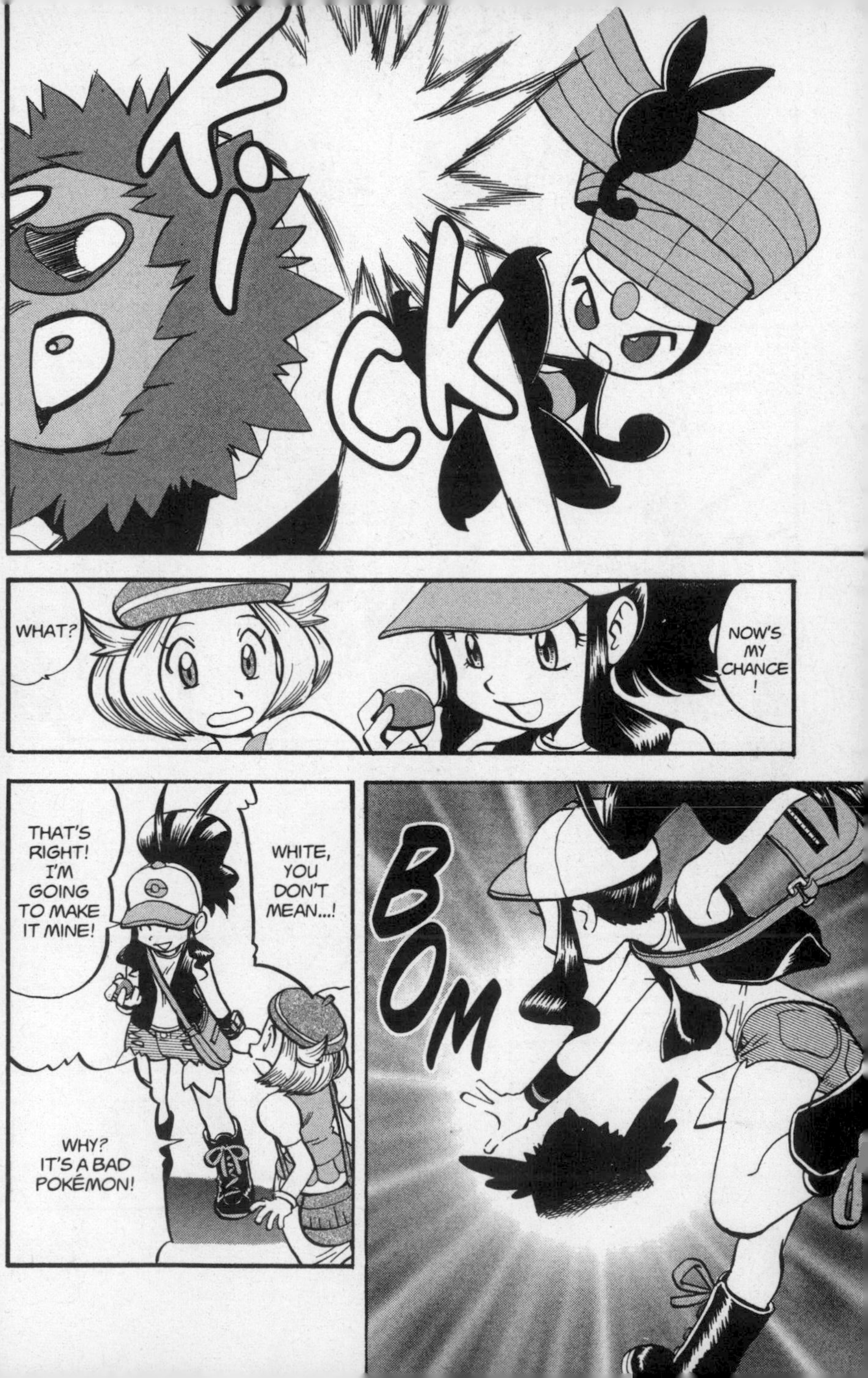
NOW'S MY CHANCE!
WHAT?
BOM
WHITE, YOU DON'T MEAN...!
THAT'S RIGHT! I'M GOING TO MAKE IT MINE!
WHY? IT'S A BAD POKÉMON!

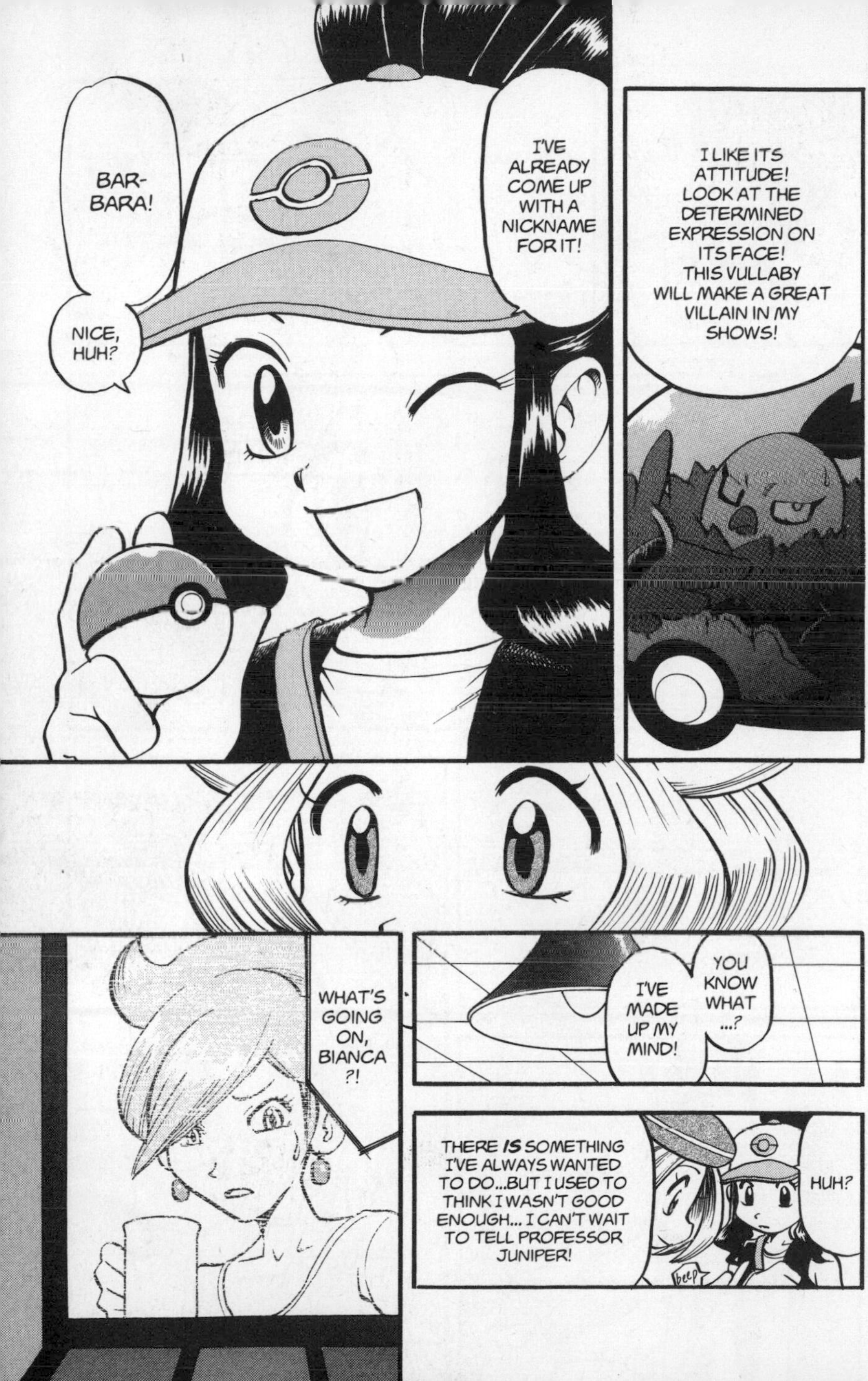
I LIKE ITS ATTITUDE! LOOK AT THE DETERMINED EXPRESSION ON ITS FACE! THIS VULLABY WILL MAKE A GREAT VILLAIN IN MY SHOWS!
I'VE ALREADY COME UP WITH A NICKNAME FOR IT!
BAR-BARA!
NICE, HUH?
YOU KNOW WHAT ...?
I'VE MADE UP MY MIND!
HUH?
THERE ***IS*** SOMETHING I'VE ALWAYS WANTED TO DO...BUT I USED TO THINK I WASN'T GOOD ENOUGH... I CAN'T WAIT TO TELL PROFESSOR JUNIPER!
beep
WHAT'S GOING ON, BIANCA ?!

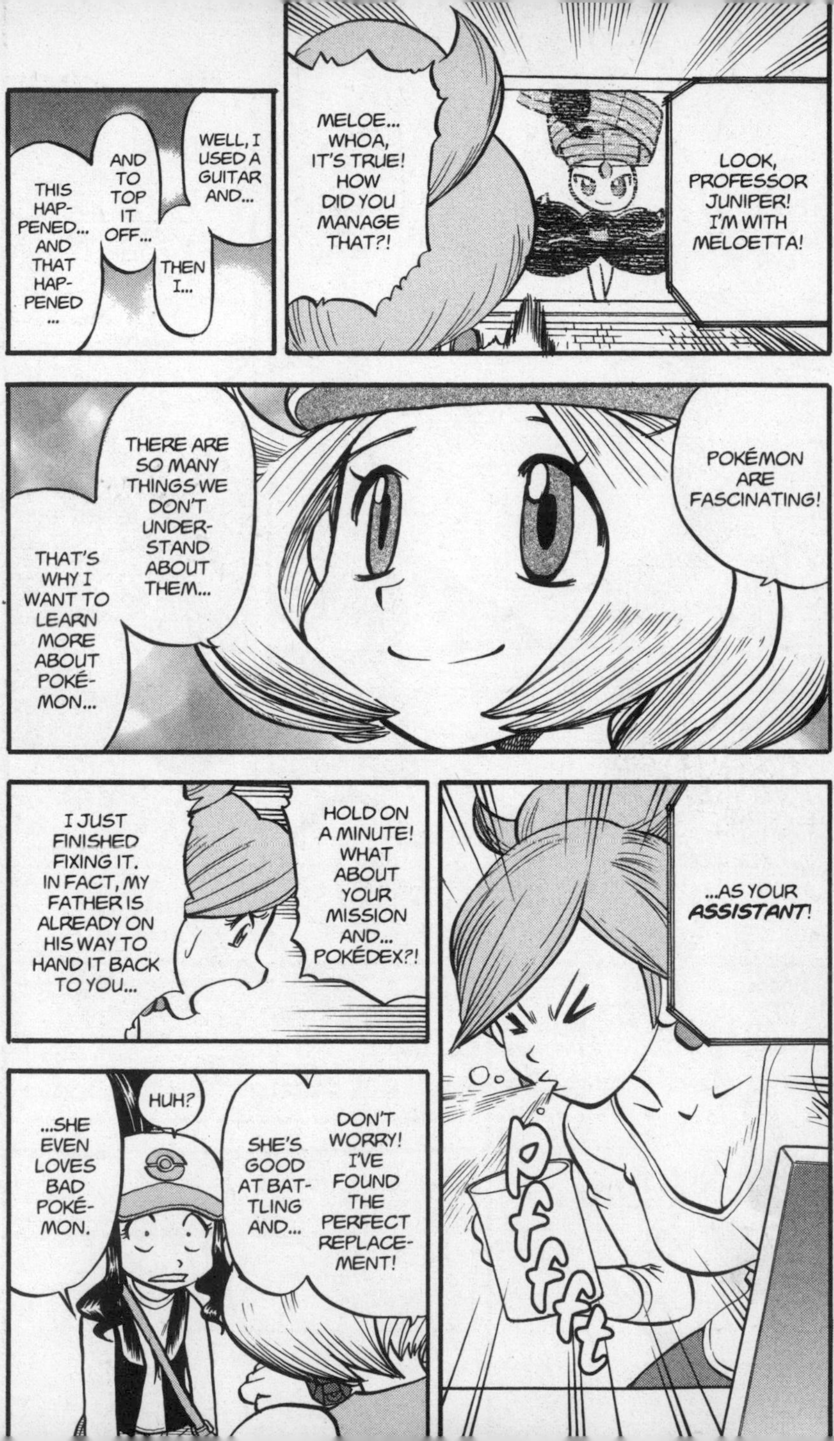
LOOK, PROFESSOR JUNIPER! I'M WITH MELOETTA!
MELOE... WHOA, IT'S TRUE! HOW DID YOU MANAGE THAT?!
WELL, I USED A GUITAR AND...
AND TO TOP IT OFF...
THEN I...
THIS HAP-PENED... AND THAT HAP-PENED...
POKÉMON ARE FASCINATING!
THERE ARE SO MANY THINGS WE DON'T UNDER-STAND ABOUT THEM...
THAT'S WHY I WANT TO LEARN MORE ABOUT POKÉ-MON...
...AS YOUR ***ASSISTANT***!
pfffft
HOLD ON A MINUTE! WHAT ABOUT YOUR MISSION AND... POKÉDEX?!
I JUST FINISHED FIXING IT. IN FACT, MY FATHER IS ALREADY ON HIS WAY TO HAND IT BACK TO YOU...
DON'T WORRY! I'VE FOUND THE PERFECT REPLACE-MENT!
SHE'S GOOD AT BAT-TLING AND...
HUH?
...SHE EVEN LOVES BAD POKÉ-MON.

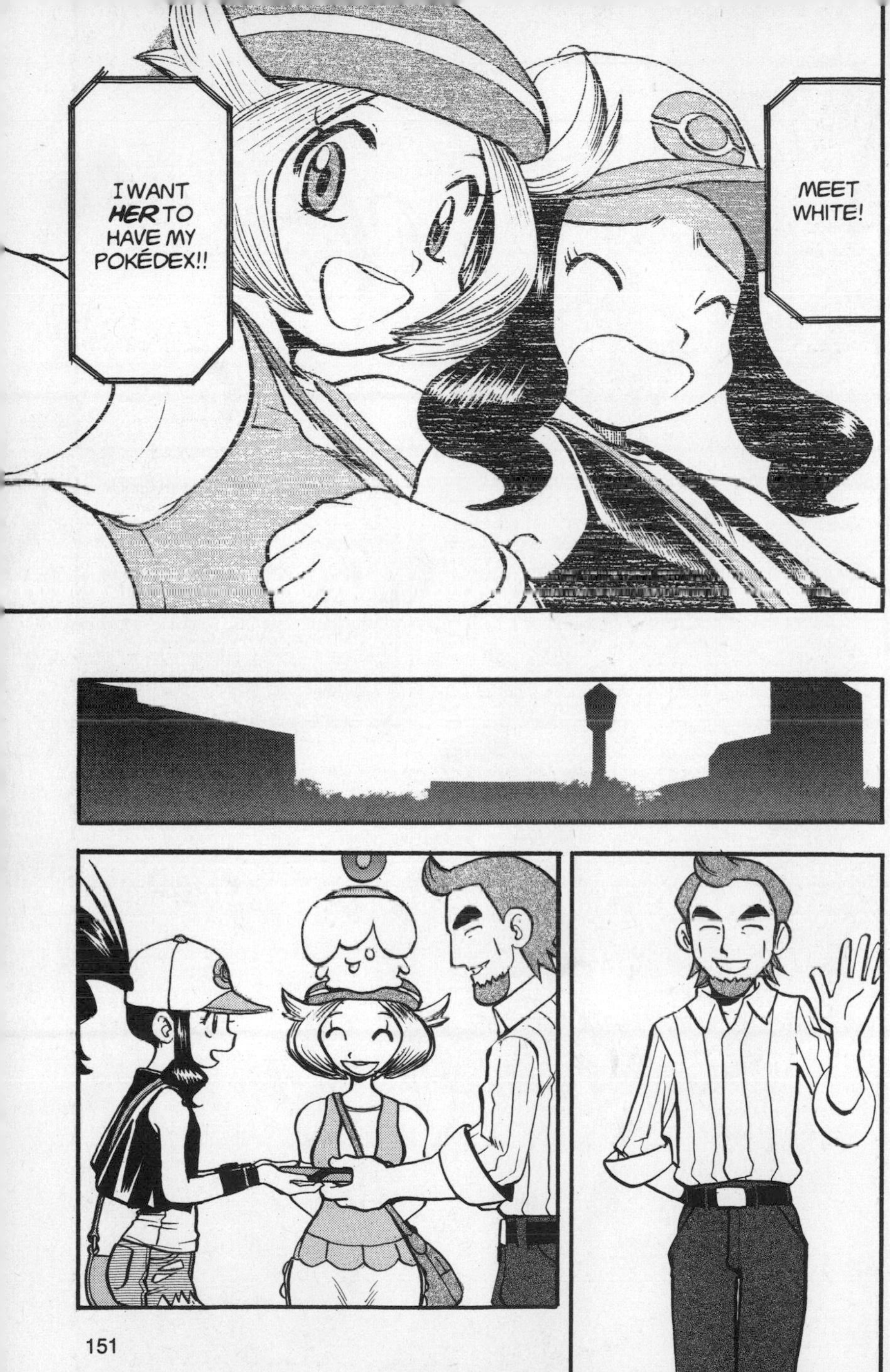
MEET WHITE!
I WANT HER TO HAVE MY POKÉDEX!!

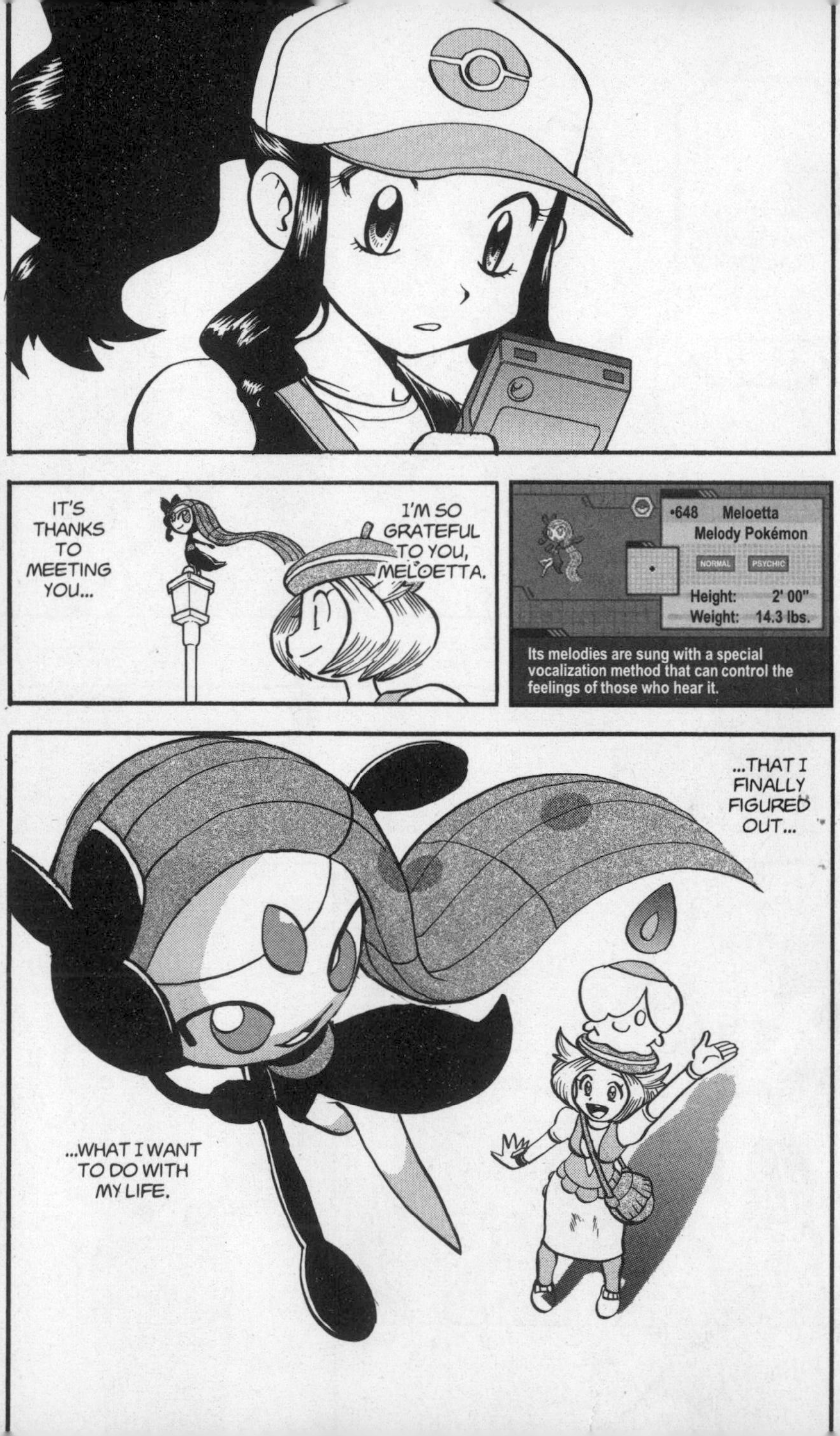
•648 Meloetta
Melody Pokémon
NORMAL
PSYCHIC
Height: 2' 00"
Weight: 14.3 lbs.
Its melodies are sung with a special vocalization method that can control the feelings of those who hear it.
I'M SO GRATEFUL TO YOU, MELOETTA.
IT'S THANKS TO MEETING YOU...
...THAT I FINALLY FIGURED OUT...
...WHAT I WANT TO DO WITH MY LIFE.

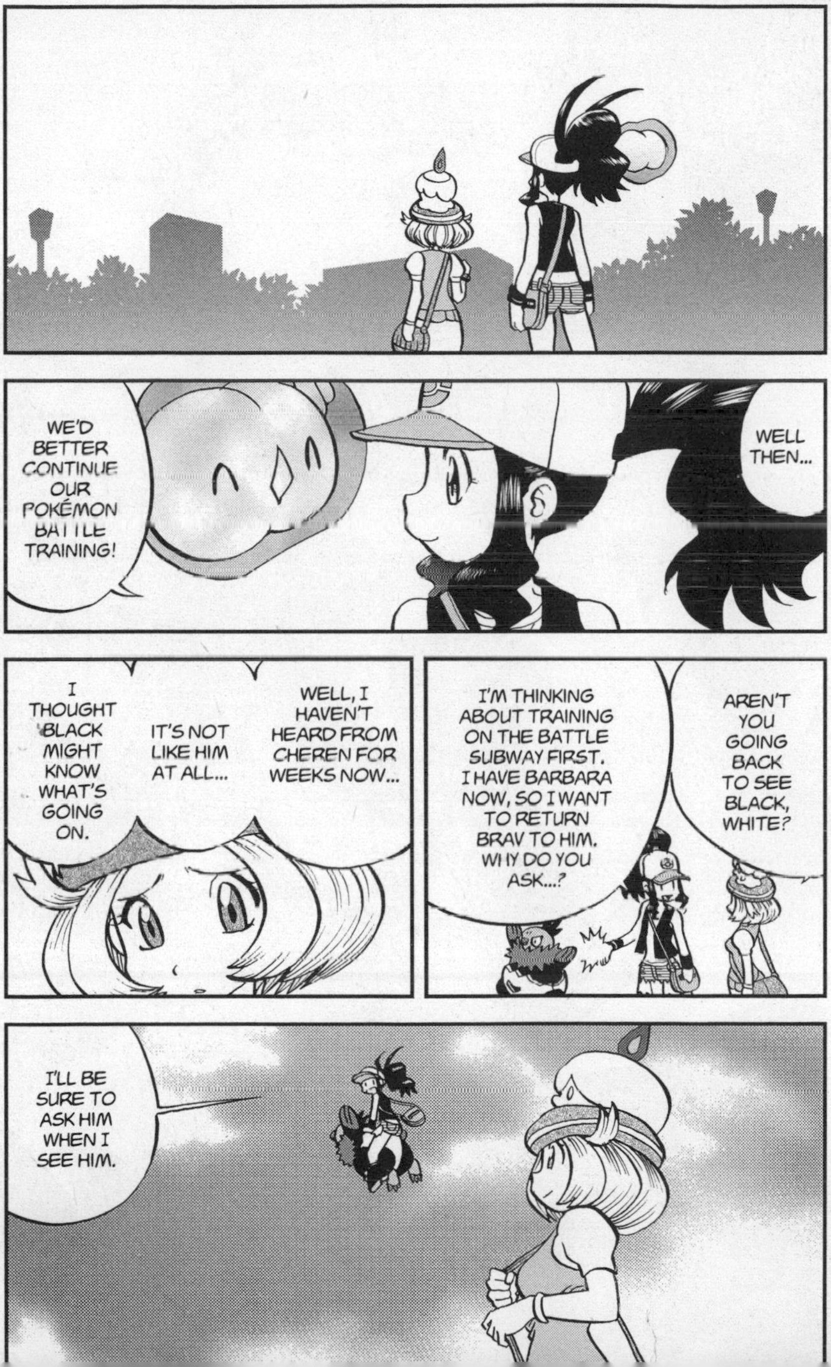
WELL THEN...
WE'D BETTER CONTINUE OUR POKÉMON BATTLE TRAINING!
AREN'T YOU GOING BACK TO SEE BLACK, WHITE?
I'M THINKING ABOUT TRAINING ON THE BATTLE SUBWAY FIRST. I HAVE BARBARA NOW, SO I WANT TO RETURN BRAV TO HIM. WHY DO YOU ASK...?
WELL, I HAVEN'T HEARD FROM CHEREN FOR WEEKS NOW...
IT'S NOT LIKE HIM AT ALL...
I THOUGHT BLACK MIGHT KNOW WHAT'S GOING ON.
I'LL BE SURE TO ASK HIM WHEN I SEE HIM.

POKÉMON™ ADVENTURES BLACK & WHITE

RUFFLET

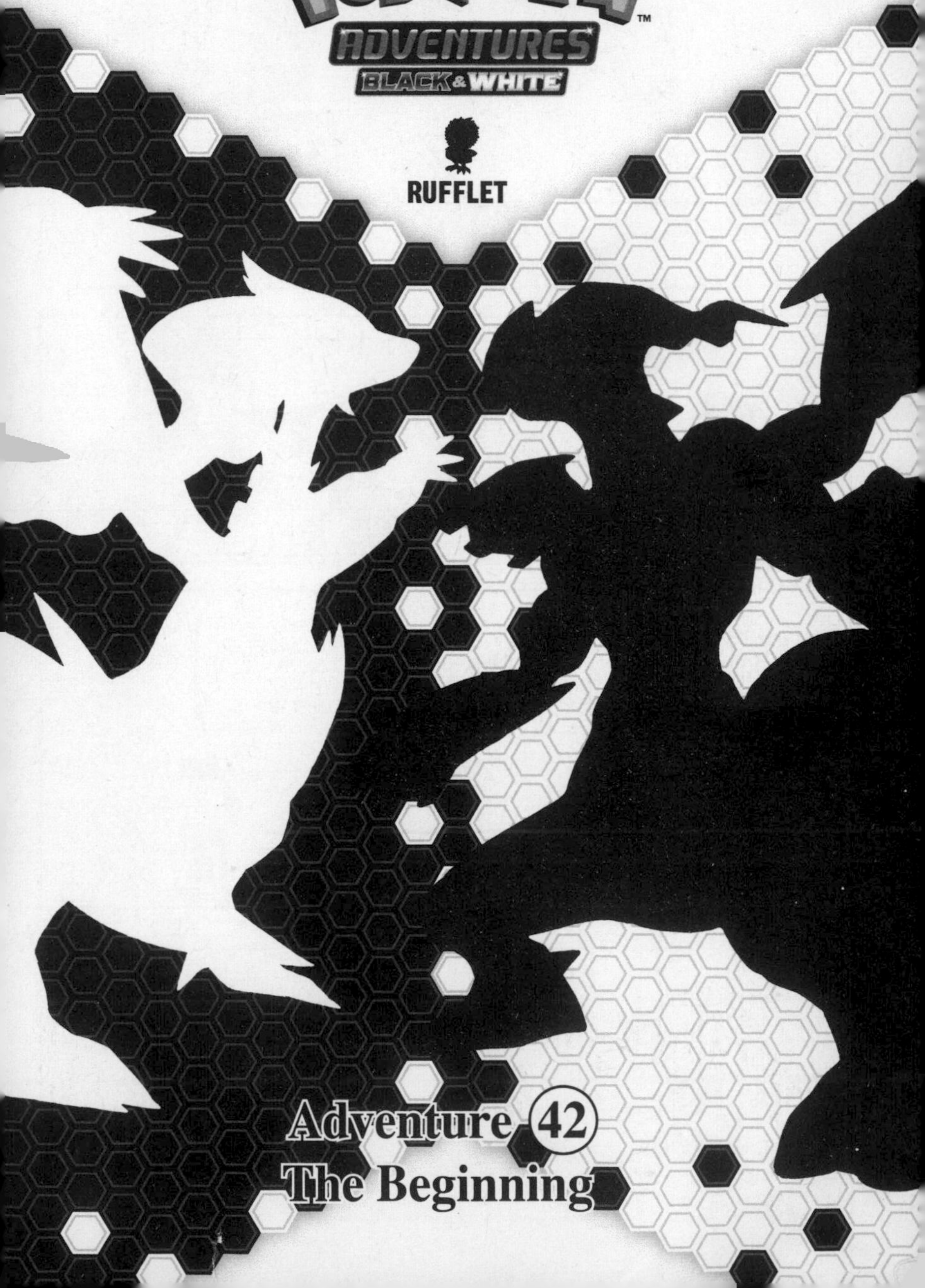

Adventure 42
The Beginning

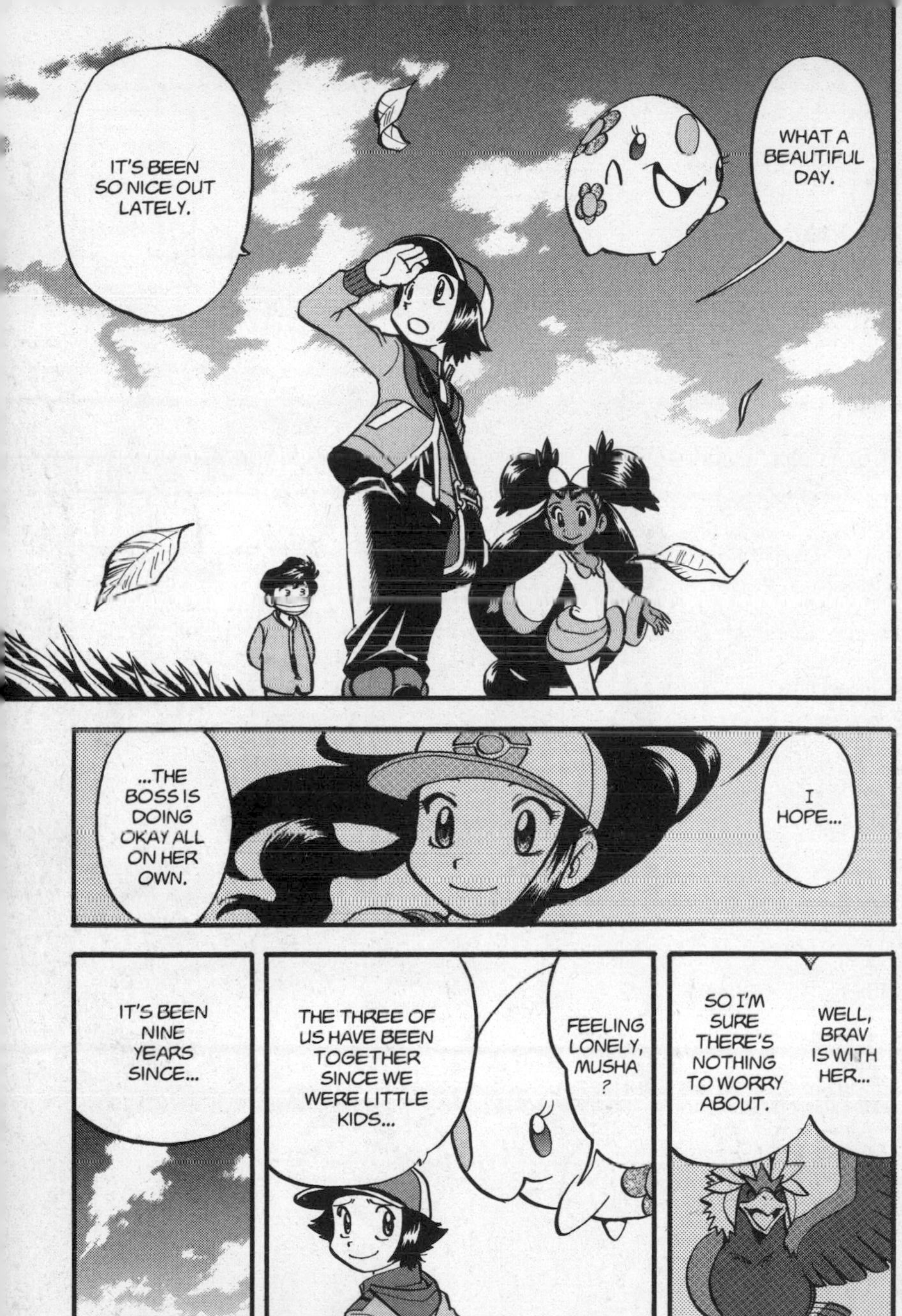
WHAT A BEAUTIFUL DAY.
IT'S BEEN SO NICE OUT LATELY.
I HOPE...
...THE BOSS IS DOING OKAY ALL ON HER OWN.
WELL, BRAV IS WITH HER...
SO I'M SURE THERE'S NOTHING TO WORRY ABOUT.
FEELING LONELY, MUSHA?
THE THREE OF US HAVE BEEN TOGETHER SINCE WE WERE LITTLE KIDS...
IT'S BEEN NINE YEARS SINCE...

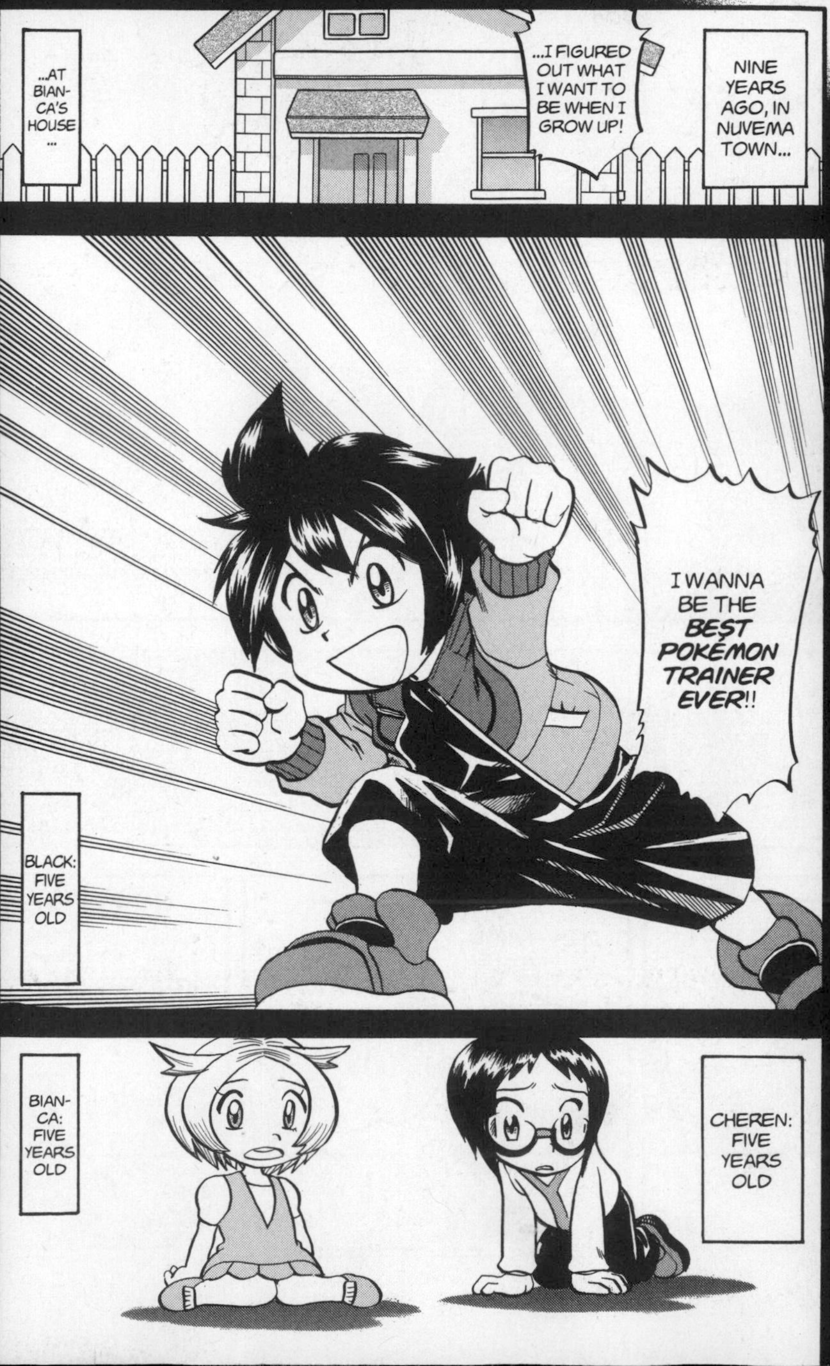
NINE YEARS AGO, IN NUVEMA TOWN...
...I FIGURED OUT WHAT I WANT TO BE WHEN I GROW UP!
...AT BIANCA'S HOUSE...
I WANNA BE THE ***BEST POKÉMON TRAINER EVER***!!
BLACK: FIVE YEARS OLD
CHEREN: FIVE YEARS OLD
BIANCA: FIVE YEARS OLD

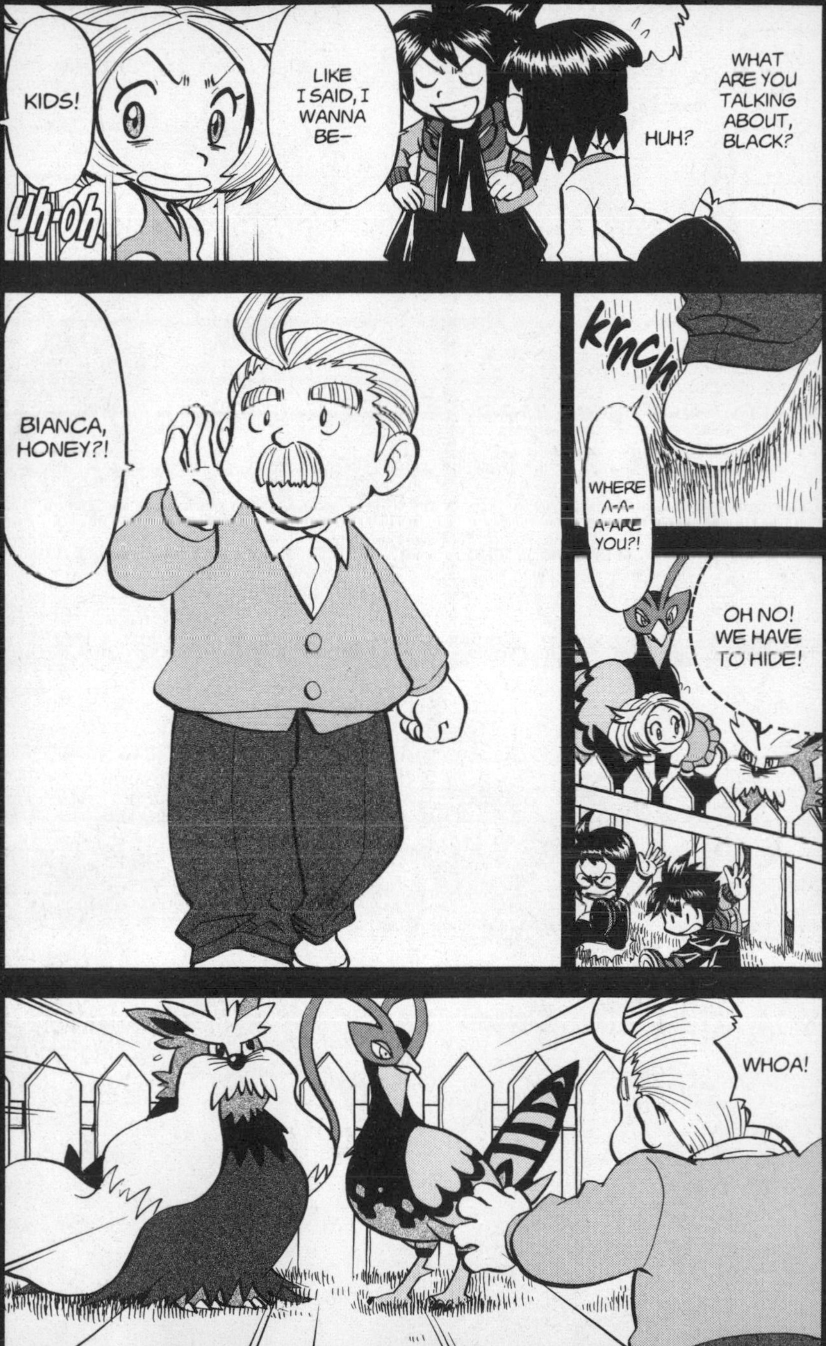
WHAT ARE YOU TALKING ABOUT, BLACK?
HUH?
LIKE I SAID, I WANNA BE–
KIDS!
uh-oh
krnch
WHERE A-A-ARE YOU?!
OH NO! WE HAVE TO HIDE!
BIANCA, HONEY?!
WHOA!

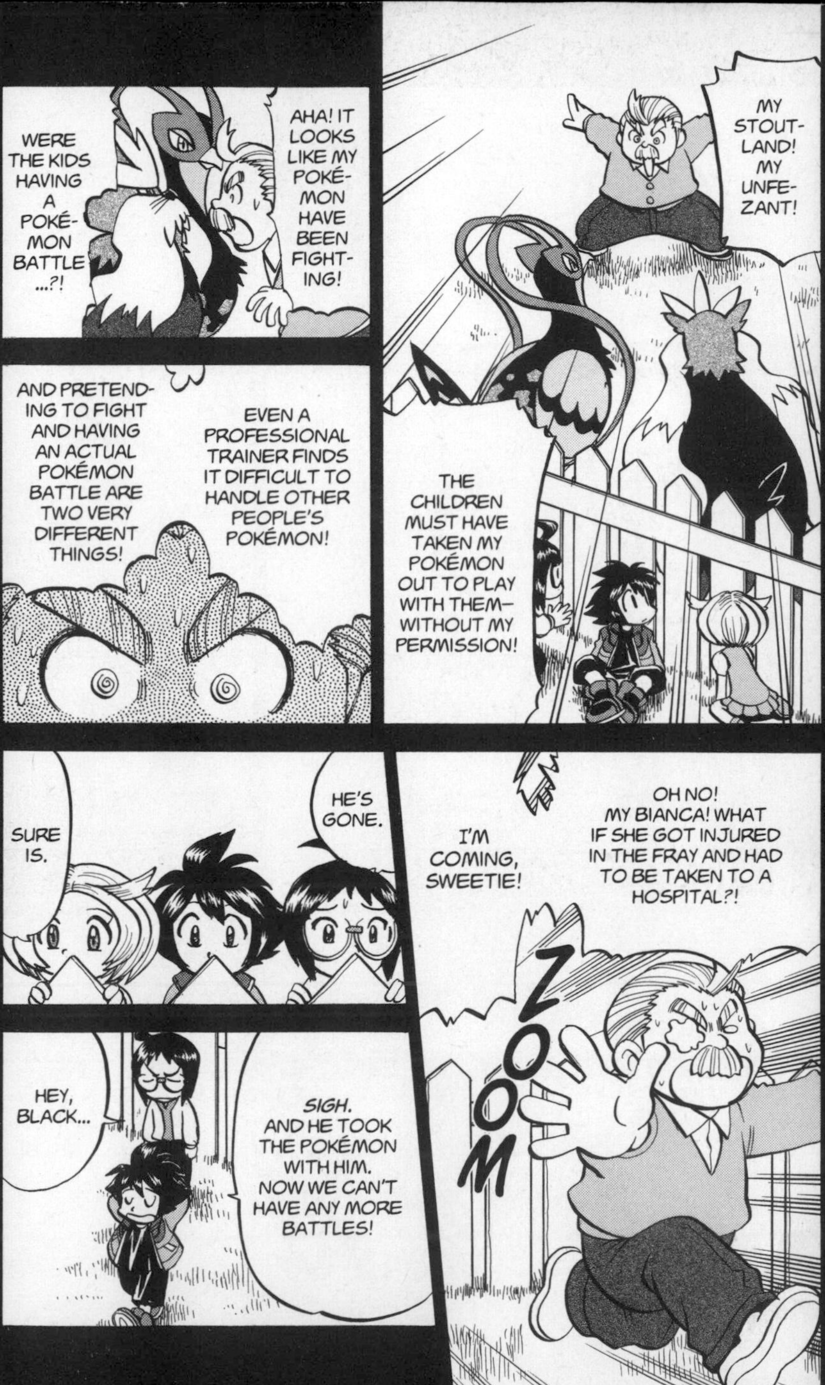
MY STOUT-LAND! MY UNFE-ZANT!
THE CHILDREN MUST HAVE TAKEN MY POKÉMON OUT TO PLAY WITH THEM—WITHOUT MY PERMISSION!
AHA! IT LOOKS LIKE MY POKÉ-MON HAVE BEEN FIGHT-ING!
WERE THE KIDS HAVING A POKÉ-MON BATTLE ...?!
EVEN A PROFESSIONAL TRAINER FINDS IT DIFFICULT TO HANDLE OTHER PEOPLE'S POKÉMON!
AND PRETEND-ING TO FIGHT AND HAVING AN ACTUAL POKÉMON BATTLE ARE TWO VERY DIFFERENT THINGS!
OH NO! MY BIANCA! WHAT IF SHE GOT INJURED IN THE FRAY AND HAD TO BE TAKEN TO A HOSPITAL?!
I'M COMING, SWEETIE!
ZOOM
HE'S GONE.
SURE IS.
SIGH. AND HE TOOK THE POKÉMON WITH HIM. NOW WE CAN'T HAVE ANY MORE BATTLES!
HEY, BLACK...

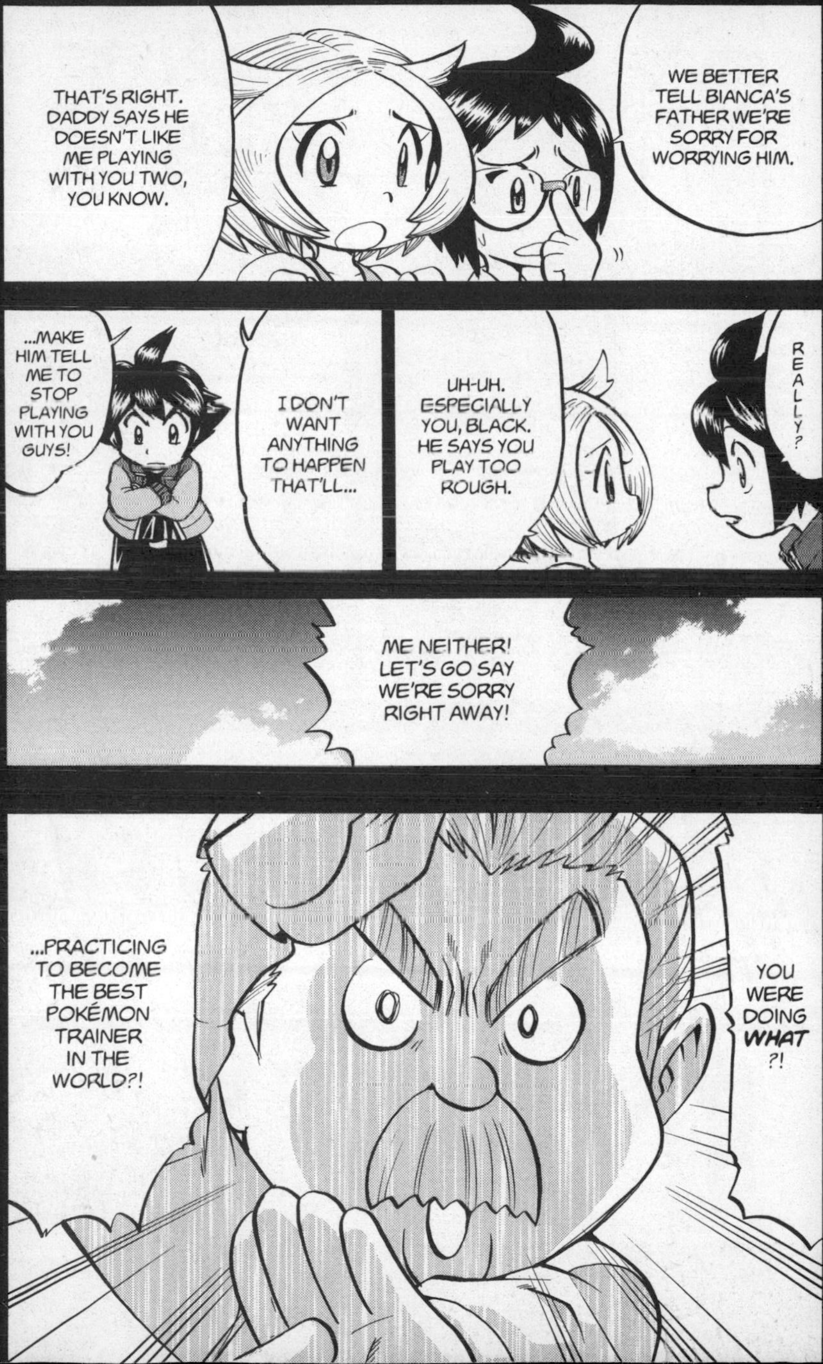
WE BETTER TELL BIANCA'S FATHER WE'RE SORRY FOR WORRYING HIM.
THAT'S RIGHT. DADDY SAYS HE DOESN'T LIKE ME PLAYING WITH YOU TWO, YOU KNOW.
REALLY?
UH-UH. ESPECIALLY YOU, BLACK. HE SAYS YOU PLAY TOO ROUGH.
I DON'T WANT ANYTHING TO HAPPEN THAT'LL...
...MAKE HIM TELL ME TO STOP PLAYING WITH YOU GUYS!
ME NEITHER! LET'S GO SAY WE'RE SORRY RIGHT AWAY!
YOU WERE DOING **WHAT**?!
...PRACTICING TO BECOME THE BEST POKÉMON TRAINER IN THE WORLD?!

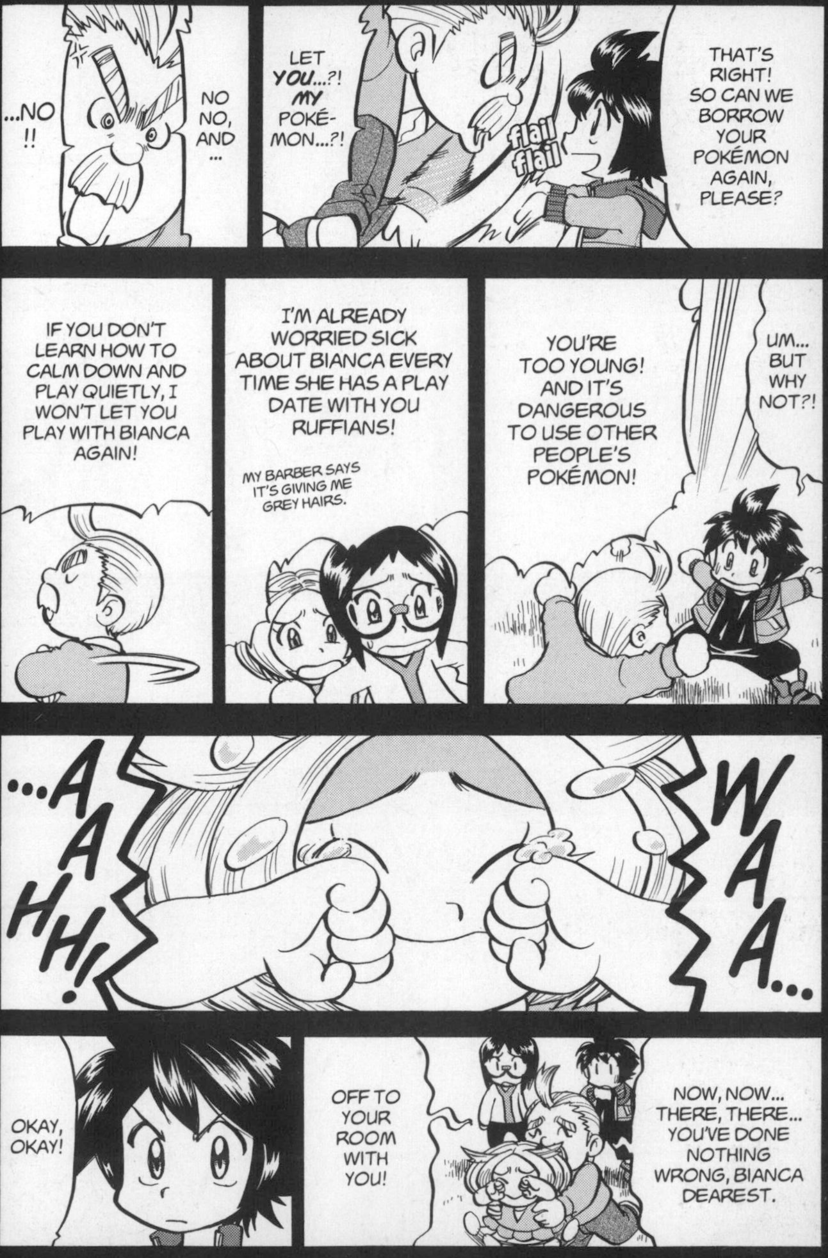
THAT'S RIGHT! SO CAN WE BORROW YOUR POKÉMON AGAIN, PLEASE?
flail flail
LET YOU...?! MY POKÉ-MON...?!
NO NO, AND ...
...NO !!
UM... BUT WHY NOT?!
YOU'RE TOO YOUNG! AND IT'S DANGEROUS TO USE OTHER PEOPLE'S POKÉMON!
I'M ALREADY WORRIED SICK ABOUT BIANCA EVERY TIME SHE HAS A PLAY DATE WITH YOU RUFFIANS!
MY BARBER SAYS IT'S GIVING ME GREY HAIRS.
IF YOU DON'T LEARN HOW TO CALM DOWN AND PLAY QUIETLY, I WON'T LET YOU PLAY WITH BIANCA AGAIN!
WAAA...
...AAHH!
NOW, NOW... THERE, THERE... YOU'VE DONE NOTHING WRONG, BIANCA DEAREST.
OFF TO YOUR ROOM WITH YOU!
OKAY, OKAY!

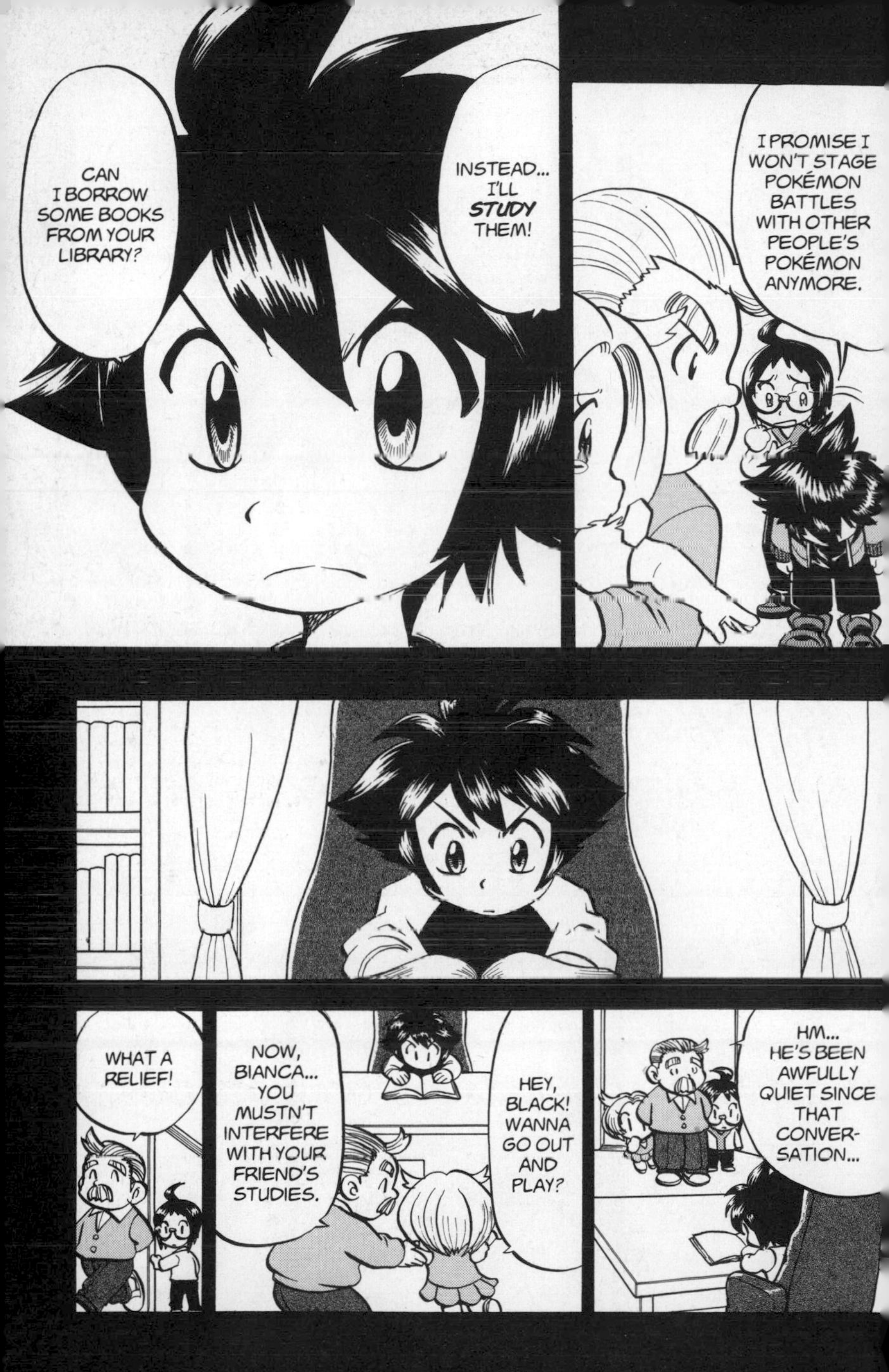
I PROMISE I WON'T STAGE POKÉMON BATTLES WITH OTHER PEOPLE'S POKÉMON ANYMORE.
INSTEAD... I'LL **STUDY** THEM!
CAN I BORROW SOME BOOKS FROM YOUR LIBRARY?
HM... HE'S BEEN AWFULLY QUIET SINCE THAT CONVERSATION...
HEY, BLACK! WANNA GO OUT AND PLAY?
NOW, BIANCA... YOU MUSTN'T INTERFERE WITH YOUR FRIEND'S STUDIES.
WHAT A RELIEF!

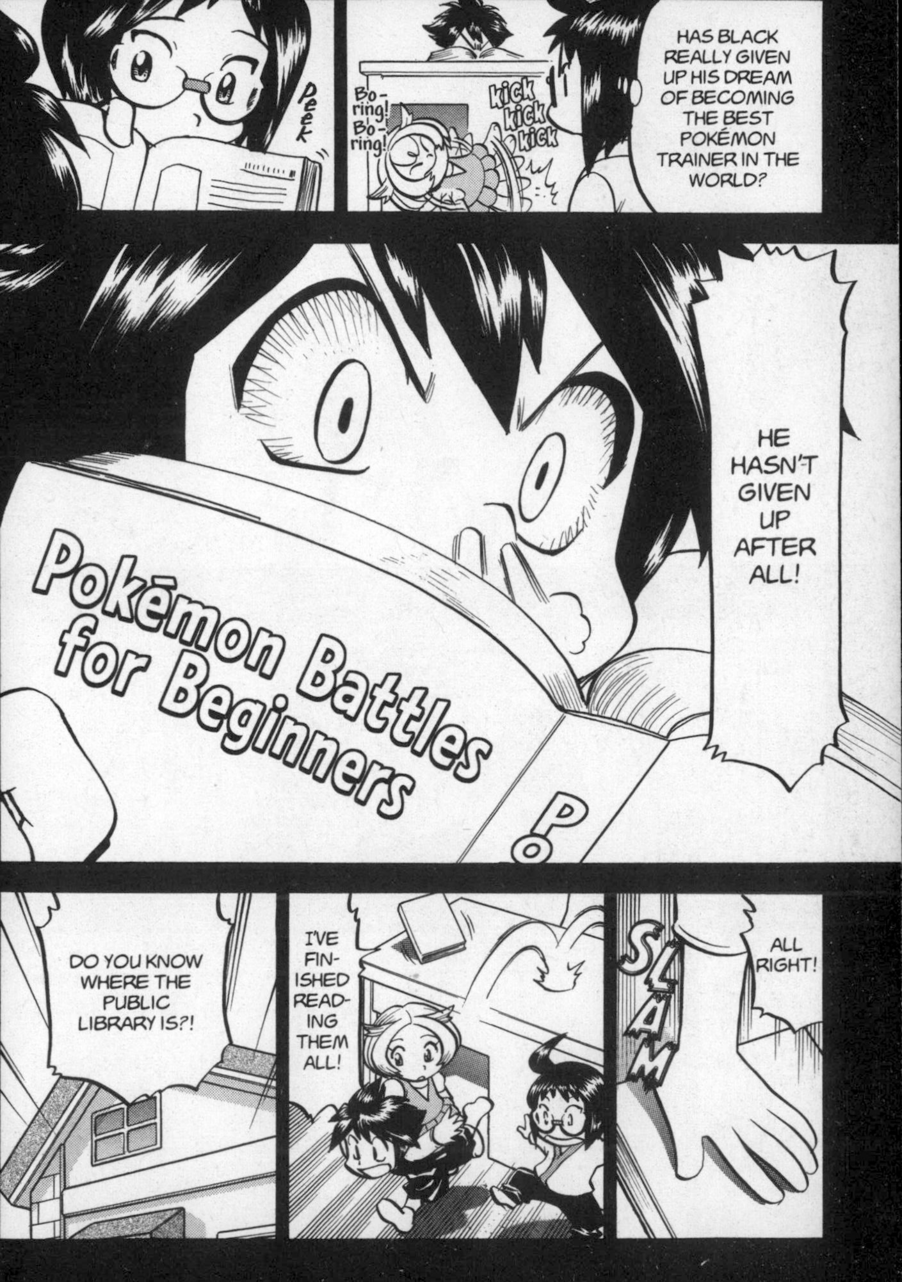
HAS BLACK REALLY GIVEN UP HIS DREAM OF BECOMING THE BEST POKÉMON TRAINER IN THE WORLD?
kick kick kick
Bo-ring! Bo-ring!
Peek
HE HASN'T GIVEN UP AFTER ALL!
Pokēmon Battles for Beginners
ALL RIGHT!
SLAM
I'VE FIN-ISHED READ-ING THEM ALL!
DO YOU KNOW WHERE THE PUBLIC LIBRARY IS?!

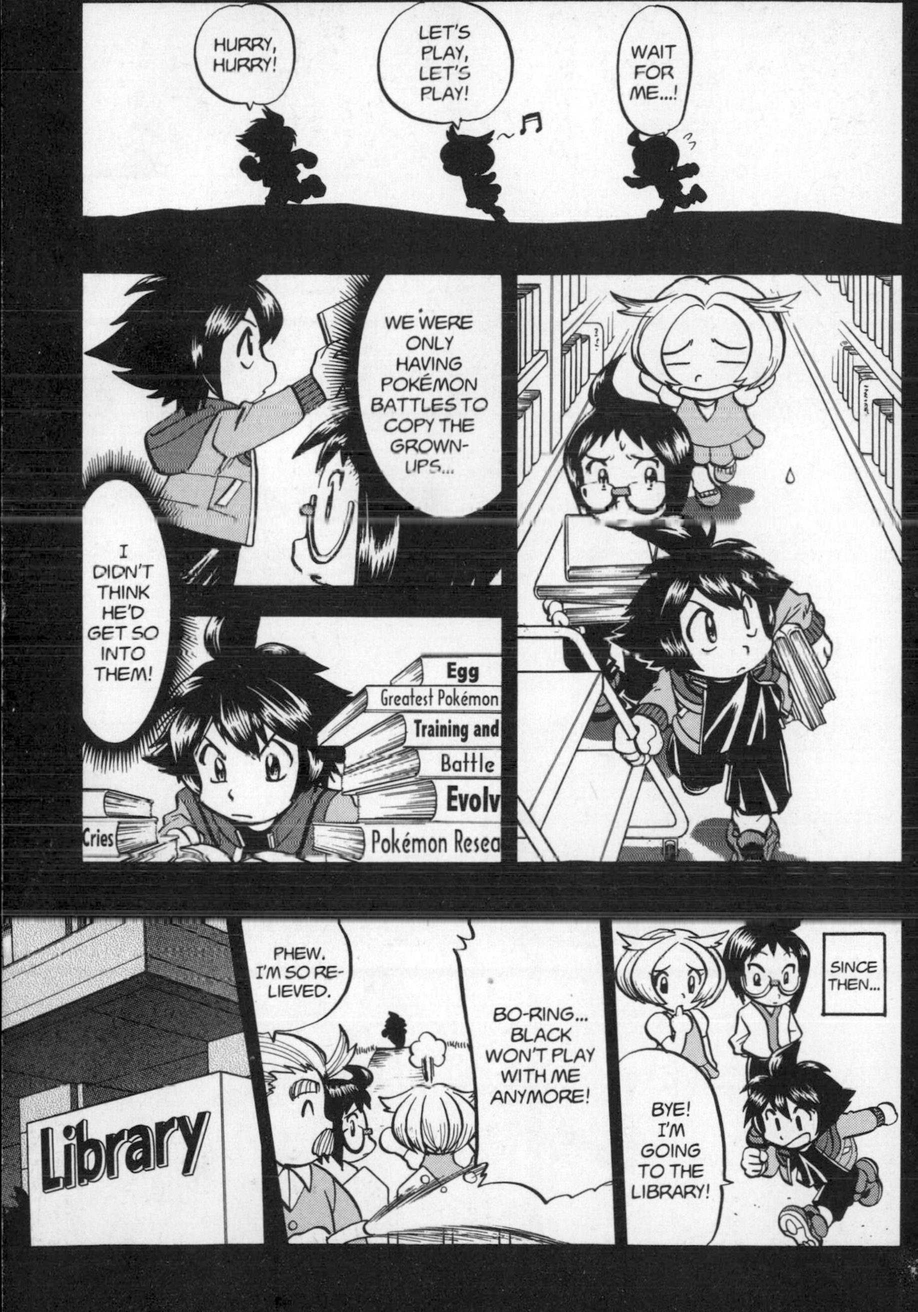
WAIT FOR ME...!
LET'S PLAY, LET'S PLAY!
HURRY, HURRY!
WE WERE ONLY HAVING POKÉMON BATTLES TO COPY THE GROWN-UPS...
I DIDN'T THINK HE'D GET SO INTO THEM!
Egg
Greatest Pokémon
Training and
Battle
Evolv
Cries
Pokémon Resea
SINCE THEN...
BYE! I'M GOING TO THE LIBRARY!
PHEW. I'M SO RE-LIEVED.
BO-RING... BLACK WON'T PLAY WITH ME ANYMORE!
Library

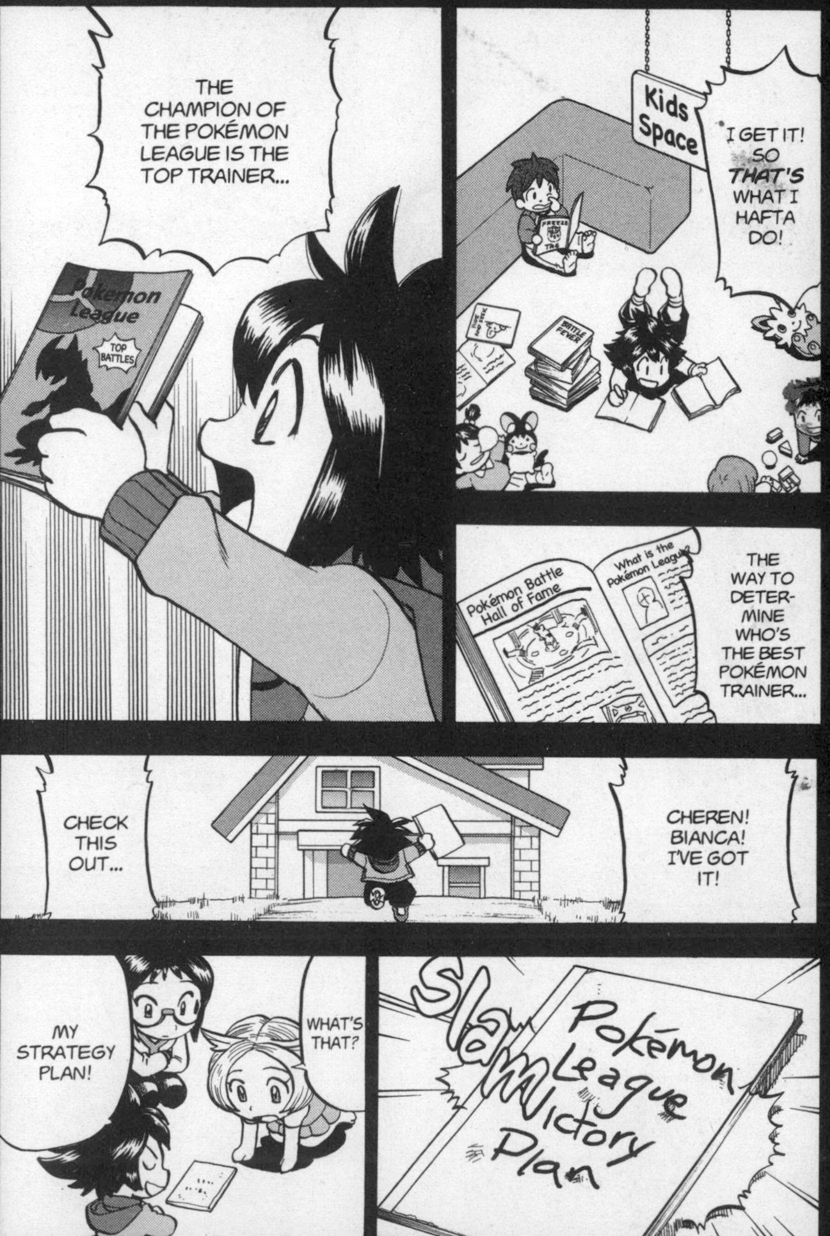
Kids Space
I GET IT! SO *THAT'S* WHAT I HAFTA DO!
BATTLE FEVER
What is the Pokémon League?
Pokémon Battle Hall of Fame
THE WAY TO DETERMINE WHO'S THE BEST POKÉMON TRAINER...
THE CHAMPION OF THE POKÉMON LEAGUE IS THE TOP TRAINER...
Pokemon League
TOP BATTLES
CHEREN! BIANCA! I'VE GOT IT!
CHECK THIS OUT...
Slam
Pokémon League Victory Plan
WHAT'S THAT?
MY STRATEGY PLAN!

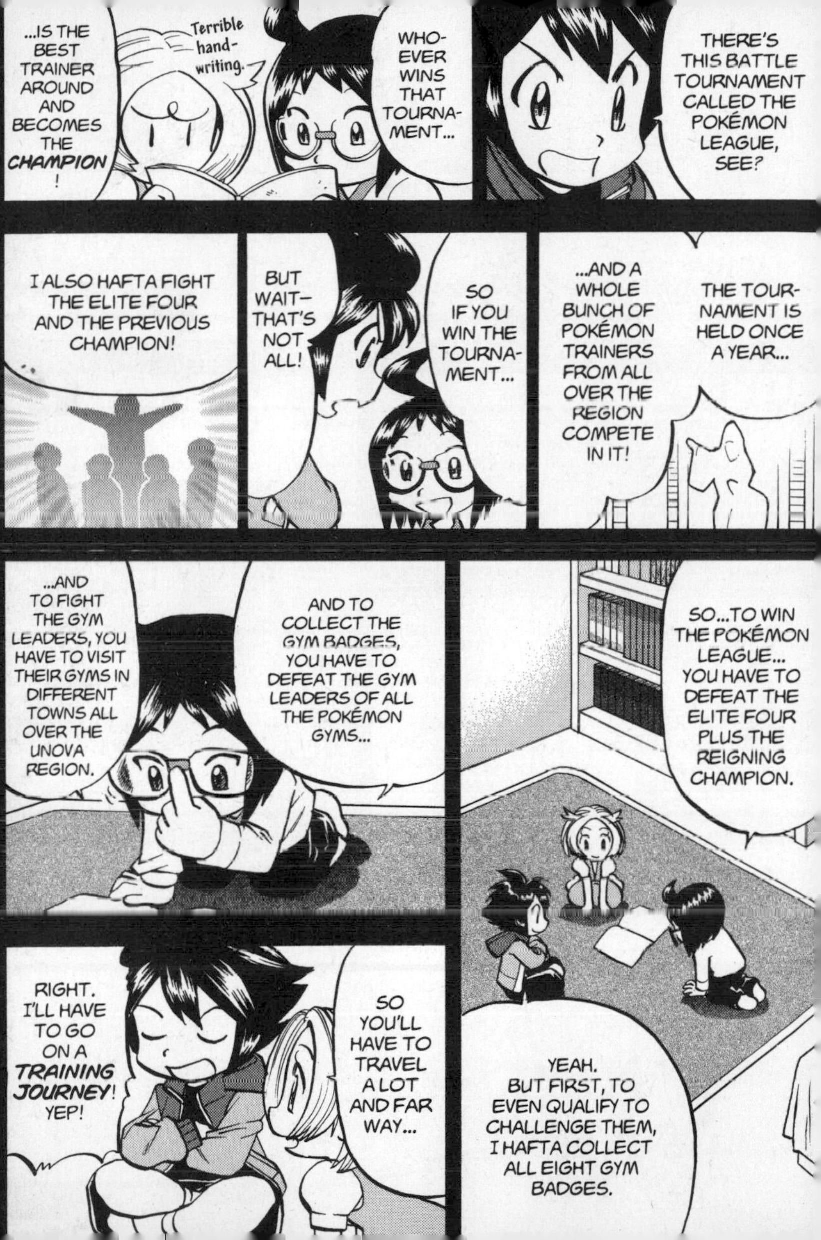
THERE'S THIS BATTLE TOURNAMENT CALLED THE POKÉMON LEAGUE, SEE?
WHOEVER WINS THAT TOURNAMENT...
Terrible handwriting.
...IS THE BEST TRAINER AROUND AND BECOMES THE **CHAMPION**!
THE TOURNAMENT IS HELD ONCE A YEAR...
...AND A WHOLE BUNCH OF POKÉMON TRAINERS FROM ALL OVER THE REGION COMPETE IN IT!
SO IF YOU WIN THE TOURNAMENT...
BUT WAIT—THAT'S NOT ALL!
I ALSO HAFTA FIGHT THE ELITE FOUR AND THE PREVIOUS CHAMPION!
SO...TO WIN THE POKÉMON LEAGUE... YOU HAVE TO DEFEAT THE ELITE FOUR PLUS THE REIGNING CHAMPION.
YEAH. BUT FIRST, TO EVEN QUALIFY TO CHALLENGE THEM, I HAFTA COLLECT ALL EIGHT GYM BADGES.
AND TO COLLECT THE GYM BADGES, YOU HAVE TO DEFEAT THE GYM LEADERS OF ALL THE POKÉMON GYMS...
...AND TO FIGHT THE GYM LEADERS, YOU HAVE TO VISIT THEIR GYMS IN DIFFERENT TOWNS ALL OVER THE UNOVA REGION.
SO YOU'LL HAVE TO TRAVEL A LOT AND FAR WAY...
RIGHT. I'LL HAVE TO GO ON A **TRAINING JOURNEY**! YEP!

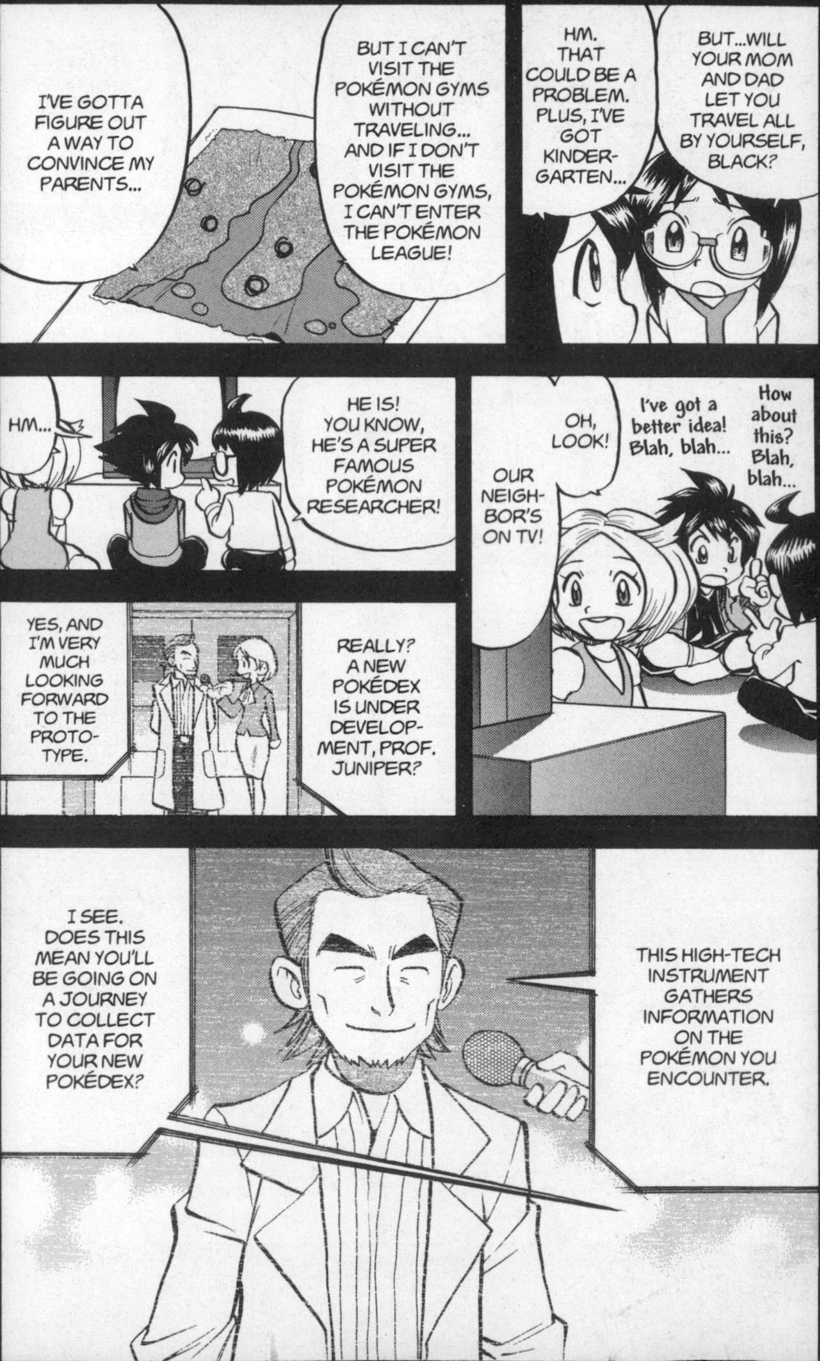
BUT...WILL YOUR MOM AND DAD LET YOU TRAVEL ALL BY YOURSELF, BLACK?
HM. THAT COULD BE A PROBLEM. PLUS, I'VE GOT KINDER-GARTEN...
BUT I CAN'T VISIT THE POKÉMON GYMS WITHOUT TRAVELING... AND IF I DON'T VISIT THE POKÉMON GYMS, I CAN'T ENTER THE POKÉMON LEAGUE!
I'VE GOTTA FIGURE OUT A WAY TO CONVINCE MY PARENTS...
How about this? Blah, blah...
I've got a better idea! Blah, blah...
OH, LOOK!
OUR NEIGH-BOR'S ON TV!
HE IS! YOU KNOW, HE'S A SUPER FAMOUS POKÉMON RESEARCHER!
HM...
REALLY? A NEW POKÉDEX IS UNDER DEVELOP-MENT, PROF. JUNIPER?
YES, AND I'M VERY MUCH LOOKING FORWARD TO THE PROTO-TYPE.
THIS HIGH-TECH INSTRUMENT GATHERS INFORMATION ON THE POKÉMON YOU ENCOUNTER.
I SEE. DOES THIS MEAN YOU'LL BE GOING ON A JOURNEY TO COLLECT DATA FOR YOUR NEW POKÉDEX?

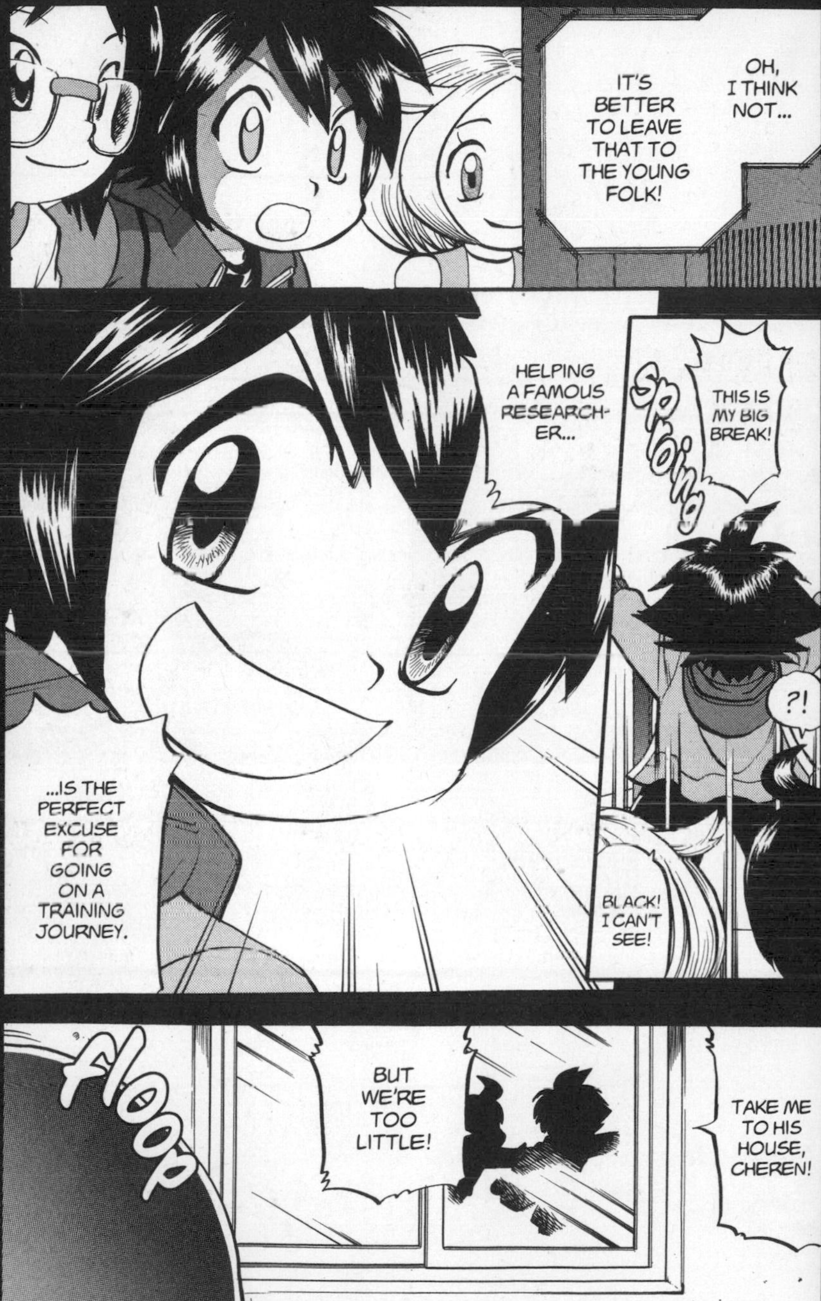
OH, I THINK NOT...
IT'S BETTER TO LEAVE THAT TO THE YOUNG FOLK!
THIS IS MY BIG BREAK!
Spoing
?!
BLACK! I CAN'T SEE!
HELPING A FAMOUS RESEARCHER...
...IS THE PERFECT EXCUSE FOR GOING ON A TRAINING JOURNEY.
TAKE ME TO HIS HOUSE, CHEREN!
BUT WE'RE TOO LITTLE!
FLOOP

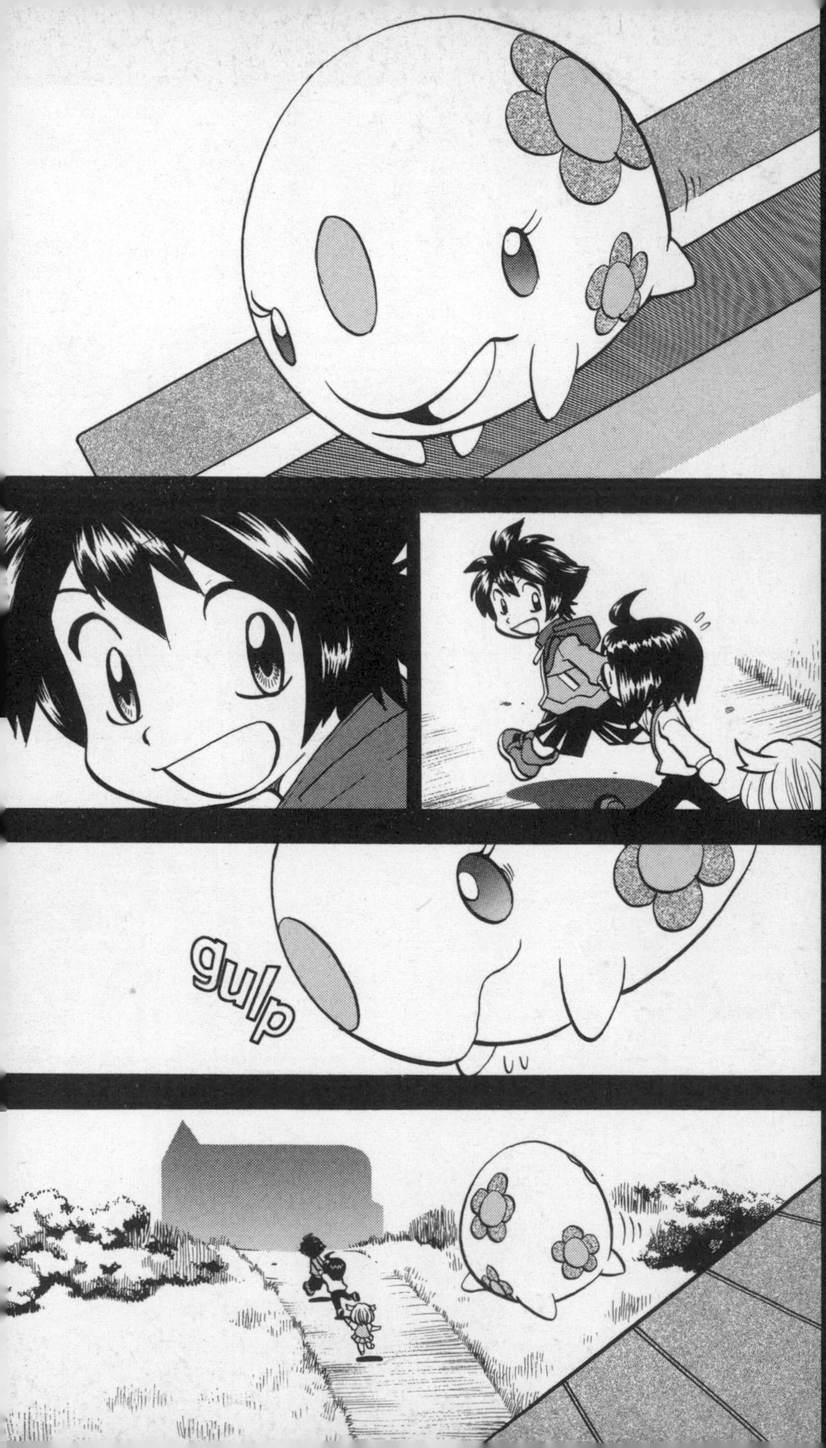
gulp

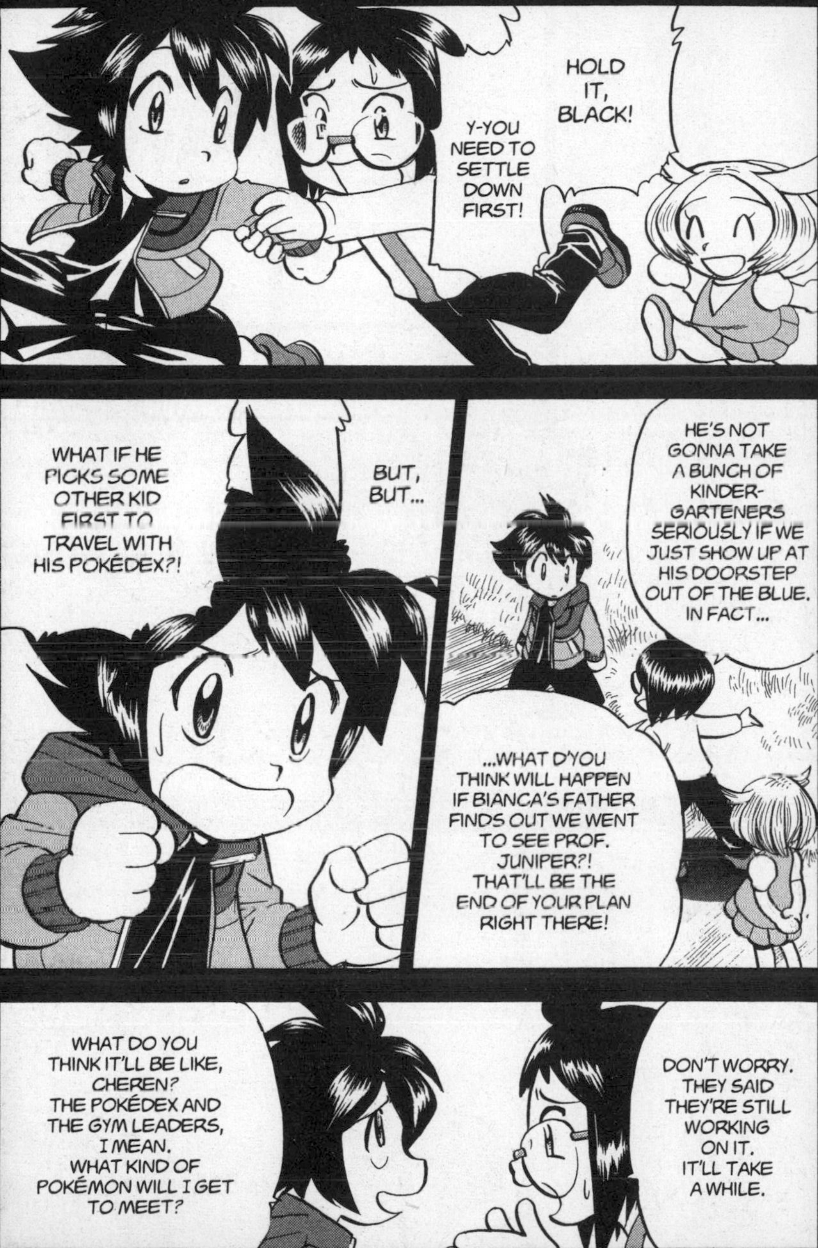
HOLD IT, BLACK!
Y-YOU NEED TO SETTLE DOWN FIRST!
HE'S NOT GONNA TAKE A BUNCH OF KINDER-GARTENERS SERIOUSLY IF WE JUST SHOW UP AT HIS DOORSTEP OUT OF THE BLUE. IN FACT...
...WHAT D'YOU THINK WILL HAPPEN IF BIANCA'S FATHER FINDS OUT WE WENT TO SEE PROF. JUNIPER?! THAT'LL BE THE END OF YOUR PLAN RIGHT THERE!
BUT, BUT...
WHAT IF HE PICKS SOME OTHER KID FIRST TO TRAVEL WITH HIS POKÉDEX?!
DON'T WORRY. THEY SAID THEY'RE STILL WORKING ON IT. IT'LL TAKE A WHILE.
WHAT DO YOU THINK IT'LL BE LIKE, CHEREN? THE POKÉDEX AND THE GYM LEADERS, I MEAN. WHAT KIND OF POKÉMON WILL I GET TO MEET?

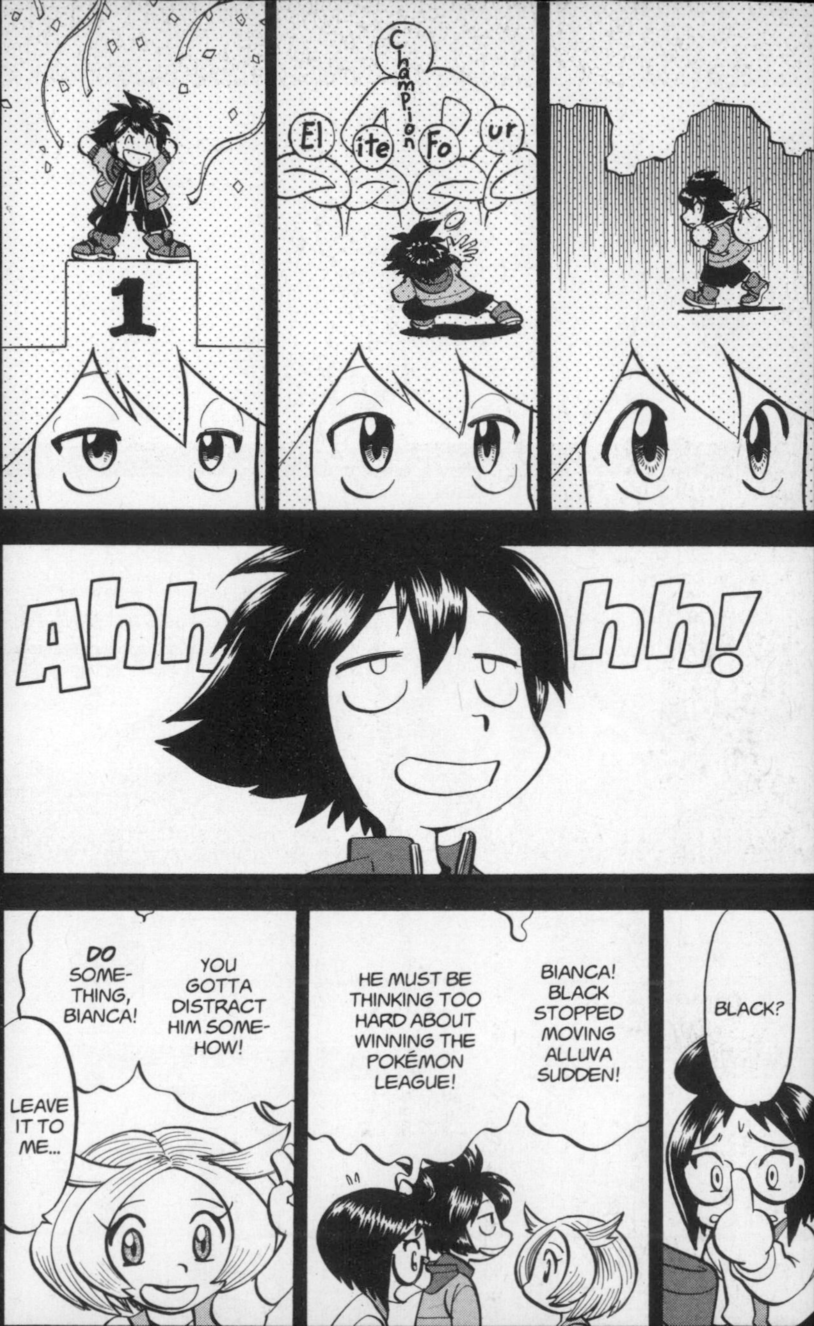
Champion
El ite Fo ur
1
Ahh hh!
BLACK?
BIANCA! BLACK STOPPED MOVING ALLUVA SUDDEN!
HE MUST BE THINKING TOO HARD ABOUT WINNING THE POKÉMON LEAGUE!
YOU GOTTA DISTRACT HIM SOME-HOW!
DO SOME-THING, BIANCA!
LEAVE IT TO ME...

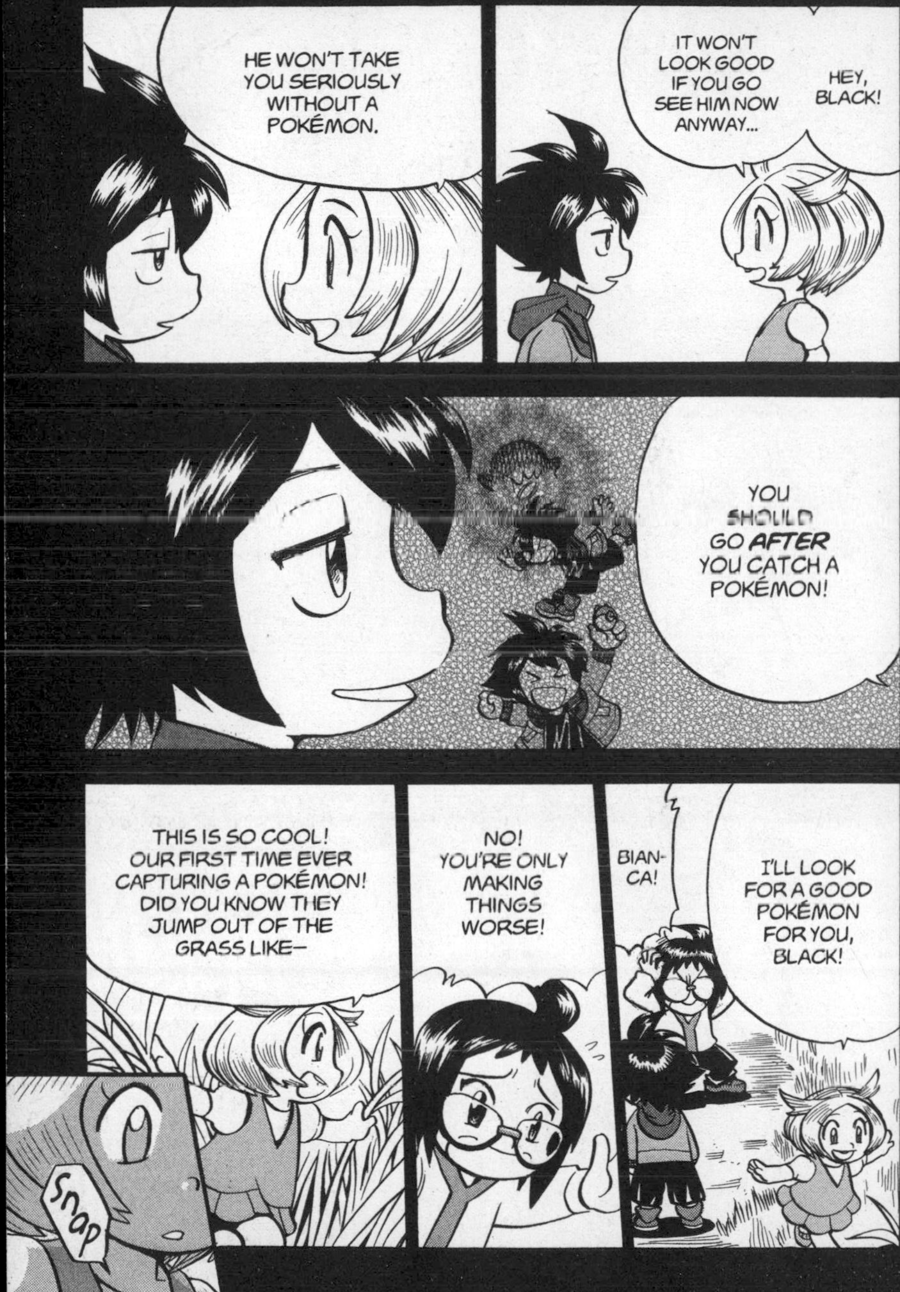
HEY, BLACK!
IT WON'T LOOK GOOD IF YOU GO SEE HIM NOW ANYWAY...
HE WON'T TAKE YOU SERIOUSLY WITHOUT A POKÉMON.
YOU SHOULD GO **AFTER** YOU CATCH A POKÉMON!
I'LL LOOK FOR A GOOD POKÉMON FOR YOU, BLACK!
BIAN-CA!
NO! YOU'RE ONLY MAKING THINGS WORSE!
THIS IS SO COOL! OUR FIRST TIME EVER CAPTURING A POKÉMON! DID YOU KNOW THEY JUMP OUT OF THE GRASS LIKE–
Snap

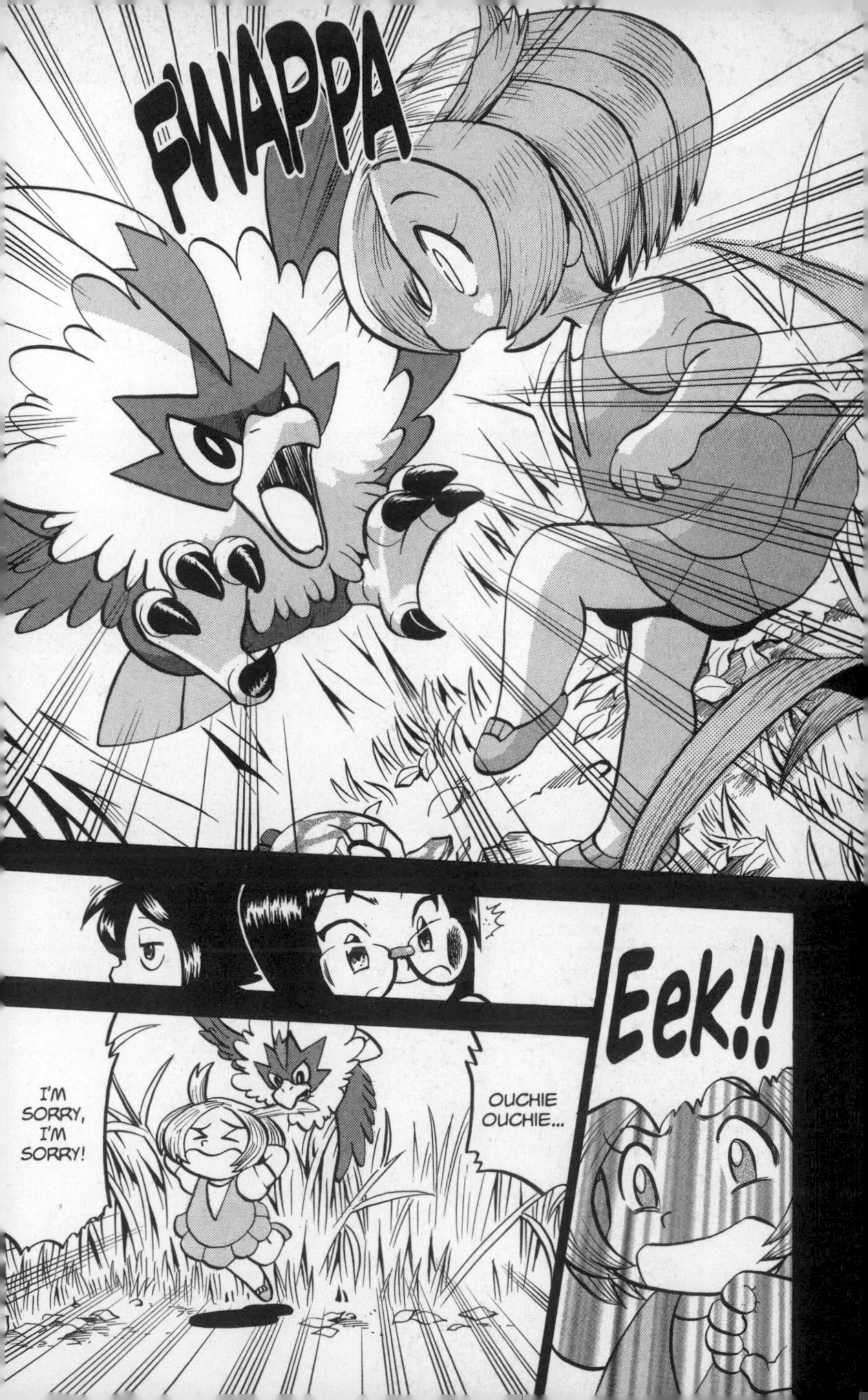
FWAPPA
Eek!!
OUCHIE OUCHIE...
I'M SORRY, I'M SORRY!

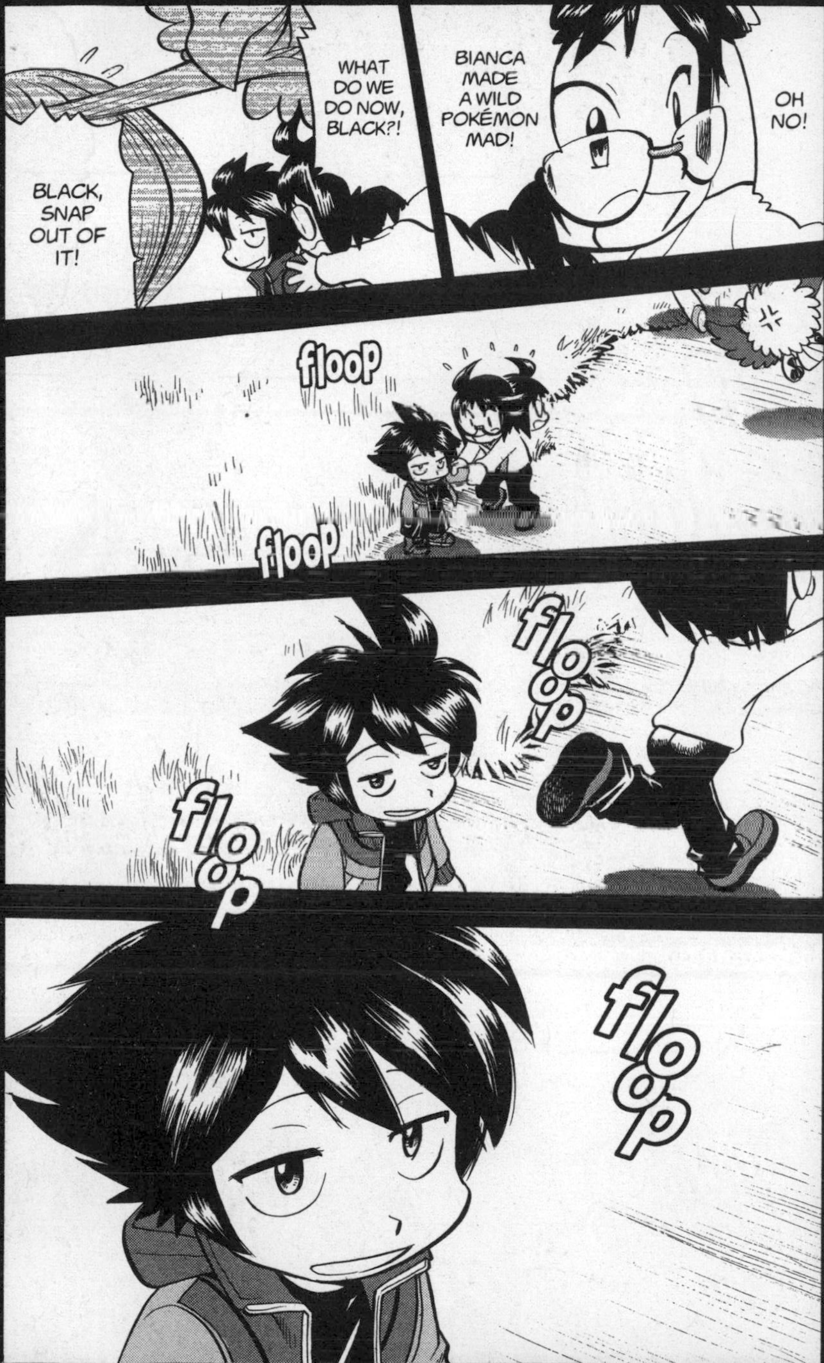
OH NO!
BIANCA MADE A WILD POKÉMON MAD!
WHAT DO WE DO NOW, BLACK?!
BLACK, SNAP OUT OF IT!
floop
floop
floop
floop
floop

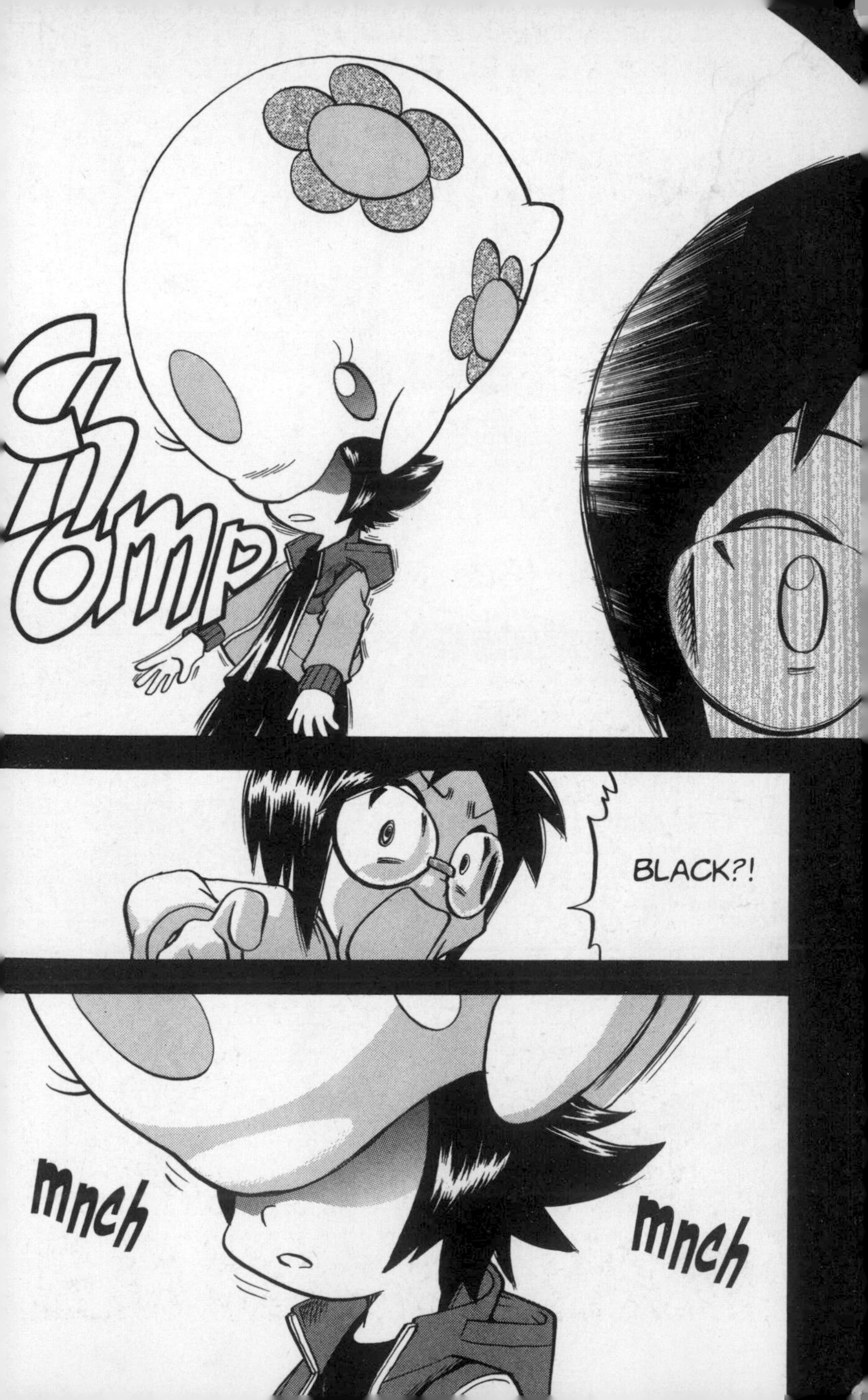
CHOMP
BLACK?!
mnch
mnch

ADVENTURE MAP

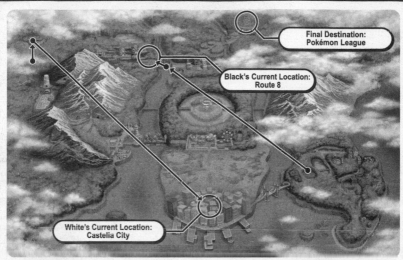

Final Destination:
Pokémon League
Black's Current Location:
Route 8
White's Current Location:
Castelia City

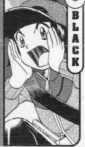

BLACK

Bo — Mega Fire Pig Pokémon
Emboar ♂ | Fire | Fighting
Lv.41 Ability: Blaze

Musha — Dream Eater Pokémon
Munna ♂ | Psychic
Lv.53 Ability: Forewarn

Tula — EleSpider Pokémon
Galvantula ♂ | Bug | Electric
Lv.54 Ability: Unnerve

Costa — Prototurtle Pokémon
Tirtouga ♂ | Water | Rock
Lv.36 Ability: Solid Rock

WHITE

Amanda — Grass Snake Pokémon
Servine ♀ | Grass
Lv.29 Ability: Overgrow

Darlene — Season Pokémon
Deerling ♀ | Normal | Grass
Lv.26 Ability: Chlorophyll

Dorothy — Trap Pokémon
Stunfisk ♀ | Ground | Electric
Lv.30 Ability: Limber

Nancy — Caring Pokémon
Alomomola ♀ | Water
Lv.30 Ability: Healer

Barbara — Diapered Pokémon
Vullaby ♀ | Dark | Flying
Lv.35 Ability: Big Pecks

Solly — Cell Pokémon
Solosis ♂ | Psychic
Lv.25 Ability: Magic Guard

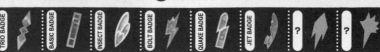

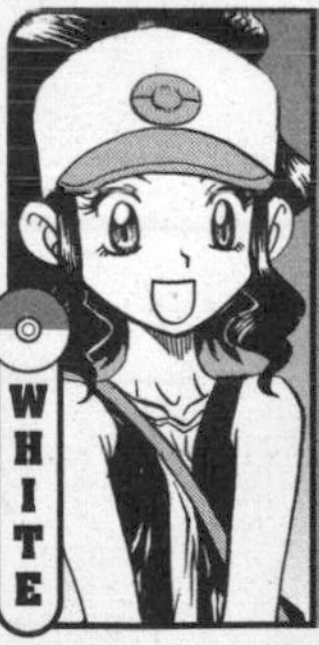

TRIO BADGE · BASIC BADGE · INSECT BADGE · BOLT BADGE · QUAKE BADGE · JET BADGE · ? · ?

Pokémon™ Adventures Black & White

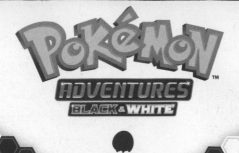

MUNNA

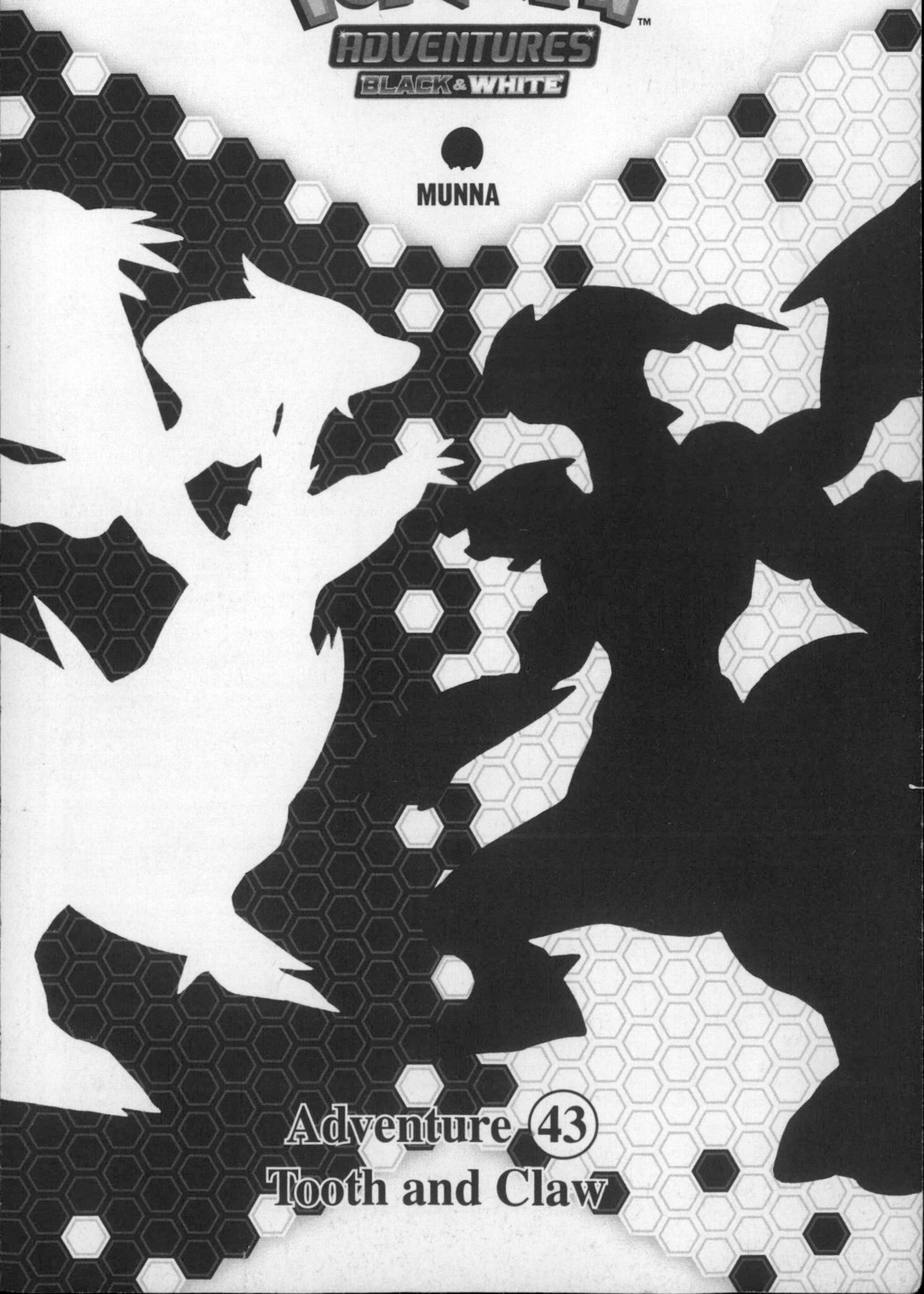

Adventure 43
Tooth and Claw

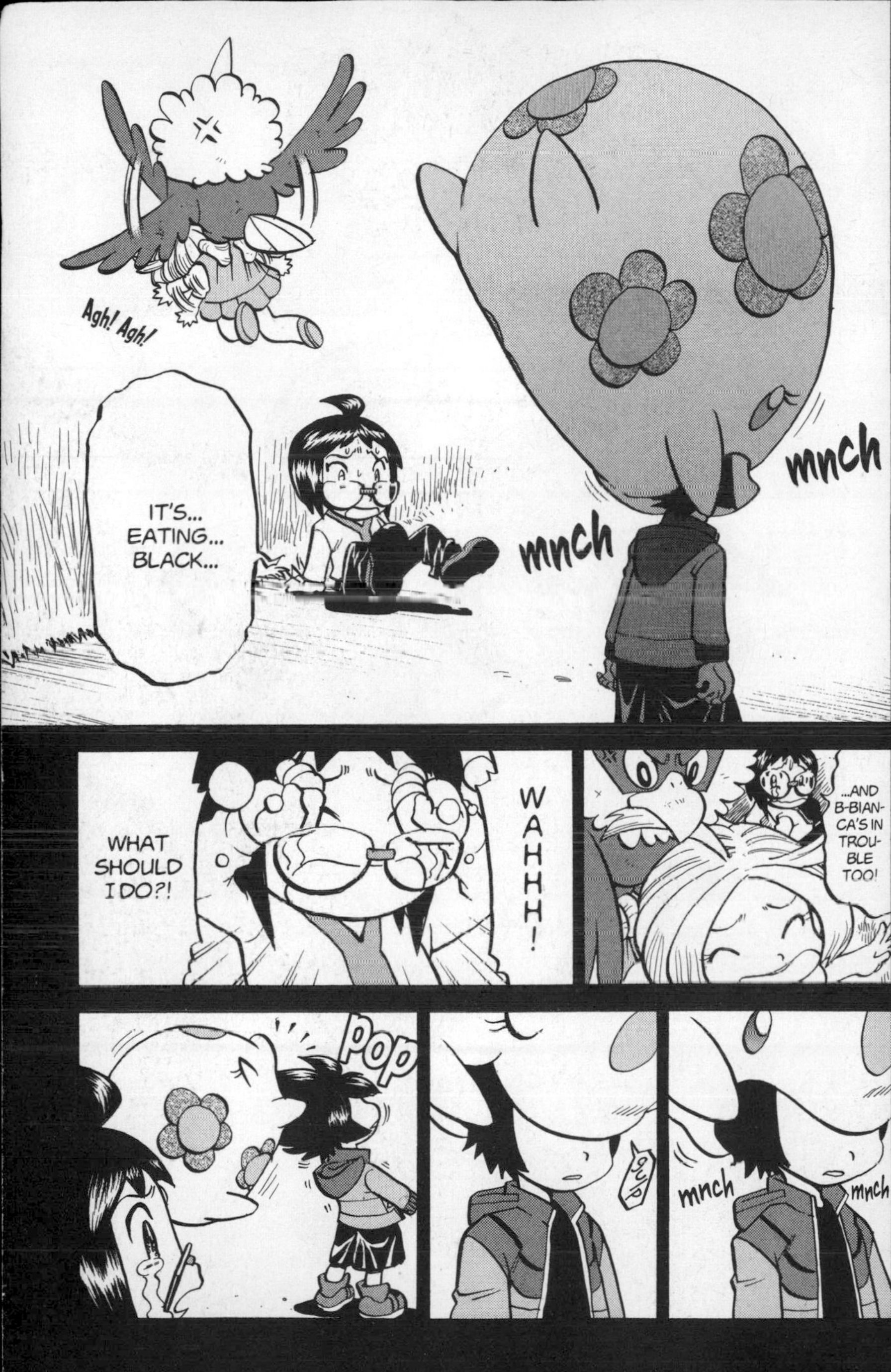
mnch
mnch
Agh! Agh!
IT'S... EATING... BLACK...
...AND B-BIANCA'S IN TROUBLE TOO!
WAHHH!
WHAT SHOULD I DO?!
mnch
mnch
gulp
pop

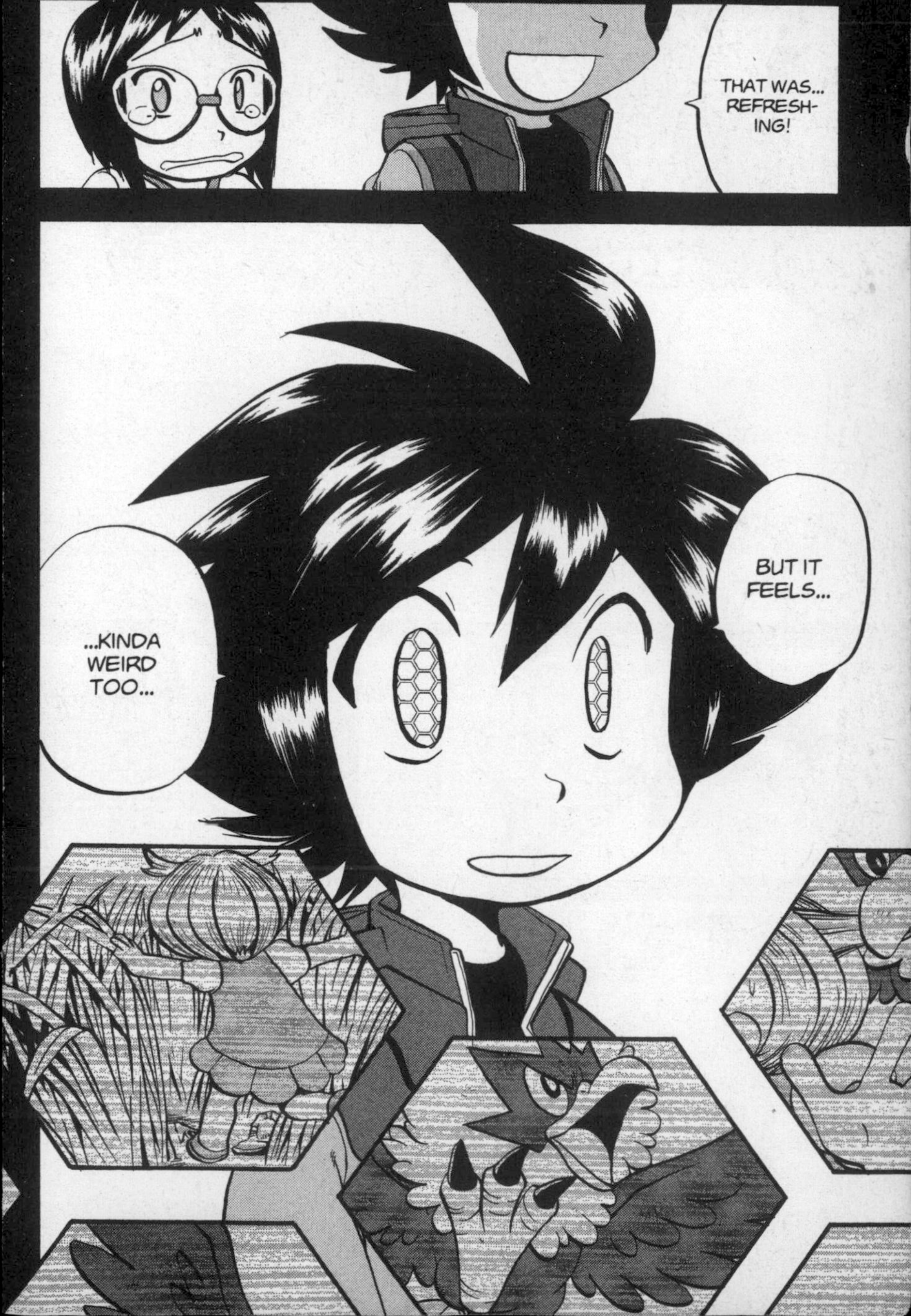
THAT WAS... REFRESH-ING!
BUT IT FEELS...
...KINDA WEIRD TOO...

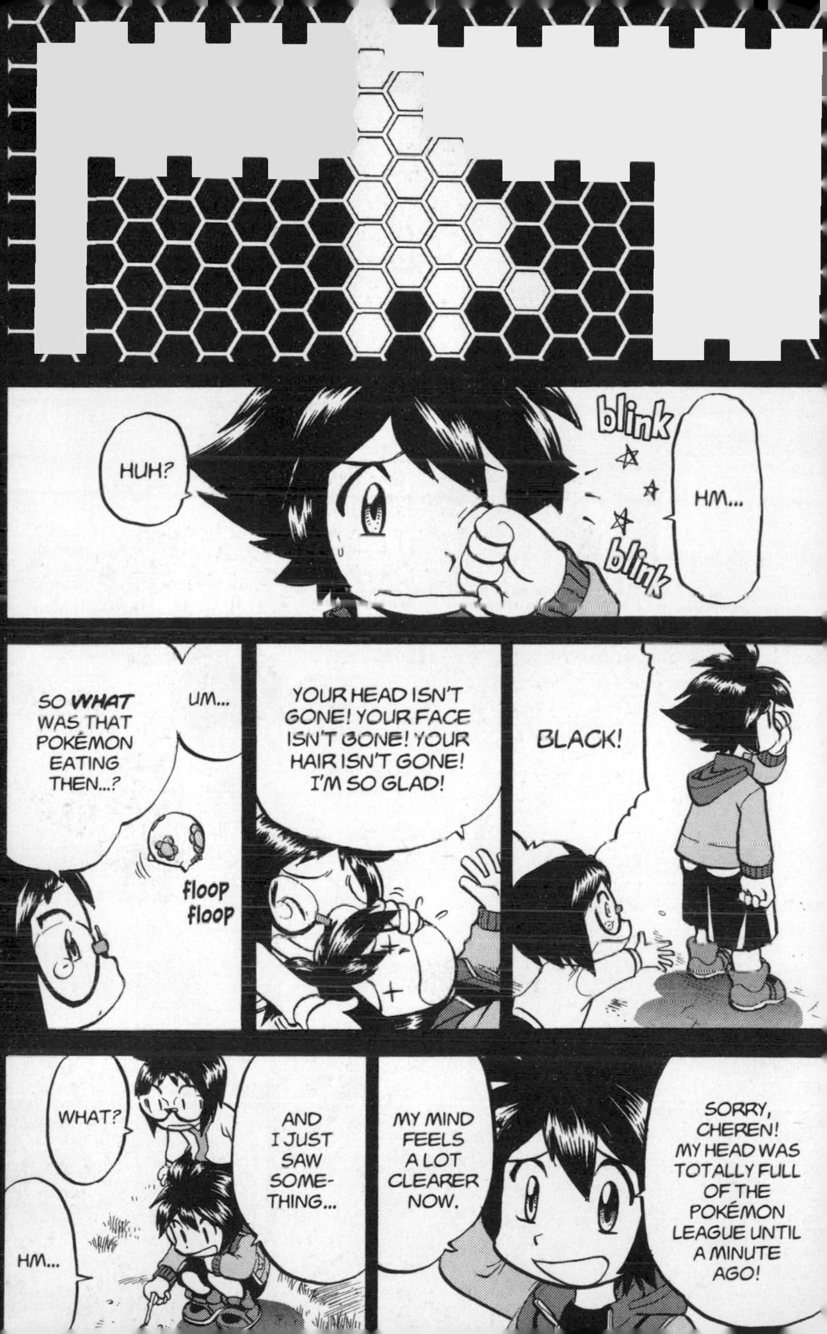

HM...
blink
blink
HUH?
BLACK!
YOUR HEAD ISN'T GONE! YOUR FACE ISN'T GONE! YOUR HAIR ISN'T GONE! I'M SO GLAD!
UM...
SO WHAT WAS THAT POKÉMON EATING THEN...?
floop floop
SORRY, CHEREN! MY HEAD WAS TOTALLY FULL OF THE POKÉMON LEAGUE UNTIL A MINUTE AGO!
MY MIND FEELS A LOT CLEARER NOW.
AND I JUST SAW SOME-THING...
WHAT?
HM...

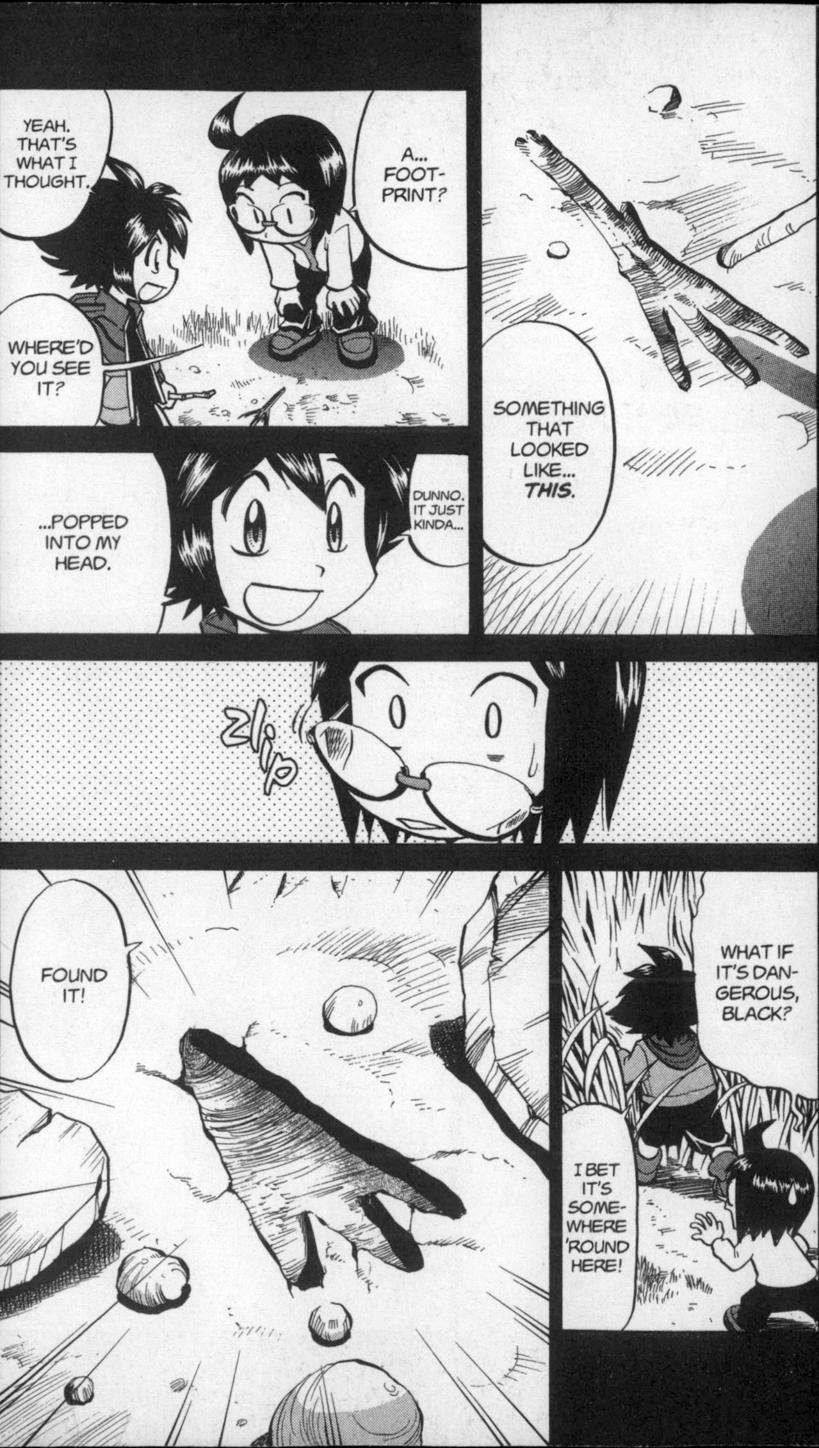
SOMETHING THAT LOOKED LIKE... *THIS*.
A... FOOT-PRINT?
YEAH. THAT'S WHAT I THOUGHT.
WHERE'D YOU SEE IT?
DUNNO. IT JUST KINDA...
...POPPED INTO MY HEAD.
zlip
WHAT IF IT'S DAN-GEROUS, BLACK?
I BET IT'S SOME-WHERE 'ROUND HERE!
FOUND IT!

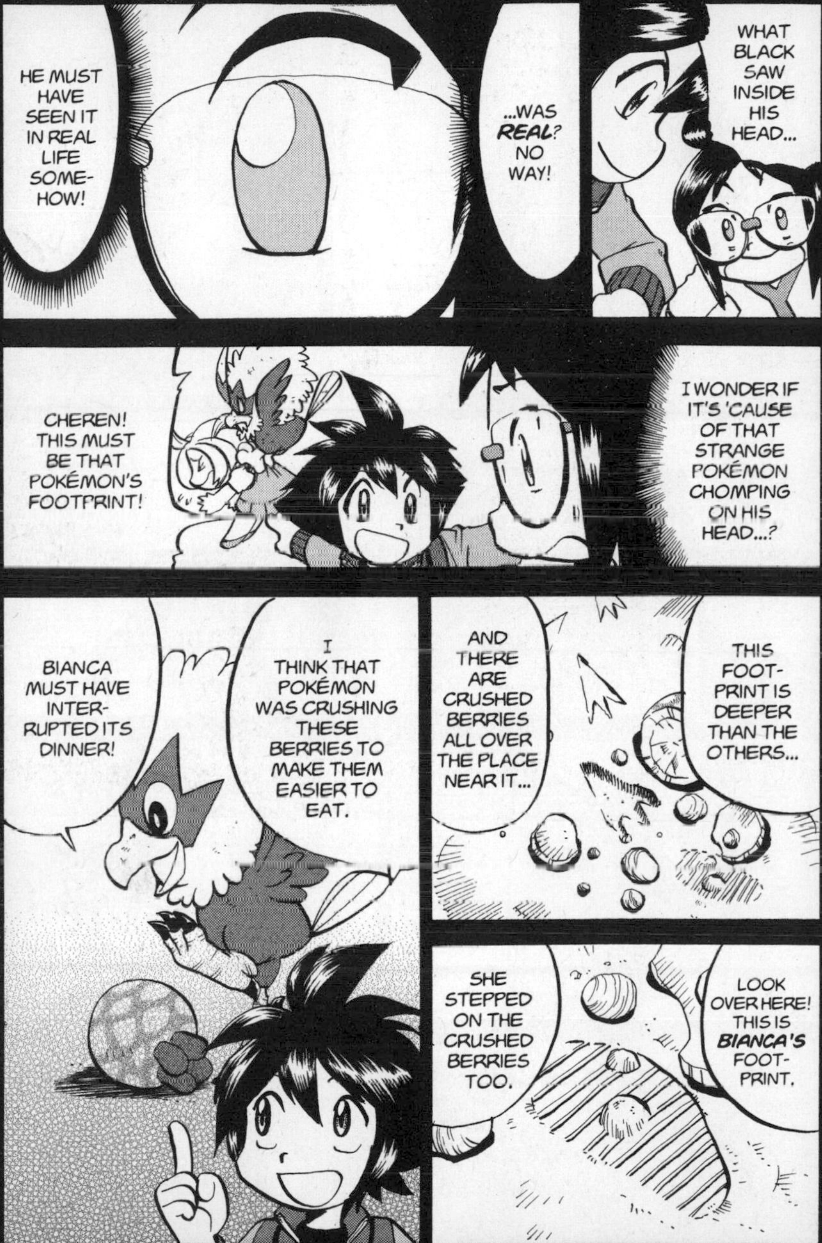
WHAT BLACK SAW INSIDE HIS HEAD...
...WAS **REAL**? NO WAY!
HE MUST HAVE SEEN IT IN REAL LIFE SOME-HOW!
I WONDER IF IT'S 'CAUSE OF THAT STRANGE POKÉMON CHOMPING ON HIS HEAD...?
CHEREN! THIS MUST BE THAT POKÉMON'S FOOTPRINT!
THIS FOOT-PRINT IS DEEPER THAN THE OTHERS...
AND THERE ARE CRUSHED BERRIES ALL OVER THE PLACE NEAR IT...
LOOK OVER HERE! THIS IS ***BIANCA'S*** FOOT-PRINT.
SHE STEPPED ON THE CRUSHED BERRIES TOO.
I THINK THAT POKÉMON WAS CRUSHING THESE BERRIES TO MAKE THEM EASIER TO EAT.
BIANCA MUST HAVE INTER-RUPTED ITS DINNER!

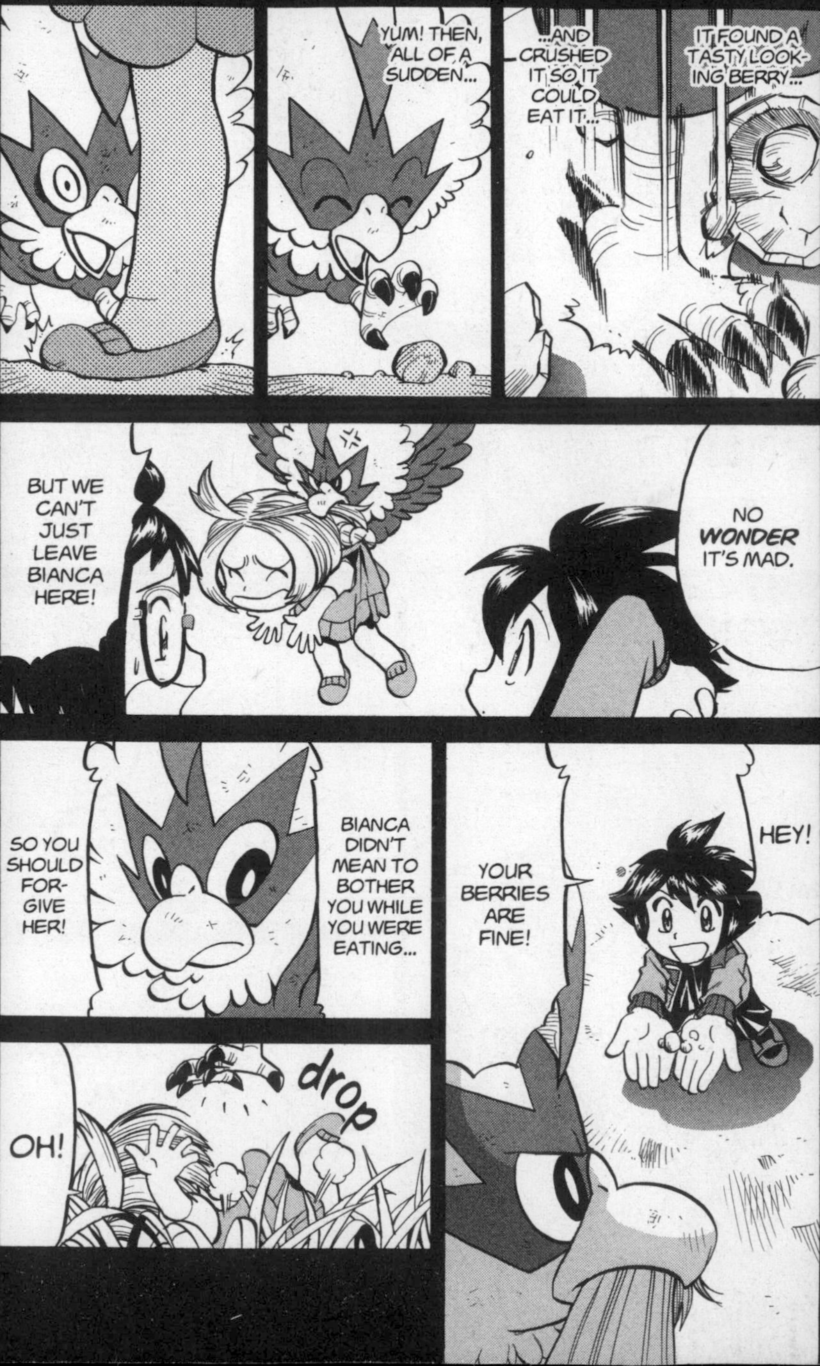
IT FOUND A TASTY LOOK-ING BERRY...
...AND CRUSHED IT SO IT COULD EAT IT...
YUM! THEN, ALL OF A SUDDEN...
NO WONDER IT'S MAD.
BUT WE CAN'T JUST LEAVE BIANCA HERE!
HEY!
YOUR BERRIES ARE FINE!
BIANCA DIDN'T MEAN TO BOTHER YOU WHILE YOU WERE EATING...
SO YOU SHOULD FOR-GIVE HER!
drop
OH!

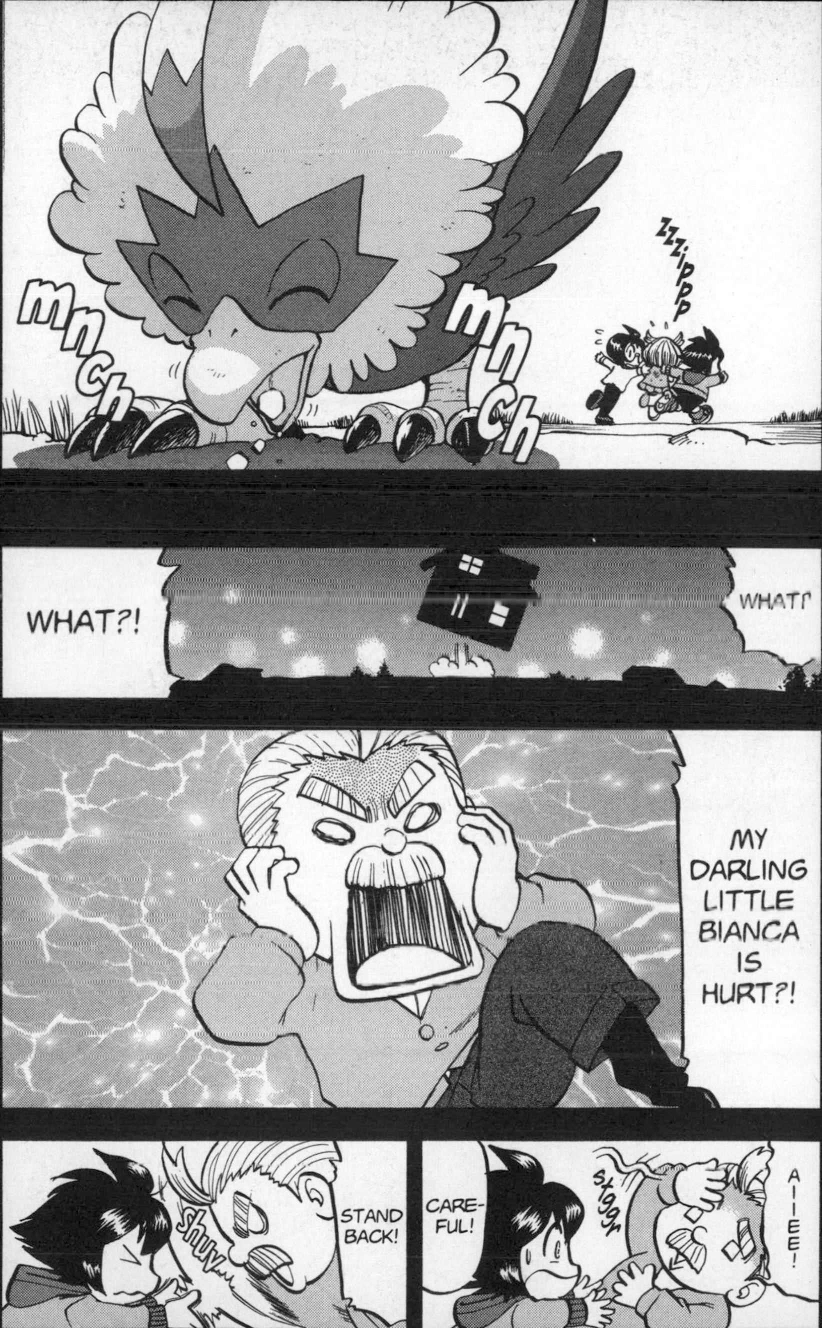
ZZZipppp
mnch
mnch
WHAT?!
WHAT?!
MY DARLING LITTLE BIANCA IS HURT?!
AIIEE!
stggr
CARE-FUL!
STAND BACK!
shuv

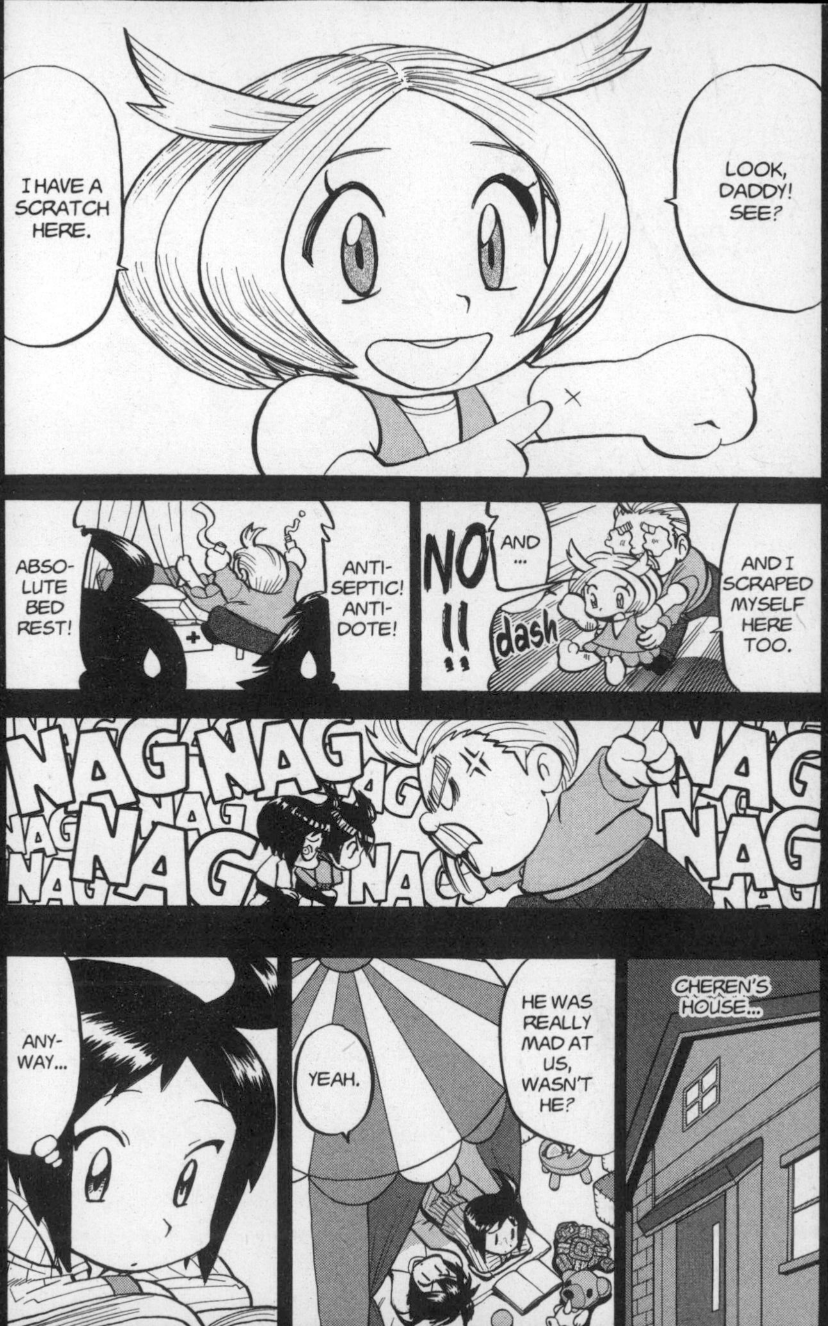
LOOK, DADDY! SEE?
I HAVE A SCRATCH HERE.
AND I SCRAPED MYSELF HERE TOO.
AND...
NO!!
dash
ANTI-SEPTIC! ANTI-DOTE!
ABSO-LUTE BED REST!
NAG NAG NAG NAG NAG NAG NAG NAG NAG
CHEREN'S HOUSE...
HE WAS REALLY MAD AT US, WASN'T HE?
YEAH.
ANY-WAY...

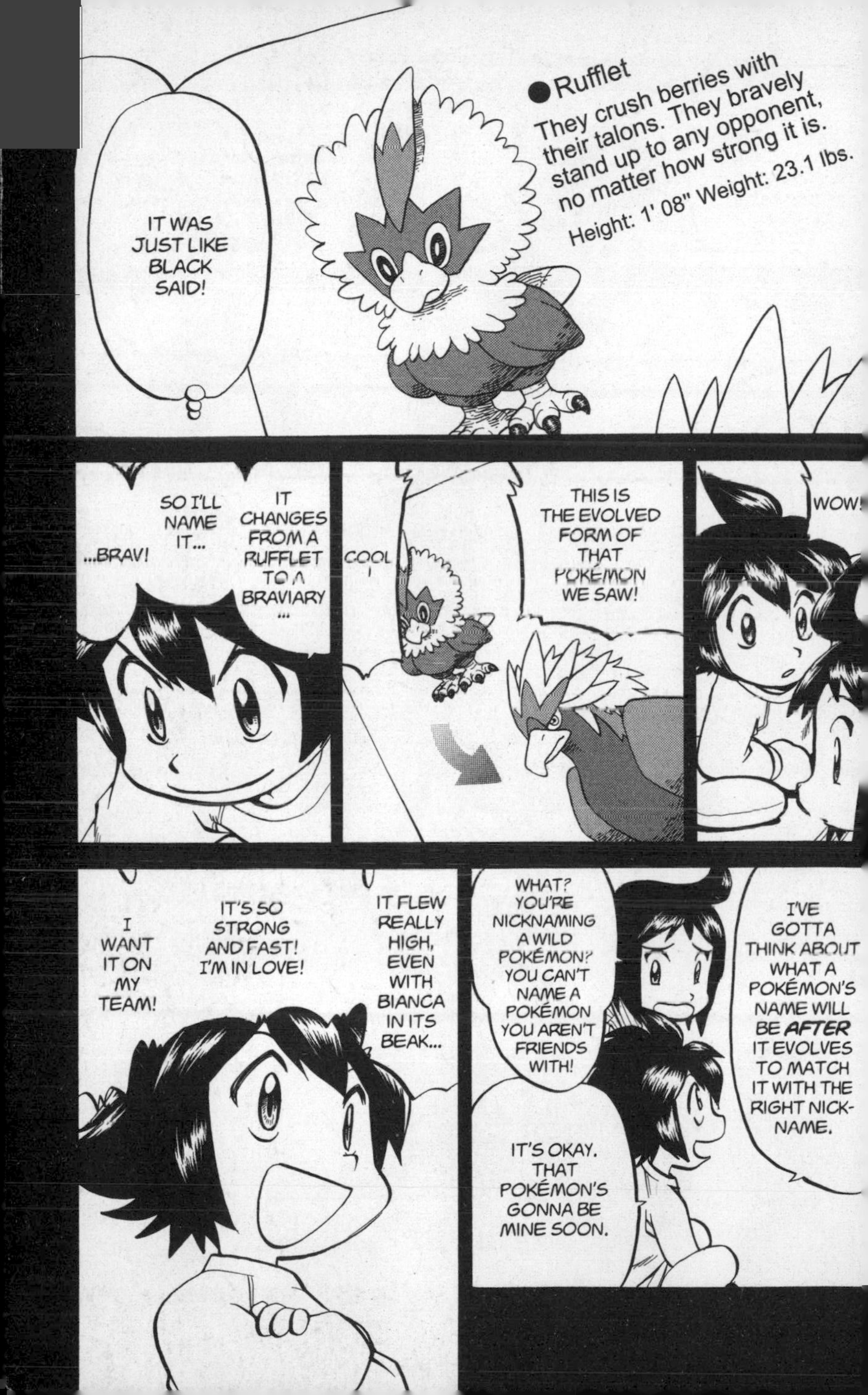

●Rufflet
They crush berries with their talons. They bravely stand up to any opponent, no matter how strong it is.
Height: 1' 08" Weight: 23.1 lbs.
IT WAS JUST LIKE BLACK SAID!
WOW!
THIS IS THE EVOLVED FORM OF THAT POKÉMON WE SAW!
COOL!
IT CHANGES FROM A RUFFLET TO A BRAVIARY...
SO I'LL NAME IT...
...BRAV!
I'VE GOTTA THINK ABOUT WHAT A POKÉMON'S NAME WILL BE *AFTER* IT EVOLVES TO MATCH IT WITH THE RIGHT NICK-NAME.
WHAT? YOU'RE NICKNAMING A WILD POKÉMON? YOU CAN'T NAME A POKÉMON YOU AREN'T FRIENDS WITH!
IT'S OKAY. THAT POKÉMON'S GONNA BE MINE SOON.
IT FLEW REALLY HIGH, EVEN WITH BIANCA IN ITS BEAK...
IT'S SO STRONG AND FAST! I'M IN LOVE!
I WANT IT ON MY TEAM!

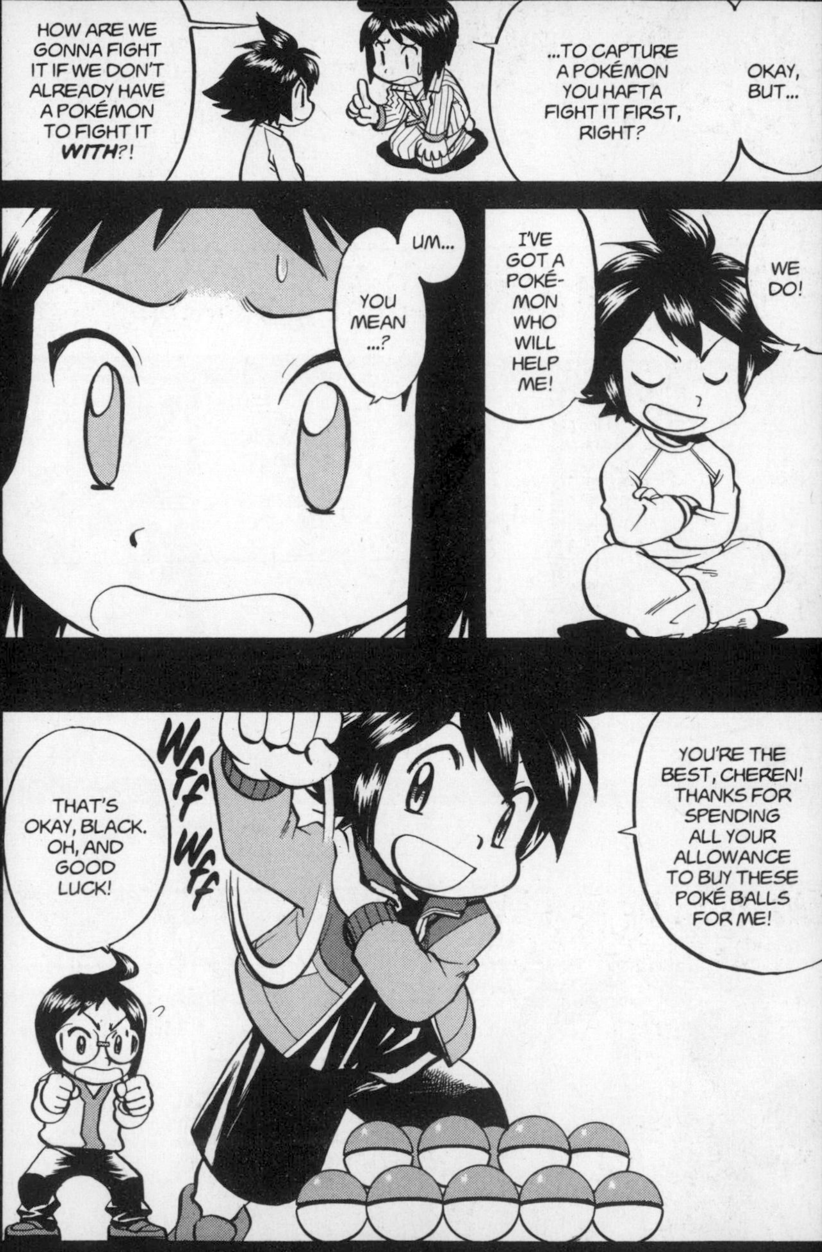
OKAY, BUT...
...TO CAPTURE A POKÉMON YOU HAFTA FIGHT IT FIRST, RIGHT?
HOW ARE WE GONNA FIGHT IT IF WE DON'T ALREADY HAVE A POKÉMON TO FIGHT IT *WITH*?!
WE DO!
I'VE GOT A POKÉ-MON WHO WILL HELP ME!
UM...
YOU MEAN ...?
YOU'RE THE BEST, CHEREN! THANKS FOR SPENDING ALL YOUR ALLOWANCE TO BUY THESE POKÉ BALLS FOR ME!
WFF WFF
THAT'S OKAY, BLACK. OH, AND GOOD LUCK!

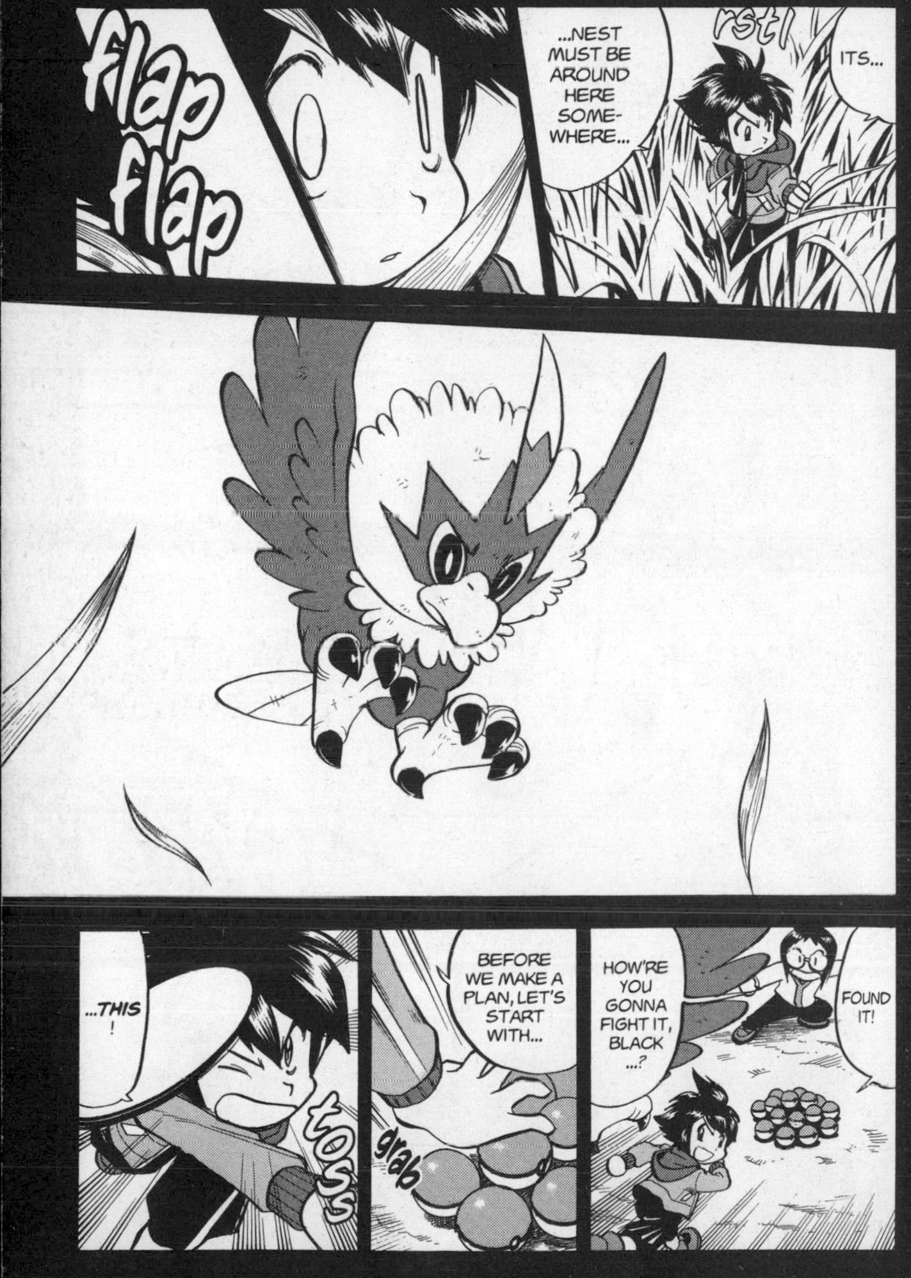
rstl
ITS...
...NEST MUST BE AROUND HERE SOME-WHERE...
flap flap
FOUND IT!
HOW'RE YOU GONNA FIGHT IT, BLACK ...?
BEFORE WE MAKE A PLAN, LET'S START WITH...
grab
...THIS!
toss

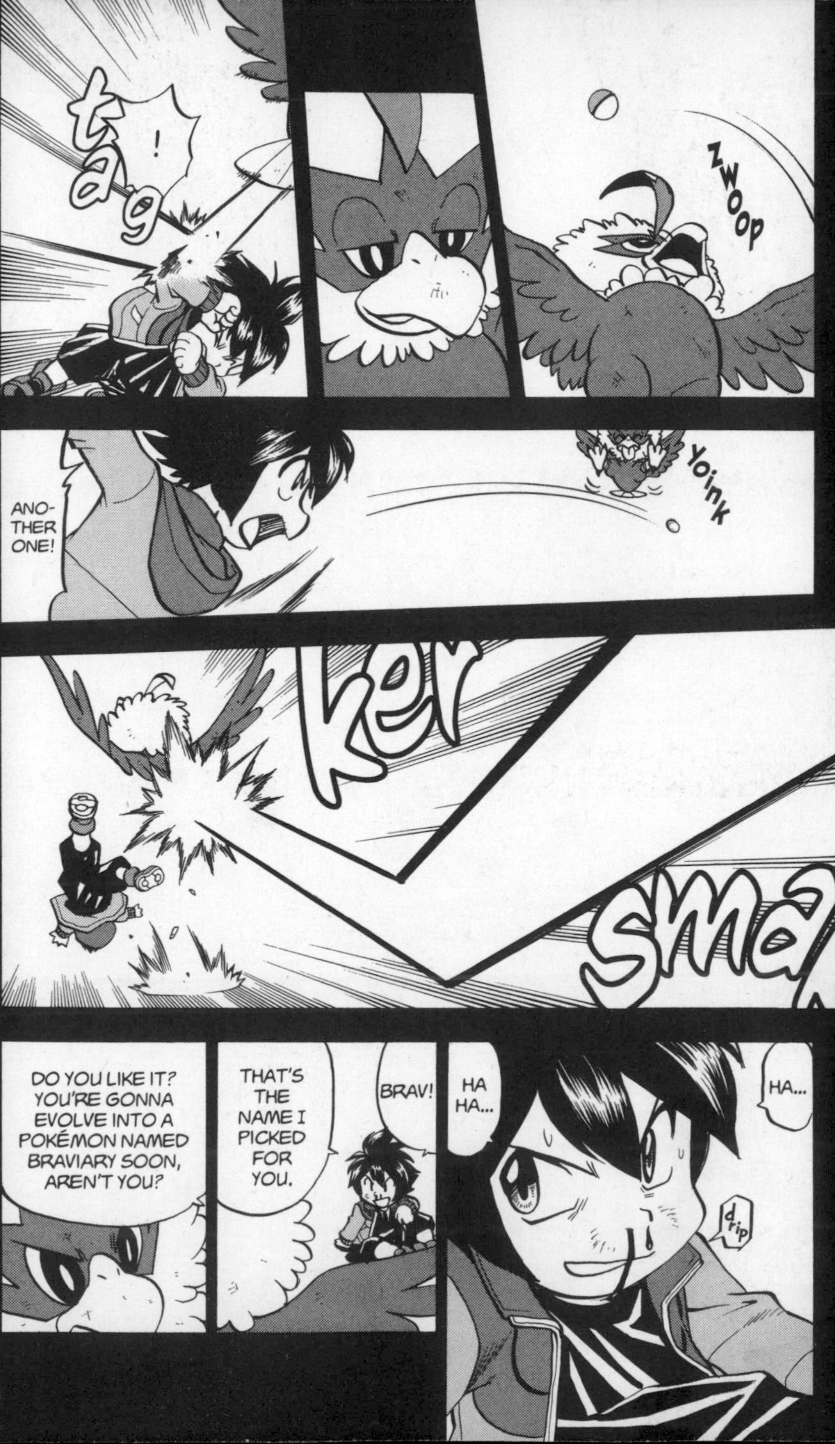
ZWOOP
tag
!
Yoink
ANO-THER ONE!
ker
smak
HA...
HA HA...
drip
BRAV!
THAT'S THE NAME I PICKED FOR YOU.
DO YOU LIKE IT? YOU'RE GONNA EVOLVE INTO A POKÉMON NAMED BRAVIARY SOON, AREN'T YOU?

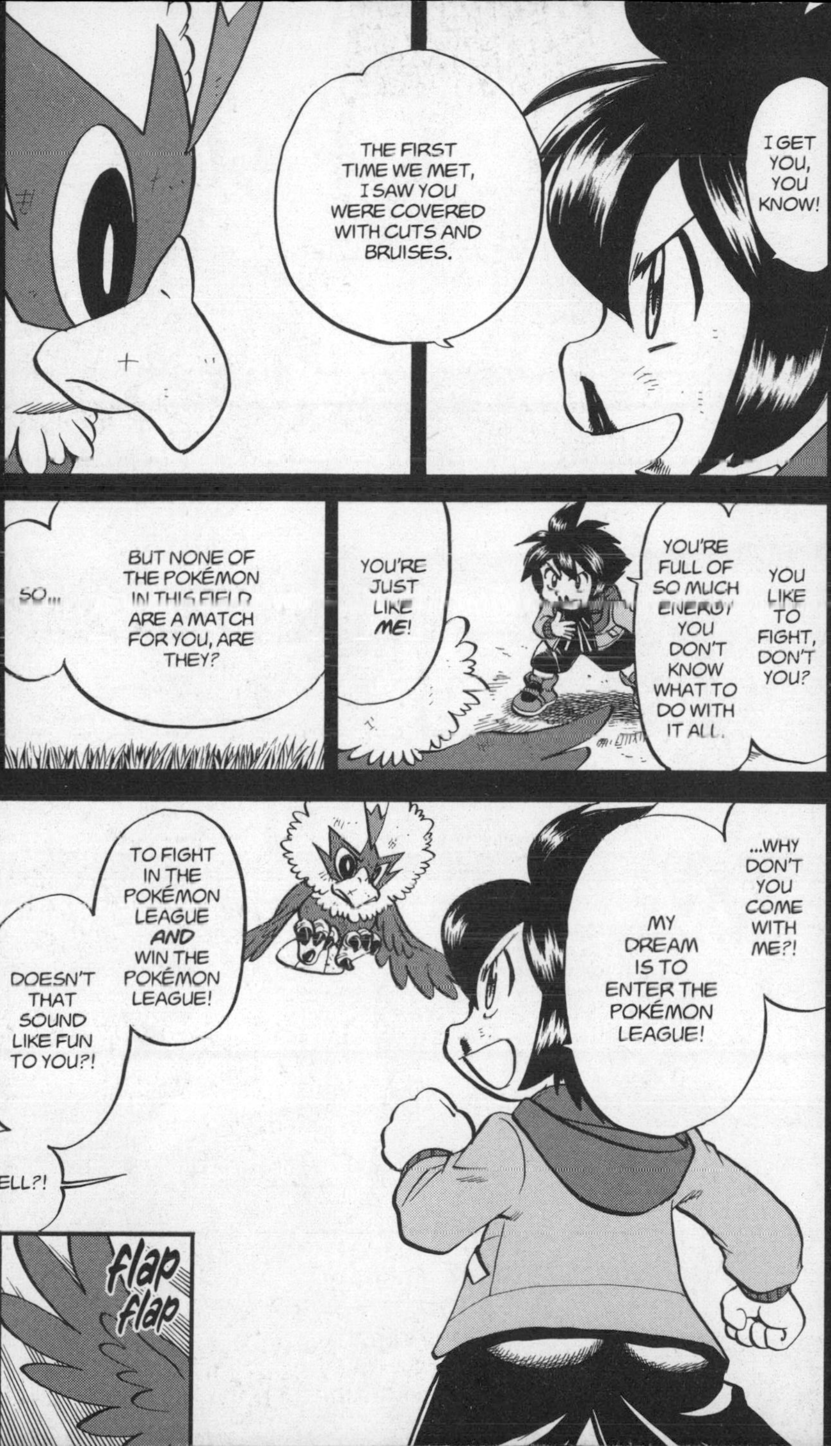
I GET YOU, YOU KNOW!
THE FIRST TIME WE MET, I SAW YOU WERE COVERED WITH CUTS AND BRUISES.
YOU LIKE TO FIGHT, DON'T YOU?
YOU'RE FULL OF SO MUCH ENERGY YOU DON'T KNOW WHAT TO DO WITH IT ALL.
YOU'RE JUST LIKE *ME*!
BUT NONE OF THE POKÉMON IN THIS FIELD ARE A MATCH FOR YOU, ARE THEY?
SO...
...WHY DON'T YOU COME WITH ME?!
MY DREAM IS TO ENTER THE POKÉMON LEAGUE!
TO FIGHT IN THE POKÉMON LEAGUE *AND* WIN THE POKÉMON LEAGUE!
DOESN'T THAT SOUND LIKE FUN TO YOU?!
WELL?!
flap flap

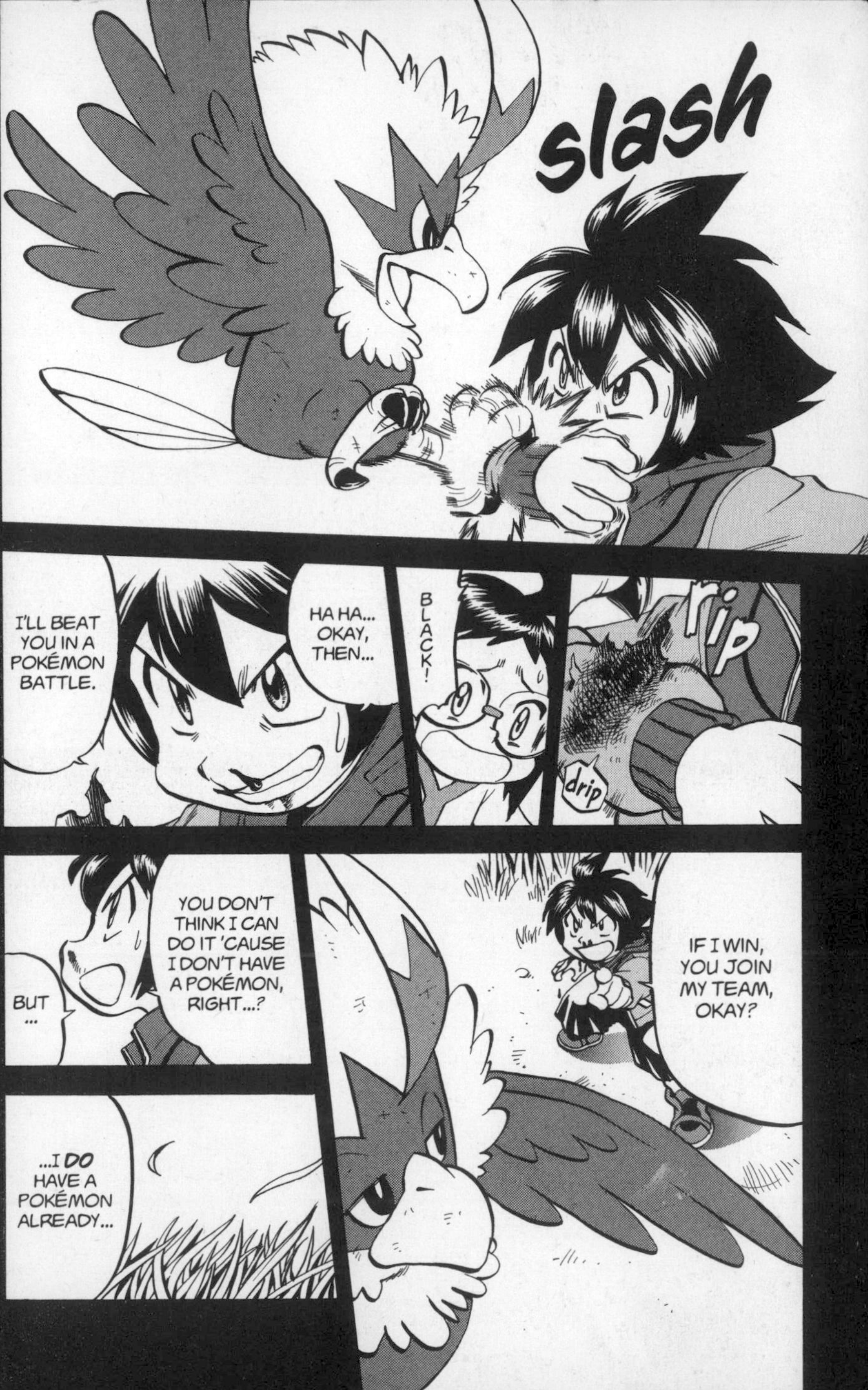
slash
rip
drip
BLACK!
HA HA... OKAY, THEN...
I'LL BEAT YOU IN A POKÉMON BATTLE.
IF I WIN, YOU JOIN MY TEAM, OKAY?
YOU DON'T THINK I CAN DO IT 'CAUSE I DON'T HAVE A POKÉMON, RIGHT...?
BUT ...
...I **DO** HAVE A POKÉMON ALREADY...

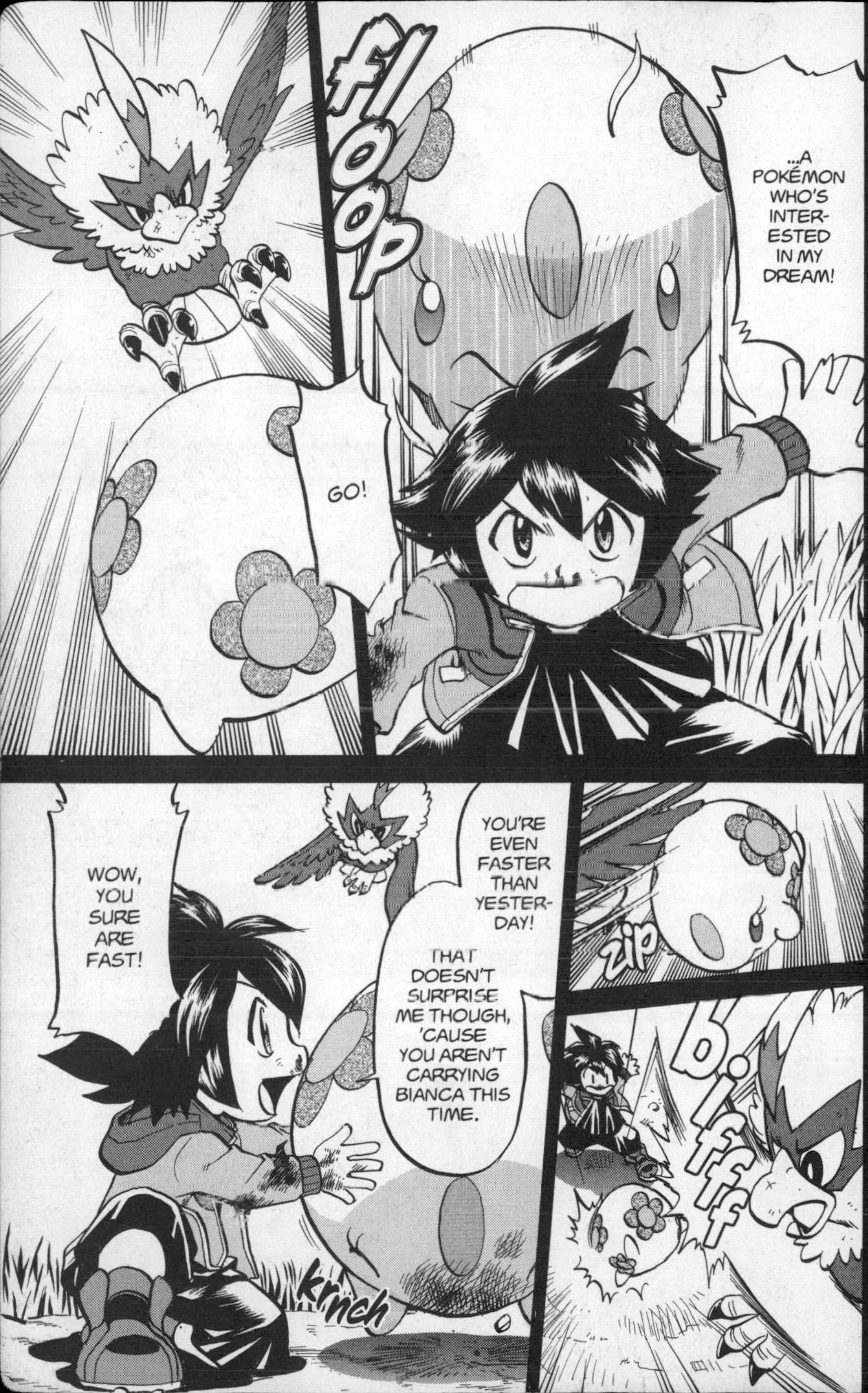
...A POKÉMON WHO'S INTER-ESTED IN MY DREAM!
FLOOOP
GO!
zip
biffff
WOW, YOU SURE ARE FAST!
YOU'RE EVEN FASTER THAN YESTER-DAY!
THAT DOESN'T SURPRISE ME THOUGH, 'CAUSE YOU AREN'T CARRYING BIANCA THIS TIME.
krnch

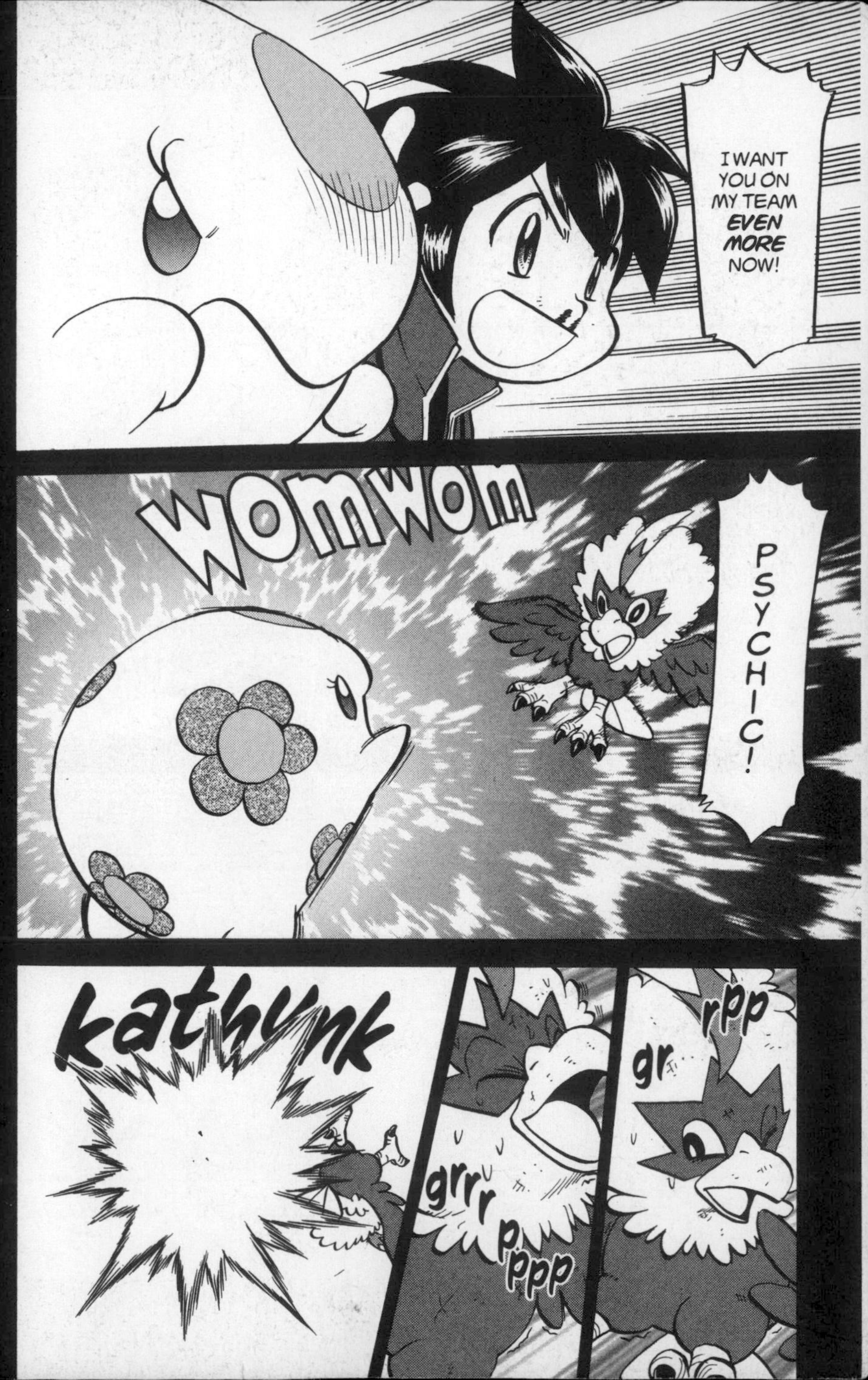
I WANT YOU ON MY TEAM EVEN MORE NOW!
PSYCHIC!
WOMWOM
rpp
gr...
grrr
pppp
kathunk

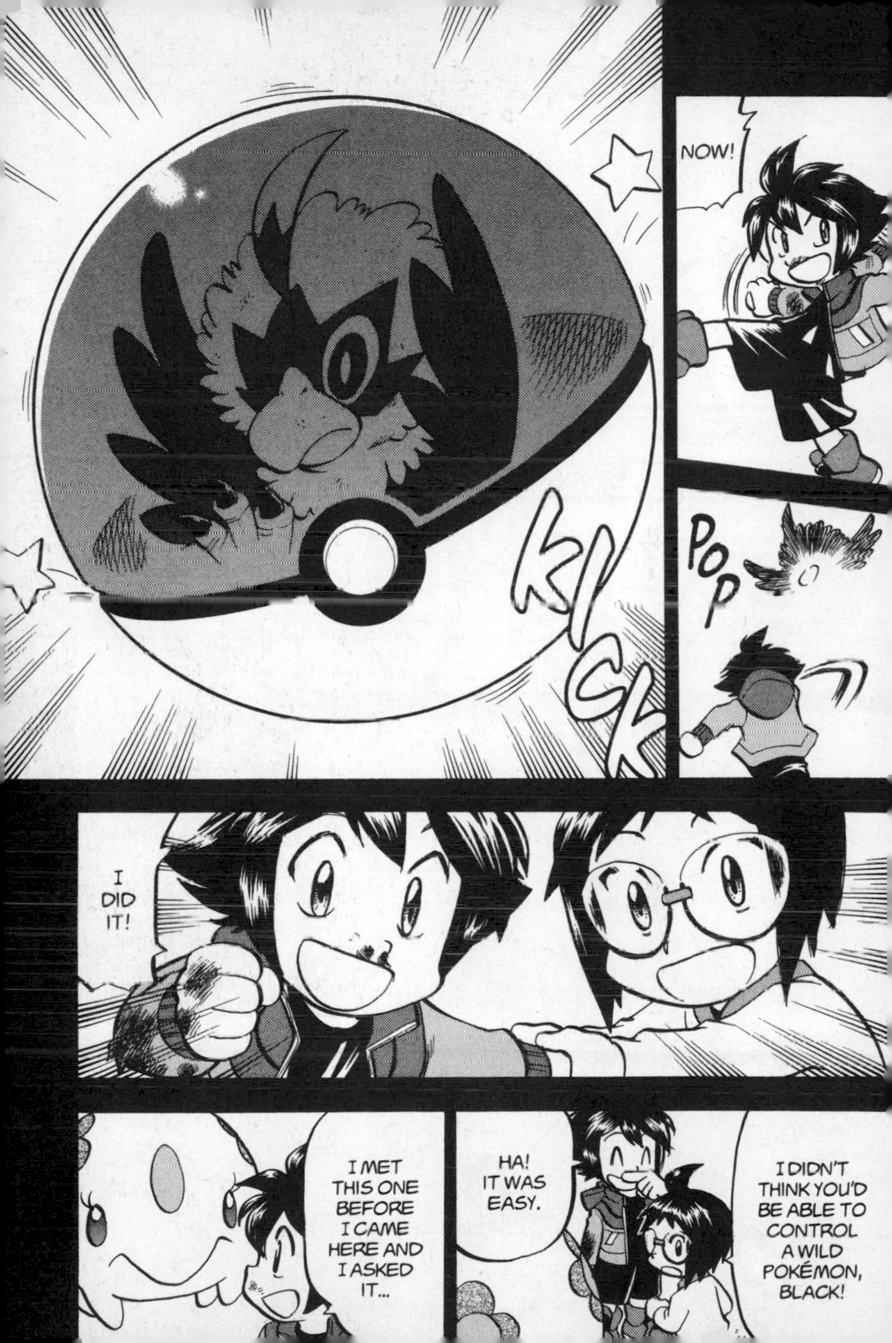
NOW!
POP
KICK
I DID IT!
I DIDN'T THINK YOU'D BE ABLE TO CONTROL A WILD POKÉMON, BLACK!
HA! IT WAS EASY.
I MET THIS ONE BEFORE I CAME HERE AND I ASKED IT...

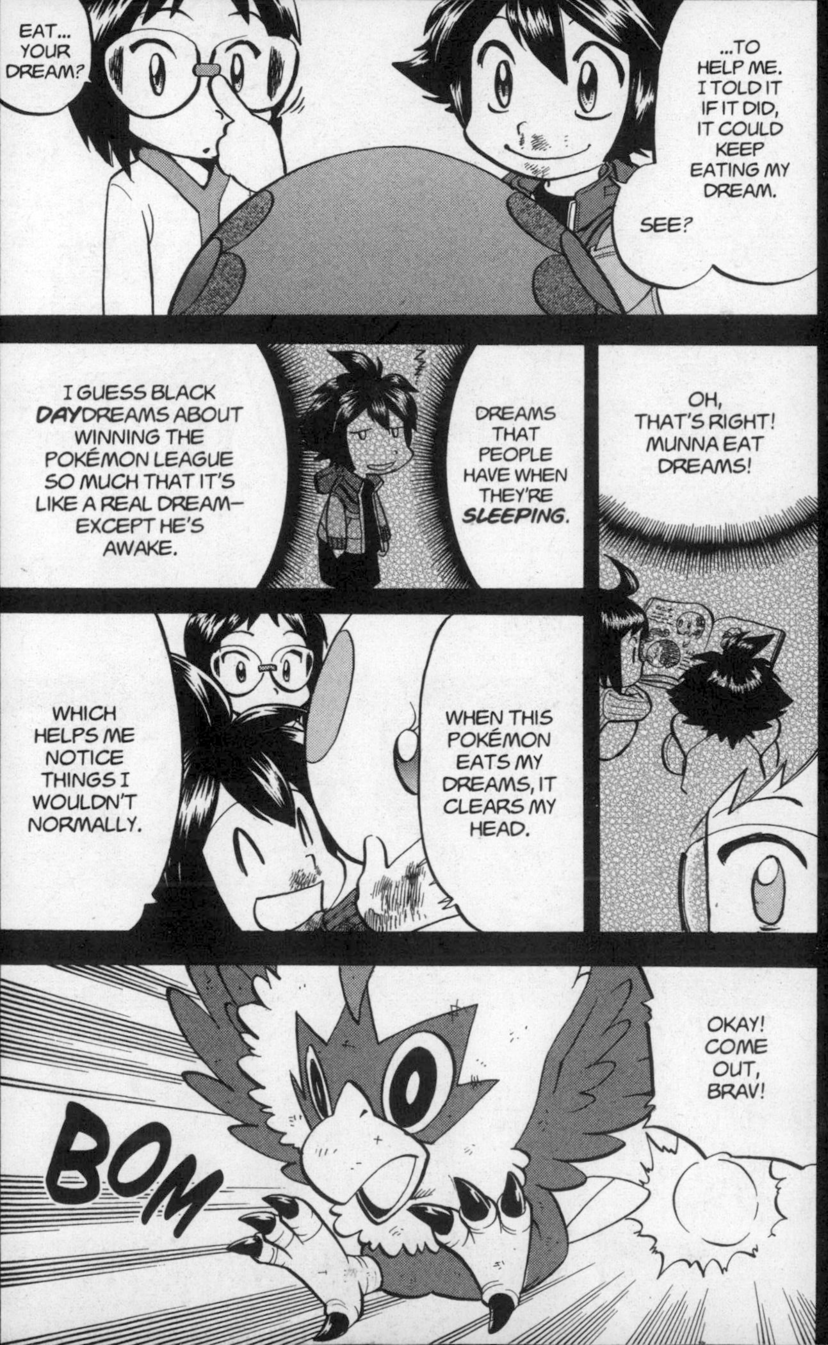
...TO HELP ME. I TOLD IT IF IT DID, IT COULD KEEP EATING MY DREAM.
SEE?
EAT... YOUR DREAM?
OH, THAT'S RIGHT! MUNNA EAT DREAMS!
DREAMS THAT PEOPLE HAVE WHEN THEY'RE SLEEPING.
I GUESS BLACK DAYDREAMS ABOUT WINNING THE POKÉMON LEAGUE SO MUCH THAT IT'S LIKE A REAL DREAM—EXCEPT HE'S AWAKE.
WHEN THIS POKÉMON EATS MY DREAMS, IT CLEARS MY HEAD.
WHICH HELPS ME NOTICE THINGS I WOULDN'T NORMALLY.
OKAY! COME OUT, BRAV!
BOM

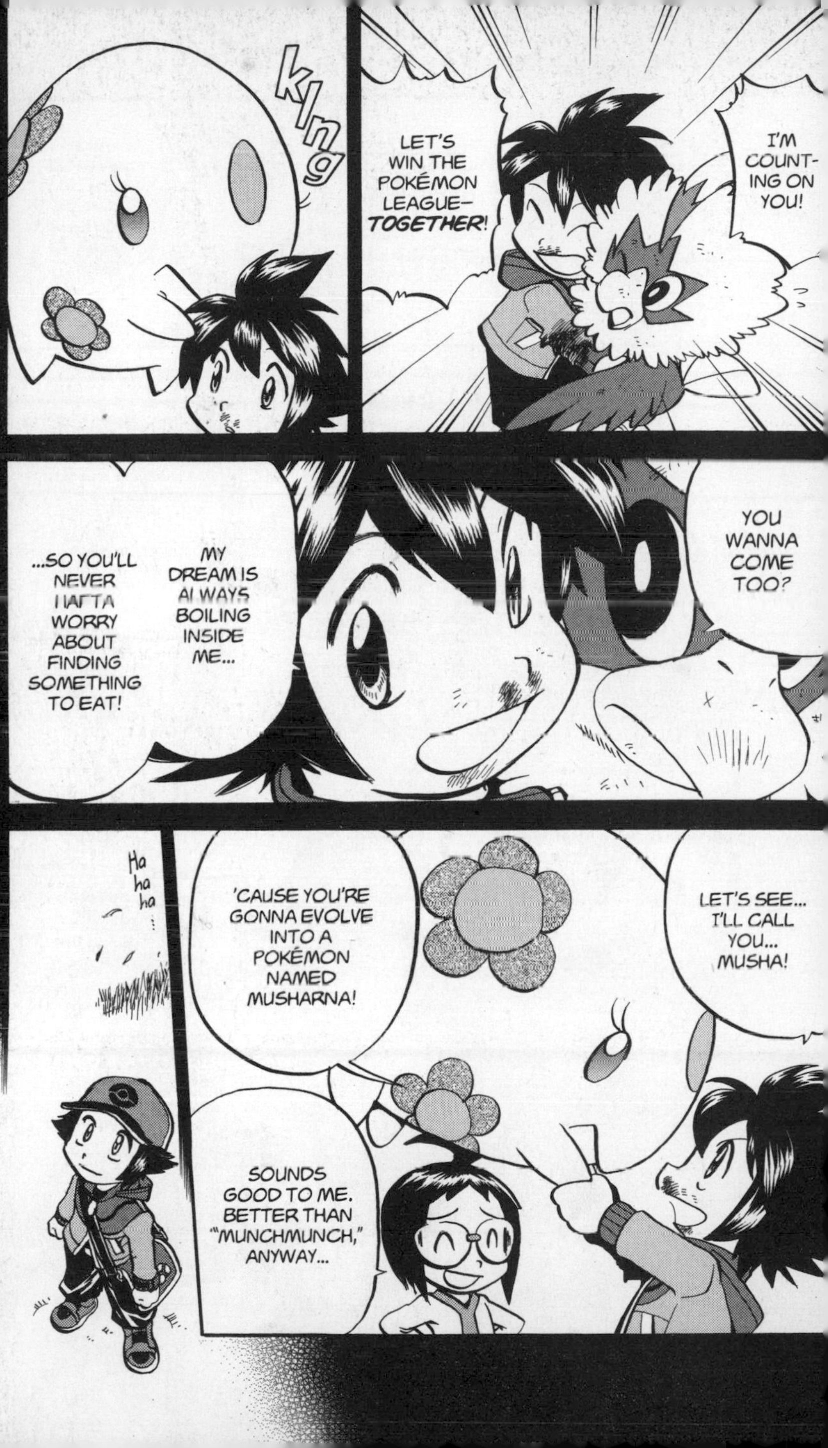
I'M COUNTING ON YOU!
LET'S WIN THE POKÉMON LEAGUE—**TOGETHER**!
klng
YOU WANNA COME TOO?
MY DREAM IS ALWAYS BOILING INSIDE ME...
...SO YOU'LL NEVER HAFTA WORRY ABOUT FINDING SOMETHING TO EAT!
LET'S SEE... I'LL CALL YOU... MUSHA!
'CAUSE YOU'RE GONNA EVOLVE INTO A POKÉMON NAMED MUSHARNA!
SOUNDS GOOD TO ME. BETTER THAN "MUNCHMUNCH," ANYWAY...
Ha ha ha...

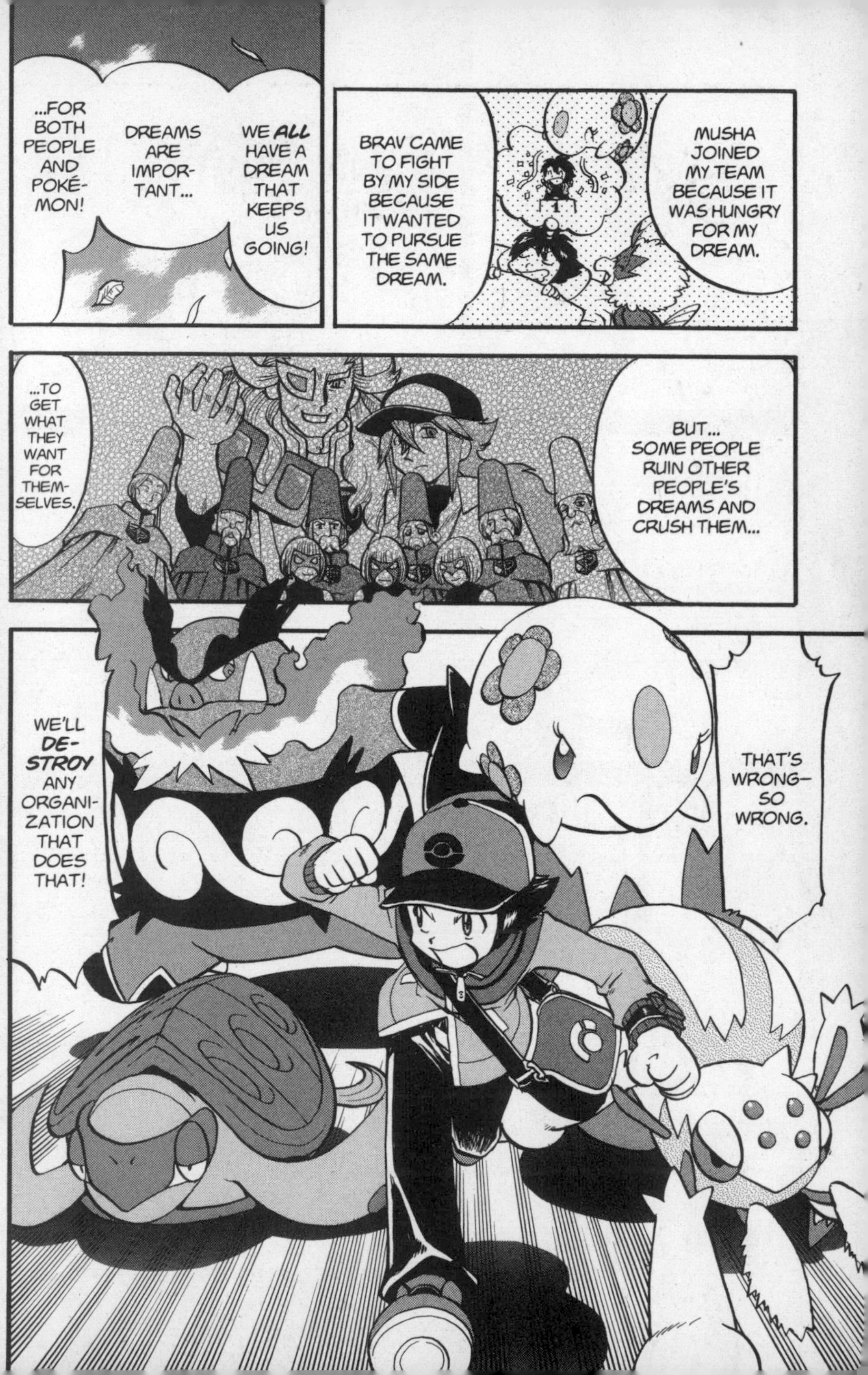
MUSHA JOINED MY TEAM BECAUSE IT WAS HUNGRY FOR MY DREAM.
BRAV CAME TO FIGHT BY MY SIDE BECAUSE IT WANTED TO PURSUE THE SAME DREAM.
WE **ALL** HAVE A DREAM THAT KEEPS US GOING!
DREAMS ARE IMPOR-TANT...
...FOR BOTH PEOPLE AND POKÉ-MON!
BUT... SOME PEOPLE RUIN OTHER PEOPLE'S DREAMS AND CRUSH THEM...
...TO GET WHAT THEY WANT FOR THEM-SELVES.
THAT'S WRONG— SO WRONG.
WE'LL ***DE-STROY*** ANY ORGANI-ZATION THAT DOES THAT!

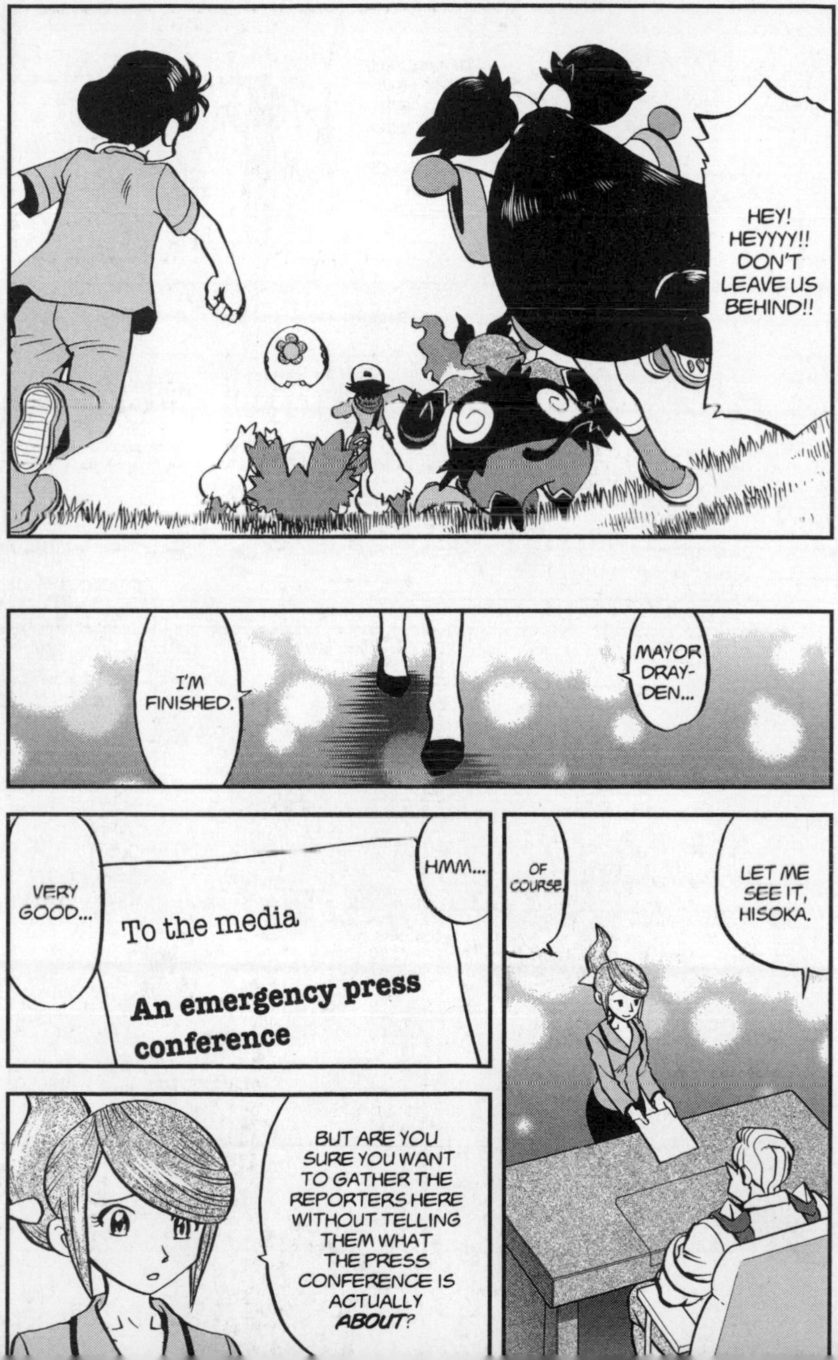
HEY! HEYYYY!! DON'T LEAVE US BEHIND!!
MAYOR DRAY-DEN...
I'M FINISHED.
LET ME SEE IT, HISOKA.
OF COURSE.
HMM...
VERY GOOD...
To the media
An emergency press conference
BUT ARE YOU SURE YOU WANT TO GATHER THE REPORTERS HERE WITHOUT TELLING THEM WHAT THE PRESS CONFERENCE IS ACTUALLY ABOUT?

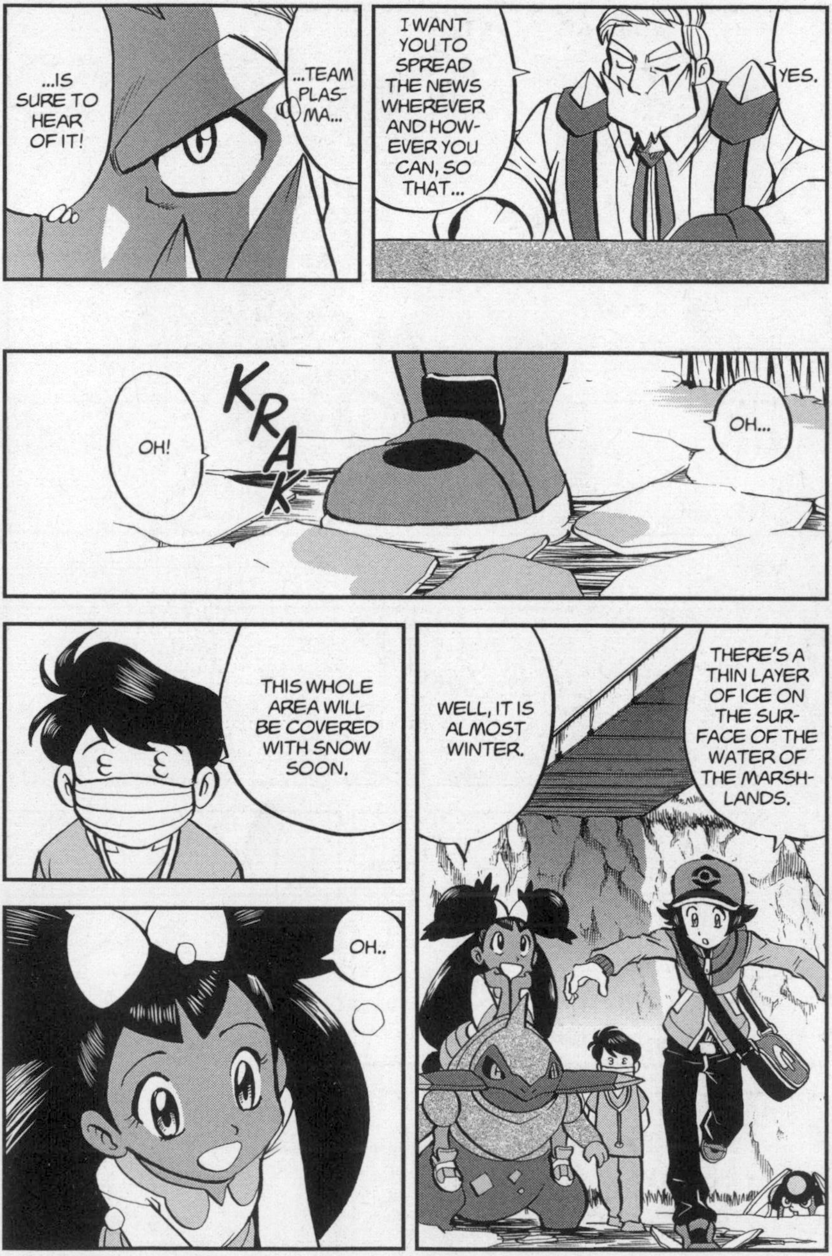
YES.
I WANT YOU TO SPREAD THE NEWS WHEREVER AND HOW-EVER YOU CAN, SO THAT...
...TEAM PLAS-MA...
...IS SURE TO HEAR OF IT!
OH...
KRAK
OH!
THERE'S A THIN LAYER OF ICE ON THE SUR-FACE OF THE WATER OF THE MARSH-LANDS.
WELL, IT IS ALMOST WINTER.
THIS WHOLE AREA WILL BE COVERED WITH SNOW SOON.
OH..

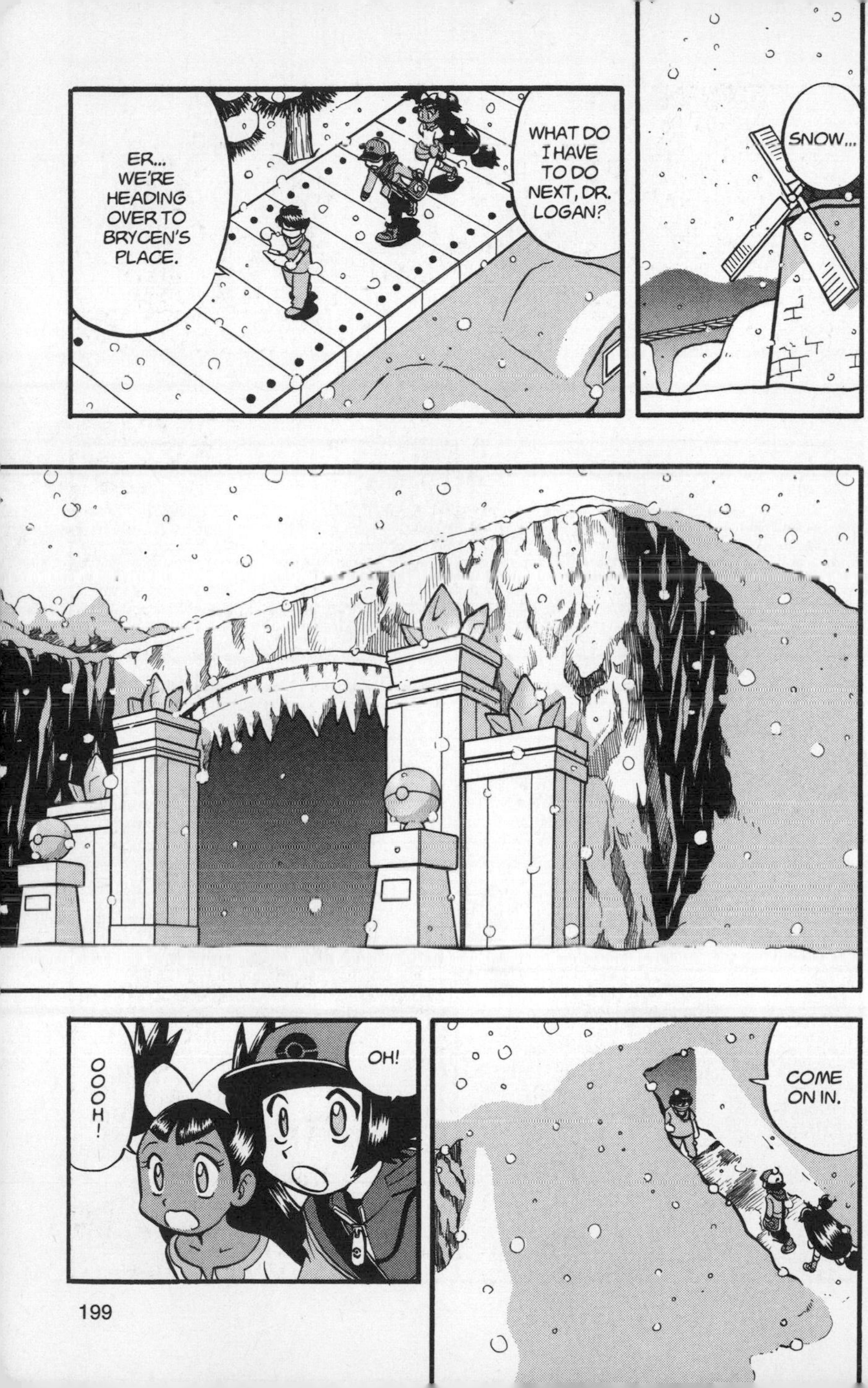
SNOW...
WHAT DO I HAVE TO DO NEXT, DR. LOGAN?
ER... WE'RE HEADING OVER TO BRYCEN'S PLACE.
COME ON IN.
OH!
OOOH!

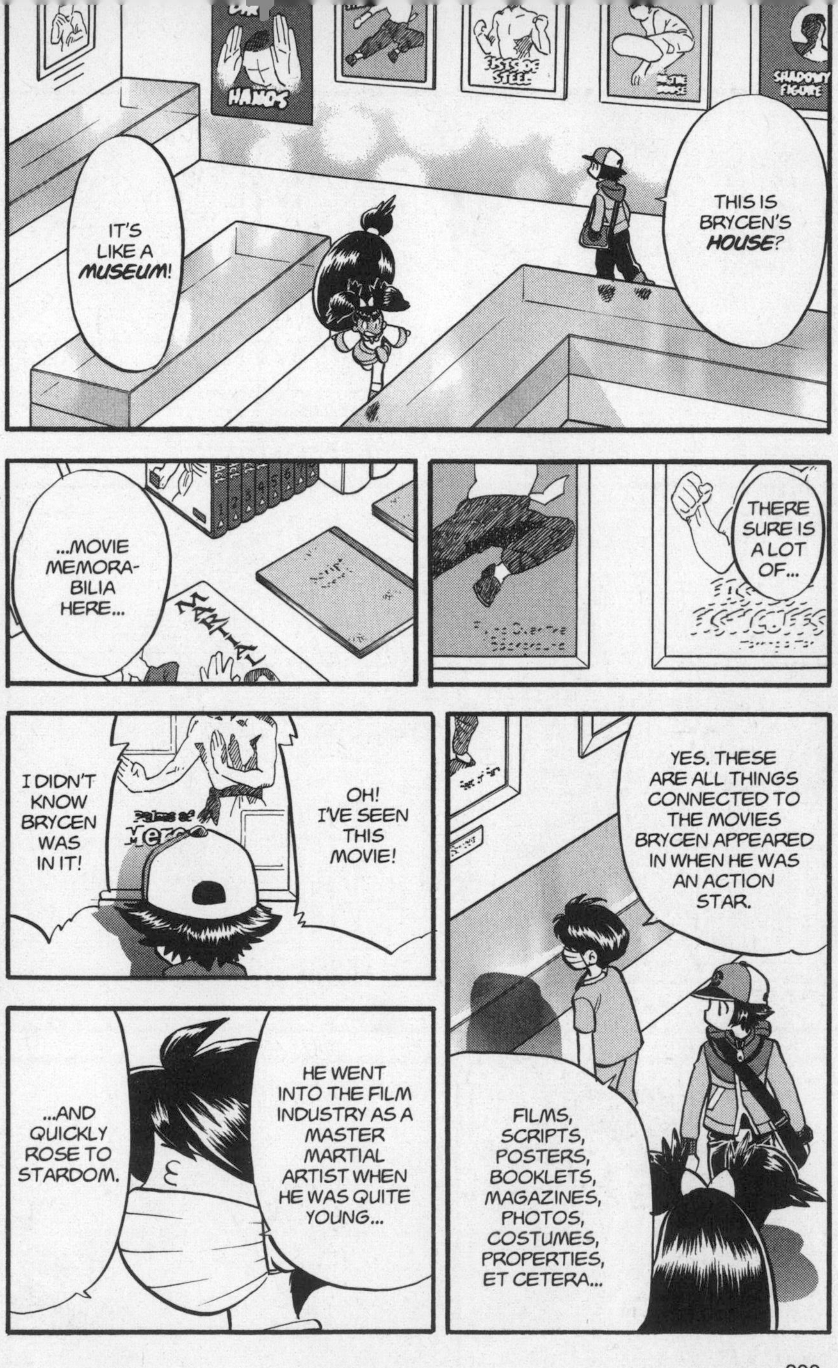
THIS IS BRYCEN'S HOUSE?
IT'S LIKE A MUSEUM!
THERE SURE IS A LOT OF...
...MOVIE MEMORABILIA HERE...
YES. THESE ARE ALL THINGS CONNECTED TO THE MOVIES BRYCEN APPEARED IN WHEN HE WAS AN ACTION STAR.
FILMS, SCRIPTS, POSTERS, BOOKLETS, MAGAZINES, PHOTOS, COSTUMES, PROPERTIES, ET CETERA...
OH! I'VE SEEN THIS MOVIE!
I DIDN'T KNOW BRYCEN WAS IN IT!
HE WENT INTO THE FILM INDUSTRY AS A MASTER MARTIAL ARTIST WHEN HE WAS QUITE YOUNG...
...AND QUICKLY ROSE TO STARDOM.

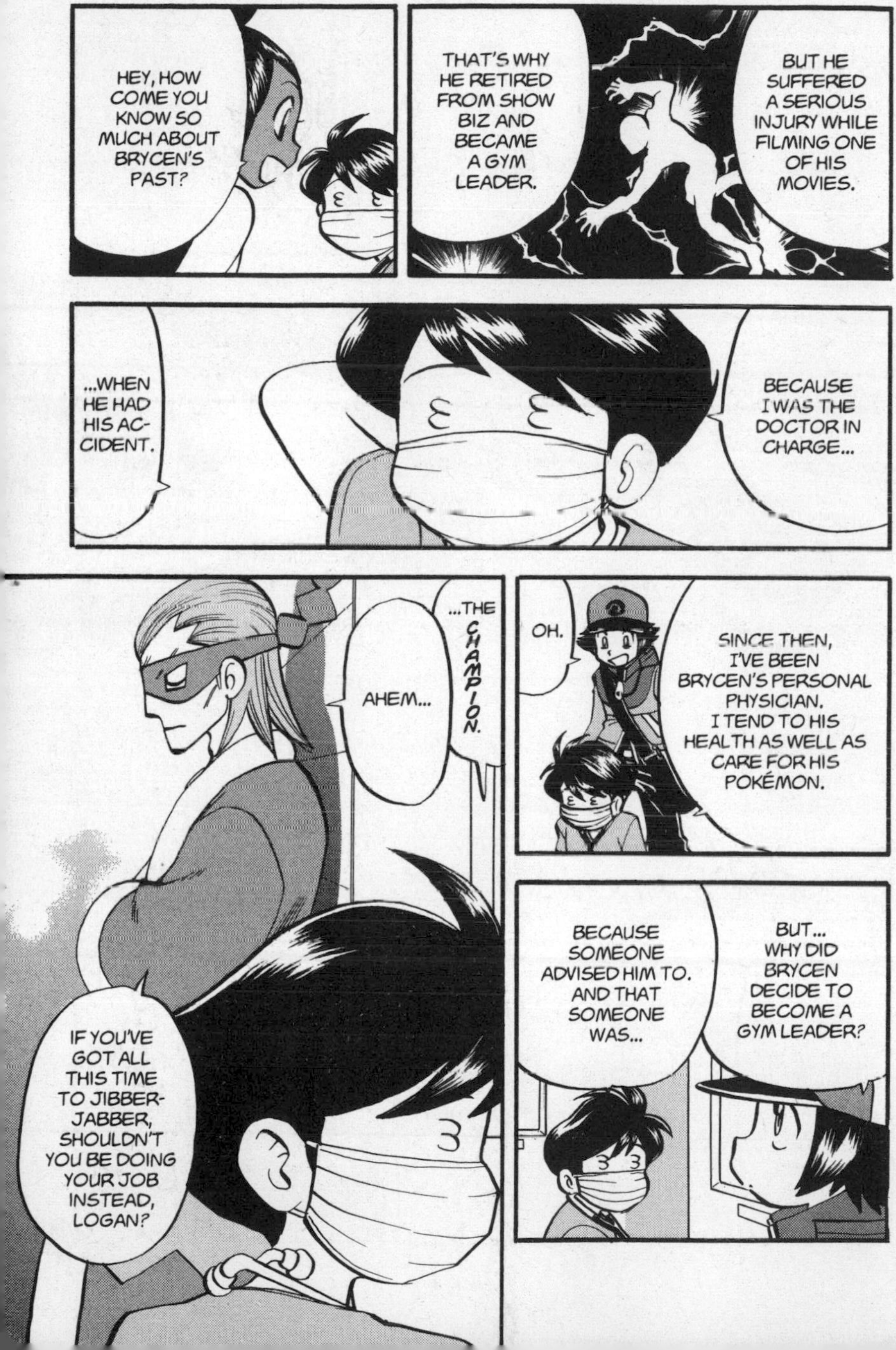
BUT HE SUFFERED A SERIOUS INJURY WHILE FILMING ONE OF HIS MOVIES.
THAT'S WHY HE RETIRED FROM SHOW BIZ AND BECAME A GYM LEADER.
HEY, HOW COME YOU KNOW SO MUCH ABOUT BRYCEN'S PAST?
BECAUSE I WAS THE DOCTOR IN CHARGE...
...WHEN HE HAD HIS ACCIDENT.
SINCE THEN, I'VE BEEN BRYCEN'S PERSONAL PHYSICIAN. I TEND TO HIS HEALTH AS WELL AS CARE FOR HIS POKÉMON.
OH.
BUT... WHY DID BRYCEN DECIDE TO BECOME A GYM LEADER?
BECAUSE SOMEONE ADVISED HIM TO. AND THAT SOMEONE WAS...
...THE CHAMPION.
AHEM...
IF YOU'VE GOT ALL THIS TIME TO JIBBER-JABBER, SHOULDN'T YOU BE DOING YOUR JOB INSTEAD, LOGAN?

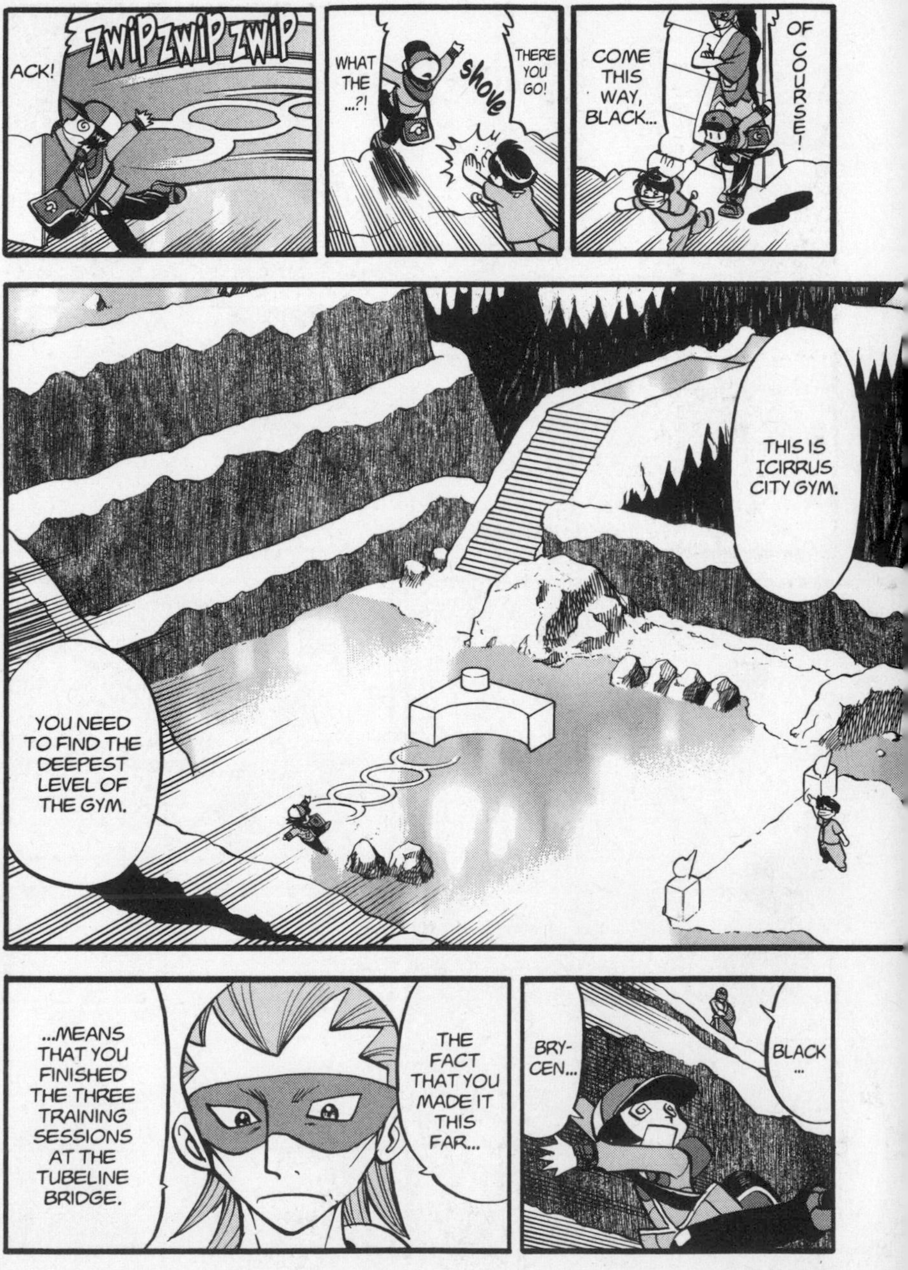
OF COURSE!
COME THIS WAY, BLACK...
THERE YOU GO!
shove
WHAT THE ...?!
ZWIP ZWIP ZWIP
ACK!
THIS IS ICIRRUS CITY GYM.
YOU NEED TO FIND THE DEEPEST LEVEL OF THE GYM.
BLACK ...
BRY-CEN...
THE FACT THAT YOU MADE IT THIS FAR...
...MEANS THAT YOU FINISHED THE THREE TRAINING SESSIONS AT THE TUBELINE BRIDGE.

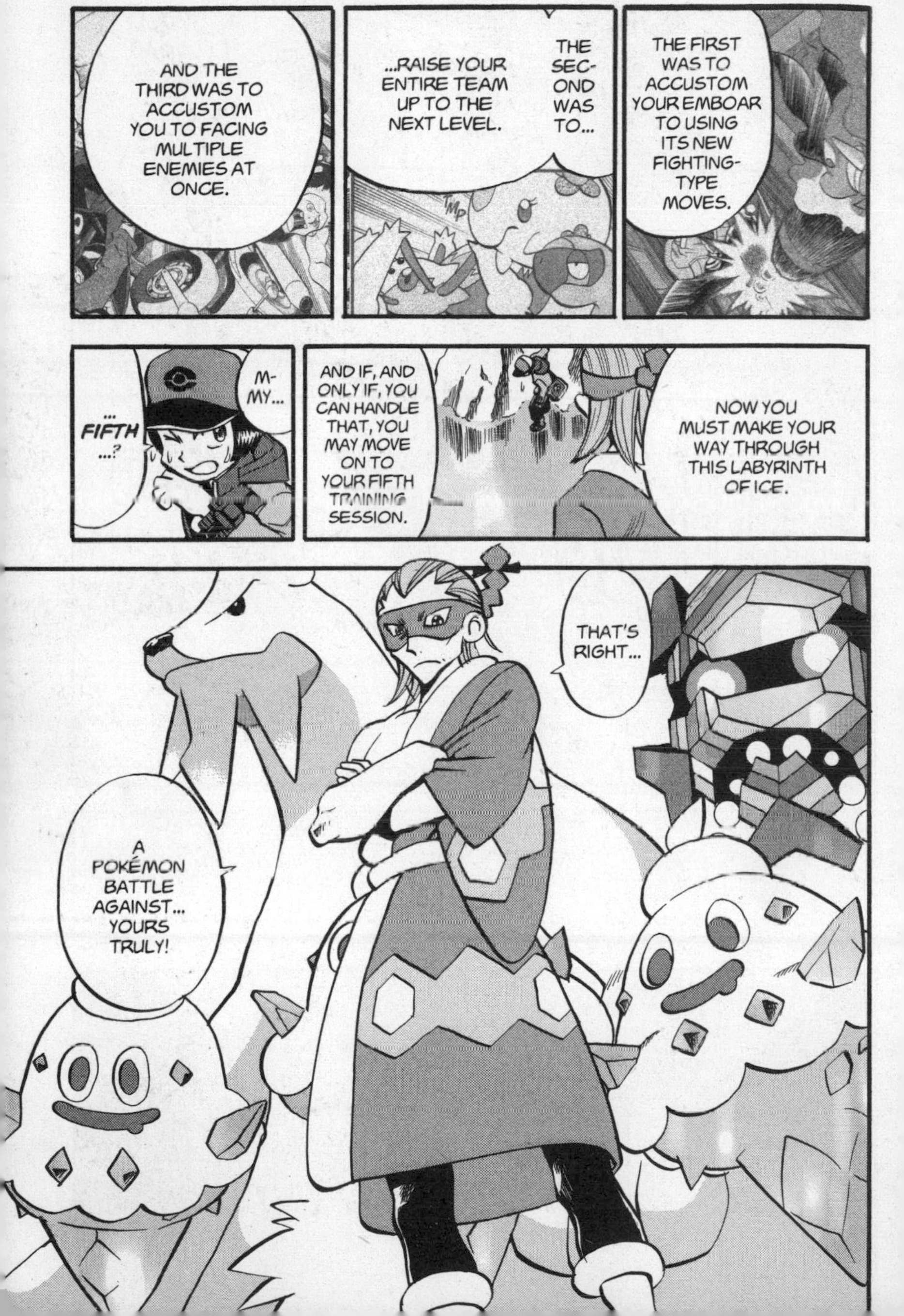
THE FIRST WAS TO ACCUSTOM YOUR EMBOAR TO USING ITS NEW FIGHTING-TYPE MOVES.
THE SECOND WAS TO...
...RAISE YOUR ENTIRE TEAM UP TO THE NEXT LEVEL.
TMP
AND THE THIRD WAS TO ACCUSTOM YOU TO FACING MULTIPLE ENEMIES AT ONCE.
NOW YOU MUST MAKE YOUR WAY THROUGH THIS LABYRINTH OF ICE.
AND IF, AND ONLY IF, YOU CAN HANDLE THAT, YOU MAY MOVE ON TO YOUR FIFTH TRAINING SESSION.
M-MY...
...FIFTH...?
THAT'S RIGHT...
A POKÉMON BATTLE AGAINST... YOURS TRULY!

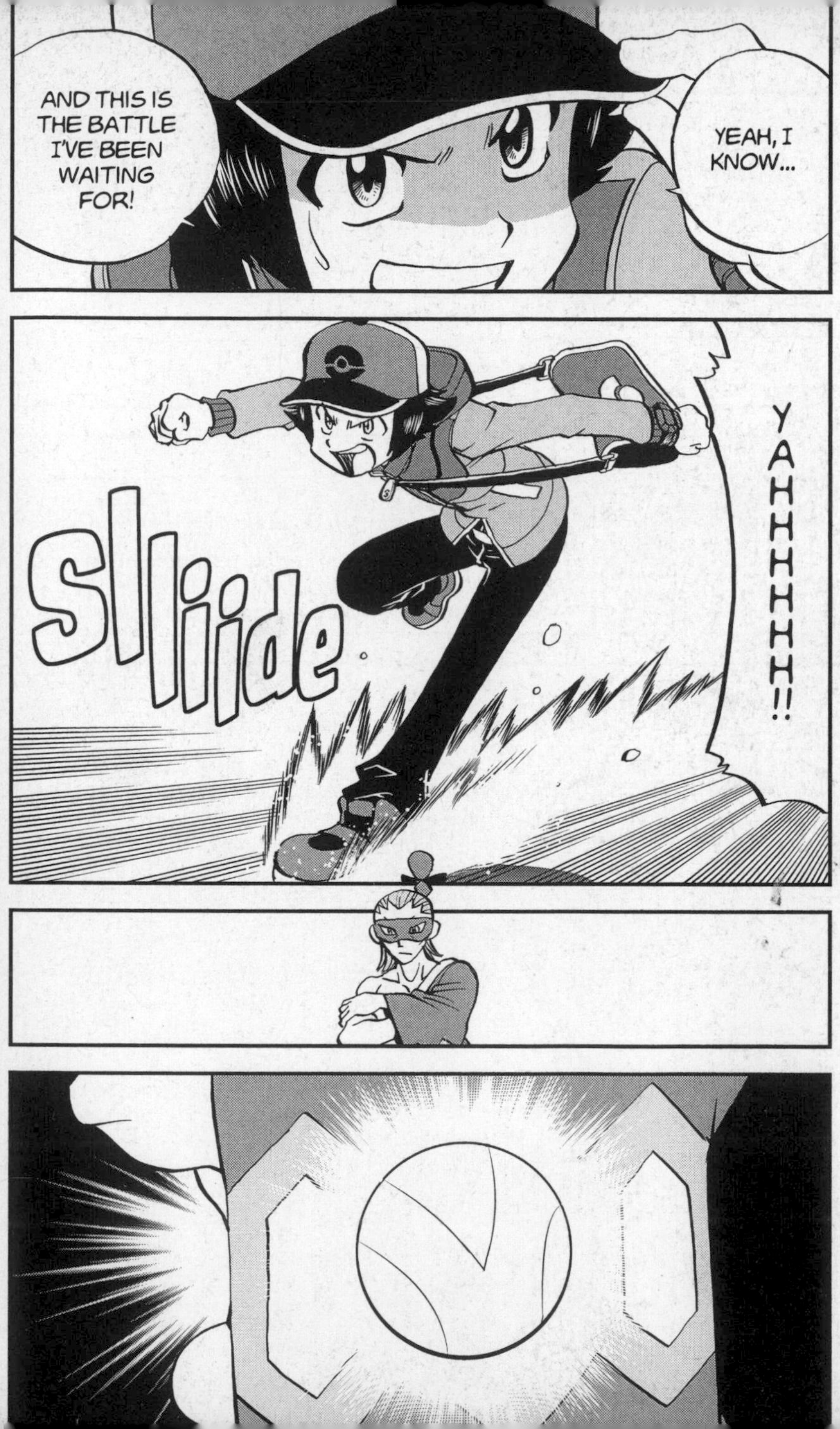
YEAH, I KNOW...
AND THIS IS THE BATTLE I'VE BEEN WAITING FOR!
YAHHHHH!!
sliide

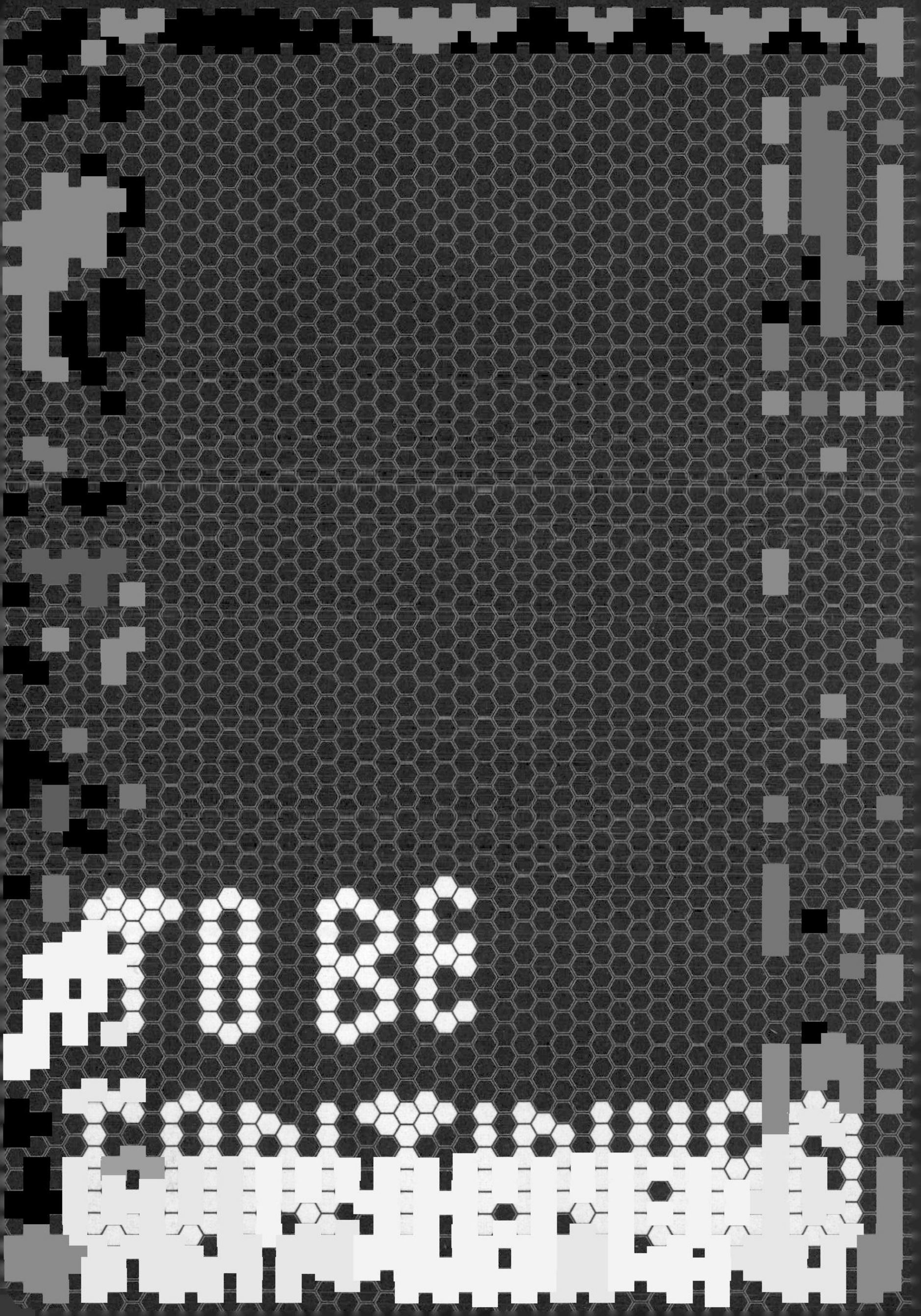
TO BE

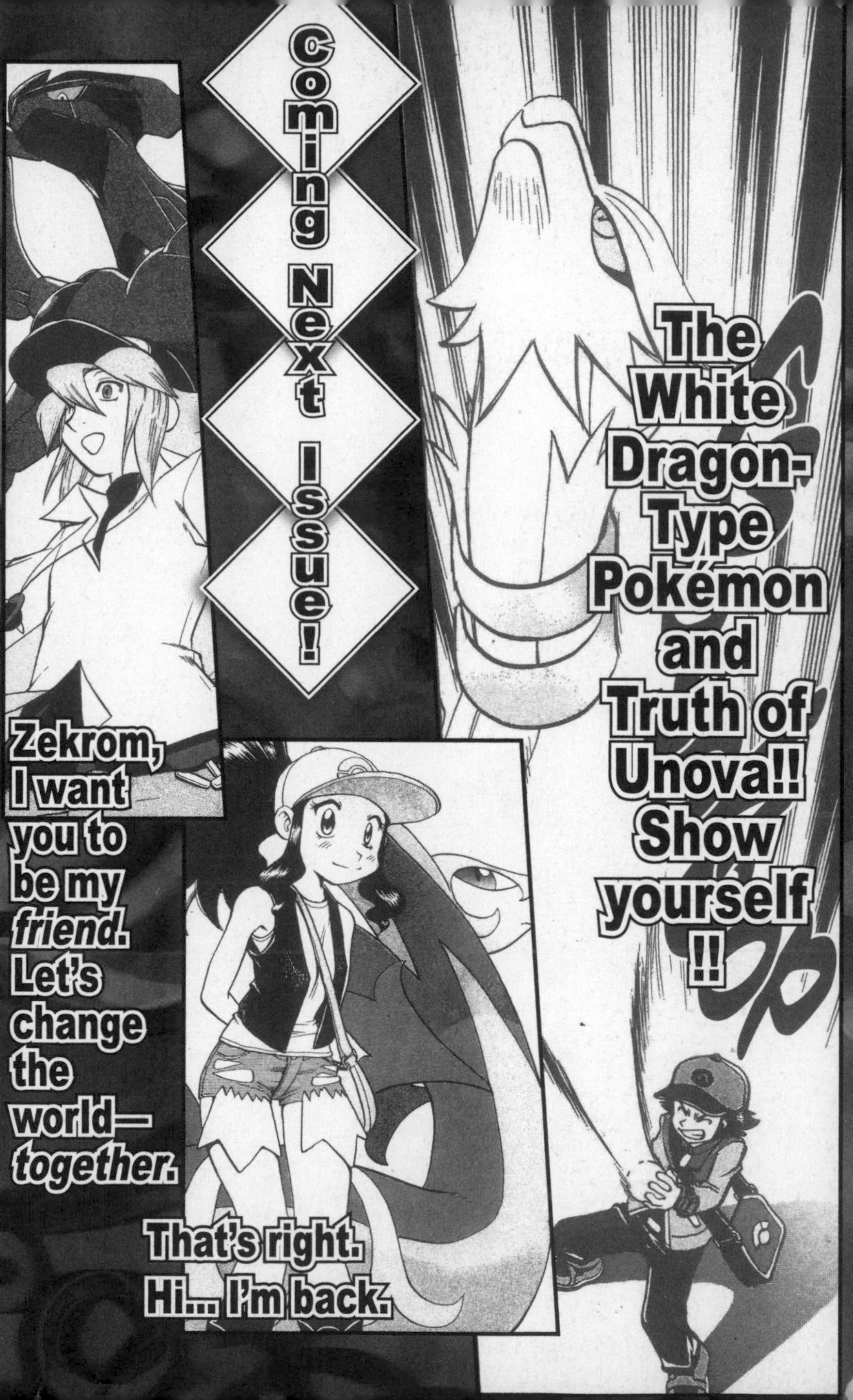
Coming Next Issue!
The White Dragon-Type Pokémon and Truth of Unova!! Show yourself!!
Zekrom, I want you to be my *friend.* Let's change the world—*together.*
That's right. Hi... I'm back.

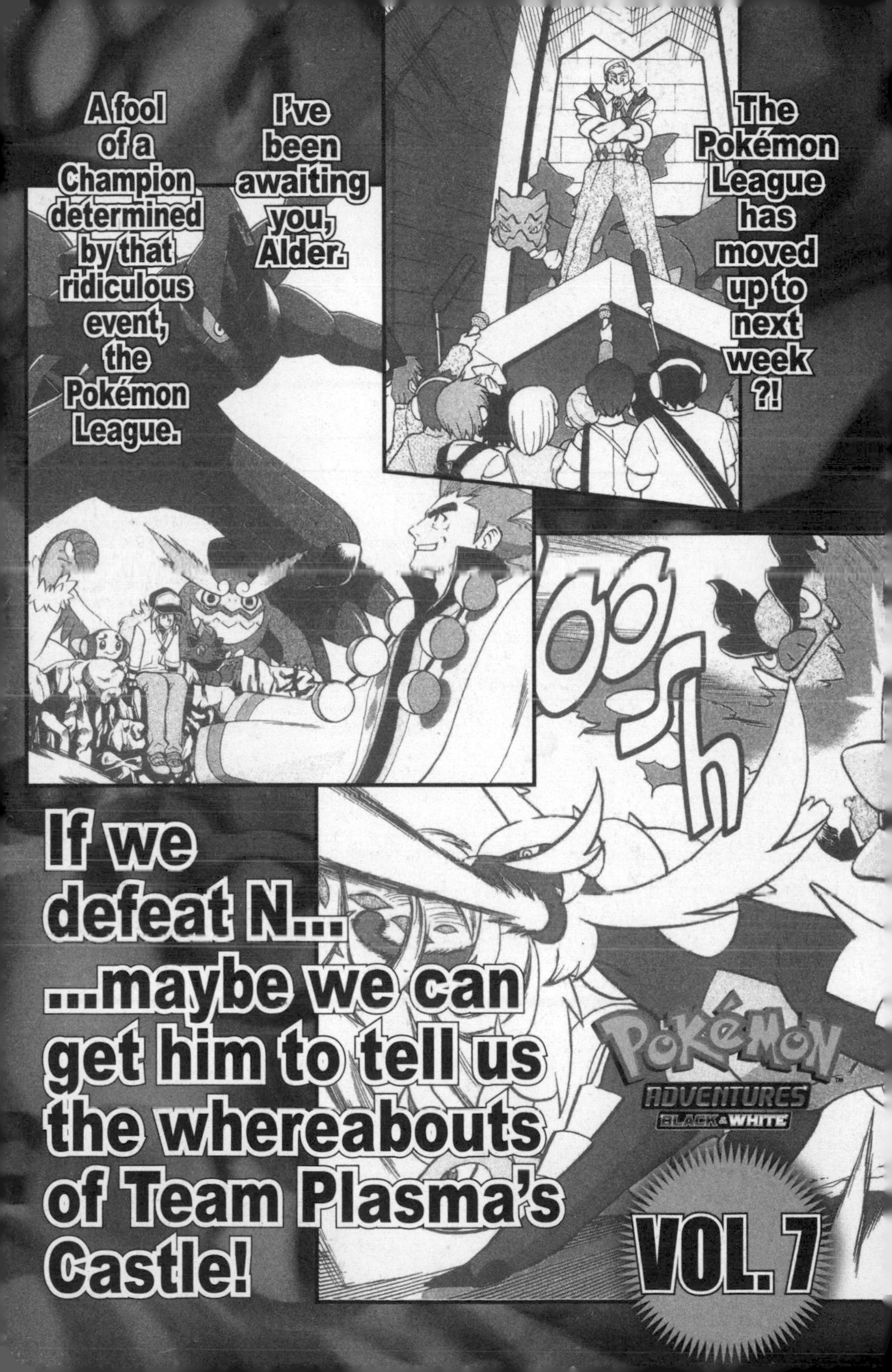

The Pokémon League has moved up to next week?!
I've been awaiting you, Alder.
A fool of a Champion determined by that ridiculous event, the Pokémon League.
If we defeat N...
...maybe we can get him to tell us the whereabouts of Team Plasma's Castle!
Pokémon Adventures Black & White
VOL. 7

Pokémon ADVENTURES
BLACK AND WHITE
Volume 6
Perfect Square Edition

Story by HIDENORI KUSAKA
Art by SATOSHI YAMAMOTO

© 2014 Pokémon.
© 1995–2014 Nintendo/Creatures Inc./GAME FREAK inc.
TM, ®, and character names are trademarks of Nintendo.
POCKET MONSTERS SPECIAL Vol. 48
by Hidenori KUSAKA, Satoshi YAMAMOTO
© 1997 Hidenori KUSAKA, Satoshi YAMAMOTO
All rights reserved.
Original Japanese edition published by SHOGAKUKAN.
English translation rights in the United States of America, Canada,
United Kingdom, Ireland, Australia and New Zealand
arranged with SHOGAKUKAN.

Translation/Tetsuichiro Miyaki
English Adaptation/Annette Roman
Touch-up & Lettering/Susan Daigle-Leach
Design/Shawn Carrico
Editor/Annette Roman

Printed in the U.S.A.

Published by VIZ Media, LLC
P.O. Box 77010
San Francisco, CA 94107

10 9 8 7 6 5 4 3 2 1
First printing, January 2015

www.perfectsquare.com   www.viz.com

Message from
Hidenori Kusaka

I received a lot of gifts and letters from readers this year. I was especially grateful for the hand-made gifts; they're so heartwarming and special. Soft fabric dolls, stone cell-phone straps, buttons and badges, dot art created with iron beads, T-shirts etc. These things are all one-of-a-kind and irreplaceable. Thank you very much. ♪(´ θ`)ノ

Message from
Satoshi Yamamoto

I bring you vol. 6, filled with episodes that mark the turning point of the Black and White story arc. I have good memories of all the adventures, but I especially like the one about Bianca. Maybe it's because Bianca's slightly annoying klutzy and carefree nature reminds me of myself. I worked every hard to draw her as a lovable character. (LOL)

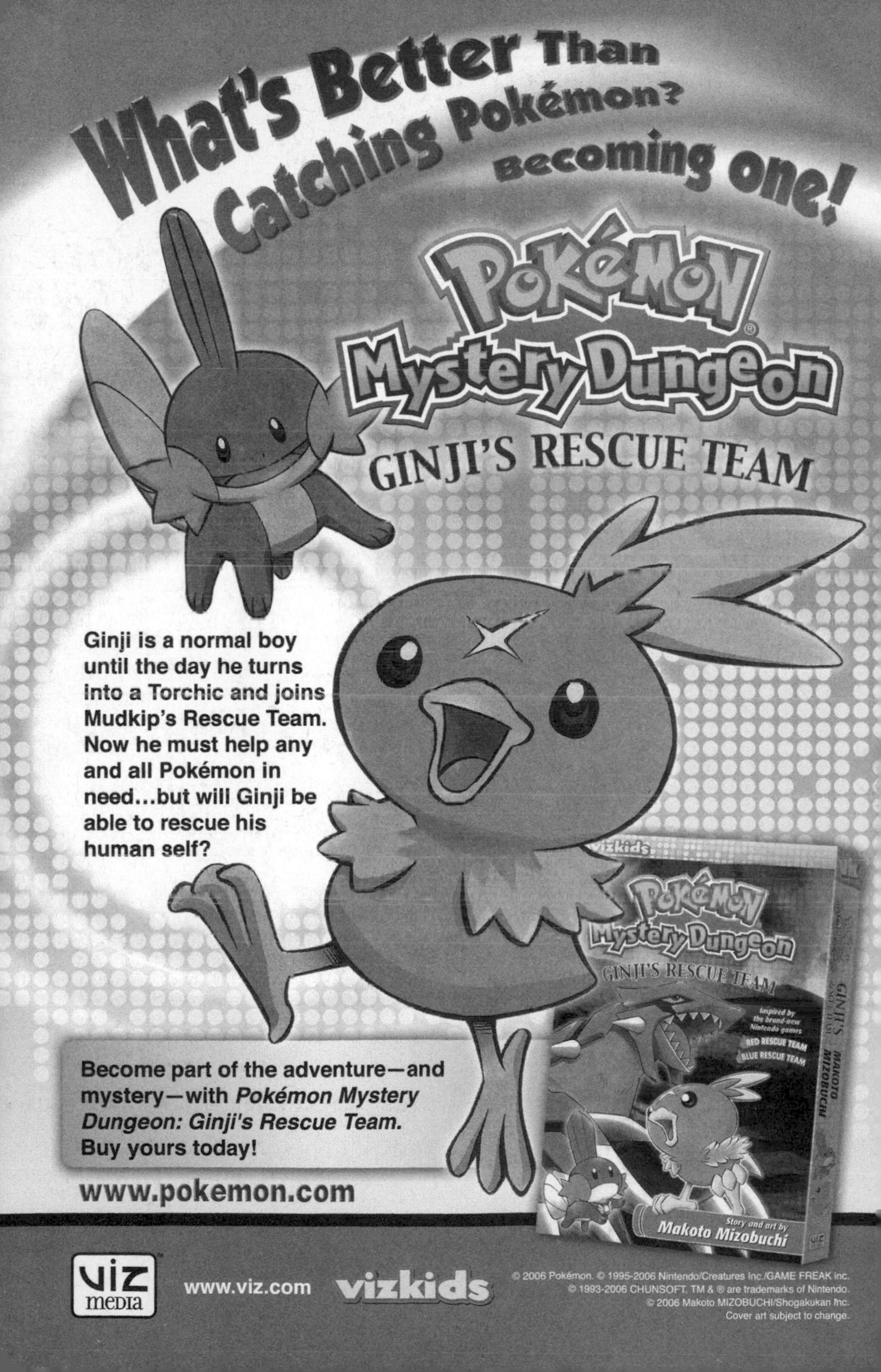
What's Better Than Catching Pokémon?
Becoming one!
Pokémon®
Mystery Dungeon
GINJI'S RESCUE TEAM
Ginji is a normal boy until the day he turns into a Torchic and joins Mudkip's Rescue Team. Now he must help any and all Pokémon in need...but will Ginji be able to rescue his human self?
Become part of the adventure—and mystery—with *Pokémon Mystery Dungeon: Ginji's Rescue Team.* Buy yours today!
www.pokemon.com
vizkids
Pokémon Mystery Dungeon
GINJI'S RESCUE TEAM
Inspired by the brand-new Nintendo games
RED RESCUE TEAM
BLUE RESCUE TEAM
Story and art by
Makoto Mizobuchi
GINJI'S RESCUE TEAM
MAKOTO MIZOBUCHI
VIZ media
www.viz.com
vizkids
© 2006 Pokémon. © 1995-2006 Nintendo/Creatures Inc./GAME FREAK inc.
© 1993-2006 CHUNSOFT. TM & ® are trademarks of Nintendo.
© 2006 Makoto MIZOBUCHI/Shogakukan Inc.
Cover art subject to change.

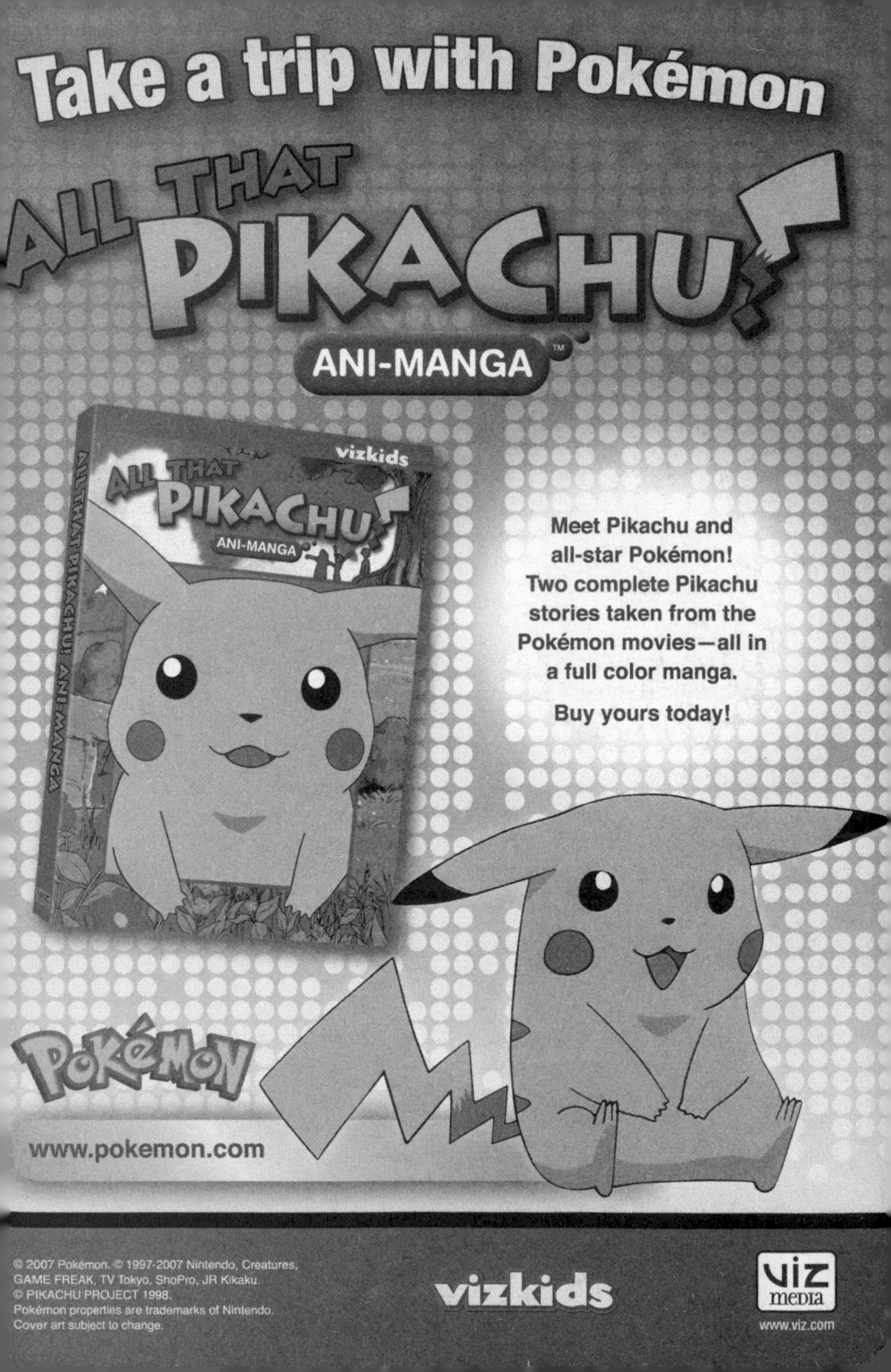
Take a trip with Pokémon
ALL THAT PIKACHU!
ANI-MANGA™
vizkids
ALL THAT PIKACHU!
ANI-MANGA
ALL THAT PIKACHU! ANI-MANGA
Meet Pikachu and all-star Pokémon! Two complete Pikachu stories taken from the Pokémon movies—all in a full color manga.
Buy yours today!
POKÉMON
www.pokemon.com
© 2007 Pokémon. © 1997-2007 Nintendo, Creatures, GAME FREAK, TV Tokyo, ShoPro, JR Kikaku.
© PIKACHU PROJECT 1998.
Pokémon properties are trademarks of Nintendo.
Cover art subject to change.
vizkids
VIZ MEDIA
www.viz.com

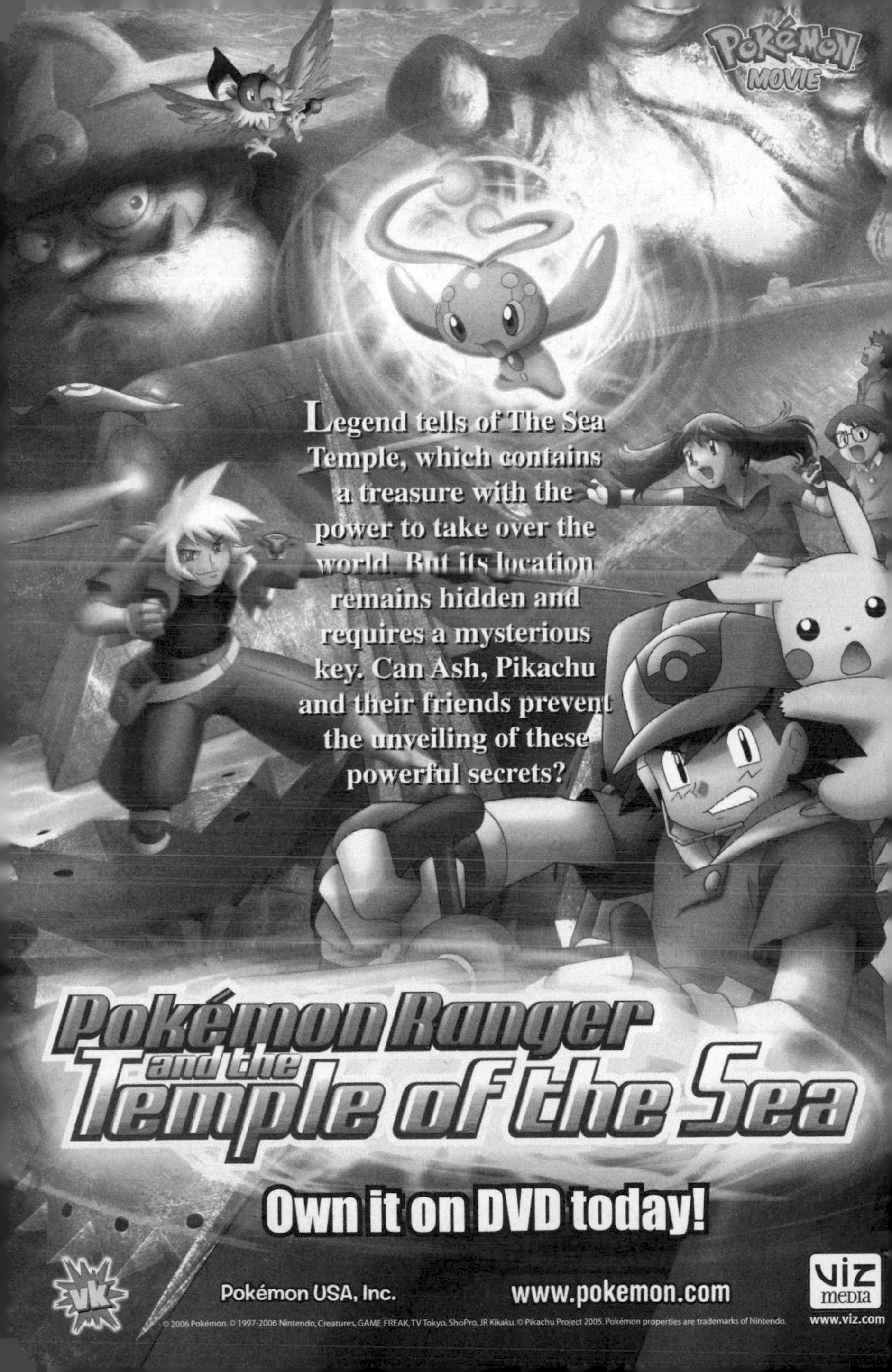

POKéMON MOVIE
Legend tells of The Sea Temple, which contains a treasure with the power to take over the world. But its location remains hidden and requires a mysterious key. Can Ash, Pikachu and their friends prevent the unveiling of these powerful secrets?
Pokémon Ranger and the Temple of the Sea
Own it on DVD today!
vk
Pokémon USA, Inc.
www.pokemon.com
viz media
www.viz.com
© 2006 Pokémon. © 1997-2006 Nintendo, Creatures, GAME FREAK, TV Tokyo, ShoPro, JR Kikaku. © Pikachu Project 2005. Pokémon properties are trademarks of Nintendo.

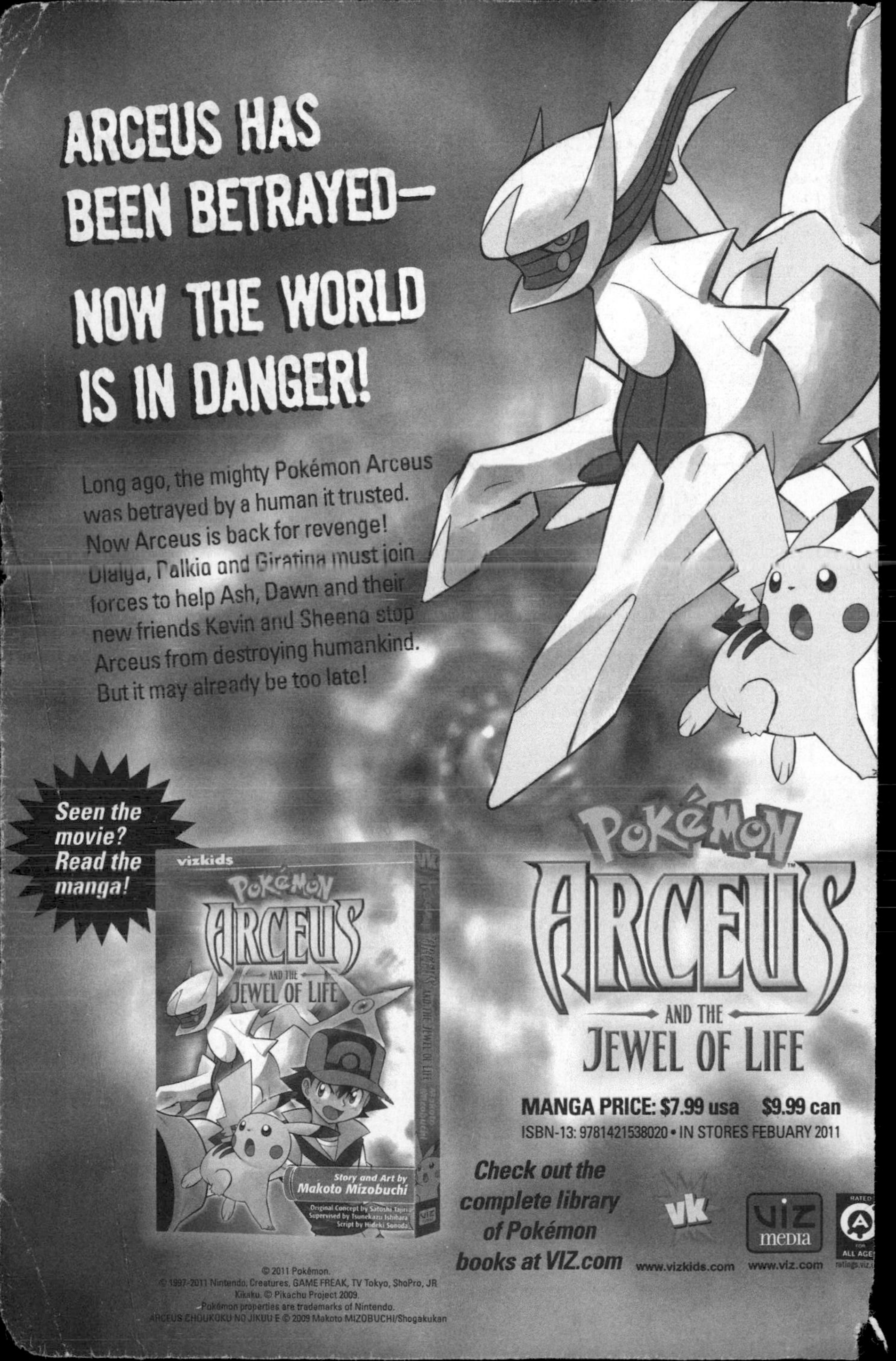
ARCEUS HAS BEEN BETRAYED—
NOW THE WORLD IS IN DANGER!
Long ago, the mighty Pokémon Arceus was betrayed by a human it trusted. Now Arceus is back for revenge! Dialga, Palkia and Giratina must join forces to help Ash, Dawn and their new friends Kevin and Sheena stop Arceus from destroying humankind. But it may already be too late!
Seen the movie? Read the manga!
vizkids
POKÉMON
ARCEUS
AND THE
JEWEL OF LIFE
Story and Art by
Makoto Mizobuchi
Original Concept by Satoshi Tajiri
Supervised by Tsunekazu Ishihara
Script by Hideki Sonoda
POKÉMON
ARCEUS
AND THE
JEWEL OF LIFE
MANGA PRICE: $7.99 usa $9.99 can
ISBN-13: 9781421538020 • IN STORES FEBUARY 2011
Check out the complete library of Pokémon books at VIZ.com
vk
www.vizkids.com
VIZ media
www.viz.com
© 2011 Pokémon.
© 1997-2011 Nintendo, Creatures, GAME FREAK, TV Tokyo, ShoPro, JR Kikaku. © Pikachu Project 2009.
Pokémon properties are trademarks of Nintendo.
ARCEUS CHOUKOKU NO JIKUU E © 2009 Makoto MIZOBUCHI/Shogakukan

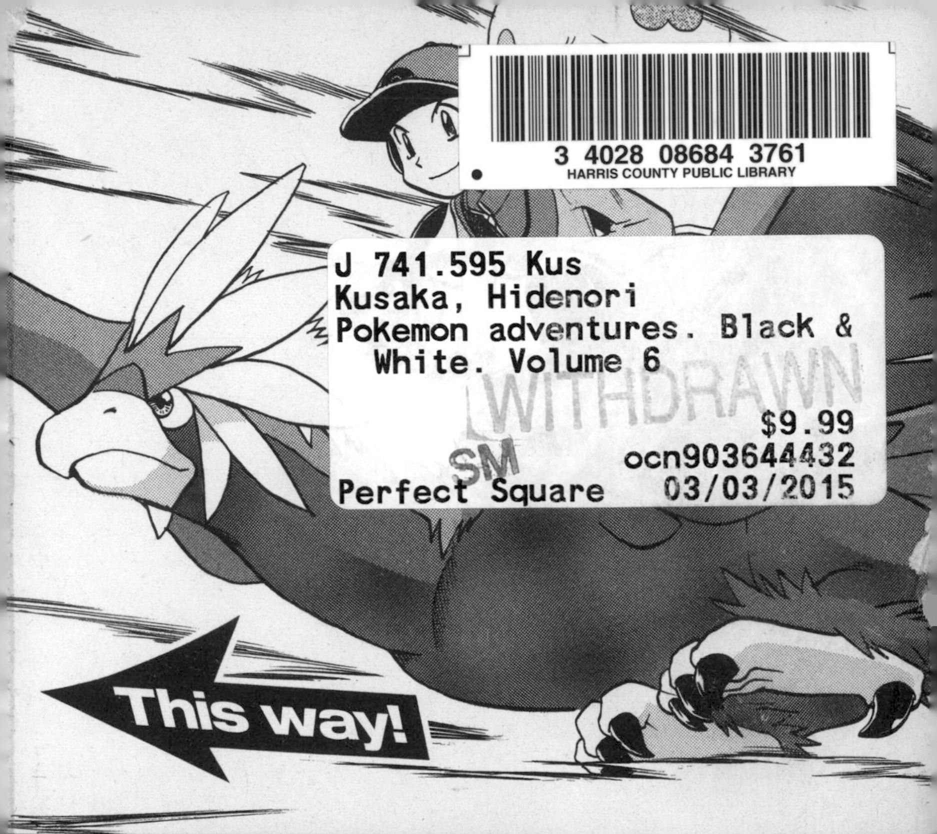
This way!

THIS IS THE END OF THIS GRAPHIC NOVEL!

To properly enjoy this VIZ Media graphic novel, please turn it around and begin reading from right to left.

This book has been printed in the original Japanese format in order to preserve the orientation of the original artwork.

Have fun with it!

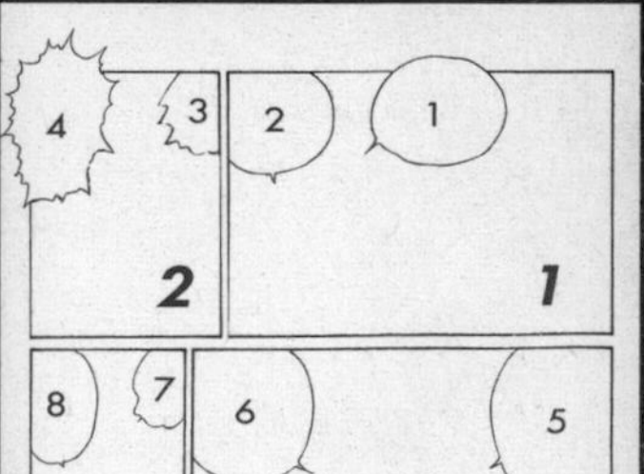

FOLLOW THE ACTION THIS WAY.

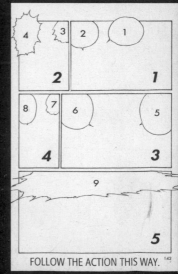